ACKROYD

A NOVEL BY

Jules Feiffer

Simon and Schuster
New York

Designed by Irving Perkins
Manufactured in the United States of America

1   2   3   4   5   6   7   8   9   10

Library of Congress Cataloging in Publication Data

Feiffer, Jules.
   Ackroyd.

   I.   Title.
PZ4.F2974Ac   [PS3556.E42]   813'.5'4   76-58872
ISBN 0-671-22502-2

For Susan Crile

. . . in investigating crime we must take our stand among the commonplace.

—HERCULE POIROT, *Murder on the Links*

I am a fatherless boy who cannot go through the regular channels; I am touchy about the regular channels. But I do greedily absorb scraps of information that are dropped, and I use them my own way.

—PAUL GOODMAN, *Five Years*

1964

April 8

Stationery and bill forms arrived today. The name that I admired so much when I picked it now seems like a foolish joke. Too late, I suppose, to do anything about it.

For the record I thought I should describe this office. But in looking about I am unable to find anything in it to describe.

April 9

Rereading Chandler. Philip Marlowe does not take divorce cases. Well, I will. It isn't my business to impose value judgments on clients. But the point is moot. So far no clients.

April 10

The classified lists 159 private detective agencies in the borough of Manhattan, some long established; most, I presume, making a profit. But not I. I have no connections in the Police Department, no connections with criminal lawyers. Corporation lawyers, yes, dozens of them, but all employees or ex-employees of my father. So that eliminates them. The question then is what steps to take to find clients.

April 11

Too often I see myself in double vision, moving through present struggles from a vantage point of some future time when I have made it as a success. Yet I profess to despise success: my rationale for escaping the family, changing names, going into the detective business. . . .

The detective business is my peace corps. Or so I choose to see it. But, if true, why do I fantasize so much Sam Spade shit? Why can't I focus more on the problems of others?

April 12

My first phone call! Looks like a case! A Mrs. Annabelle Plant. Sounds very nervous on the phone, talks as if she is afraid of being listened in on, refuses to discuss her problem but agrees to come by the office at ten tomorrow morning.

April 13

Her name is Annabelle Plante. Her features, while individually perfect, are spread very far apart so that it's more like looking at a face on a movie screen than a face in person. Green eyes, expressive of hurt—hurt in women gets me all the time. I sit staring, not listening, wondering if I'm bothered that she has crow's-feet around the eyes—not much, just a trace, but no question, crow's-feet. And the beginning of age lines on the neck. A battle between love and revulsion. I want her perfect! So I redefine perfection to include crow's-feet and neck lines.

How old can she be? Thirty-five? Does she think I'm too young to be a good detective? *And what the hell is it she's saying?* I've got to learn to listen!

"I think I get the picture, Mrs. Plante. Let me ask you why you haven't gone to the police."

"I'm not even sure it's a crime."

I nod thoughtfully and sneak a look at my note pad for a clue to what she's talking about. I have drawn a doodle of an empty bird cage. "Theft," I remember.

"I can't go to the police about a parakeet. In any case, it's the emotional price I'm concerned with. Josh is a very sensitive boy."

"What brought you to me?"

"I saw your ad in the *Saturday Review*. First of all, that a private detective should advertise in the *Saturday Review*. That made me curious. Then your name. Roger Ackroyd. Is that your real name?"

I smile as if we are both in on the joke. Her eyes express doubt.

"I didn't expect you to be this young."

I nod in sad agreement; it is a disappointment we share in common. "Why don't you run it over again from the top, Mrs. Plante? The first time I like to get the total picture. The second time I may want to ask questions."

She launches into it, more relaxed now, making it easier on both of us. I turn the page of my legal-sized yellow pad and, almost feeling professional, begin jotting down notes.

"I told you my husband is Oscar Plante."

"What does your husband do?"

She looks at me with some surprise. "The sports columnist!"

"Oh, that Oscar Plante!" I write down a name I never heard of.

"Josh took our separation very hard. He's nine, very adult for his years, but he's always hated any kind of change. Hates to go away in the summer, hates to come home in the fall. Won't let anyone disturb the surfaces in his room. Won't even let the maid in to clean his clubhouse. He's very much like his father that way. It sounds crazy that a marriage can break up because I removed a photograph of the 1944 Brooklyn Dodgers from the wall in the bedroom and hung it in his bathroom." We exchange stares: hers defensive, mine reassuring. It gives her the stamina to go on in that provocative manner she has where every sentence seems to be a dressing for her emotions.

"He can be a terrible bully," she says angrily. "He's never beaten me," she says apologetically. "Only with words," she says bitterly. "Josh is no different," she says in self-pity. "Except he also hits," she says dryly, almost self-mocking. And on and on in the same way.

"He has tantrums that can be absolutely—the worst was when he discovered the parakeet gone. He didn't show very much reaction when his father left us—but when Snoopy disappeared . . ."

"Snoopy is the parakeet?"

She nods. "He was uncontrollable. Uncontrollable."

"Who gave him the parakeet?"

"His father, officially. He doesn't have time to buy him gifts so I buy them and say that they come from him."

"Where did your son keep the parakeet?"

"In his bedroom."

"Is it a big house?"

"Four bedrooms. My bedroom, Josh has a bedroom. There's the maid's room. My husband has—had a study. And there's a guest bedroom, and then Josh used to have a playroom in the basement but that's been empty since my husband's book sold to the movies and we put up a clubhouse in the back yard. Is all this important?" She smiles. I am beginning to feel very much at home with her. I wonder how I'll get the nerve to bring up the subject of money.

"Tell me about when your son first missed his parakeet."

"Five days ago. He woke me screaming. The first thing he

14

does before school every morning is play with Snoopy. I went in to look. The cage door was open and no Snoopy."

"Who feeds the bird?"

"Sometimes Josh, mostly the maid."

"Might the cage door have been left open the night before?"

"Josh is very responsible about that."

"Any windows open?"

"There have been several burglaries in the area during the past year, so every night before turning in we check to see that the front and back doors are bolted and chained and all the windows are locked." She points a gloved finger at my door and window to help me understand what she means by doors and windows.

"The parakeet never turned up?"

Her face disappears behind her features. "I promised Josh that while he was at school I would call the police to look for Snoopy and that I was sure that by the time he was home from school Snoopy would be home too. Then as soon as the bus picked him up I drove down to the pet shop and found a parakeet that was so much like Snoopy that I hoped Josh wouldn't notice the difference."

"Did he?"

She says a barely audible no and bows her head and plays with the hem of her Pucci. In a small guilty voice, she says, "I told him we found Snoopy on the roof. He was very happy going to bed. But the next morning the parakeet was gone."

"The new bird was gone?"

"Josh was grief-stricken. He made me climb the roof. I swore to him Snoopy would return just as he had yesterday." She takes a deep breath and crosses her legs. They are beautiful but marred with small shaving sores, which would have gone unnoticed had she not crossed her legs. "He's a quiet boy. Very self-contained. I think he thinks I drove his father away. I don't know what his father tells him. He never had time for the boy, but Josh forgets . . . And to top it, this business with the parakeet—" A deep crease has formed between her eyes; it ages her and makes her look cross-eyed. I'm not sure I like the way she reacts to crises. "I had the pet shop order for me a half dozen parakeets, all as close to Snoopy in size and color as they could find. I left five of the parakeets in the store and took one home with me, in a cage identical to the one Snoopy has. I put it in my husband's study; Josh hasn't set foot in that room since he left us," she says proudly. "An hour before Josh was to get up I got up. I looked in his room and, as I suspected, the cage was empty. I substituted the new parakeet in the new cage. Josh didn't notice a thing. Every morning for the last five mornings, the cage has been empty and I make another substitution."

"The boy doesn't suspect?"

She brushes the flat of her hand across her lap and then turns it palm upward in a plea. "How long can I get away with it?"

"Do you have any idea who's taking the birds?"

She pounces on the question, making it clear to me that she's been lying in wait for it. "His father!"

"How?"

"I don't know. But it fits the pattern."

"Have you confronted him?"

She all but cringes. "He's only a hint away from saying I did it. But he's doing it and I want you to catch him at it."

The hate in the air gives me a backache. I stand up and pace back and forth behind my desk, for the moment not wanting to look at Mrs. Plante. "How does he get into the house?"

She makes a sour face at me. "He's getting back at me through Josh. There's nothing he's not capable of when he's in this frame of mind! I don't know how he does it but he does it. What do you charge?"

"Where is the maid right now?"

"Home."

"She does your shopping?"

"Yes."

I push the phone over to her. "Call her please."

She wants to know why while dialing. I don't answer until she gets the maid. "Ask her if she's noticed over the past week that she's going through more bird food than usual. Ask her if any boxes of bird food are missing."

I listen, with rising complacency, to the answer.

"She says yes, a box is missing. And one box that she just opened is nearly finished. How did you know?"

I wind my watch for no particular reason. "Ask the maid to go out to his clubhouse and report to us if she finds anything unusual. Tell her you'll hold on."

We wait five minutes in silence, both of us staring life into the phone. It finally takes effect. Mrs. Plante brings it up to her ear. "Thank you, Walda. Hold on." Then to me: "There's nothing out of the ordinary in Josh's clubhouse. This is all too vague. What is it you're looking for?"

I ignore her tone of criticism, though it does piss me off. "Send her down to the part of the basement your son used as a playroom. Same instructions. Tell her you'll hold on." A two-minute wait this time, then the phone shakes in Mrs. Plante's hand. She starts to get rid of it. "Wait! Tell her to say nothing to Josh when he comes home from school."

She hesitates, but does it. Her face, on hanging up, is closed, guarded. "How did you know?"

"How many are there?"

"Five parakeets. It's a holy mess down there."

"One of them is Snoopy."

She looks betrayed. "I guess so." She shifts uncomfortably in the chair. Her expression suggests that I put the birds in her basement.

"The way I figured it, he wouldn't kill the birds. He might free the substitutes, but he wouldn't free Snoopy, and the chances are that he wouldn't free any of them. Kids hate to give up what they get their hands on, and with the boy feeling a strong sense of loss over his father, he would hide the birds, not add to his losses."

Her face is almost black. "Are you accusing my son of these thefts?"

"It's not you. It's not your husband. Who's left?"

"It *is* my husband!"

"Why would he hide the birds in the basement?"

"So that Josh would find them and blame me!"

"O.K., after he leaves, how does he bolt and chain the door or lock the window he used to gain entrance?" She gives a little smile as if she knows but won't tell. "I'm sorry, Mrs. Plante, but if we try to get at the answer unemotionally we have no choice but to ask who had the best opportunity. Josh. Which leaves us to ask, What does he do with the birds? Hide them. Where does he hide them? Where only he goes. His clubhouse or the playroom in the basement."

"You sit there very pleased with yourself."

She may be crazy but she's right.

"You're so smug."

She stands up, trembling wildly. "You're hateful! You're incompetent. He wouldn't do that to me! After I went out and bought all those damned birds! You're a crook! I won't pay!" She clamps a hand over her mouth. I am afraid she is going to pass out or vomit. She does neither. She just leaves.

I peel a bill form off the pad in the top drawer and type out my first bill. Fifty dollars? Fuck it, brilliance deserves its day, make it a hundred. Only then do I remember that I hadn't taken her address.

There is no Oscar or Annabelle Plante in the Manhattan directory. Wait a minute. She indicated they lived in the suburbs. What suburb? I didn't ask. Her husband is a famous sports writer. For what paper? I didn't ask. He published a best seller. What publisher? I didn't ask.

I wish I knew a good detective. I'd hire him to find my client.

April 14

I have lost Annabelle but I have found Oscar Plante. Journeyman detective work led me to *The New York Times,* and there he was, hiding out on the sports page: high-toned for a sports writer. Cool. British. A little pretentious. But he draws you into his world. I like parts of his novel, which is a serio-comic thriller about a foreign correspondent who smuggles pornographic literature into Russia and dissident literature out. It's perfect for the movies, and now that he's rich, if he doesn't pay me I will sue him for every cent he's got.

I send my itemized bill in care of the *Times,* wondering as I drop it down the mail chute why I feel such animosity toward the man. I never heard of him until yesterday. Is it Annabelle? But she's too old, too pathetic and too crazy. Perfect. Just my type.

I diddle around the office past midnight entertaining the hope that she'll call to apologize.

April 21

A cheating wife caper. Not much but better than parakeets. The client's name is Logan Jessup and this time, first things first, I get his address.

He and his three-year bride, Deborah Jessup, live on East Thirty-fifth Street, three-room apartment on the twenty-second floor. Photograph shows her to be a knockout. Blond, fat lips, thick, smoky eyes. How he ever got her I'll never know, but little wonder he finds himself in trouble.

Jessup is in his middle forties, tall, slender, walks like a drunk pretending to be sober, combs his hair like an elder statesman. Handsome, unlined face. Off-putting eyes with the color and firmness of grapes and as hard to meet as is the man himself. Sits as if he's standing. Stands as if he's about to fall down. I only hope he's solvent. Should be. Says he's a fund raiser for the American Cancer Society.

So for fifty dollars a day I am to keep an eye on his wife from the time he leaves in the morning until he gets home from Cancer at night. Report on whom she sees, where she goes, the usual.

I feel sorry for Jessup. Hope he's wrong about his wife. But there's something about him that expects the worst and past observation indicates that these guys usually get what they expect.

A check for fifty dollars from Oscar Plante. On the back where the endorsement goes it says: "Full and complete for services rendered." I knew I didn't like the son of a bitch.

April 28

A week of Mrs. Jessup. Discomforting. It didn't show in the photograph, but in life she reminds me of Annabelle Plante. She's younger, shorter, blonder, skinnier, and looks entirely different but she gives off that same aura of quivering strength and near-breakability.

I wonder what future there is for me in this business if I keep falling for my clients or their wives.

And Jessup, the cad, has done the girl wrong. She is above suspicion, beyond reproach and pure as the driven snow. This week anyhow. I have tailed her to Bloomingdale's, Henri Bendel's, the dentist's, lunch at the Russian Tea Room, and five movies in seven days. And so what if they are all blue? What she does with her mind is her business; my assignment is to cover her body.

April 29

Jessup sits across from me with a face that wants to cry. He goes through my report slowly, indicating through long heart-stopping silences that I am a great disappointment to him. It is, I know, a dull report. Blue films, for reasons of my own puritanism, have been upgraded to Doris Day. Nothing remains of interest unless you are a Bloomingdale's nut.

Jessup tries and fails to smile. "You discovered nothing."

"Nothing so far."

"But you did discover my wife."

"I have every reason to believe so."

Jessup shakes his head. "Shopping, shopping, movies, movies—this describes a suburban matron. This is not Deborah, Mr. Ackroyd. Is it conceivable that you followed the wrong woman?"

I hand Jessup the photograph he had given me. "I followed the woman in this picture."

He compares the picture to the report, looking for a resemblance. Apparently he finds none. "If you insist." His smile suggests compassion.

All the confidence drains out of me. Desperately I say, "She was wearing a brown suede jacket, a dark green skirt, brown leather boots."

Jessup waves the description aside. "I never notice what she wears. I'm sorry."

"But it could be her."

"It could be." In a tone that implies it could also be Kim Novak.

"She is blond?"

"Mm." He studies the ceiling.

"She is brown-eyed?"

He pauses for a moment. "Possibly."

I feel like a contestant on a quiz show. "About five feet, four inches?"

Jessup brightens. "The wrong woman! No question! Deborah is my height. In heels, taller."

I go to my notes. "It says here five-four." I hand him the notes. "This is your own description of your wife given to me a week ago."

Jessup looks them over. "This four could be an eight."

I take back the notes. The four could not be an eight. It could be nothing but a four. "Are you saying that she's five-eight?"

Jessup nods, depressed. "You see, it *was* the wrong woman."

"But you're over six feet. You just said she was your size. In heels, taller. Six-inch heels, Mr. Jessup?"

Jessup stares through me. "I like them in high heels," he says so low I have trouble hearing him.

"You're saying the woman I should have followed looks exactly like the woman I did follow except she is four inches taller and wears heels that make her six-two."

Jessup folds his hands across his chest and looks like he has very recently died.

"I'm going to have to ask you to level with me, Mr. Jessup."

He goes back to the report and studies it. "Perhaps it was my wife."

"It is now a possibility."

"It's possible that the way you see her is not the way I see her." We smile at each other. "Yes, now that I think of it, that must be the explanation." He gets to his feet. "In a few more days I'm sure you'll see her more clearly." He smiles again from the door. "Keep up the good work."

May 1

Jessup now stops by every night for a report. I find a great time lag between my comments and his responses. It is as if he's listening to several people at one time and I am but one of them. More and more he gives the impression of a man put together with building blocks. Or the Tin Man in *The Wizard of Oz*.

He skims my report. And why shouldn't he? It could appropriately be entitled "Son of Bloomingdale's" and is not much worth bothering with. He puts the report back on my desk and I do not have the nerve to look at it. He has, by doing nothing and saying nothing, made it a failure. I am reminded of my father.

May 2

8:00 A.M.: Jessup on his way out as I arrive to take up watch. Looks bigger, more impressive/aggressive out of doors.

Walk has a strut to it that he doesn't bring into a private detective's office. Stares through me in my telephone repairman's jump suit.

Station myself in service hallway outside Jessup's back door. Wedge service door open with stick of wood so I can see who comes and goes out of both Jessup doors. Quickly into my telephone toolbox, remove one can dark yellow paint, one paint brush and coveralls. Slip coveralls over jumpsuit and proceed to spread yellow over the shit-brown walls. So pleased with my craftsmanship I nearly forget to keep my eye on front door of Mrs. Jessup.

10:00 A.M.: Speculation: If Mrs. Jessup has a lover he does not come from outside but inside. He lives or works here in the building, meaning he is either unemployed or a freelance or a member of the building custodial staff. Possibilities: doctor, dentist, actor, writer, artist, salesman, teacher, super, handyman, doorman, elevator operator, porter . . .

4:00 P.M.: No lover, but hall is coming along beautifully. Mrs. Jessup opens service door to throw out garbage. Close up in a tight-fitting everything, she is the low-cut lady of my dreams. I investigate her garbage. Not much. No love letters. Only one letter of any kind and that a bill addressed to Miss D. Jessup. Some magazines, all addressed to D. Jessup. Assorted used toilet articles, three yogurt cartons, two prune juice cans, yesterday's *Times,* and that's it. What to make of it? One thing: Where is Jessup's garbage?

9:00 P.M.: As I finish typing out my report, Jessup appears like my confessor. I deliver my report in the traditional monotone and with the certain sense that I am drowning. I finish, and he gives me a look which, if audible, would be a sigh. He lights a cigar and drags on it with respect; the most formidable object in my office. With each drag he sucks more life out of the office. By the end of his cigar he will have inhaled my desk, my chair and my gold-leafed name on the door. To divert the gloom, I hand him the building directory. "Will you go through this directory for me, Mr. Jessup, and mark down the tenants whom you know?"

Jessup tosses the directory back at me. "Don't know anybody." He looks as if I have stripped him bare.

"How long have you lived there?"

"Two, three years."

"I notice you're listed in the directory under your wife's name."

He gets thoughtful. "Under her thumb, why not under her name?" The ash from his cigar falls on his lap. He smiles at it.

"What can I do? I love her. I would die for her. I expect to die for her. See that you find this man. He must be warned. There is no sense in two of us dying for her."

Lip-moving a silent goodbye, Jessup brings his stiff body to its feet and carts it off. I envy Jessup. His misery has just a touch of triumph about it.

May 3

At home with the Jessups. Nothing till noon when Mrs. J. unlocks the service door. She is in leather, a remarkably fine body but not one I'd willingly die for. She fiddles with the garbage longer than necessary and I feel her examining me. My heart stops. I paint as if I'm trying to break into the union.

"I wonder if I could ask you for a very small favor? Do you know anything about hooks on doors?" She wrinkles her nose at me.

"What about hooks?"

"I'm a disaster with my hands." She sticks out her hands as if to show they don't match. "I've been trying all morning to put a couple of hooks on the bathroom door and it keeps coming out."

"What does?"

"The screw." She wrinkles her nose. Is it a tic?

"I don't know . . ." Then, grudgingly: "O.K. Let me take a look."

I follow her through the kitchen which is a mess, through the dining room which has all the homeyness of a subway platform, through the bedroom which looks like an open wound, and finally into the bathroom where she keeps most of her furniture. She holds up a silver hook and points to a bathroom door riddled with screw holes.

"It won't stay in," she moans. Her eyes tell me that she knows this is silly and that she is silly but that silly people can have problems which to them are nonetheless serious. My heart melts. I examine the door. It is a flush door. Hollow except on its frame, which is why the hook won't stay.

"Do you have smaller screws?"

She goes off obediently to look. While she looks for screws, I scout the bedroom. The closet reveals a forest of clothes, all hers. Dozens of shoes, all hers. Where does she put Jessup? I imagine him living out of a footlocker in the foyer. Maybe the bathroom hook is for his suits.

Still . . . it's hard to see Mrs. Jessup enslaving anyone. She reminds me too much of Annabelle Plante. She returns, looking sweetly triumphant, holding two tiny screws. I start on my task, feeling haunted, proceeding with care. One false move and the door crumbles.

Intense concentration. The phone rings. Deborah says "Excuse me" and goes to an extension in another room, although a phone lies a few feet away on a bed table. I lift up the bedroom phone with the care of a surgeon. I hear sobs. Deborah is crying.

"But where does that leave me?" she is saying. "I don't think you really care."

"Darling . . ." Said with a sigh.

"I'm sorry, Rags. I know you have a lot on your mind."

A long pause.

"Then I'll see you later, Rags, O.K., honey?" Another long pause. "Bye," says Deborah, as if it's a question, and quietly hangs up, as do I, not knowing if Rags is still on the line or not.

She is a long time getting back to me and her eyes are newly made up and her breath is scented with Scotch. "You've got it in."

"Yop."

"Will it stay?"

"As long as you don't put anything heavy on it."

"But towels are all right?"

"As long as they ain't wet."

She gives up on the problem and moves two dollars in my direction without looking at me. I thank her. She returns the thanks, and with her face half turned away escorts me through the apartment, back to my wall.

How to write a report informing your client that he is officially a cuckold. Three drafts get me nowhere. Hard-bitten language in the first draft lapses into sociology in the second draft until, in the third draft, I emerge as Max Lerner. I am saved by a ringing telephone. My answering service, with the very first messages they have ever taken for me! Annabelle called. Three times. Says she will call back. Jessup sits in the client's chair for five minutes before I notice him.

He folds the report, then unfolds it, then folds it again, then, seeming not to know what to do with the remains, folds it many times over, pinches the bottom, flares open the top and makes it into a fan. "She knows."

"She knows what?"

"Who you are."

I shift uncomfortably. "I don't think so."

He smiles at my innocence. "She already has you doing jobs for her. Tomorrow that hook will be off the door and she will make you do it again. And again. It will go on for days. Until you have lost all sense of pride or dignity."

I wonder what you have to do around here to get a normal client. "What about Rags?"

"Rags?"

"The man on the phone to your wife."

Jessup stops fanning himself. "I'm sorry, he's not our man."

"You know him?"

"Her brother." He fans himself. "Actually her half-brother."

He is at the door, fanning himself slowly with my report. "Do what you can." He opens the door. "I have very little hope."

10:00 P.M.: I hyperventilate. Can't catch my breath walking east to Downey's, can't breathe when I see her sitting in the corner of a booth, don't see her when I see her. She tugs at my jacket as I pass by. "Mr. Ackroyd!"

She looks dark and lost and heartbreaking and exotic and my fantasies rise so high in my mouth that I can't use it for words. I order a drink quickly. Slowed to a trot after my second martini, my vision clears well enough for me to know her again if I happen to pass her on the street.

She is wearing a suburban wife's day-in-town dress and I am unpleasantly reminded of my mother. She wears enough rings on her fingers to cut a man to pieces. I contain my rage and try to put it in some rational balance with my infatuation. She *does* look beautiful. But no less troubled, no less fragile. I notice once again that it takes a while for me to be able to hear what she's saying.

"—looked everywhere. I'm worried sick."

"How long has he been missing?"

"Six hours."

"Have you looked in the basement?" She nods impatiently. "In his clubhouse?"

"That was the first place I looked."

"He's disappeared again?"

"Why do you say 'again'? He's never disappeared before!"

Has the woman gone crazy? "Snoopy?"

"I'm talking about Josh!"

I clasp both my hands to my chin to look thoughtful, when what I really want to do is put them over my eyes to hide. "Have you gone to the police?"

"I don't dare. He'll use it against me."

"Who will?"

She groans—either at her fate or my stupidity. "My husband! He'll take Josh away from me! That's why he's got to be found before he finds out."

27

"Why wouldn't you come to my office?"

"I didn't want to come to you as a detective, I wanted to come to you as someone I could trust."

I restrain a sneer but not a comment. "Someone you called incompetent and a crook."

She bites her lip. "I never would have said a word to Josh if you hadn't told me he stole the parakeets. But I did and now he's gone. I know you're not a crook. And you know you know that. And for you to bring it up now—" She pauses, as out of breath as I was when I arrived. "I don't know what you expect of me. All I ask is for you to find my son before his father hears about this. I think you owe me that much. If you have any sense of responsibility . . ." She brushes a hand against my forearm, then leaves it there, then takes it away. I feel more tired than after a full day's painting.

"When did you discover Josh missing?"

"Walda couldn't find him for dinner."

"That's the maid?"

"He had milk and cookies when he came home from school. And that's the last either of us have seen of him."

"You told him you knew he took the parakeets?"

"Yes. Thank you very much for that."

It isn't worth the effort so I let it go by. "How did you tell him?"

"I don't know. Is there a good way? I waited a week. Every day I had to come up with a new parakeet. I could see that to him it was really only a game. So I decided the way to tell him was to make it a game. I told him I knew a magic place that parakeets went when they flew away. I thought I was doing fine but he didn't react very well. He refused to go with me to the basement to find the magic place. He got hysterical. Said he hates me. He does hate me. He swore he was going to jump off the Empire State Building. He started to hold his breath—"

"The Empire State Building?"

"For two weeks he's threatened. You can imagine what a joy that is to live with."

"Has he ever been there?"

"You always ask the most— How should I know? In school, I suppose. Doesn't everyone get the Empire State Building? King Kong. It's his father's favorite movie. I can't guess how often they see it. It's the only thing he and Josh do together. You'd expect a father would share some other experience with his son. Baseball. Football. Especially if he's a sports writer. But I never could get him to budge an inch. Not him. 'You're the one who wanted kids,' he'd lie so smug on that couch and tell me." She is off and flying. I think of interrupting but think again. "He used to be hard, but he's gotten so soft and selfish. Thinks only of himself. Rags has to come first. That's all he ever thinks of."

"Who?"

"My husband."

"What did you call him?"

"Rags. That's his name."

"His name is Oscar."

"If you were named Oscar, wouldn't you want to be called something else? He's been Rags forever. Rags for ragweed. Ragweed Plante. I used to think it was because he had hay fever. He doesn't have it; he gives it."

Rags. Plante. Life, my son, is a circle. "Could Josh be with your husband?"

"How would he get there?"

"Your husband wouldn't take him without your knowing?"

"No."

"Not even as a misunderstanding?"

"My husband only misunderstands to his advantage. He sees as little of Josh as he can get away with. He—"

"Have you spoken to your husband since the boy left?"

"And give him ammunition? Please, try to help, Mr. Ackroyd."

She wants me as a friend but talks to me like a servant. Life, my son, is a paradox.

"Is he a popular boy?"

"Very. He has dozens of friends. Mostly fair-weather. He makes the wrong friends. Anyhow, he has his own interests."

I get dizzy with her change of pace. "Give me a list of his friends."

"I've already called them. What do you think I am?"

I think you're crazy. "I'd like a list anyway. I may want it for later."

"You think he's dead!" Her eyes pop.

"I don't know what I think but I don't think he's dead. Maybe he just went off for repairs."

"What does that mean?"

"A kid who feels a lot of pressure—"

"I don't pressure Josh."

"I mean a broken home—"

"I know very well what you mean, and I demand an apology."

I say nothing. Incapable of talk. My plan is to find Josh and run away with him.

"I knew I shouldn't have given you a second chance." She grabs her bag and walks out on me.

I pull what I can find of myself together and pay the bill. On Eighth Avenue, behind a cordon of prostitutes, I uncover a newsstand and check *Cue*'s movie listings. No *King Kong*. I hop a cab to the Empire State Building, walk around outside, inside, question the night security men, ride up and down all the elevators and hang around the observation tower. No kid. I hop a cab to Central Park and patrol the zoo. The animals are quiet. The muggers are quiet. No kid. I hop a cab and give him the Bronx Zoo as an address. The cab driver is not quiet. I promise him a round trip and a five-dollar tip. He agrees to take me, but not graciously. Along the way I wonder about Rags.

The Bronx Zoo is closed, fenced in and devoid of interest except for a dirt-stained nine-year-old trying, with no luck, to climb over the fence. I tell the cab to wait. He says, "I got all night." We hold a brief negotiation over whether I am to pay him before setting foot out of the cab. I hand over to him, as a sign of my good faith, a fat wallet stuffed with blank paper. He accepts the wallet and I stroll over to the kid.

Josh, if he is Josh, is small for his age. He is also fragile, scared, slightly effeminate and in a very bad temper. He charges the fence like a bull, leaps at it, clawing the air, slices up his fingers, falls on his ass, jumps up and goes at it again, clearly committed to not making it.

I dislike him on sight. What I see in him makes of me every grownup I've ever hated. "You!"

He freezes, taking me for the cop I am trying to sound like.

"Over here where I can get a look at you."

I watch his face undergo a sleight of hand, dissolve into a collage of different faces—one of them his mother's—until he arrives at no face at all. Flight having taken place inside him, he approaches, looking cooperative.

"Let's have it."

"What?" He tries a smile on me.

"The money."

"I don't have any." He smiles again.

"Did you hide it or spend it?"

"I didn't take any money! Look!" He starts to empty his pockets.

"She says you did. Last night."

"Who?"

"The Negro lady."

"I didn't do it." He talks out of the smile, his lips barely move.

"She says you stole it from her."

"I don't even know her." All reasonableness behind the smile.

"She says you hit her."

"I never hit anybody." The smile broadens. It is like interrogating a photograph. "I can prove it."

"You can't prove anything."

"I was home last night. That proves it."

"You need witnesses. Was anyone with you last night who can prove you didn't hit the Negro lady?"

"I can prove it because I was watching television." His smile no longer comes off as an expression—more the absence

31

of an expression. He launches into the plot of a show called *The Virginian*.

It is too painful to watch so I put a stop to it. "That's not proof. You need a witness. Let's go downtown."

The smile breaks. The photograph of Alfred E. Neuman fades into a flesh-and-blood little old man. "My mother was with me."

I take out a pad and pencil, just like a real cop. "Where does she live?"

He looks hungrily at the zoo, a wizened nine-year-old. "Home."

"Where's home?" Silence. "Where's home?" More silence. "Let's go downtown."

"Larchmont." His face whitens. "Forty-three Poplar Road, Larchmont." He begins to tremble violently.

I guide Josh gently into the cab and break it to the driver that we are headed for Westchester County. I sit back, untroubled by the antagonism on all sides. I have outwitted a nine-year-old and I have found out where Annabelle lives.

May 4

Jessup arrives at nine, later than expected, wanting to know why I am in the office this morning instead of out painting his hallway. His eyes stare softly and disappointedly into mine.

"This man Rags—" I begin.

Jessup smiles. "Not him again."

"How long have you known this man whom your wife claims as her brother?"

"Oh, Mr. Ackroyd, Mr. Ackroyd, what's going to become of us if you go on in this way?"

"Well, if that question doesn't interest you, let me ask you this: How long has your wife been intimate with Oscar Plante?"

Jessup laughs, truly delighted. "Now how in the world did you come up with *him?*"

"You know Oscar Plante?"

"The novelist? How in the world would I get to know some-one like that?"

"Your wife doesn't know him?" Jessup seems relaxed, comfortable, enjoying himself. "His nickname is Rags."

"My brother-in-law? I told you that."

"No. Oscar Plante."

"Oh, for God's sake, Ackroyd, we don't want my brother-in-law and I'm sure we don't want Oscar Plante. I'm not an actuary. I have no idea of the statistical count on men named Rags in the city of New York. For all I know, thousands." Jessup rolls his eyes in boredom.

"Where do you get your mail delivered, Mr. Jessup?"

"At my residence." Apparently to ease his boredom he extracts a Havana out of his cigar case and lights up.

"I was curious because I checked through your garbage. Lots of mail for Miss D. Jessup or Miss Deborah Jessup. No mail for Mrs. Jessup. No mail for Mr. Jessup."

"I take my mail to the office in the morning."

"Is that where you also keep your clothes?"

Jessup smiles patiently. "Pardon?"

"I ask because not only is your name not listed with your wife's in the building directory, not only is there no record of your receiving mail there, but you don't seem to keep your clothes there. Correct me if I'm wrong, Mr. Jessup, but from all indications, one could not help but draw the conclusion that you don't live with Deborah Jessup." I open my desk drawer and blindly feel my way to Oscar Plante's novel.

"For the purpose of argument, let's say Mrs. Deborah Jessup is, in fact, *Miss* Deborah Jessup. That she is not married. That she has a lover. That this lover sleeps, but does not live, with her. That he is Oscar Plante, the novelist, as you call him, or the sports writer as most people seem to know him."

I take Plante's novel out of the drawer and place it on the edge of the desk nearest to Jessup. It is badly balanced and falls to the floor. Jessup dives after it and returns it solicitously to the desk. I pick it up and turn to the photograph of the author on the back. It is Jessup. Smoking a Havana. I hold the photograph up for my client to see. His pudding eyes glow with good humor.

"This calls for a drink," he says.

"You take the drink, I'll take the explanation." I bring half a bottle and a clean glass out of the drawer used for files, if I had any.

"You want an explanation. You shall have it. Do you smoke?"

I accept the cigar. He clips the end and hands it to me, then lounges elegantly in the client's chair in a manner totally foreign to Jessup.

"I have a gift for saying things that are misunderstood. It's a common gift. I find that when I think I am complimenting someone it often turns out that I have hurt his feelings. So I hesitate to compliment you on a job well done. Other than to say I am impressed. May I say I'm impressed without giving offense?" I frown, waiting for him to get at whatever he thinks he is getting at. "You *are* offended."

"Why the masquerade?"

"To discover if your talents go beyond finding lost parakeets. And they do. I am pleased to say that they do."

"Are you telling me that the whole Jessup charade was for my benefit?"

Plante pauses. "You read my book?" I nod. He picks up the book. "This has changed my life. Did you like it?" His eyes ask, not without self-mockery, that I say yes.

"It wasn't *War and Peace*."

Plante puts down the book. "You're direct." I am back to failing him. "I have three dear friends. We get together and talk about writing. We've been doing this on and off for years. But nothing gets written. Books get written, but not by us. The way some friends have the war in common, we have in common our unwritten novels. That was before I wrote this—" He picks up the book. "—which, sad to say, is not *War and Peace*. My friends' names are Otis Kaufman, Wally Burden and— Why aren't you taking this down?"

"Why should I?" I look at him blankly.

"It's a case."

"I'm being hired for another case?"

"This is the case I intended to hire you for all along once I made sure of your credentials." He puts his book down.

On a legal-sized yellow pad I write out the names Otis Kaufman and Wally Burden. "Who are the others?"

"One other: Emmett Cornwall. Emmett is a newspaperman, possibly the last stylist in the business. We worked on the *Telegram* together. Wally Burden is a press agent, a truly witty man who chose a profession he had a low opinion of so he'd have time to write, but has never written. Otis Kaufman is my oldest friend. We date back to grammar school. In high school he was the star athlete and I was the star reporter. We made each other local legends."

"What does he do now?"

"He is a fund raiser."

I smile. "Cancer?"

He smiles back. "Jews. He works for the UJA. He drinks to forget it. As do we all. All my friends are heavy drinkers. But they handle it and I don't. I black out. I lose hours. That's why I do my serious drinking only with close friends. So I'll be in safe hands. The point is I'm not anymore. This is very difficult. I value these friendships." He pauses, his eyes watering.

"I have an idea for a new novel. It is still only an idea—several pages of notes written in the bathroom of a bar while I was drinking one night three weeks ago. I was with one of my friends. I remember thinking at the time: I've broken through, this will be the best that I have in me. If I am capable of producing art, this will be art. I remember thinking that. And that's all I remember. I don't remember the idea and I can't find the notes."

"What day are we talking about?"

"April eighteenth."

"Which friend were you with?"

"I don't know."

"But it was one of the three?"

"Yes."

"And you suspect him of taking your notes."

"No."

"Then what happened to the notes? Could you have lost them?"

"I never lose notes."

"Do you remember showing them to anyone?"

"I remember deliberately not showing them. I remember sitting in the bathroom, feeling ill, suddenly inspired to write. Ten or fifteen pages of notes. I remember coming back to the table determined not to talk about it, not wanting to rub it into him that I would soon have two novels while he didn't have any."

"Who?"

"I can't remember."

"Are your friends jealous of the success of your novel?"

"They treat the whole thing as a lapse in taste."

His eyes suddenly brighten. "Someone in one of the bars said something—made an observation that was word for word out of my notes. Word for word! Remarkable! That's why I told him! So he wouldn't think I stole his idea! So to prove I had the idea first I showed him my notebook."

"You remember this?"

"I was relieved that he wasn't put out. I remember a surge of great affection. I think he must have liked my idea." Plante beams with pleasure. "Yes, he liked it!"

"Who liked it?" I ask quickly.

Plante shakes his head. His eyes twinkle, warning me he is not to be caught easily. His face still basks in the pleasure of the memory of his friend, the thief, admiring his notes.

"Your friends aren't aware you suspect them?"

He looks at me with surprise. "I don't suspect them."

I relight the cold cigar he has given me. "Why don't you tell me what you do remember of the night, how it began, who you met, drank with, etcetera. Try not to leave anything out."

After fifteen minutes of tooth pulling, all I manage to get are the names of four bars: P. J. Clarke's, Bradley's, the White Horse, Elaine's.

"Your friends are known at these bars?" Plante nods.

The phone rings. I could let the service get it, but I need a breather. It is Annabelle Plante. "This isn't an easy call for me to make."

"I'm with a client," I say with some degree of titillation. "Give me your number and I'll call you back." Without argument, she gives me her number. I hang up, hide a smirk, and look for Plante, who is not in his chair. I find him standing at the door.

"I'd better give you a couple of numbers where you can reach me."

I smile. "I found out on my own where I can reach you. It seemed simpler that way."

Plante's laugh is infectious. I fight hard not to grin.

May 5

It amazes me how many waiters, barflies and bartenders have near total recall when it comes to Plante and his cronies. Anyhow, after a long, lackluster night of pub-crawling, this is my reconstruction of Plante's doings on the night of April eighteenth. Times are, of course, approximate.

Six-thirty: Plante meets Otis Kaufman at P. J. Clarke's. Waiter claims them as regulars. Kaufman is described as a genial but incoherent giant. "All wind-up and no pitch," according to the waiter. He says that alone Plante and Kaufman talk about childhood, with the others present they talk about things he can't make head or tail of. But they are good customers and don't make trouble. Drink a lot, don't get drunk. Kaufman leaves, no one knows when. Plante has a drink alone, makes a couple of phone calls. So much for Clarke's.

Eight o'clock: The White Horse. Plante and Emmett Cornwall drinking heavily. They talk about corruption which, according to the waiter, is what they always talk about. Both extremely bitter. The difference between them, says the waiter, is Plante laughs a lot at Cornwall's jokes but Cornwall does not laugh at Plante's. "Deadpan," "poker face," are the waiter's descriptions.

Eleven o'clock: Bradley's. Plante, Cornwall and Wally Burden. Burden is characterized as an amiable fat man who talks like a book but means no harm by it. Burden and Cornwall are putting down Plante, who is cheerful. Argument seems to be over a column Plante wrote on the Boston Marathon. They pick up unidentified girl whom they ask to moderate. She sides with Plante. Cornwall insults girl. Plante challenges Cornwall to step outside. Manager accompanies them outside to see that they don't get hurt. They involve him in argument over the second Liston-Clay fight. They go back inside to find girl gone and Burden disconsolate. Last conversation waiter recalls is on suicide and whether you have the right to do it if you have children.

Twelve-thirty: Elaine's. Plante, Cornwall, Burden, Kaufman and four celebrity regulars who are not pertinent because they leave early. Burden and Plante in an argument over William Faulkner. Plante's turn to be despondent. Burden buys him a drink. Plante knocks it over. No one is talking to anyone, which is when the four celebrities leave. Plante gets hiccups and goes off to john. After a half hour Burden goes off to retrieve him. They return best of friends and Plante buys drinks for the table. By this time he is apparently incoherent but he puts everyone in a festive mood.

One-thirty: Clarke's. They close the place. Plante is doing all the buying and most of the drinking. Waiter reports others are unusually glum. But Plante cannot stop talking. Waiter reports every other word out of his mouth is either "art" or "artist." Plante, who lives close by, decides to walk home; others share cab.

Typing the report develops in me an enormous thirst for Annabelle. I try not to call her—whenever I tried calling yesterday her line was busy. I let her phone ring a dozen times, then hang up and dial Plante's home number. No answer. I dial Deborah Jessup. After five rings a Negro voice answers: "Mizz Jessup's residence."

"Is Mr. Plante there?"

"Is that you, Ackroyd? Have you found out anything?"

"I found out you do imitations; I also found out how you spent the night of April eighteenth. Should I come over?"

"You're at your office?" I say yes. Long pause. "I'll be there in twenty minutes."

More than enough time to try Annabelle again. On the fifteenth ring she picks up. "What in God's name are you doing calling me at this hour?" She yawns all through my explanation. "I'll talk to you tomorrow," she says, and the line goes dead, as do I from the neck down.

Plante doesn't get past the White Horse. He drops the report in his lap and pretends it isn't there. "I have to accept this, I suppose."

"All those waiters and bartenders could be lying."

The report slips from his lap onto the floor. "I can't read the thing. I don't know these people, I don't want to know them. I am going to assume, for the purposes of this investigation, that it is true. I can't disprove any of it, but I know of no reason on this earth why I should be forced to relive it." His complexion is yellow.

"It seems clear now that you wrote the notes for your novel in the men's room at Elaine's. You were alone there for roughly half an hour. Burden went back to get you. It's not clear how long you and Burden were alone together. From the time you and Burden joined Cornwall and Kaufman you were never alone with any one other person for the rest of the evening."

Plante shakes his head. "It's not Wally."

I point down to the report. "If you don't want it, would you mind kicking it over here?" Plante retrieves the report from between his legs and hands it over to me. I scan it. "At Clarke's at the very end you were riding high talking about art and artists. Do you remember that?"

Plante puts a hand to his head. "Was I? My God! No!"

"The others were very depressed. Might that be a reaction to your having told them about your idea?"

"I know I didn't tell all of them. I might have been baiting them." He gives it a moment's thought. "It can't be Wally."

"I think I have a way to prove it to you." Plante shakes his head. "I want you to set up separate meetings with your friends just as you did on the eighteenth. I want you to meet Kaufman first at Clarke's, leave him and go to meet Cornwall at Bradley's, then Burden at the White Horse. I want you to relax and have a good time with them. I want you to seem to drink."

Plante stares down at his hands. "And seem to black out," he adds.

I grin. "But only seem to."

"And you'll be there watching the whole shameful performance."

"I'll be at the next table. Wherever you go, I'll be at the next table."

"And what will all this deceit prove?"

"I assume you have a new notebook. May I see it?" Plante draws a three-by-five, green-covered spiral memo pad out of his inside jacket pocket. "At some point late in the evening, when you're with all three of your friends, I want you to go to the john; I want you to return after fifteen or twenty minutes very excited, publicly brandishing your notebook so they can't possibly miss it, and say something like: 'It's incredible! It all came back!' You don't have to say much more than that. Then I want you to start celebrating. Do you think you can do that?"

"You don't seriously believe this will work?"

"You won't do it?"

He rises from his chair so stiffly I am afraid he won't make it. "What you're talking about is entrapment." We exchange stares. "These men are my friends. Would you do this to your friends?"

"Friends who I don't trust, I'd do it to them."

"How can you keep friends you don't trust?" His face seems to fade in and out of focus, trying to settle on an expression. The expression is disgust. Aimed at whom? At me? At himself? At all of the above?

May 6

Annabelle calls: "Please forgive me for last night. I know all I do is apologize, but I was on Seconals and they depress the hell out of me. What do you take to sleep?"

"Company."

She lets that go by. "Listen, do you think there's any chance of our ever getting together and being nice to each other? I'd really like to try."

"Fine with me."

"Oh, good! I was sure you'd hang up on me. How about tonight?"

"Terrific."

"About seven?"

"Where?"

"The Algonquin?"

"Swell."

"You won't stand me up?"

"Why would I do that?"

"How come you're so dear on the telephone and so ominous in person?" I don't believe it and I don't know how to answer it. The other line rings. Mr. Ackroyd wanted on two! I put Annabelle on hold and switch over. It's Plante. It's all set up. He's meeting Kaufman at Clarke's at six-thirty and from then on, the others in the right places in the right order. I groan and tell him terrific.

I switch back to Annabelle. "Listen, something's just come up. I'm afraid I have to call it off for tonight."

"I can't say I'm surprised. What happened? A better offer?"

"Can we do it tomorrow?"

Icily: "Can we stop playing games?"

May 7

To get past the worst first, my notebook has been stolen. It is nowhere in the office. And I am sure I had it with me when I shadowed Plante last night. I remember having it in Clarke's.

But it is not in my coat pocket or my jacket pocket or my pants pockets—I have gone through them all a number of times—it is not anywhere on my desk or in the desk drawers or under the desk, nor has it slipped under either of the chairs. And it is not in the john down the hall. I looked when I threw up.

So the first question is, where is my notebook? The second question is, why did I come back to the office to sleep? The third question is, where was I last night?

No question, I am hung over. But I didn't have that much to drink. In any case, I handle liquor well. I don't get sick. And I don't black out. Still, the fact remains that I woke up at five-thirty slumped over my typewriter, my face pockmarked with key indentations, my teeth dying to fall out. And I am nauseous, I am sweating, my hands shake, my stomach crawls with worms, my head is a sack of meal, my body, a deadweight.

Could I have been doped? Was my drink (drinks) fixed? When? Where? By whom? Who was I with? My mind is a blank. Brain damage?

The phone clangs. I miss my first try at it and then give up. I don't want to talk to anyone. I particularly don't want to talk to Plante. What can I possibly say to him?

I sit, staring into space, trying to drill messages into my brain. I do remember Clarke's. A little. A hazy vision of Plante sitting opposite a great bruiser of an apparition—no features, no characteristics other than size. I wouldn't recognize the man if he walked in here, but he must be Kaufman.

Panic surges. I know I've been poisoned! Why have they done this to me? Why can't I remember?

Calm. I must collect myself. If Kaufman poisoned me—and who can it be besides Kaufman?—I can only bring him down if I collect myself, work out the sequence of events, act like a detective.

If I am to accept the assumption that Kaufman drugged me (of all the suspects only he was at Clarke's), then I must accept the second assumption that he knew who I was, knew the whole scheme from the beginning. But how? Who tipped him off? How did he slip me the drug?

I stare at the litter on my desk, the contents of my pockets strewn about during my search for the notebook. Among the familiar items, a number of unfamiliar ones: matchbook covers from Elaine's and scraps of paper napkins with cryptic, difficult to decipher, pencil scrawls. The hand that made them was unsteady, but recognizably my hand. I gather the scraps together and organize them into a small, threatening pile.

PB fite ③ nite bsbl!!
P try blow nb!! read 2C J save day: Hooker bit ✓ ✓
PB on jocks ✓ ✓
P crazy!!
PC on VN!!
J pay bill 75!!
B on star fuk!!
PC fite ② Rocky!!
P xx!!
PK on Salinger ✓
J: Tolsty bit 2 KBC ✓
C stiffs J!!
C on JFK!!
PJ john Pxx: no nb!! Give mine ✓ ✓
PK fite–wife!!
Pxx calls me A!!
CB vs PK: Mailer!!
CB xit!! J bring bak ✓ ✓
PK on Hemwy ✓ ✓

Nineteen notes in all, obviously on-the-spot reminders to myself scribbled on scraps and meant to be embellished with detail later. So my first deduction is that Kaufman lifted my notebook sometime after Plante and his cronies arrived at Elaine's. It is a run-of-the-mill deduction but it puts me in a more relaxed frame of mind: I am back in control. I can deduce. I can handle it. I examine the scraps of code with a confidence approaching euphoria.

I proceed with the simplest deductions first: 2 is shorthand for to, except when it is inside a circle when it probably means two; the checks are positive signs put there to indicate that things are going well; the double checks mean to tell me that things are going very well. The double exclamation points speak for themselves: they look like bulging eyes under astonished eyebrows, depicting shock, surprise, disapproval.

I work for forty-five minutes, through three more phone attacks, trying to establish a time sequence for the notes. Impossible. So I give up chronology for an attempt to analyze the notes singly, sorting them out on a name basis. P is obviously Plante; B is Burden, the publicist; C is Cornwall, the newspaperman; K is Kaufman, the poisoner; A is for Ackroyd. There is also a J. The only previous J on record is Deborah Jessup, but that's impossible: this is strictly a men's group, and the reference to P and J in the john plus another, which has J paying the bill (*J pay bill 75!!*) proves he's male. But what male?

Even more disturbing is the note *Pxx calls me A!!* Did Plante expose me? Did he identify me as a private detective to his friends? The double-x can only stand for double-cross. Altogether three references to double-cross. *What does it mean? Can it be that Plante set me up?*

A slow, cumulative rage develops toward Plante. Why would he want to get me? Has he found out about Annabelle and me? But what is there to find out, except my intentions? Then why double-cross me? Does it all add up to the fact that the notebook business is one more phony like the Jessup busi-

44

ness? Could all this be a set-up? Is Plante really working for my father? Was it Plante who drugged me, tried to fix it that I fail—not Kaufman, but Plante?

Sweat glands erupt on the crown of my head. My forehead burns. I am running a low fever.

Calm. I must be calm. Without calm I lack control. Without control I can't restore order. Hate, however justified, is nonproductive. If Plante is, in fact, my father's agent, I must treat it as a test, an opportunity. Whatever the truth of this matter, I must turn it to my advantage.

I go back to work, line up the shorter notes, expecting them to be easier to break down.

PB on jocks√√ Plante and Burden talk about jocks. Apparently with my approval. *P crazy!!* Like a fox! *PC on VN!!* Who is VN, and why is he marked negative? *J pay bill 75!!* *C stiffs J!!* Who the hell is J?

I concentrate on the notes mentioning Cornwall. *PC fite* ② *Rocky!!* Who is Rocky? Does ② mean fight number two? Plante and Cornwall's second fight? Their second fight over Rocky? *C on JFK!!* Was Cornwall criticizing President Kennedy? Could Rocky be Rockefeller? *CB vs PK: Mailer!!* Cornwall and Burden fight with Plante and Kaufman about Norman Mailer. *CB xit!! J bring bak* √√ Cornwall and Burden exit, that is, they leave Elaine's. Another appointment or the result of a fight? In any case, the day is saved by the elusive J who brings them back, winning himself a double check.

I am working well now. Cool. Under control.

Every reference to Cornwall is marked negative. Meaning what? Was he my prime suspect, or was it merely that I didn't approve of his opinions on Kennedy and Rockefeller and VN? Could VN be Vietnam?

Under control.

Burden, according to the notes, talked to Plante about jocks (good marks), night baseball (bad marks), and star fucking (bad marks), which left Plante's literary conversation in the hands of Kaufman. Hemingway and Salinger are discussed without acrimony (good marks). The one bad mark for Kaufman reference: *PK fite—wife!!* An unpleasant fight over a wife. Surely Kaufman's. Otherwise, I would have probably written Annabelle or some cryptic abbreviation thereof.

An awful lot of fighting going on at that table. They lost control. A lesson to be learned from that.

P try blow nb!! read 2C J save day: Hooker bit ✓✓ Once again the mysterious J. A disheartening suspicion that J is the key to everything. If so, I'm in serious trouble. And what the hell is nb? *It can't be a name! Names are capitalized!*

Cool. Restore cool. It's going to be all right. This is only a test.

In a sudden brain-congealing overview, the entire note coheres into an explanation, the harrowing truth of which sends me off to the john for a renewed session of vomiting, retching, and near-suicidal impulses.

What have I done?

I sit in the john, trembling, conclusions riddling my skull like shell fragments: nb, of course, is notebook. Plante tried to read his notebook to Cornwall but J interceded. How did J save the day? By diverting Cornwall's attention with an anecdote: the hooker bit. The reference is distressingly clear: the hooker bit is mine, a story I tell, have told and retold for years, my ticket of admission into the party, how I win new friends through charm, smut, and self-deprecation. God help me, I was a member of Plante's party: I was J.

I stifle a second rush of nausea. Why did I join them? And, having joined them, why did I humiliate myself by telling that awful story? My first visit to a prostitute. Drunk, out of control, impotent. So I gave her a fifty-dollar tip, my school allowance for the rest of the month, not to inform on me to my friends. Why do people find that story amusing? Why do I tell it almost every time I get drunk? Why can't I conduct a professional surveillance?

I am a flop. A fuckup. I am everything my father said I was. He may call me his enemy, but, in truth, I am his ally. I have done my best to prove that he is right about me.

No one drugged me. No one had to. I drugged myself. I did it all to myself: got drunk, blacked out, lost my notebook. I am the Quisling in my own ranks.

Fresh wave after wave of self-hate. It goes on for almost an hour: Byzantine, sensual, inspired. . . . It makes me hot: thoughts of sex with Annabelle Plante and Deborah Jessup. The result of failing Plante is that I want to screw his wife and girlfriend.

I will run away, change my name again and start all over. I will not be a detective. I will be a garbage man.

Out of control, I ramble back over the years to resume an ancient quarrel with my sister, Elsie, who always took my father's side in arguments, not because she agreed with him— she agreed with me—but because she was in terror of losing him. Well, she didn't lose him; she lost me!

I seethe as I hear Elsie, in residence inside my head, take on the job of Plante's counsel: All I am to Plante is a service organization, yet I'm bitter that I'm not recognized as an equal; is that why I had to get drunk last night? Because in a circle of successful men I am not a success; because among sophisticates I'm an outsider? Is that what goaded me to join his table? Elsie demands to know.

Wretch. The wretch retches. Calm. Sanity. Sanity is good. Panic is bad. Panic prevents deduction and deduction is the only thing that's going to get me out of this.

A pertinent thought interrupts my confrontation with Elsie. On the evidence of the notes, Plante was about to break up the party. He was about to send everyone home before he pulled his notebook act in the john. He was *not* going to pull his notebook act in the john; he was chickening out! And so the succession of quarrels: Vietnam, night baseball, Rockefeller, Mailer, the pretext was unimportant. That's why I horned in —not out of envy—but to save the day!

Okay. Good reconstruction. Take a deep breath. Where are we? *P try blow nb!! read 2C.* . . . Plante tried to read the decoy notebook to Cornwall—but that's not possible: it was blank. No, not blank if he was able to read from it. Read what? Stay calm. *PJ john Pxx: no nb!! Give mine* √√ What did Plante do in the john to screw things up? *He didn't bring the decoy notebook!* That was his little surprise for me in the john! "Sorry, can't go through with it, forgot my notebook." So I gave him mine! Which is why it's missing: I handed it over to Plante!

Cool now. The notebook. We came back from the john and Plante wouldn't play, forced me to set the stage: *J: Tolsty bit 2 KBC* √ I did it all. Told Kaufman and Burden and Cornwall that Plante had confided to me his brilliant idea for a new novel, dozens of pages of fresh notes, best novel since *War and Peace*. So I've entrapped his friends, not him. He's out of it; in the clear; sweetheart of a guy.

It takes so long for him to answer his phone that by the time he picks it up I have finished wanting to kill him.

"What in the world were you up to last night?" His voice, a blurred monotone, bristles with reproach. "I must tell you I am shocked! As little as I can recall of last night I cannot manage to black out your egregious plagiarism. As if it's not painful enough to have my novel stolen, you add insult to injury by stealing my name. Logan Jessup, indeed! In the future, kindly leave in my possession those few creations I am sober enough to still lay claim to."

Midway through his diatribe I realize he has blurted out the meaning of J. J is Logan Jessup! Why? Why of all names did I have to pick the one most likely to provoke him?

Plante interrupts my orgy of self-recrimination with a coughing fit that goes on for thirty seconds. I instinctively close my hand over the receiver to deflect his germs and his anger. By the time he returns to health I have re-established calm. "I specifically asked you not to drink," I say, unconscionably, "but since you ignored my request, I guess I had better remind you of what went on. Your meeting with your friends was so out of control that it looked like the whole evening was about to be blown. That's why I used the name Jessup. To restore calm and to remind you of our purpose. Furthermore, I had to lend you my notebook. You had forgotten your decoy. Now I need those notes so I can type up my report."

Plante responds with a dry, humorless chuckle. "Am I to understand that you have lost your notebook?"

Ten minutes of unpleasant wrangling produces the information that Plante does not have my notebook. If not Plante, then who? The thief? If the thief has the notebook, I think I have the thief. I tell Plante but he refuses to act pleased or even interested. Just the opposite. Insists that he has to get off the phone to write a column. I manage to inveigle him into a six-o'clock date at the Algonquin. "I'll need every detail of conversation you can dredge up from last night, no matter how trivial. It's really important."

"But you were there!" he complains wearily. "Even without notes you can't possibly have forgotten more than I."

"I always like to double check," I tell him.

Because we are at the Algonquin, Plante is quicker at remembering what Dorothy Parker said to Robert Benchley than what Burden and Cornwall and Kaufman said to him. He's wearing a gray flannel oscillating pinstripe. His soft, pleasant face, his gray suit, his Havana cigar refuse to stay in focus. He drinks a Bloody Mary while I drink a Scotch to replenish my calm.

After a half hour of teeth-grinding digression, I maneuver him onto the subject of last night at Clarke's.

"Our first watering hole, so I can report every word." He looks pleased with himself. "One topic we discussed was writers and alcoholism. O, or Big O, as he is known within the confines of our small fraternity because of the vast amounts of him, quoted the Fitzgerald remark, 'First you take a drink, then the drink takes a drink, then the drink takes you.' I responded that serious drink led to serious guilt and that serious guilt led to literature. This led O to hope that I didn't become so serious that I ceased to entertain. To move us away from his bruising innocence, I reminisced on O's high school exploits in Old Saratoga, venturing the theory that being a writer was, to me, mere sublimation for not having played football before cheering crowds on Saturday afternoons. Writing, I explained, was mainly an attempt to out-argue one's past; to present events in such a light that battles lost in life were either won on paper or held to a draw. I remember O smiling throughout the course of our conversation, a tic he displays when he doesn't understand a word said but does not want to appear rude."

I tell Plante how well he is doing. He bows his head at my approval and offers, in response, a second round of drinks. I restrain my need to say yes and encourage him to report on his conversations with Cornwall and Burden. He leaps into it now with an enthusiasm born out of my flattery. "Cornwall is in the habit of seeing all life with the sort of remove that turns one's personal disasters into gossip, tragedy into farce, and apocalypse into a two-alarm fire. If you wish to be sincere with Cornwall you must do it in the anecdote form. He took umbrage at my remark that Robert Kennedy was unqualified for the vice presidency because as the highest legal officer in the land it was his duty to try Lyndon Johnson, not run with him. We took turns offering outlandish versions of the assassination conspiracy, offending O and depressing Burden. Some foul words were exchanged on Vietnam but I can't recall whether Cornwall was for or against it. I suppose that depended on the position I took; I wish I knew what it was."

His eyes glitter, seeming to beg for good grades. My anger cannot stand up under the oddity of the situation: his conversion of our interview into a classroom quiz. I encourage him to talk about Burden. "Burden's complaint is that he lives in the wrong century and should rightfully be dining with Dr. Johnson. In his view, the art of conversation consists of a lecture by Burden, spiced on occasion with brief questions from the rest of us. Since, of the rest of us, O alone cooperates, conversation with Burden is, shall I say, spirited. I do not listen to him and he does not listen to me, but we enjoy outshouting each other. I seem to remember an uninformative dispute on the aesthetics of night baseball. If we touched on more enlightened matters, I assure you it was a mistake."

Back in the office with three containers of black Chock full o'Nuts coffee to stoke my fires I collate Plante's information with my drunken notes.

The evidence, to say the least, is inconclusive, but it's all I have, so I draw conclusions. On April eighteenth each of Plante's pals had opportunity to steal his notebook: Kaufman was alone with him at Clarke's, Cornwall was alone with him at the White Horse, Burden was alone with him in the john at Elaine's. Last night, during the period that counts (if I am to believe the evidence of my notes), only Kaufman was alone with him. Admittedly, that's a shaky surmise, but it is buttressed by Plante's testimony.

Kaufman is the one friend Plante naturally confides in. Cornwall? Too cynical for serious talk; they get witty over politics. Burden is an egomaniac, a snob; doesn't listen and, if that's not enough, restricts his conversation mainly to sports.

But Kaufman? The least flashy member of the crowd, the low man on the totem pole. Plante speaks of him with condescension, has known him half his life, knows he's interested in his writing, is able to discuss books with him, no doubt relies on him for uncritical approval. Who better to trust with a fragile new idea?

Tenuous, perhaps. Built on shaky facts, perhaps. But were I still a drinking man after last night I would raise a glass to Logan Jessup II.

It is shortly before five. I look up the UJA in the Manhattan book. Before dialing I try for a mental fix on Kaufman: at this very moment what shape is he in? What did he think when he opened the notebook and found not the plot for Plante's novel, but Jessup's diary? Does the diary give me away as a detective? Does he know he was set up for a trap? As I dial Kaufman's number I wonder which of us is entering this conversation with less reliable information.

"Mr. Kaufman?" Breathing on the other end. "This is Logan Jessup."

More breathing. Then: "Yes?" A soft voice, furry at the edges, very deep.

"We met last night at Elaine's." Breathing continues. "Mr. Kaufman, I wonder if you have some free time? I'm doing a doctoral thesis on 'American Writers and Their Use of the Vernacular'—I already have hundreds of pages of notes—and I'd like to interview you on Oscar Plante."

A long pause. "A doctoral thesis . . ."

"What opinions you have on the role of ordinary day-to-day speech in a writer's work. The sort of conversation I couldn't help but overhear last night, for example—"

The breathing escalates into a singsong rhythm. "I don't know if I can be of much help."

"I promise not to take too much of your time."

A long pause. "Where are you taking your doctorate?"

I am prepared for the question. "The University of Hawaii." Another sustained bout of agonized breathing.

"We met at Elaine's. Logan Jessup. When can I see you? Do you have some time now?"

"No, I don't know—"

"It won't take long."

I hear small noises, desk drawers opening and closing on the other end. "Not here," he says in a near whisper.

"Clarke's?" No answer. "Say, in twenty minutes?" I wait.

"Make it a half hour," Kaufman whispers. I do not answer. A windstorm of heavy breathing. "Are you still there?" I don't answer. "Jessup." I don't answer. More breathing, a click; the phone goes dead.

I give Kaufman plenty of time to get there before me, dreaming him into a huge writhing mass of anxiety: Big O, two hundred-odd pounds of nerve-racked plum pudding, putting away two drinks at the very least before my arrival, desperately ill over my phone call. No such luck. I wait in an unlit corner in Clarke's, one eye on the door, the other glued to the glass of Scotch on my table to make sure it stays put. No Kaufman. I case the joint to see if I could have missed him. Not a chance. No one here alone except me, growing lonelier. No one near the size reputed to be Kaufman's. I sip soda and fume. Clarke's is crowded with my generation, my class: sleek, flitty, unserious. Not a trace of character on any face in the room. Not a face on any face . . . Resonating voices gifted in chalk talk. Gibble gabble. My fingers move toward the Scotch.

"Anyone here named Logan Jessup?"

My mood of superiority is replaced by a sudden urge to make a break for it. A tall, lanky waiter of twenty or so, wearing a black bow tie and a white apron, leans against a telephone booth next to the bar holding the receiver in his hand. His manner hints that he will ask for identification. About six feet tall, unruly brown hair, a pinched baby face with gray insolent eyes, he stands more like a judge than a waiter, the receiver jutting out of his fist like a gavel. Only when I am on top of him does it occur to me that my animosity toward him stems from his striking resemblance to me.

"Mr. Jessup?" It's a woman's voice on the phone, low, resonant. She introduces herself as Esther Kaufman and informs me that Kaufman is standing me up—"unavoidably detained" is the way she puts it—but that he would be pleased to see me at some other time, for example tomorrow at seven-thirty at their apartment for dinner. A regal assurance to her voice makes it somehow all right that a suspect invite his pursuer home to dinner.

"I don't think that would be appropriate." I hold out, ill at ease because I haven't a clue to the lady's relationship to Kaufman.

"I can assure you we don't bite," she says, obviously mocking me and thereby settling the matter. I ask for an address.

Elsie has found me. Hadn't thought of her for months until this morning and now she shows up. A former classmate of hers at Bard turns out to live one floor below me here at the Excelsior. Elsie and her network of informants!

Should I take her along as my date to the Kaufmans? If he can protect himself with family, why can't I retaliate with my big sister? She can embarrass me over hors d'oeuvres, expose me over soup, and betray me for dessert.

So far, however, she is on her best behavior, hasn't mentioned our father, hasn't asked me to go home. As usual, she offers me money. As usual, I feel ashamed when I turn it down.

May 8

I try Kaufman's office three times. Each time the girl asks "Who's calling?" and, on being told, says he's out. I think of calling a fourth time and leaving a different name, but if I did get him, then what? I don't want to panic the man, and he already gives signs of being trapped. Is that the point of tonight's family scene? A bid for pity? Kaufman surrounded by his loved ones?

Kaufman's loved ones. Spouse: Esther, five foot two, brown-black eyes, thick black hair cut short in a pageboy. A slender, boyish body in a tailored silk blouse and black skirt, not unsexy for a woman of her age. Olive complexion, thick lips, large white teeth that take over the room every time she smiles.

Older daughter: Naomi, short, squat and fierce. Can't be much past twenty. Dark and hairy features, eyebrows like Nixon's. Her body, bound tightly in a brown tweed suit, looks like an instrument of war. Could easily be mistaken for her mother's mother.

Younger daughter: Tina, a knockout. Sixteen years old, close to six feet tall. Must take after her father, but as slim as or slimmer than a fashion model. Tiny head, all torso and legs. Moves like sea grass in a light wind, sits in T-shirt and jeans in physically implausible positions. Lighter in color than her mother and big sister. Doesn't talk. Doesn't smile. Not sure she even listens. If she ever lost balance it is probable that she would not fall down but float up to the ceiling. Not that she's ethereal, just aerial.

Kaufman: there is no Kaufman. He is—guess what—late.

Esther has my hand in her small, strong one and guides me to a little chair, black leather and angular and cushioned low enough to the floor for me to have to view her and her brood from between my knees. The Kaufman women sit together in tableau on the low, black couch, mother the centerpiece, Tina drifting in and out of focus, Naomi planted low and dark, not very different in appearance from the furniture.

Apologies from Esther. Otis is expected momentarily, you know how it is in his business, and what business are you in, young man? I'm a student. Tina, get Mr. Jessup a drink. Tina unwinds, is off to the kitchen, drifts back with a Coke. Naomi lights a Tiparillo with a long wooden match and exhales more smoke than I've ever seen in one drag. Tina's long fingers meet around the glass. I sip my Coke and smile comfortably at the Kaufman women. I've been thinking of going into writing when I get out of school; has Mr. Kaufman ever wanted to write? Warm laughter from Esther. Oh no, my goodness; Otis, I suppose, could do anything he put his mind to and he'd have our support. He does write occasional letters to the *Times*. Naomi glowers. What's such a big deal about Rags Plante that you want to write about him? Thus, I am tipped off that Kaufman has briefed his women. Mr. Plante is very talented, or don't you think so? Her fingers drum softly on the sofa counting out beats against me. I never thought about it. I smile at her, shooting charm. Did you like his book? My charm is obscured by an enormous exhalation of Tiparillo smoke. Esther lays a gray hand on Naomi's fat bronze knee. I do think it's wonderful that you want to write; what do your parents think? My mother is dead. Oh, I am sorry, what does he do, your father? In business. Aren't we all; what sort? Aerospace. Oh, that's a good business. Out on Long Island? No. California. San Francisco? Los Angeles. Oh, Los Angeles, that's a wonderful place to bring up children. How are the schools in Los Angeles? I went to school in New York. But you said you come from Los Angeles? My parents are divorced, my mother moved to New York. How sorry I am, a broken home. I know how lonely that is for a child. Her eyes wrap around me like a comforter, reminding me of all that is solid and good in Jewish mothers and all that is barely discernible in Wasps. My own mother fades into the shadows, a pretender, next to Esther no mother at all; the gaunt white lady who came into my room three times a week to say be responsible. Kaufman is later and later. It's rude to our guest to make him wait for his dinner, how do you take your roast beef, young man, unless I miss my guess you take it rare. Wine? No, the Coke is fine. More than fine if I were to be frank; it is acting on me like a truth serum. A black teak dinner table, wooden handled silver, candles doing shadow play on the oak paneled wall. Blotto on Coke, or is it the Kaufmans? Esther's dark, round face glows in the candlelight. Tina and Naomi, tall and short shadows on either side. Aren't you a little old to be a student? Well, I'm doing this paper. But you're no longer a student? Well, yes, the paper is for school—it depends on how it works out—if Mr. Kaufman can help me; you don't find many friendships that last as long as his and Mr. Plante's. Then this paper you're doing is not for your thesis? Do you like strawberries? I haven't had strawberries in years. Well, we'll correct that right now. You must excuse me if I sound confused but how can my husband possibly be of help to you? Do you take cream with your strawberries? You see, Mr. Plante says Mr. Kaufman is the only one he will discuss his writing with and he's reluctant to discuss it with me but he said I could get what I needed out of Mr. Kaufman, including his notebooks— My husband keeps no notebooks. Mr. Plante's notebooks. What would my husband be doing with Mr. Plante's notebooks? I don't know, but Mr. Plante said it would be all right for me to see them. So it's not their boyhood you want to ask my husband about? More cream and sugar? Yes, that too. But mainly you're interested in notebooks? Well, I don't separate the two, I'm interested in the whole relationship. Well, I don't know anything about notebooks, this is the first I've heard. More coffee? A drink, then? Tina, get Mr. Jessup a—what do you drink, Mr. Jessup?

1:00 A.M.: What hit me? Esther hit me. She unpeeled me like a banana. And what did I get out of her? Dinner. But what a dinner! Okay. So far, not too much harm done. If I can only learn to keep my mouth shut with her then I might turn this to my advantage. If I can't get to Kaufman directly maybe I can get to him through Esther.

Somewhere Kaufman lurks: Big O turned into Invisible O, his family surrounding him like a palace guard. Hopeless to strike from without, but to penetrate from within, to befriend Esther! If she can be convinced that my interests are, in the end, her interests, that if Kaufman keeps the notebooks he undermines the security of her home.

Elsie has moved in downstairs with her friend who turned me in. Brought her up to my room at three in the morning. For protection? I was up anyway. Astonished how baldly she flirts with me in front of strangers.

May 10

I call the UJA. No Kaufman. Hang around outside his office for three hours, before, during and after lunch. No Kaufman. On a long shot I call Esther. Can she do anything to put me in touch with her husband? Why don't I come over for lunch, we can discuss it then. I file a counter-offer: Let me take her out to lunch. We make it for one at the Plaza.

Pain is in her face: Something is disturbing her husband, he won't confide in her, he has always confided in her, she wonders if it has anything to do with me. Her eyes take over mine. I can't stare away. I notice, peripherally, a small tremor in her hand. It is holding a daiquiri and the liquid shivers. My professional cool shivers with it. An extraordinarily powerful desire to confess, to throw myself on her mercy. I muster the dregs of my resources.

"Mrs. Kaufman, I have to tell you frankly that I think it has to do with those notebooks I mentioned the other night. Did you ask your husband about them?"

Her stare reaches deep into my vitals. "What is it you're not telling me, Mr. Jessup?"

Every time she calls me Jessup I want to pull the tablecloth over my head and hide. "The question isn't what I'm not telling you, it's what your husband isn't telling. Are you sure he's being straight with you about those notebooks?"

She smiles thinly at me: a smile that says she had hoped for better of me but that she is prepared to forgive if I will only come clean.

"Look, Mrs. Kaufman, it seems to me a fairly simple matter. I want to talk to your husband about his boyhood friend, Rags Plante. I have Mr. Plante's go-ahead to do so. I also have Mr. Plante's go-ahead to look at some notebooks he says Mr. Kaufman is holding for him. Now, who am I? A kid at a bar whom Mr. Kaufman was introduced to as Logan Jessup and to whom you'd think he'd be perfectly free to say 'Go to hell' if he didn't want to be bothered with me. But instead he says he will help me out, breaks two dates with me and drops out of sight. What's the threat? That's what I ask you to think about. Is it from me? I swear to you, Mrs. Kaufman, you are a woman I respect and admire: I'm not the threat. That's crazy! So the threat must be elsewhere. He doesn't want me to see those notebooks."

Her eyes move off my face for the first time in minutes. She looks down at the lunch rolls. "You won't mind if I ask what must seem to you a foolish question?"

"Right," I say, half listening, trying hard to keep in order what I just said.

"You mentioned your first meeting with my husband—"

"My only meeting."

"Yes. And you alluded to your introduction in a way that gave me reason to wonder if your name is really Logan Jessup. I'm sure it is. I just want you to clear that up for me because your phrasing—"

"You're right, Mrs. Kaufman. I was deliberately being ambiguous. My name is not Logan Jessup. It's Roger Ackroyd."

"I see," she says so quietly I can hear the ax whistling toward my neck.

"Because your husband met me as Jessup, I didn't want to confuse matters by using another name on him so I continued as Jessup. The deception wasn't deliberate; I slipped into it out of convenience and—I don't know—the whole business of explanation—it seemed impossible at the time. But that's beside the point—"

"Is it? Is it really?" Her eyes narrow. "You come to my home as a guest using a false name, making up a story about notebooks—"

"I didn't make up the story about the notebooks."

"And you didn't make up the story about the thesis?" I nod, tight-lipped. "Another convenience?"

"Yes."

"Like the name." An arrow pierces my heart. "You apparently will say or do anything to get what you want; why you want it is no concern of mine. What is my concern is to free my husband from your harassment." Her voice has lost all friendliness; it is the voice of a woman who has survived much, will survive more and is not going to have too hard a time surviving me.

"I don't want to make an enemy of you, Mrs. Kaufman." My own voice, I notice in near-panic, is barely under control.

"You have a strange way of showing it."

I try to get back on the track. "Look, I could have said anything and made you believe it. But I couldn't with you because it didn't seem right, so I'm paying now for telling you the truth, not for lying. I just wish that for one minute you could try to see my side of it; you and I don't start out from the same points of departure. You see this from your husband's point of view; I see this from another."

"*Whose?*"

"I'm not free to say."

"Oscar Plante?"

"I'm sorry."

"Did he put you up to this? If he thinks Otis has his notebooks, why doesn't he come to him like a man and ask him for them?"

"He doesn't know anything about what I've done. No one has to know. If your husband would only surrender the notebooks." I am pleading.

"Oscar Plante hired you to get my husband's notebooks."

"They don't belong to your husband."

"After picking at Otis's bones for years he now wants to strip them bare. But he's not big enough to face Otis man to man. So he hires you—what are you? A lawyer?"

"I'm not a lawyer."

"No, I wouldn't think your kind would be admitted to the bar. A private detective, then. Shameless! Shameless!" She fires at me one last eye-burst of lead. Seconds later the table is empty. Except for my remains. Last rites don't take long. No one shows up, they are all too embarrassed.

Big fight on the phone with Elsie. Told her she'd better start calling me "Roger," no more "Bobbie." I won't see her again until she calls me "Roger." Her friend Jeanie came up to reason with me but I didn't let her in.

May 11

Mad as it may seem, I think I am infatuated with Esther Kaufman. Not that I am about to take it seriously. Up half the night composing letters in my head to her explaining my side of the notebook affair, but the more I explained the more questionable my case. How can I rationalize my persistence on a job that the client himself doesn't seem to take seriously? And why is Plante so cavalier in his attitude?

Stakeout Kaufman's apartment, not expecting results, not certain that I would recognize the man if I saw him. All I can be sure about is his size. It is a perfect spring day and I am in a euphoric mood, perhaps in reaction to my self-disgust of yesterday. I couldn't be happier. I fantasize a stroll along the East River with Esther, tugboats tooting, she and I rambling on about our lives. She is a wonderful listener in my fantasy; I tell her things I've never told anyone. I am pissed off that, after an hour and a half of platonic idyll, Naomi, the dour daughter, a physical violation of spring, galumphs out of the building, walking east as if she has skis on. Of the three Kaufman women, I remember Naomi as being the most hostile the other night, meaning something perhaps about the depth of her involvement with her father. On a hunch, I follow her.

An easy tail job: With her thick fullback's body decked out in a bright orange and yellow plaid suit I couldn't lose her in Yankee Stadium. We board a Second Avenue bus, take it eight blocks to Fifty-seventh Street, transfer to a crosstown for seven blocks and get out at Seventh Avenue. By this time, I have no doubt in my mind where she's headed. I wait for her outside Kaufman's office building. Only a ten-minute wait before she comes out carrying a stuffed nine-by-twelve manila envelope. I am so excited by our progress that I want to rush up and congratulate her as if the two of us are in on this together. Instead, I take up my position a half block behind and let her trudge stiff-legged (she must hate walking) over to Columbus Circle. The man she meets at Columbus Circle is sitting on a park bench munching pretzels.

A gray fedora pulled over dark glasses hides his face. A camel's hair topcoat buttoned for February with the collar turned up hides the rest of him. He is as inconspicuous as a polar bear and not very much smaller. I am embarrassed by how they greet each other: far too emotional, by my standards, for father and daughter. They hug, they clutch, they do everything but roll around in the grass. From behind my lamp post station, thirty yards away, I hear anguished sobs that infuriate me. Nobody's prosecuting. The man is not going to jail. Purest bullshit melodrama! All the son of a bitch has to do is turn over the goddam notebooks and I will get out of his life.

Fifteen minutes of intense touching and clutching and whispering and moaning is, thank heaven, time enough for them to complete their business. A bearhug from Kaufman sends Naomi plodding east. He conceals the bulky envelope under his camel's hair coat, confirming to me that inside are the missing notebooks, and takes off at a brisk clip, looking from a half block behind like someone I know. We arrive at an underground garage at Sixty-third and Amsterdam before I settle on whom: of course, Plante. While Kaufman gets lost in the maw of the garage, I flag down a cab on Amsterdam and explain the nature of our mission. Five minutes later Kaufman comes gliding into view encased in a '64 Olds convertible with the top down. The illogic of it is enchanting. For a man in hiding he might as well take out ads.

I stay amused at Kaufman's ridiculousness until I realize we are on the Cross Bronx Expressway, undoubtedly headed for Larchmont. I get less amused the closer we come to Annabelle's. By the time Kaufman pulls into the driveway on Poplar Street, I have to resist my impulse to provoke a fight with the cab driver over out-of-town rates.

I stake out Annabelle's house in a mood of quiet, cold fury, grateful that I was fortunate enough to have the blow softened by my sudden infatuation with Esther Kaufman. That Annabelle, who it was in the cards for me to sleep with, should be hiding, perhaps shacking up with the man who stole her husband's notebook: rage and incredulity combine into an emotional hash. I hike ten blocks to an outdoor phone booth and put in a collect call to Plante. He refuses the call. I scream through the long-distance operator that it's an emergency. He still refuses the call. I hike another half mile to the center of Larchmont where I locate a bank across the street from a pet shop displaying (I can't help but notice) parakeets in the window. With five dollars' worth of quarters from the bank, I try a second time for Plante. He apologizes for not accepting the call: he was in the middle of writing a column. I tell him that Kaufman has stolen his wife in addition to his notebook. He acts uninterested, even has the gall to suggest that I am trying too hard. I tell him that I have irrefutable proof. Plante remarks that he doesn't want proof, only his notebook. Nothing I say will alert him or convince him. By the time he eases me off the phone I am half convinced that Kaufman is at Larchmont for nothing more serious than high tea with his old friend Annabelle. I take the New York Central home wondering if I'm trying too hard.

May 12

Plante, appearing with all his emotional baggage—blurred face, vacuum in the eyes, air of dependence—is waiting for me as I open the office. No apologies. He follows me inside already in the middle of a monologue on trust, friendship, betrayal, the works . . .

Now it's not only a matter of getting back the notebooks, he wants to know what's going on between Kaufman and his wife, not that he believes anything is, not that he believes Kaufman stole the notebooks. He is a saint, believes only the best of anyone he isn't married to, acknowledges the sinfulness of Annabelle but further acknowledges that it is his fault. He is generous, he forgives her, but he is also a realist: I may as well take pictures of Kaufman and her together; not that he intends to make use of them, but for future reference, a record, in order to know what's going on . . .

I tell him I'm tired of fighting cab drivers and need money for a car rental, also money for a camera and, while we're at it, bugging equipment. He vetoes the electronics, gives me six hundred in cash, looks at me, eyes all water, the money in my hand the sign of his continued trust, the mist in his eyes the sign of his expected disappointment.

1:00 P.M.: Larchmont, courtesy of Hertz. I am the proud owner of a 500mm Nikon, so classy, precision-made and efficient that when I use it I feel in a state of grace; the cross as a tool. I rejoice, click away, snap everything in sight: snap

Annabelle, busy in and out, with Josh, with the maid, never with Kaufman.

I desperately hope Annabelle will spot me so that we can have it out, so that she can tell me that she is putting up Kaufman only to get back at Rags, so that she can tell me that he sleeps alone in the basement.

At three-thirty the front door opens and Josh is thrown out the door. He turns and argues with his mother, who is hearing none of it. She firmly shuts the door in his face. A moment later all the curtains on the front side are drawn. Josh sits morosely on the stoop. The door opens; Annabelle throws out a bunch of comic books. Josh at first ignores the comic books, then, one by one, tears them apart. He kicks the pieces all over the lawn, then walks around to the back of the house.

I follow Josh around to the back. It is a spacious yard and Josh is standing stock still in the middle of it staring at me. I wink at him and hold a finger to my lips. He holds a finger to his nose and in a very loud voice starts to sing "Puff the Magic Dragon."

The curtains in back have been drawn. I trample the geranium border to get as near to the windows as possible. No break in the curtains but I hear voices, nothing audible, but a man and a woman are definitely talking. Josh's singing doesn't help. I turn to look at him. He hasn't moved but he has changed tunes. He is singing "Rudolph, the Red Nosed Reindeer." I work out a mental floor plan of the interior of the house, reload my Nikon and, not without fear, reach for the kitchen door. It is locked. I am not to be trifled with. I turn back to Josh, once again put a finger to my lips and, just as I expected and hoped, he raises his pitch to a decibel level loud enough to drown out the sound of glass breaking in the kitchen door. The song is "Santa Claus Is Comin' to Town," and when he gets to:

> He knows if you've been bad or good,
> So be good for goodness sake,

I am inside the house, splintered glass at my feet. The maid is bent over the kitchen sink, humming and singing along with

Josh. It is hard to believe my luck will hold long enough for me to get by her unseen but, bless Josh, it does.

I prowl the living room, thin yellow walls and Design Research furniture, listening for Kaufman and Annabelle. I hear only a reprise of "Puff the Magic Dragon." I am about to try a closed door when it is flung open and Annabelle bursts out, all fury, obviously ready to add one more percentile to the statistics on battered children. She is in white shorts. I spot her bare legs and Kaufman, all twelve feet of him, by her side, at the same time. I scream: "Kaufman, you philandering son of a bitch!" and in a matter of seconds shoot off a roll of film capturing for posterity the emotional binge unleashed on their two faces: shock, consternation, guilt and collapse.

If I feared violence from Kaufman I misconstrued. Annabelle is the violent one in this crowd, sneers at my threat to use Kaufman as a corespondent in a divorce suit, shrieks betrayal, violation of ethics that I have gone to work for her husband while I am still employed by her(!). Demands not just the films but my brand-new camera, then says to hell with the pictures, to hell with me, to hell with Rags, do what I want with them, she couldn't care less.

I am in sympathy with her outrage, believe in her innocence, want to be alone with her to explain I'm on her side but my guilt is child's play next to Kaufman's.

He is not quite as large as he looked at Columbus Circle but he's none the less intimidating. Emasculating. He sits in gray business suit and blue tie taking up most of the couch, red-faced, his eyes swollen from lack of sleep, his mouth drawn in bitterness and self-contempt, looking like a magnified mirror image of everything I've been feeling about myself this past week. His hair is close-cropped red and graying, his complexion less red but quite red, lots of flesh, blurred features, handsome in the beefy manner of over-the-hill jocks, boyish looking for all his size and age, unfinished for all his finesse as a fund raiser. I look him over and feel apprehensive for Annabelle. He is broken, helpless, in flight. Am I wrong that she finds this irresistible?

Kaufman's statement follows: "I am not a nothing. I am not a millionaire but I am not a nothing. I am not famous, celebrated, never will be—all right, but my family, my children, by all means, look upon me—*looked* upon me as some kind of —as some*one!* Nothing too good for me. My daughters at least. Naomi more than Tina. Tina, I don't know what it is, but Naomi! And now—the way she looks at me. I can't— I won't— I am a young forty-nine, it's not over. By no means. But Naomi, that at least, her father, what else, she's no beauty, if not a core to hold on to, what? When that goes—and you see it going everywhere, high and low—oh yes, I know—but when it goes, the faith by which we hold our lives together— And what's left? For Naomi—I know her shortcomings—without a father to look up to? What? No, this is intolerable. What you've created. No, it's intolerable. I know, I know what you want, but the means and the ends? You have no right to do that, now you undo it. You undo it and I give you the notebooks."

The man talked slowly, even more disjointed than what is recorded here, six thoughts for every word, head cluttered with garbage, unable to make sense or talk sense. His problem becomes my problem. How, after all this, do I get back the fucking notebooks?!

I say to him: "Return the notebooks, I'll stop hounding you, your life will revert to normal."

Annabelle, for the fifteenth time, orders me out of her house. She doesn't listen, only reacts. Kaufman absorbs what I've said, absorbs words like DDT, by now anything said to him is that much more poison.

"You brought me down. You must restore me in the eyes of my family. You have a responsibility. Rags and I—what business is it of yours? I'm willing to go halfway. Am I asking too much? Tell me if I am. I don't think so. Those are my terms."

I ask him how I can possibly restore him in the eyes of his family. He answers with a sob. His sob shakes the couch. Annabelle flies to his side, puts an arm around him, glares at me with a disdain that reminds me of Esther's. The only two women I've cared about in more than a year were met through this case and both of them hate me.

"Does your wife know you're here?"

Honest to God, he whimpers!

"Ackroyd, I'll kill you!" says Annabelle.

Kaufman looks up. "I thought his name was Jessup."

So he doesn't know anything; doesn't know I'm a detective, doesn't know about my lunch with Esther, doesn't know shit. "When did you last speak with your wife?" I try to say it gently but he flinches. Annabelle screams at me. I also scream at me: Out, I want out! I went into this business to be Sam Spade, not Hitler. I stand up. "Look, I'll come back later. Maybe we'll both think of something." I leave Kaufman, leave the house and leave Larchmont. I am accompanied by background music. Josh is singing "Jingle Bells."

Back in the office I call Plante and tell him I've quit. "No matter," he says and hangs up. In order to do something I try to type up my notes but type gibberish. Too much anger. Too much confusion. I pick up the phone to call Plante and apologize; instead of a dial tone I hear Kaufman.

"I've thought it all out. This is what I want. A testimonial dinner." I wait. "They should all be there. Emmett and Wally, you met them the other night, and Rags. It should be in a private dining room somewhere. The Regency. It should be very formal. I have a birthday coming up. It should be a surprise for my birthday. My family is to be invited. Also some celebrities. I know a few, Rags and Wally know everybody. I am to be the guest of honor. I don't want presents; I just want them all to be there. I don't think it's too much to ask after all these years. You set it up. Tomorrow I'll give you a guest list. You can't come."

I call Plante. "I want to take back my resignation. At least until I can talk to you. Something new has come up. Can we talk?"

"I'm in the middle of writing a column."

I grunt; Plante picks up on it: "I don't mean to sound abrupt. I can't afford another curse."

Elsie now never fails to bring Jeanie with her for protection. Calls me "Roger." Swears she won't tell Father where I am. My hunch is she's already told him. And he doesn't care. Too bad for Elsie.

May 13

"I wish I got along better with people," Plante begins as soon as drinks arrive. His is ginger ale, mine is club soda. The waiter at Bleecks evidently knows Plante and serves us with compassion. "You, for example. I don't know what to make of you, and not knowing that disturbs me." He does not look disturbed. He looks fit, cheerful, in no way defensive about not having called me back last night; altogether in better shape than all the shapes I'd seen him in since he first approached as Logan Jessup. "I'll tell you what I feel," he goes on. "I feel that you judge me. I wish you'd stop. It upsets me terribly to be judged.

"We're so quick to form opinions of others, aren't we? And what do we form them out of? We base our opinions of present people on previous judgments of past people. So we're always arriving at final judgments one person too late. Differences blur and we are stereotyped. It disturbs me to be a type. I don't want to go down in anyone's book as a particular type."

I am tired of Plante. More and more I wish Kaufman was my client. "How long has this thing been going on between Kaufman and your wife?"

"What thing?"

"You deny they've been having an affair?"

"You have evidence that they've been having an affair?"

"You don't consider their being together at your house as evidence?"

"Only that something now exists between them. But no, not evidence of anything up until this time." He smiles cooperatively. "Perhaps I'm unimaginative."

"You didn't leave your wife because she was having an affair with Kaufman?"

Plante falls back in his chair. "You amaze me!"

"Very little information gets volunteered around here. I have to pry."

"Absolutely right. Forgive me. Please go on." The man acts like a visitor to his own case.

"Why did you leave your wife?"

"I see. You want to talk about Annabelle. This might surprise you, but I don't mind. What would you like to know?"

"How you met."

"*Newsday.*"

"She worked on *Newsday?*"

"Ah, yes."

"And that's when you began dating?"

" 'Dating.' I disapprove of the word. No, we never 'dated' on *Newsday.*"

In my head I begin singing "Puff the Magic Dragon."

"When did you date?"

"Years later."

"You were still on *Newsday?*"

"I must have been on the *Times* by that time."

"Mrs. Plante too?"

"Oh no, Mrs. Plante had given up work. She was too busy running around with Buddy Pasternak."

"Who?"

"You're not serious."

"Has Buddy Pasternak come up in this case before?"

"Mr. Ackroyd, the gaps in your education— Buddy Pasternak is the Giants' quarterback."

"The football Giants?"

"Surely not the baseball Giants."

"Mrs. Plante was Pasternak's mistress?"

"This need you have for labels plunges me into despair. Do you mind if I give you a brief lecture on labels? Labels are a means of communicating without getting close to the subject.

69

Labels are untouched by human thought; that is their purpose. Once we have labeled an idea we have caught it, put it in irons, disarmed it of all ambiguity and consequently never have to give it honest consideration. Labels are a blow to literacy, truth and manhood. They are the death of the soul and the curse of nations. Without labels we would not have murder. Without labels we would not know war. To call my wife Pasternak's mistress is to say something about her that simply isn't true."

"Did your wife live with Pasternak?"

"For a while."

"How long?"

"A year. I must admit it surprised me. Still waters run deep."

"And now she's off with another football player."

Plante winces.

"What has Kaufman got against you?"

Plante looks genuinely surprised. "What gives you the idea he has anything against me?"

"Are you willing to concede that on the basis of the available evidence he has mixed feelings?"

Plante smiles. "You're asking me to judge. I'm sorry, I can't and I won't."

"He wants a testimonial dinner." Plante squints, not getting it. "Kaufman says if you give him a testimonial dinner he'll give you back your notebook. He says he deserves it. He says it will restore him his place in the eyes of his family."

The muscles under Plante's cheeks do a little dance. "You can't be serious."

"He wants you and Burden and Cornwall and lots of celebrities. At this very moment he's probably making up a guest list."

Plante waits a long time, his eyes hazed over. He takes out one of his Havanas, rolls it around in his hand and puts it back in his case. "He wants a testimonial dinner?" I say yes. "A testimonial dinner," Plante repeats and has a coughing fit. He collects himself, blows his nose, looks at me with damp eyes. "It's my fault. The price of one goddamned notebook! Who's going to care in the long run? Say it turns out to be as good as

I'd hoped, my second book; the critics will hate it. They always hate the second book. I don't know why I dragged either one of us into this mess."

"You want to drop it?"

Plante makes a sour expression with his mouth. "Any move I make will be a mistake. So I'll make the one that does the least damage." He starts decorating the table with wet rings from his glass.

After a dozen rings I say, "Kaufman's waiting for me to get back to him. Anything in particular you want me to say?"

Plante talks to the rings he is making. He paces himself slowly, as if dictating. "Tell him no damage done, I'm still his friend. I hope that someday he'll feel better about being my friend."

Plante watches me write it all down. "I see you have a new notebook."

On the other end of the phone Kaufman sounds as if he is taking the news hard.

"He doesn't want it?" His breathing is hoarse and loud.

"He says it's not worth all the trouble it's caused."

Nothing but breathing on Kaufman's end, then Annabelle's voice on the extension: "It's a trick! He's screwing you out of your dinner."

Kaufman (*doubtful*): "But he's letting me keep the notebook."

Annabelle: "No one gives a hoot about the damned notebook but everyone will know about the dinner!"

Kaufman (*petulant*): "Well, I've changed my mind about the dinner."

Annabelle: "Is the notebook more important than your dignity and your family?"

Kaufman (*irritated*): "I don't understand you, Annabelle; I think Rags is acting generously under the circumstances."

Annabelle: "It's always Rags, isn't it?"

Kaufman (*cold*): "Let me worry about my family."

Annabelle: "My pleasure!" And she clicks off.

Kaufman breathes deeply into the phone. "Listen, can I come and see you?"

"I'm off the case. It's closed. I don't see the point."

"I'd like to clear up a few things. It's important that I talk to you."

"I'm sorry, Mr. Kaufman, but I'm on my own time now."

Kaufman takes a while in answering. "I'll bring back your notebook."

"When?"

"An hour?"

"I'll be here," I say and dictate the address.

Kaufman sits in what I have come to think of as Plante's chair, looking creepily like Plante writ large: the same way of holding himself as if his trunk is Scotch taped to his body and might fall off at any moment. Size without presence: the closer he gets to you, the smaller and lighter he becomes, so that seated a few feet away he appears virtually transparent.

"What I wanted to say," he begins, "is that it's not what you may think, and I'd like that communicated to Rags, about Annabelle and me. There isn't anything—she offered to help and I took her up—I haven't tried or done anything . . ." He trails off, sips from a healthy measure of Scotch I poured for him.

"If you knew me at all—I don't play around— My marriage is a sacred thing to me, my family. My wife has put up with so much, how could I pull anything on her? I'm not worth—after high school—her little finger— She's the best thing that ever happened to me. I count my blessings. She sticks."

He shuts himself up with the rest of the Scotch. I pour him a new glass.

"Do you want to tell me why you took the notebook?"

Kaufman's color rises; his chest heaves; he empties his glass. I refill, examining him for signs of drowsiness.

"It's not— I've never taken anything in my life. I come from a good family. My mother, was she strict! Listen, if I brought a piece of chalk home from school and it wasn't mine, she'd make me take it back, imagine! She drilled honesty, honesty, honesty into us—the truth, so help me—I must be the only fund raiser in the human race who doesn't pad his expense account.

"If you want to know—I never let anyone treat me. Kids always wanted to, but no, it wasn't the way I was brought up. I had to set an example because you know how many Jewish families there were in Saratoga in those days? So I had to not only be good, but excel! Gee, didn't we have some fun though! In those days I was the big shot. But I don't care what you think, it's not that." He empties his glass and in virtually the same motion holds it out for more. "All you have to know is one thing only: I had no choice." At which point, just when I'd lost all hope, he passes out.

I bound out of my chair and into his suit. My notebook is in Kaufman's right-hand jacket pocket. A second notebook is in his inside jacket pocket. I turn to the first page and see Plante's name, address and telephone number at *The New York Times*. Kaufman snores loudly, giving promise of sound health despite the sodium amytal I mixed with his Scotch. I type Plante's home address on a manila envelope, enclose his notebook, seal it and stamp it and step out in the hall to mail it.

I type a note to Kaufman confessing that I doped him and have recovered the notebooks. I assure him that his secrets, what there are of them, will go with me to my grave. I tell him that the key to the john is on the desk and if he uses it to please return it and, on leaving, to do me a final kindness by making certain the office is locked. I slip the message in the pocket that previously held Plante's notebook. Kaufman's breath is pure poison. I open a window, turn off the lights, then reconsider and keep one on for Kaufman when he wakes.

May 19

Late dinner with Elsie and Jeanie. I talk to Jeanie while Elsie eats herself into a stupor. Says she's going home. Seems intimidated, downcast. Can it be my good spirits? I let her pay for the dinner. It was the one part of the evening that pleased her.

Finally get around to reading the contents of my kidnapped notebook after a week of avoiding it. Lingering shame, I suppose.

I append them to the record.

Six-thirty: Clarke's. Plante sits with his well-tailored back to me, sipping a martini. He is fawned on by the waiter. Little does he know I'm going to date his wife! I call Plante's waiter to give an order but he's too busy lecturing Plante on basketball.

Plante is really in his element. Success emanates out of him. He releases the waiter who goes to the bar, but not for my order because he hasn't taken it yet. I am desperate for the drink which I didn't want when I sat down ten minutes ago. Is that how alcoholics are made?

Plante jumps to his feet, nearly knocking his chair into mine, to greet a man three times anybody's size in the entire joint. "Rags, goddam it!"

"The Big O!"

The two grip hands and exchange shit-eating grins. Kaufman's grin is bigger because he's bigger. His shoulders span the width of the table. He sits down and the silver rattles on all the nearby tables. He looks years older than Plante but his eyes are light and boyish and his hair thin, graying and close-cropped, face very red.

For all their disparity in size I have the impression I'm watching brothers. I wonder who gave the other his posture. No doubt, Kaufman to Plante, athlete to scholar.

They both laugh. Kaufman starts on a bourbon. Plante is finishing off his first martini and has two more lined up. I wish he'd slow down. Boring sports commentary during which I get a chance to order. A double. I know the way the system works around here.

Halfway through Plante's second drink his face bursts into sudden glow. "Remember Tessie Toga?"

Kaufman frowns. "I sure do."

"Tessie Toga, the girl of our dreams."

"That's right."

"That's right." Plante empties his glass, begins on his third. "You don't miss Tessie? I sometimes miss Tessie."

"Tessie's dead," Kaufman says.

"Is she? Poor Tessie. No, Tessie Toga will never die. And her faithful Indian companion? You don't miss him? Now what was his name again?"

"Damned if I know."

"That's not right. Damned-If-I-Know is no name for an Indian. Poor Tessie. We used her when we needed her and now disparage her memory. It's hardly fair."

"You think Josh plays games like that? He's a quiet kid, isn't he?"

Plante doesn't answer for a long time. "When did you see Josh?"

"We had Annabelle over last week."

"I didn't know that."

"Do you mind?"

"When was the last time you had *me* over for dinner?"

"You and Esther make a great combination."

"I don't start it."

"Like two cocks in a pit."

"True, but hers is bigger than mine."

They laugh without pleasure. In fact, the last few minutes have been very tense indeed. When did it start?

Plante and Kaufman get to their feet in slow motion. This is where Plante ditches Kaufman and goes on alone to Bradley's. He tosses me a side glance to show he's still under control. Then to Kaufman: "I'm supposed to meet Emmett at Bradley's. What do you say?"

Kaufman checks his watch. "Just for a quickie. I'll have to call Esther."

I glare at Plante. He pretends not to see me. What's the son of a bitch up to?

1965

February 15

Plante, dapper in a gray pinstripe, wanders through the multitudes as if looking for an exit. His eyes, when he greets his guests, flick on and off: warmth and indifference. He is fifteen years older than anyone else in the room. Others are all smiling, toothy mannequins: fresh, well dressed, strong odor of on-the-make. Was I ever like this? O.K., once. I learned and they'll learn. Everywhere I turn, mind-boggling girls in minis. What is it in Plante that attracts the young? He doesn't *do* anything. Is it fame? Is it age? Someday I'll be Plante's age —style isn't hard to come by, it's a matter of waiting.

In the meantime I attract booze and booze attracts me. Some of my best thoughts come to me under booze, some of my finest moments. And if I black out it doesn't matter anymore because I write it all down. Everything gets written down, I miss no trick; my pockets are stuffed with notes, scribbled on matchbook covers. I've learned to put it all together, before I go to sleep. If not, scratch it, the next day it's blank.

79

If only all these assholes knew what I thought of them they'd run out in the streets screaming.

"What are you laughing at?" a pretty girl asks me.

"Inside joke," I say, deliberately omitting the charm, walking away from her. If she wants me she'll follow me to the bar; if not, better to know it in front; once it's all out in the open, no excuses for anyone getting hurt. The girl does not follow me. I laugh.

I size up the room: picture windows on the East River and the rest is books. Books not just in bookcases where they belong, but everywhere: on coffee tables, end tables, arms of chairs, the piano. Instead of decoration Plante has books, is promiscuous with books. I also like to read—but *so many books?!*

Miserable as I am at it, honest appraisal leaves no doubt that I am built for the private detective business. Why? Because I am invisible. Seventy-five people mingling, drinking, rubbing shoulders, getting acquainted, arguing, talking, prefucking—and to every last one I am invisible. I can move at my ease—it doesn't matter where—and no one pays attention. Not a single word spoken to me all evening by a single person.

Yes, *one* single person! That snotty girl who asked me what I was laughing at. "You!" I should have said. Or something sharper. Not that it wouldn't bounce right off her. People won't be insulted anymore. Why is that?

Plante wants a report on what people are saying about him at the party. Impossible. All that people here talk about are movies I haven't heard of that aren't out yet. Plante's crazy.

In my own defense, this time around I did try to ship him off to another private detective. Plante didn't bite, said that he had tried two others before me. True? Or was he trying to piss me off? Anyhow, he claimed they lacked the sensibility and subtlety for a job of this nature. Which means what? Probably that they laughed him out of their offices. I told him if he couldn't find a detective to take the job maybe he should hire a psychiatrist to find out why. For once I got to him; definitely not amused.

I don't need him anymore; I almost made a living this last quarter: on small jobs, drudgery, but neatly handled drudgery —no crazy clients. All four of them well satisfied. Another year and I am likely to be financially independent. If I don't chuck it and go to law school. I like being a detective until I come to parties like this and then I would rather come as a lawyer.

I wish I had a machine gun. Not much in this room would survive. Just the books. But the way Plante exploits his books some books might have to go too.

Four and a half hours of this. Unbelievable! And I'm still on my feet, moving from corner to corner, comfortable now in my boredom—it rests at ease with my hate—I am, if the truth must be told, on the edge of having a good time. Being a smart detective I have come up with a clue to parties. The clue is fantasy. No one walks into a party without having a far better party going on inside his head. Every party is going to be that party until we get there. So the key to the boredom and tension at parties is that no one wants to be at the party he's at, he wants to be at the party he's missing.

I tell my theory to Plante and his eyes fog. "What have you heard?"

"Nothing."

"Nothing at all?"

"Some of them think Brando's over the hill; some of them don't. That's about it."

Hard to believe, but he looks at me with relief. Is he bull-shitting me? Difficult to know with him, especially here, allegedly in his own element, the one man in the room with the right to have a good time. A final squeeze on the forearm and he disappears into a sea of celebrants.

Where, I wonder, are Plante's old drinking buddies, Burden and Cornwall? I didn't expect Otis Kaufman, but I did expect the other two clowns; or has Plante dropped them for his youth brigade; or does he confine them to his weekly tour of bars? And who, come to think of it, is Plante's girl? Can't tell from his manner; he displays a sort of tight-lipped affection toward all the ladies, acknowledges their come-ons like a reluctant royal presence: Phil the Greek—he even looks a little like him. Is that what does it? Cool? My problem with cool is that it has a habit of slipping, unnoticed by me, into indifference. First mine, then the girl's. By the time I get hot and bothered they are long gone. Passionate in absentia, that's me.

All this comes to one part of my mind because the other part of my mind is focused on a six-foot, extraordinary-faced, flat-bodied girl of nineteen or so who I can't take my eyes off. *Her* eyes are wide and brown—at first impression, sedate; at second impression, screaming for help. I volunteer and infiltrate the periphery of her circle. Two young blades whom she is obviously dying to get away from blow pipe and cigarette smoke at each other while trying to win her heart by the strength of their opinions. They are in conflict over the relative merits of Fellini as opposed to another Italian director named Antonioni. She plays talk show host to the two of them, turning from one to the other and repeatedly asking, "Do you think that's true? I don't know if I agree with that or not. What do you think?" For one who does not know she certainly nods a lot, says, "uh-huh" and "I see" a lot, says it continually throughout all the idiotic cross-conversation, no matter which pompous ass is doing the talking. She has room to do all this and still take note of my arrival, nodding once or twice at me as if, with me too, she does not know if she agrees, although I haven't said a word. She is just a little taller than I am and, as I look at her, keeps growing taller; appears, in fact, to be rising, her long torso floating in graceful astral rhythms toward the ceiling. Her hair is long and thick and glistening black; from the way it hangs off her head it looks charged with electricity. Her dress is that of a nineteenth century upper-class Russian peasant. The dress is long and pleated and hides black stockings and long, skinny feet in black ballet slippers. She wears no makeup and, except for what I take to be a case of raging narcissism, is, in my book, out of this world, not of this time and perfect. She cannot have been at the party long. I may, from time to time, be a diffident detective but it is humanly inconceivable that in four hours I could have overlooked her.

I make my bid to cut into the conversation. "I understand Rags is going to do a film with Fellini." My aim is to move them off Fellini and onto Plante. It is not achieved by virtue of the fact that all three act as if they have not heard me. The girl does not even say "uh-huh."

Tired and bored by not only being invisible but valueless, I abandon the girl to her peers. With the next group I come to I recklessly surrender my wallflower stance and plunge into conversation. Party guests are notoriously unwilling to discuss any matter bordering on substance, but I prod, push and, to the extent that I am able, intimidate. What the wallflower detective draws from the wallpaper guests is that Plante is generally admired: appraised as sexy and remote; also a genius and an ex-alcoholic, driven to drink when his wife, a fabled beauty, ran off with his best friend. The consensus is that she later turned lesbian. Plante himself is suspected by some, denied by others, to be a closet queen and subject to fits of despair during which times, if he is not institutionalized, he will try to do away with himself. Some report having seen the scars on his wrists. His best friends are reputed to be Hugh Hefner, whose Chicago orgies he regularly attends, and Johnny Carson, who has been quoted as saying Plante is the only writer whose books he can't put down.

By three the bar is closed, the guests are gone, the girl has vanished—not that I tried very hard to keep track of her. I have a fair notion of my limits and she is past them. Plante sits between his books and empty plastic glasses, gray-faced, distracted, neat as a pin, a middle-aged duplicate of his guests.

I offer myself a drink, the first of the evening. One swig and I am alive with bad humor. Plante, the gifted journalist who notices nothing, does not notice.

"I'm exhausted," he begins. And that's it for a while. To entertain myself I put ice in my glass.

"Tough being adored."

Plante looks interested. "Was that your impression?" The tightness leaves his body. "What did you hear?"

I report his desertion by his lesbian wife, his suicide attempts, his institutionalization, Johnny Carson, Hugh Hefner, and the consensus that he is a remote, sexy, genius closet queen.

Plante gets up from his chair and stretches. He takes a walk to his picture window. "Do you like the view?"

"Very nice if you like teenagers."

He does not chuckle. "I guess that's all then." He stands at the window, his back to me, rubbing his hands together, lording it over the East River. I sneak a quick second drink while he's in his trance. Plante turns, a sheet of paper in his hand. "Ackroyd." He holds out the paper. I am meant to come to him and take it. I stand in place. Plante too. Then, moving forward as if he's moving backward, he hands me the paper. "This is a list of names. I made it out for you this afternoon. Every name on that list was invited to the party. If you like, you may call it my 'A' list." Plante's mouth is self-mocking, his eyes serious. "They didn't come. I knew they wouldn't. Some called to say they couldn't, others didn't bother. I want you to find out why these people won't come to my parties."

Restraining the temptation to collapse in hysterics, I glance over the paper. There are a dozen names, ten of them famous. The other two are Wally Burden and Emmett Cornwall. "You said 'parties,' plural. You give a lot of these?"

Plante swings over to the defense. "One or two a month. A writer can't afford to be insular. It was a way of paying back invitations. This, however, is no longer a problem." He looks at me, eyes shimmering. He indicates the list. "These are all close friends. Some new. Some old. Some very old. I want to know why they're cutting me. Quintana Kilmartin," he says, mentioning one of those ladies whose picture is always in *Women's Wear Daily,* "has not given a dinner party in nine months without inviting me. I was not asked to her last three. I want you to find out why." He takes a check out of his shirt pocket. It is damp with sweat. "I trust your discretion."

February 16

What I really want to do is call up every name on Plante's list and say: "My name is Ackroyd, I'm a private detective hired by Oscar Plante to find out why you aren't coming to his parties anymore."

And why not? Possibly because there's a statute of limitations on my passion for resentment. Not word one from the bastard after the return of the notebook. After he told me to give up on the case; never expected to see it again. But do I get a bonus check or, short of that, a letter of thanks, a post card, even a phone call!? Does he indicate in any way, shape, manner or form the smallest recognition of a job well done? Didn't need me anymore, so why waste his energy. Use it where it can do the most good: on his fucking parties!

Rage is dissipated by malice. I call Cornwall and Burden. They are not number one on Plante's list—Quintana Kilmartin is number one—but they are number one on mine. Will they know the man who spent seventy-five dollars on them at Elaine's? And will I know them? I reach Burden at his P.R. office, Cornwall at *The New York Post*. I tell them I am Miles Undershaft, a free-lance for *Time* magazine assigned to do an intimate profile on their close friend Oscar Plante. Neither sounds particularly interested, but when I suggest a joint interview in a joint of their own choosing they relent. Cornwall chooses Tim Costello's; Burden groans, but goes along.

When it nears time for me to go along I play with the notion of changing the part in my hair and affecting dark glasses for a disguise. But the hell with it; I will go in the disguise of Ackroyd playing Undershaft. It is enough; probably more than enough. That's the way it is when you are invisible.

Costello's is an ex-famous newspaperman's bar peopled almost entirely by Madison Avenue. Its claim to distinction is that James Thurber once drew on the walls. Nine o'clock is just past the dinner rush and I am suffused in an atmosphere of evening letdown. I sit in the back, last in a row of near-empty booths, keeping tab on the door. I have drifted into my second Scotch when Burden and Cornwall falter in. Burden is bald and appears fat at first glance, but it is not real fat but the ghost of recently dieted fat. He wears an expensively unkempt brown suit and a creased shirt and tie that he's probably had on for days. He has the face of a worldly cherub. Cornwall is about two inches taller than Burden's five-eight and looks every bit as sour as I expected. He is round-shouldered, pot-bellied, skinny-armed and hulking. His green sport coat smells of ashes. His eyes appear to be the only part of him not under sedation.

I wait, during an exchange of dogged pleasantries, for them to recognize me, but in order to recognize someone you have to look at him. Not Burden: he is eyeing the blonde at the table behind me. Not Cornwall: he is glowering at the bowl of pretzels on our table. Burden's first sincere acknowledgment that I am present is when I unflap my notebook. "Attribution, at last," he murmurs.

I open with a brief description of my assignment, which must bore the pants off them because in the middle of it they start talking about *Time* style, Cornwall arguing that *Time* invented a style to cover up its bad writing. I use the implied insult to introduce Plante into the conversation.

"Oscar Plante is well known for his style, wouldn't you say?"

"A great stylist, but we are a nation of great stylists," says Burden to the blonde as drinks arrive. "When content becomes banal we are only too happy to trade it for form."

Undershaft: "Are you implying that Plante's work lacks content?"

Burden (*to the blonde at the next table*): "I was referring to Warhol. Cultureless culture and standardless standards. Gentlemen, I give you America!"

Cornwall has a habit of half-pulling, half-wiping his nose every time he disagrees. He says to the pretzels: "Don't blame Warhol, blame Kennedy."

Burden (*to the blonde*): "Kennedy brought Frost to the White House."

Cornwall pulls his nose. "He brought a chill to the White House. Frost never made it past the podium at the Inaugural."

Burden: "He brought Edmund Wilson."

Cornwall: "He may have brought him, but he didn't read him. He read James Bond. You want the inside word on where it all started to crumble? When Kennedy took his style off James Bond. If he didn't read James Bond there wouldn't have been a missile crisis."

Burden: "He brought urbanity and wit."

Undershaft: "Do you see as much of Plante now that he's a big success?"

Cornwall: "If Camelot is wit, then you can charge it to Kennedy."

Burden: "I concede he was a politician."

Cornwall: "He was an image hustler. Cary Grant in the White House. You get a pop President in Washington, it follows you get a pop culture in the country. This is a country that takes its standards off Washington."

Burden: "I beg to differ. Hollywood."

Cornwall: "The same difference. One-industry towns living off gossip, bullshit and pimping for power. The only difference between Scotty Reston and Hedda Hopper is the name of the town they work in. Without Truman we wouldn't have had Willy Loman; without Eisenhower we wouldn't have had theater-of-the-absurd; without Kennedy we wouldn't have had Andy Warhol."

Undershaft: "Plante has Andy Warhol to his parties, doesn't he? What are they like?"

The blonde gets up to leave. As she passes our table, Burden signals the bartender for another round.

Cornwall: "You want to know what ruined Rockefeller? His divorce. If Rockefeller had kept his lovelife out of his marriage, like any sane politician, he'd be President today."

Burden (*staring at where the blonde was*): "His family was his base. He opted for freedom. Now he's rootless and grounded."

Undershaft: "You all started out at about the same time. Do you resent Plante for outdistancing you?"

Burden: "Does a nation deserve to survive when its head of state is a megalomaniac with an inferiority complex and its most influential arbiter of taste is Johnny Carson?"

Undershaft: "Do you ever wonder why Plante has made it and you haven't?" Someone must have ordered another round because it arrives.

Burden: "We deserve Johnson. He is our self-hate writ large; the seamy underside of our virility; that machismo which gives a good name to impotence."

Cornwall practically pulls his nose off his face. "Don't blame Johnson, blame the Cold War. Americans are used to winning but we don't win anymore. We stalemate."

Undershaft: "Plante surrounds himself with a lot of phonies, or don't you think so? Do you think he's changed, or has he always been that way?"

Burden: "The American problem is that we are passionate only in regard to show business. When Warhol paints it is not to make art but to make the cover of *Time*."

Cornwall: "That's all art is, a tryout for show business. It's America's New Haven."

Undershaft: "Don't you find all the too too clever people Plante knows—you know, the Algonquin Roundtable sort of thing—just a little bit boring?"

Burden: "The American dream is to make it. The American truth is to be trivialized and cannibalized as the price for having made it."

Cornwall calls the waiter over for one more round. I break in and demand the check. I can't cut into the party but I can cut my losses.

I am mind-whipped and wit-whipped. If they are all that bright and funny, why do I feel they were trying to kill me?

Jeanie wants to know why we have such long silences. She wants too much.

February 17

Some things will never change. Plante, as usual, hates my report. He mutters as he reads: "No, no . . . they can't be serious . . . this is too much . . . laughable . . ." We are in my office bedroom and he is sitting in the only chair, I am at my usual post on the bed. Plante sniffs the air. "Not very much, is it? No, not very helpful."

"You travel in fast company," is my single comment. I am in a sour temper over his friendship with Cornwall and Burden. Verbal diarrhea. With friends like that you don't need enemas. Let that smart-ass Burden come up with a better one than that.

"You were angry with them." Plante smiles in recognition of the emotion.

"I was trying to get a rise out of them. It was part of the job."

"But you were furious."

"I was frustrated."

Plante scans the report. "It is good fun. They gave you a fine run for your money." He hunches his shoulders and crosses his legs so that the shoe-tip of the crossed leg touches the floor. The impression is of a man holding himself together. "Why do you think they won't talk about me? They are absolutely determined not to. Aren't they?"

Plante's self-pity rides so close to the surface that I am hungry for a drink to drown it. I get one; all it delivers is sadness. Plante looks comfortable, almost prim in his despair. He fits into his mood changes as if they are custom-made. Whatever the emotion it looks right on him. That, I suppose, is a description of class.

"Curious how much of their conversation concerns celebrities," I comment.

Plante smiles sourly. "It's their business."

"Burden calls this a time of standardless standards."

"Warhol is a pet aversion of his, as he is of mine."

"You're positive he's referring to Warhol?"

"He says Warhol. I assume he means Warhol."

"Let's assume no such thing. Let's assume he means Plante."
I pick up my copy of the report and flip through it, taking
my sweet time. Plante's wounded eyes follow my motions but
I pretend not to notice. "Let's try something. Let's accept as
a premise that Burden and Cornwall are trying to pull off
something more ambitious than Quote of the Week in *Time*
magazine. Let's see how this report reads if we assume as a
premise that they are trying to strangle you without leaving
fingerprints." I notice, in a side glance, Plante's mouth twitch.
"What if we check out this interview as if all these names—
Warhol, Kennedy, Reston, Rockefeller—are, in fact, code
names? Why don't we see what happens if we go through this
report and substitute *your* name for their names?" I look up,
smile speculatively. Plante's face is white-on-white, seconds
away from heart seizure.

I proceed: " 'Cultureless culture and standardless standards.'
What if they don't mean Warhol? What if the reference here
is to you and your work; in particular, your novel?" Nothing
about Plante moves.

I proceed: "Kennedy as an 'image hustler' who reads trash.
Our first 'pop President,' 'Cary Grant in the White House.'
What if the trash Kennedy reads is not James Bond but a
cover for their opinions of the books *you* write? Trash that,
in their opinion, has turned you into an image hustler, a pop
celebrity, the Cary Grant of the publishing world." He listens
so hard the room aches.

I proceed: " 'The only difference between Scotty Reston
and Hedda Hopper is the name of the town they work in.'
What if they mean you and not Scotty Reston; that through
your movie sales, your TV appearances, your socializing with
celebrities you have sold out to show business." Plante's body
looks like it has been plugged into a wall.

I proceed: "O.K., Rockefeller's divorce. 'His family was
his base. He opted for freedom. Now he's rootless and
grounded.' Is that Rockefeller they see that way or is it you?
Your parties: rootless. Your old friendships: grounded."

"Not my parties." His voice is low, hoarse, hint of a death

rattle. "It's my writer's block. I have not been able to write—write well—since leaving Annabelle. That's it, you see, it's my writer's block."

I proceed: " 'Does a nation deserve to survive when its head of state is a megalomaniac?' "

Plante leans forward and says, "Or one of its more prominent writers." His elbows are on his knees, hands clasped and rubbing against each other. Color returns to his face.

I proceed: "Johnny Carson. That 'most influential arbiter of taste.' Do they mean Johnny Carson or do they mean you? Your influence on young people?"

Plante picks up a copy of the report and turns to the page. "No. They mean Carson. Until a short while ago I was on his show twice a month." He rips through to the next page and reads: " 'When Warhol paints it is not to make art but to make the cover of *Time*.' "

I cut in. "Warhol or Plante?" He smiles so tightly I feel it in the back of my neck.

He grabs the next one: " 'That's what art is, a tryout for show business.' "

"Whose art?" I inquire.

Plante flushes. "Plante's art!"

I plunge on past him. " 'The American dream is to make it. The American truth is to be trivialized and cannibalized as the price for having made it.' "

Plante is on his feet. "My writer's block! Once again! God help me for taking them into my confidence, they can't get enough of my writer's block!" He devours the report, squeezing the life out of the pages. "Rich stuff. Rich!" His body is electric, his eyes bright, his teeth flashing incandescently. Altogether the picture of a very dynamic man.

What have I done?

February 23

According to Jeanie, I am a better lay than I am a companion because, to me, talking is more of a threat than screwing. By use of this ploy she forces me, though half asleep, to tell her about the case. But scoring points in companionship loses me points in morality. She is shocked by my "exploitation" of my unnamed client's paranoia. So I am backed into a corner, citing—inventing!—evidence to prove Plante's suspicions are not paranoid.

She now looks at me with such intensity it makes me want to turn over in bed to see who's lying behind me.

February 25

Plante gives a party tonight. He has invited his entire "A" list, half of whom have declined. Plante predicts that none of the others will show up either. He wants me to find out who's giving the party that he wasn't invited to. I concentrate on Burden, Cornwall and Quintana Kilmartin. I will tail Burden. I sub-contract Cornwall and Kilmartin to two other private eyes culled from the classified. (1) Conrad Farr, fiftyish and an ex-cop, has Cornwall; (2) Dominic Stasio, sixtyish and ex-FBI (he says, but I doubt it), gets Kilmartin. They pull fifty plus expenses for the night. I, therefore, will pull nothing but the satisfaction of knowing that at last I am a corporation. Farr is beefy, whiskey-voiced and red-eyed; Stasio is swarthy, balding, and spits when he talks.

I stake out Burden's East 84th Street brownstone in a Hertz rental, motor throbbing, heat turned up as high as it will go but not high enough for the 17-degree weather. Fantasies of carbon monoxide poisoning inspire me to open a window. A quarter-inch is, within seconds, a mistake. A chill locks into my hips and deploys itself in small, tingling waves up and down my back and legs; I am embalmed in ice. I wait, with hate, for pneumonia. Burden's Disease. I will leave a note on the wheel naming him. He will never tell another epigram in this town.

At nine-thirty—two and a half hours of wheel time—I pull

what is left of me out of the car and jump up and down on the sidewalk, trying to draw blood back into my body.

"Watch it!" mutters a small, squeaky voice out of a thick fur coat and I am nearly knocked over by a short, stocky woman who walks as if she's kicking small children out of the way. She crosses over to Burden's side of the street and pushes her way into the brownstone, the only person to come or go all evening. Twenty minutes after her arrival the lights on Burden's floor go out.

February 26

So now I know how legitimate detectives write reports. First of all, they file-number their cases. Bad business on my part; I've yet to make it past eight. Cornwall and Quintana Kilmartin, according to private detectives Farr and Stasio, are "the subjects." Subjects do not walk, stride, amble or meander. They "proceed." They "proceed north," "proceed west," they "complete phone calls to person or persons unknown," they "enter domiciles," and sometimes "residences," they don't meet, they have "liaisons with attractive, Caucasian female, approximate age 25, who accompanies subject to Sardi's, arriving at 9:05 P.M. and departing at 11:15 P.M." This is Cornwall, who, after Sardi's, accompanies his Caucasian female to a place of residence at 29 West 75th Street, where subject remains until 2:00 A.M., then departs alone to P. J. Clarke's, where subject remains until 3:00 A.M., then departs alone to subject's own place of residence at 45 Jones Street.

My other man, Stasio, had a more colorful evening than my man Farr. Subject Kilmartin hosted a dinner party at *her* domicile, 17 East 61st Street. Guests numbered 20 and wore formal dress. Stasio was able to engage various chauffeurs in conversation and came up with such names as Mr. and Mrs. William Paley, Mr. and Mrs. Bennett Cerf, Mr. and Mrs.

Clifton Daniel, Senator and Mrs. Jacob Javits, Mr. and Mrs. Otto Preminger, and Mrs. Katherine Graham and her escort, Mr. Truman Capote.

Plante stares, frozen-eyed, at the Kilmartin report. He stiffens his already stiff back, tucks his chin hard into his neck and sits so rigid in the client's chair that one can easily envision a stroke. He closes his eyes. "It's pathetic. What is she trying to prove?"

February 27

Jeanie and I talk all night. Nice feeling. Went to bed exhausted. No sex. Still I felt fine waking up. Then very good sex. Morning sex may be the answer to my Jeanie problem.

Quintana Kilmartin is not an easy lady to get ahold of. Her line is continually busy, and when her line is free you get her secretary who is continually busy and puts you on hold where you are stuck for as many minutes as it takes to get impatient, hang up, dial again and be put on hold. Half a day of this and I very nearly get through, but not quite. I am put on hold every three seconds. "My name is Undershaft and I"—hold—"am assigned by *Time* magazine to write a story on Mrs. Kilmartin's good friend"—hold—"good friend Oscar Plante, and I would like to interview Mrs. Kil"—hold for almost two minutes after which the secretary comes back on and says, "Mrs. Kilmartin makes it a policy to never give interviews to the press. I'm sure you will underst—" She hangs up on herself while talking.

Seventeen East 61st Street is a townhouse stolen out of Henry James, the lobby all fluted marble columns with a floor resembling inlaid gold. I inch open a heavy oak door at the far end of the lobby and find myself in an office which is eighteenth century Goldsmith Brothers. A one-dimensional young lady sits behind a desk the size of a Cunard liner, talking on a World War I German telephone. Her face is Styro-

foam. Her dress is Formica, and when she spe
between a set of Smith College teeth which
She hangs up, looks inches above my head and
want.

I go into my dance. My name, this time aroun
royd, my job is with the Guggenheim Foundation; we considering Oscar Plante for a grant and he has listed Mrs. Kilmartin as one of his character references. I, Ackroyd, have
stopped by to check him out. The young lady makes a note
with a silver-plated ballpoint pen. "How much is the grant?"
she asks the space above my head.

"Twenty thousand plus a house and studio in Majorca."

The secretary rises as if to walk on water and passes through
a tooled oak door at my right. She is back in less time than
I can say Charles de Gaulle. *She* says, "Follow me."

I follow so close on her heels that I all but take off her
shoes; I may be invisible but she will know I was here. I am
guided into a painting by Mary Cassatt, in the middle of
which, small and virtually unnoticeable because of the pat-
terns on the couch, rests Quintana Kilmartin, with a head
the size and close to the color of a raisin, a briar patch of kinky
curls, eyes lost in creased, gray patches and a red kewpie-doll
mouth turned down in repose. She looks like a hand puppet
with the hand missing, no sign or semblance of body discernible beneath a dressing gown made up of yards and yards of
Oriental silk folds. She points with a liverish hand to a delicate-
looking antique chair, and I sit. The same hand points to a
silver cigarette box on a marble-top end table.

"Do you mind?" I get up and bring her the cigarette box.
She opens it and finds it empty. "God in heaven!" she says
and points to a humidor atop a grand piano. "Sometimes
they're in there."

I try the humidor and find it empty. "It's empty," I say.

A weak growl. "I'm sorry, I'll have to borrow one of yours."

"Sorry, I don't smoke."

A sigh. "Will you mind terribly going into the office and
asking the girl for a pack of L&Ms: I know I'm a pain." I start

ward one of the three paneled doors in the room. "You might also tell her for me that I can't go on this way."

I go into the office, get the cigarettes, tell the secretary she's going to have to shape up, and return to Mrs. Kilmartin, who then sends me back to the secretary for a book of matches and, after the matches, sends me down the hall into the kitchen to query the maid on what she has done with the ashtrays. On my return I find Mrs. Kilmartin flicking ashes on her dressing gown and glaring hypnotically at the chair I am about to sit in. Her glare persists after I'm seated but it's not aimed at me; I don't think she knows I'm there. She clears her throat with a grumble which comes out sounding like "Unforgivable," flicks more ashes on herself and adjusts her focus to let me in.

"I shouldn't really be talking to you, I hope you know that," she says gravely. "This morning I got a call from *Time*. They're doing a story on Oscar and now you want to make him a present of God knows how much and did I hear right—a house in Majorca?"

I nod and say, "Twenty thousand dollars." Though I can't know for sure, I sense her staring at me.

"What do you want me to say? He's talented, but everyone is talented today. Everyone is brilliant and everyone is gifted. Give them all grants. What do I care? Give me a grant. No one has ever offered me a grant. Why is that? Will you put my name down for some money?"

"You have to apply."

"Can't you apply for me? No, you'll say you'll do it but you won't; you're just like the rest. All I ever see are promises. No one ever gives me a house in Majorca. I don't much like Majorca anymore. Would you care for a drink? The bar is there, through that alcove. I'll have a Scotch with just a tiny bit of soda, lots and lots of ice."

I return from the bar with two healthy Scotches. Quintana sips hers as if it is brandy. It brings forth a tear. "Let me warn you, it's not one of the great pleasures in life to be taken for granted." A small swallow, a small tear. "Well, that's the way it is and you forgive people because they *are* people and what can one expect?" She kills her half-smoked cigarette and lights a new one. "Why come to me for an opinion on Oscar? You should go to his new friends. You must have a very old list. Yes, a very old list." Four puffs and that cigarette is gone. She lights another. "He used to call me up in the middle of the night and read me his latest column. I can live without that I suppose." She plays for a while with the silk folds of her robe. "God knows, he works hard enough for what he wants. Do you know what he wants? I don't. He mystifies me. He was at me for months to go on Johnny Carson with him. When I finally broke down and said yes, not another word out of him on the subject. Isn't that extraordinary? Don't you find that extraordinary behavior?

"Do you know his new friends? I don't. I couldn't get to one of his parties. Is that a good reason to treat me like a pariah? He's probably embarrassed. He should be." She lights a new cigarette forgetting to kill the old one. "My godson, Neal Fletcher, has literary ambitions. I don't read anymore. Everyone I know says I have excellent taste but the print is too small and at my age I've heard it all, but I gave Oscar Neal's novel to read to see what he thought of its chances— the boy's been five years on it. I know a half dozen writers more successful than Oscar who would have been more than happy to read it for me and when a month went by, one entire month during which time I had Oscar to two of my dinner parties and not a word out of his mouth. Charming as ever but what about poor Neal? Well, I brought it up. With great embarrassment I might add. Am I foolish for taking this sort of thing seriously? I suppose I am. No one else seems to. Oscar denied I'd given him the book. Is that possible? Isn't that shocking? In this very room, on *this* couch I gave him the manuscript! He was sitting next to me! Next to me! Am I going mad? He denied it ever happened! It's all so puzzling. And then dear old Pierce Baker! Over seventy and very content—one of the few who are—why should he have to write his autobiography? The thought never entered his mind until

Oscar put it there—right there—he was seated right there and dear Pierce got so excited, he trembled, actually trembled with excitement. Oscar said he'd have his editor at Scribner's call him the next morning. Three months have gone by and dear old Pierce is still waiting. Still waiting. Maybe it's me. It must be me. I'm sure it is. Give him his grant. By this time he has more money than I do but I'm sure he deserves it."

February 28

Up all night trying to read *Nova Express*. Not able to; thinking about friends, women, celebrities, a code of values. Fruitless.

I am good in bed with Jeanie because I don't let myself get that involved. But not getting involved makes me a bad companion. Jeanie wants good sex and a good companion. It is like patting my head and rubbing my belly at the same time. It is a trick that I can master but would rather not bother.

I type up a report to Plante, complete it by 6:00 A.M., shower, shave and go out to deliver it. He's technically a working man; all working men should be up by seven.

I hail a bent cab and reread Quintana Kilmartin on the way over. I now know two celebrities: her and Plante. Maybe I should throw a patry. . . . I pay off the cab in front of his house, forgetting what to tip because of a dark, disheveled girl, all in black, waiting to get in on the other side. I stand there and watch her climb in—tall and skinny, she does it in sections: fold along line A. Her face is long and white and sickly looking. As the cab pulls away it dawns on me who she must be: the girl in my life from Plante's party, more beautiful in my mind's eye than my eye's eye. Which eye do you trust? I follow on foot for two blocks, until I find an empty cab and order it to tail my old cab. Why am I doing this? I ask myself.

The girl gets out at an East Sixties highrise, looking even less like my heart's desire: round shouldered, sullen, nine years old. She doesn't smile back at the smiling doorman. Just my type: a bitch. I am reminded of Annabelle.

I rent a Hertz and drive up to Larchmont. Stalled on the Cross Bronx Expressway, I wonder what I'm doing. Traffic rolls and I have no trouble finding my way. It is as natural as going home and about as threatening. I park nostalgically in my old spot across the street and wait. The house has a new coat of paint. White with blue trim. More cozy, more livable. It is past nine, Josh must be at school. Will she kick me out? What will I say?

"Standardless standards," Burden said about Plante. He had him dead to rights. Screwing teeny-boppers. I make a mental note to call Burden as soon as I get back to town. And to buy the complete works of Shaw. I too can be witty.

Nothing stirs in the house across the way. I shut my eyes and try to envision Annabelle. A void. I don't remember the color of her hair, eyes, anything. Suddenly I'm not that certain I have the right house. I cross the street and check the mailbox. Ackerman. I drive back to New York.

This time there is no question I have the right address but Deborah Jessup is no longer in residence at it. A three-year-old-sounding child answers her old telephone number, says "Ding-ding-ding-ding-ding" to me, shrieks and hangs up. No new listing for her in the directory. Information has a restricted listing. I go through three supervisors to liberate it; after forty minutes spent nagging, crawling and insulting, my passion is depleted. Why Deborah Jessup? I'm not sure I'd know her if I saw her.

Plante's face is long, complexion waxen. He sits as if nailed by the shoulders to the client's chair. Pull out the nails and he will slide to the floor; on the floor he will dissolve into a puddle; the puddle will feel sorry for itself. "So much for friendship; drowned in trivia," he says of the Quintana written up in my report.

"What seems trivial to you may be important to her."

"Along with everything else, have we done away with objective standards for trivia?"

"Would you call holding a kid's novel for a month and then denying you ever got it trivial?"

"That's her story. Do you care to hear mine? Or is your mind made up?" I wait. His face is a combination of sadness and bitterness so mixed together it is impossible to guess which one is on top. "Did she bother to tell you how she behaves when she consents to put in an appearance at my parties? If she did it is not in here." He waves my report at me. "Mine is always the middle party of the evening. After the dinner party and before the good party. She shows up with her entire retinue, none of whom are invited. She promenades in, chooses a corner, stations herself and her crew and for one solid hour neither moves, nor meets my friends, nor speaks to a soul outside of her immediate circle. She sits and waits for me to pay court. Eventually I stop paying court. I find it insulting to pay court. And that is the last I see of her at my parties." He waves the report. "But that's not in here. Why isn't it in here?"

I get the sinking feeling I am in for a long session. "What about that business with her nephew?"

"Why didn't she ask Capote to read it? Five hundred gangrenous pages of self-absorption and I, of all her lists of notables, am assigned to do the book report. Why me? Think about it."

"What about this old man you talked into writing his autobiography?"

Plante bristles. "Do you know who that old man is? He is a former U.N. ambassador. Do you think he needs me? Do you really think he needs me? She certainly caught a live one in you, didn't she?"

March 5

Everyone to his own "A" list; Plante's would not be mine. A glossy bunch, deep tanned in March, groomed to the point of petrifaction, marbles in their mouths as if language is an imposition. Plante snorts his way through their depositions of grievances.

Number two says Plante volunteered to get her son a copy boy job on the *Times,* assured her over a period of weeks at Quintana's party, Ivor's party and Curt's party that job interviews were set up for the next day. Personnel Department never heard of the kid, denied knowing anything about the interviews.

"Bureaucratic incompetence," says Plante.

Number three says Plante volunteered to get him into Hugh Hefner's mansion as a house guest, assured him it was all set up, only for the poor sap to fly out to Chicago and be turned away at the door.

"A running gag between us, how was I to know he'd take it seriously?" says Plante.

Number four says Plante volunteered to put him in contact with Burden when he heard the man was in public relations trouble. Called Plante half a dozen times to set up an introduction. Plante never returned the calls.

"Burden didn't return my calls. What was I supposed to do?" says Plante.

He sniffs and snorts his way through five, six and seven. "Bedtime reading" is his definitive comment as he drops the report on the floor. "Grown people, supposedly people of substance, and what do they come up with? Surely they can't expect to be taken seriously? Or can they? Assuming we accept the justice of their complaints, what in God's name do they amount to? Friends forget to return calls all the time. Or don't they? Am I the first? Do you suppose that no one on this list has ever broken or forgotten a promise or failed to return a phone call? Tell me, you saw them, what do they genuinely want of me? With the best of intentions in the world I volunteer (you use the word repeatedly in your report), I volunteer to perform services for friends. How many on that list have volunteered to perform services for Plante? How many hours in a day? How many friends queued up for favors? No, when all is said and done what do I owe them? The truth is that they are taught to expect so little in the way of human kindness that when you throw them a bone their fevers rise and they tear you to pieces."

I wait for him to simmer down. I wait for me to simmer down. "That's not the picture I get. The picture I get is of a lot of famous people with shaky egos who have been made to feel that they don't fit in."

"By me."

I nod. Plante nods.

"I see. When Burden and Cornwall refuse to talk against me you take it to imply a brutal, personal assault; when my other friends indulge in a brutal, personal assault you accept it at face value."

"I call them as I see them."

"Tell me about the Carson show. The Carson show has canceled my last two bookings. Is it possible that Carson thinks he doesn't fit in? Then tell me about Bantam Books? Don't they fit in? Is that why you can forage this entire city and find not a bookstore, news kiosk or airline terminal that stocks the paperback edition of my novel? What's behind it do you think? Is it possible that my novel—two hundred thousand sales in hardcover—all at once my novel doesn't fit in?" Plante leans back, crosses his legs fragilely. "It's perfectly clear what's happening. I'm blackballed, blacklisted. But the question is why? On what ground? Have you heard anything?"

I count slowly in my head to twenty. "Nothing that I haven't reported. But that doesn't mean much. The stuff they pass to a stranger isn't likely to be as good as the stuff they pass back and forth among themselves."

Plante pales. "What stuff?"

I count slowly in my head to fifty. "You know the way people are."

Plante brings a cigar out of his case and rolls it between his fingers. "A smear campaign? Are they spreading stories?"

"I'm only suggesting it as a possibility."

The cigar rolls so fast in his hand it is hard to see what he's holding. "What do you think? A rumor?" He turns his back to me and doesn't move for a time.

I make funny faces at his back and say, "It sounds farfetched to me."

He turns front, skin shiny, eyes cold. "Farfetched?" The cigar has come apart in his hand. "Apparently everyone has heard it except you and me. What is it? Who's spreading it? Why should we be the last to know?"

March 6

Plante walks circles around the client's chair. "It's not your fault," he says with reproach.

"I only saw the girl twice and that was a year ago," I mumble, annoyed with myself that he's got me on the defensive.

"And it was cold. She was bundled up," he adds quickly. "You did write in your report that she was bundled up the other night?" He has inexplicably switched to my defense counsel. He rereads my description and chuckles. " 'Small, squeaky voice . . . short, stocky . . . walks as if she's kicking small children out of the way.' I've known her all her life and yet I let it slip by. You caught her perfectly, you know." He jerks his head as if in salute and grins shyly.

We are speaking of Naomi Kaufman, daughter to Big O. Plante spotted her arm in arm with Wally Burden at one of the dwindling series of cocktail parties he's still invited to.

"So blatantly obvious! Not Wally's part but hers. I'm certain Wally is loyal, but Naomi—what does she have against me?" His stare, wide-eyed, vulnerable, begs that I be kind to him.

"She could just be in love with the guy. It could be as innocent as that." I know by now the best way to provoke him.

Plante's skin is drawn so tight on his face I get the impression of looking at raw bone.

"Do you honestly see them as a love match? Andy and

103

Candy Panda in the wee hours with the lights out? Highly unlikely!

"And where, in all this, is her father? Naomi is nothing if not her father's daughter. Like Sherlock Holmes's famous dog that did not bark, Kaufman's total lack of connection to this case may turn out to be the most significant fact of all."

March 7

Kaufman again. I fiddle with his number, half dial, then hang up. A dozen or more times. I doped the poor son of a bitch. For what? A notebook! Last year's crisis: a notebook. This year's crisis: a guest list. Does Plante mention the notebook now? Does it make the slightest difference to his life if the goddamned thing was recovered? No, he is too busy worrying about parties. Parties!

Extract from my diary, May 8, 1964:

> Younger daughter: Tina, a knockout. Sixteen years old, close to six feet tall . . . as slim as or slimmer than a fashion model. Tiny head, all torso and legs . . . sits . . . in physically implausible positions . . . If she ever lost balance it is probable that she would not fall down but would float up to the ceiling. . . .

Poor Plante. Poor Kafkaesque figure worried sick over what they have on him. And all they have is that he's a lousy friend. But that's not good enough for Plante. He knows that there has to be more; it is not the rumor I was hired to bring back. It is not the rumor circulating inside his own head.

But if he is that frightened, why doesn't he drop the girl? He dropped Annabelle, no sweat. Deborah? Out of sight. Why not this one? Possibly because she happens to be Kaufman's younger daughter?

Kaufman, all-size and a yard wide, greets me wearing a blue terry-cloth robe and striped red pajamas (though it is four in the afternoon), eyes red and happy, a warm smile on his face, a handshake that leaves me arthritic—would you believe it, I am welcome! With one hand on my elbow, he leads me into the living room—no, he says, too public—into the study for a good talk—where we won't be disturbed by the ladies. I ask for Tina. Not at home. I do not ask for Esther.

He offers me a drink. A bar in the study, a small refrigerator under the desk full of ice and chilled glasses. On the desk, open file drawers, multiply indexed, overflowing. A finished page in the typewriter and next to it on one side, three mounds of typed manuscript, one yellow, one pink, one white; on the other side a pile of books; Martin Buber sits on top.

Hard to tell but he looks fat under his robe. His complexion is less florid, his hair longer, very little red left, mostly silvery gray. His old boyishness a thing of the past, he sits with corporate grandeur in an over-sized office swivel chair, arms at rest, drinks, his and mine, in both hands. The look he gives me—has the man turned queer?—is one of affection!

He hands over a drink and we exchange suppressed smiles at my hesitation in accepting it. I immediately drain the glass in order to prove that (1) I don't think he'd dope me just because I doped him and that (2) if he has doped me it is only what I deserve. This gesture is followed by an endless pause checked finally by Kaufman swiveling his chair toward the typewriter. "I have to finish this page. All right?"

"You work on that, I'll work on *this*," say I, indicating the bottle.

From the back he does not look like a man, but some ominous science fiction shape: giant, hulking, blue-and-red-striped. The impression given is one of intense seriousness and concentration. But nothing happens. I remember Kaufman to be a loud breather but now the silence is awesome, closing in fast on actual pain. Seconds before reaching my threshold of breakdown he begins erratically. I am hostage to his typewriter, rigid during pauses, easing off as he builds up a steady rhythm. Within minutes he is going as good as a real writer (Plante?). When he hits the margin on the bottom of the page the bell rings, ending the round. He whirls around to face me, all the boyishness returned. My turn to pour the drinks. We both chuckle. Whatever it is we are in, we are in it together.

I look around. "This must be a great place to work."

His smile has guilt written all over it. "I keep the door closed. Nobody is allowed in when the door's closed." A sudden trapped look. "What—to what do I owe the pleasure?"

"This is difficult for me but— I was at a party a couple of weeks ago and met a girl I was very attracted to. I didn't even get her name. But yesterday I was passing by and I saw her getting out of a cab and going into this building. And then I remembered where I'd met her before and that she's your daughter."

Kaufman stiffens. "Naomi?"

"Tina."

He begins rocking back and forth in his chair.

"I thought of calling her up for a date but then it occurred to me, all things considered, that you might have strong objections."

Kaufman rocks slowly and blinks a lot, as if he has trouble getting me into focus. "You're actually asking my permission?"

"It's not as if I hadn't intruded plenty enough in your life. . . ."

He laughs out loud. "Aw, come off it!" A long, thoughtful head scratch. "What say do I have over it? Asking permission! I feel damned silly!" Never taking his eyes off me he pours himself a drink. "Tina is very independent."

"Maybe I'm too old for her. Whatever you say."

Kaufman blushes. "I'll be damned! Listen, even if I ordered Tina to—she doesn't listen to what I say. No, it's nice of you—damned decent—but I can't, you can't ask me to take that responsibility." He pauses, takes a drink. "She dates boys twice your age. That's the way it is in that business. So they tell me."

"What business?"

A low mumble: "Fashion model. Her mother wants her to finish school and if Esther can't control her, don't ask me to fix it up for you."

"I didn't! I don't! That wasn't even on my mind."

"She makes three hundred a week. Seventeen years old. Beyond my depth. No, look: this isn't the nineteenth century, you two have to work this out for yourselves. You sure you don't mean Naomi? Naomi's not as tall as you."

"No, I remember Naomi."

"Naomi's closer to your age, had straight A's, whizzed right through Spence and then on to Radcliffe, then went out and got herself a great job in public relations. Works like a dog and Tina does half the work, makes twice the money."

"Don't you have friends in public relations?"

"Wally Burden. That's who she's working for. Or he says he's working for her. But if you're suggesting— I didn't lift a finger. All on her own and Wally says she runs the office. His words, not mine." He rocks back and forth, frowning. "No, listen, you were doing your job. Why am I so special? I'm like anyone else. Others can be the privileged characters. I wasn't raised like that. Of course, how you raise them today— well, you can't, because there's too much—look at tradition, all gone. Roots, wiped out. The family. Exists in name only. God, no less. We weren't religious, sure, we observed the high holy days but other than that—but today. It's not anywhere like it. That's the problem with these kids, Tina too. Structure has disappeared. Structure. Separation. Dislocation. If I can get it down it's what I'm trying to write about. Structure and dislocated man and key relationships. I won't go so far as to say it's an original work—who am I?—but in lay language. Here—" He takes a page, looks at it, puts it back. "No, it's this way: when you're born—an infant, what does he know? He knows that nipple. And sustenance. And warmth. The mother. That's a key relationship. Not just the milk. They've done studies on the effect on children when they're denied maternal warmth and affection. Autistic children. At every stage of development, in some form or another, that direct line connects, for example, the farmer to the land, the fisherman to the sea. That constant process of feedback that went on, that key relationship—it was an announcement, a sort of declaration of existence. And now it's lost.

107

"These are generalizations but you get what I'm driving at. Man leaves God in order to become God. Internalizes God. The ego. Incorporates into his own self his key relationships. So he doesn't need them anymore. So *he* thinks. It's the beginning of exploitation. Capitalism. Slavery. That dislocated state of mind.

"That's why I took a leave of absence. I felt it like everyone else, the need to make sense of it. And also ways of doing something—alternatives. Not just to say: That's it and aren't I wise for showing you?" He waves at the mounds of paper.

"It sounds as if you're writing philosophy."

Kaufman's red face reddens. "Call it—does it have to be called anything?—a study or an analysis. Anyhow I'll never finish. Listen, I know this is boring, would you like to see some of it?" He hesitates when I say yes, then plunges his hands into the middle of the white mound and pulls out what threatens to be several hundred pages. He laughs. "You didn't know what you were getting into. Does it bother you if I watch while you read?" He reaches over to a floor lamp in the corner and plants it over my left shoulder. "Light," he says. He pours two new drinks. "Wait." He places a small end table to my immediate right so that I have some surface other than his manuscript to put down my glass. He rocks, fidgeting, breathing noisily.

I'm about to get going on my third attempt at the first sentence when he jumps out of the chair with a suddenness that makes me half-wonder if he hasn't decided to beat me up after all. "Door." He lunges at the open study door but not before I catch a glimpse of Tina, pony-tailed, black turtleneck sweater, green plaid skirt, passing by. On her way in? On her way out? I spring to my feet forgetful of Kaufman's life's work, at one moment in my lap, at the next all over the floor. "Christ, I'm sorry," I mumble to Kaufman.

He drops to his knees, mumbles, "My fault," and starts grabbing pages. I follow him to the floor, trying to make it up to him by grabbing at his pace. No way: Kaufman's long arms grab pages to the left, right and in front of me. I fall far behind, ludicrously outgrabbed. He is three-to-one, maybe four-to-one in pages ahead of me. I deliver over my minuscule bundle. He puts it with his, examines the pages, flipping through them quickly. A small whimper: "I knew I should have numbered them."

Back on my feet I watch him, still on his knees, shuffling pages. "Maybe this isn't the best time—"

His head jerks away from the mess on the floor. "You don't want to read it?" His eyes are like a child's.

I am friendly, but all business. "It's getting late."

He is back on his feet, towering over me, edging me away from the door. "Have another drink. Have dinner with us. Have you made plans?"

My plans are to have dinner with the Kaufmans. "Nothing I can't get out of."

"Get out of it. You want to make a call? There's a phone. You want to be in private? I'll go outside." He opens the door and steps out into the hall.

"I don't want to kick you out of your own study. Is there another phone?" We slide past each other; now I am in the hall and Kaufman is in the study. He only half looks up as I close the door on him.

I start down the hall, officially in search of a telephone. It's not in Esther's closet; it is not in Kaufman's closet; I find one in the master bedroom next to the king-sized, chenille-covered bed, cutesy white as is every other object in the room, including the picture frames; I also find one in the room next door, apparently Naomi's, apparently vacated, no clothes in the closet except for a tattered bathrobe and a pair of blue jeans. Glum portraits of childhood depress the walls: a lot of years spent in camp.

The next door I open has to be Tina's. I ease it open, an apology and an introduction programmed on my lips. Yes, a phone but no Tina; and very little of anything else, unless you count four walls of maps: Rand McNally tearsheets of the five continents; Esso, Socony and Mobil regional road maps, most of them tacked up so long ago their colors are faded. I sit on

109

the edge of a wicker chair, waiting in vain to catch my breath, dialing a number—I can't think of whose—until I hear Plante's voice on the other end. "Yes?"

People who answer the phone with "yes" make me want to hang up on them. "Ackroyd. I don't have much time. I'm at Kaufman's. I thought you'd want to know: daughter Naomi not only sleeps with Burden, she works with him."

"What does that mean?"

"She's his assistant. I wonder if you find that as interesting as I do."

"What are you getting at?"

"One more thing. Kaufman is out of the UJA. Leave of absence. I bet you can't guess what he's doing with his time." I wait, knowing Plante does not want to ask "What?" but has very little choice. He finally asks. "He's writing a book."

"You're not serious."

I know exactly what Plante must look like at this moment: grim, frozen, bone-white complexion. "Can't talk now. I'll try to call back later." I hang up, not a moment too soon. Tina slouches into the room munching on a peanut butter sandwich. She now has on a faded Beethoven sweat shirt and blue jeans. Her long feet are bare, high-arched and very bony.

She stops in the doorway, two round spaces for eyes.

"You must be Naomi." Why let her start with an advantage?

"I'm Tina."

I point to an Esso map. "I see you've been to a lot of places. I envy you."

"Don't I know you?"

"My name is Roger." A short pause to give her time to say: "That's right! You were at Rags' party two weeks ago." She does not take advantage of the pause. "There are two schools of thought on travel," I push forward. "One is that you run around to a lot of places fast and get sort of an overview, a general picture. The other is that you settle down in one place for weeks, maybe months, and get to know it well. And by knowing one foreign place well, you get more of a clue as to what other foreign places are like."

She says, "Uh-huh." Her eyes, like her mother's, seem to circle around me, coming at me from behind.

"I don't mean to suggest that one place is like another, not at all." I wait for her to say something: I am prepared to wait forever and I almost do.

"I don't know if I agree with you or not. My mother's not home yet."

"I'm here to see your father."

"He's in his study."

"I was using the phone." I point to the phone. See and say. She says, "Uh-huh."

"But I'm curious: why the maps? Places you've been or places you want to go to?"

"Or both?" she asks. Is she being ironic with me?

I smile, encouraging her to go on. But no, it is definitely going to be a one-sided conversation. "I do a certain amount of traveling myself. Not for pleasure; I don't have the time. But that's the way it is in a job like mine where your office is more or less in your hat—clients sometimes ask you to travel, the demands of a case—"

"Uh-huh," she says, infuriating me.

"For example, I had a client last year—I can't mention his name—who had me running back and forth in the course of a couple of days to Larchmont and back." No response to Larchmont. "It's not very far, you wouldn't call it travel, but I got to know Larchmont in a way few others get to know it."

She stares at me as if I have lost several of my screws.

A rabbit hole. It opens beneath my feet. I drop. Observing with greater clarity as I fall. Invisible once more, consequently invulnerable. I will climb, hand over hand, out of the darkness and put into operation the process which will ultimately result in her falling in love: More mystery, less talk, more enigma, less open, more cool, less compassion. I am, have always been, a slow starter. I rise like a phoenix out of my rabbit hole. On earth again I hear shouts. Somewhere down the hall. Esther's voice. Loud. Ominously recognizable. *"I won't have that man in my house!"*

111

Esther has lost weight and ground. Can you imagine her giving in to her husband a year ago, ten years ago, ever? But here I am seated on her right at the dinner table, wolfing down roast chicken and there she is on my left, no visible sign of stress, no physical change at all that I can remember, except for the loss of five pounds—my heart goes out to her—but no question: she is not in command or, if in command, not with the degree of authority once held in this house.

Kaufman, changed into a charcoal gray suit, Esther wears black, Tina in her Beethoven sweat shirt. Conversation:

Esther: "Mr. Ackroyd, are you still—I'm afraid I've never known what exactly it is that you do?" A silent eye exchange between Kaufman and Esther.

Ackroyd: "I'm a private detective." She smiles; it bodes ill.

Esther: "Are you working at the moment?"

Ackroyd: "You mean am I on a case? Well, sort of."

The three focal points at the table strike three contrasting attitudes: from Kaufman, a warmth that borders on gratitude; from Esther, bare tolerance; from Tina, nothing, nothing at all.

Esther: "What sort of case are you working on?"

Ackroyd: "Most of my business is a matter of routine. I must say it's pretty boring."

Esther: "I imagine you will find ways to make it interesting." She sits with emasculating good posture, her eyes protectively on Kaufman, who smiles gamely.

Ackroyd: "I'm not as committed to it as you may think. I'm not even sure I want to stick with it. Lately I've had law school on my mind." Short of breath, I turn to Tina. "Do you find modeling interesting?"

Kaufman consults Esther's eyes to see if it's all right that I talk to Tina. She half-lowers her lids which must mean "yes" because Kaufman says, "Tina, Mr. Ackroyd asked you a question."

Tina: "Huh?" She is virtually nonexistent, her body so screwed into her plate it is practically part of the meal.

Ackroyd: "How do you find modeling?"

Kaufman: "She's off in another world."

Tina: "Fine." Her voice is disembodied; her body is disembodied.

Ackroyd: "Bet it brings you in contact with interesting people. Celebrities—and you go to parties. As a matter of fact, I think if I'm not mistaken I saw you at a party a few weeks ago."

Esther: "Anyone we know?" Said too fast, too anxious.

Ackroyd: "I don't know. Some party. Do you like parties, Tina?"

Esther: "Does your work take you to so many parties?"

Ackroyd: "A lot of it is just sitting outside in the cold. You know how it is."

Esther: "It must require a peculiar turn of mind to find satisfaction in that sort of work."

Tina: "Well, he just said he wasn't satisfied. Not everybody's satisfied, you know." Eerie. She unfurls out of her plate like a genie out of a bottle. "I might like to be a private detective. But not on murder cases. Are there only murder cases?" She *looks* at me! "What about divorce cases? I could help on divorce cases."

Ackroyd: "Loads of divorce cases."

Tina: "Do you need an assistant?"

Ackroyd: "You're hired."

Esther: "Tina's joking." She looks unfazed, in fact better than at any time since we sat down.

Tina: "What about disguises? What about a gun?"

Ackroyd: "I wouldn't worry about guns."

Tina: "If I can't have a gun I don't know if I'm interested." Eyes back on her plate.

Esther: "She's teasing you, Mr. Ackroyd."

Tina: "No, I don't know if I'm interested or not, but I could be." Eyes now full on me, a glint, small but nonetheless a glint, of excitement.

Ackroyd: "Anyhow, if you're interested I'll be glad to talk to you about it." Casually stated, meant to woo Tina, retain Kaufman, not further alienate Esther.

Kaufman: "Not out of high school and already she's a private detective."

Ackroyd: "It might be a good idea to finish high school, Tina."

Esther: "That *is* a good idea. Thank you."

I restrain my urge to thank her for thanking me.

Tina: "Well, I was only kidding anyway. How do we always end up on school?"

Ackroyd: "I didn't like school that much either." All of us, faces down, fool with our food. "I felt just like Tina only a few years ago." Said to Kaufman but meant for Tina, in an attempt to recover lost ground.

Tina: "I suppose I'll outgrow it, right?" Her torso unwinds.

Ackroyd: "I wouldn't want to be the same person five years from now that I am now, would you?"

Tina: "I don't know what you were five years ago and I don't know you now so I don't mean to be offensive but what difference does it make?" She has grown seven feet, quivers, looks translucent in the candlelight.

Ackroyd: "I think you misunderstood me, Tina. I was talking about change. Everyone wants to change. Basically I'm in agreement with you but from a different perspective. We share a lot of the same feelings; it should bring us together, not divide us."

Esther: "If we use people for purposes of our own choosing, how can we expect to receive the sort of trust that is a prerequisite for coming together?"

Will the woman never let me be?

Ackroyd: "I know how much people can change because I know from my own experience how much I've changed. Whether anyone else accepts that or not—well, I think it's worth the risk. Otherwise, we end up too separated, too dislocated."

Kaufman: "I hope you got something out of that, Tina."

Tina: "Right, I'll think about it. I have to make some calls."

I am on my feet, rising with her from the table, trying with no luck for eye contact.

Ackroyd: "I'll think about what you said too." I sit; it is

a long, vulnerable way down to the chair. It is now the three of us at the table. Or the two of them and me.

Kaufman: "If it's a parent they don't listen. What you said is what I've been trying to say for some time."

Ackroyd: "I suppose it's only a phase but she's picked up some pretty strange ideas. The sort of people that a girl as attractive as Tina meets at parties, they can sound very convincing." I push back my chair. "Will you excuse me for a moment?"

They think I am going to the john. I am, but it is mainly diversionary. What I am really after is the telephone. I slip into Kaufman's study and dial Plante's number. He picks up before the end of the first ring. "Yes."

"I'm still here. I've only got a minute. I just wanted to tell you I've managed to read part of Kaufman's book. It's good."

"Don't hang up." All urgency in the voice. "I want to know more about it."

"It's philosophy."

"A philosophic novel?"

"It's not a novel. I'd better go."

"Get it for me, I have to see it."

"It has nothing to do with you."

"How do you know?"

"I read part, I told you."

"And you also told me about your meeting with Quintana. If you missed the point once how am I to know you're not missing it again?"

"You're asking me to steal the man's manuscript?"

"What if it's based on my notebook? He never wrote a line before this."

"You think he stole his ideas from you?"

"One more thing: You say Naomi works for Burden. Are you aware that Burden's office handles publicity for Scribner's and Bantam? And that Burden books clients for the Carson show?"

"Are you implying that it's Burden who's blackballing you?"

115

"Perhaps not."

"Naomi?"

"Perhaps. It's possible that she's using Burden."

"You think she's the source of the rumor?" Anxious silence from the other end. "Any idea what the rumor is?"

Plante clears his throat. "How many pages has he written?"

"Over four hundred." A gasp at the other end. I hang up during the endless interval after the gasp.

I return to the dining room in high spirits, full of nervous energy, anxious to get on with the juggling act. I am not disappointed to find Esther lying in wait, alone at the table. Small on her way to black in the fading candlelight; her presence is far more imposing than when we sat down to dinner.

Esther: "My husband would like to read to you aloud from his book. He has gone to get it. He doesn't have many people to share his ideas with." I can't read her stare in the gloom but I assume it is not friendly.

Ackroyd: "I enjoy talking to him."

Esther: "Is that what brought you here today?"

Ackroyd: "Partly."

Esther: "There is another part?"

Ackroyd: "I had an idea that you and I could get along better."

Esther: "Since you have changed so radically in the last year the least I can do is reciprocate?"

Ackroyd: "You're not taking me seriously."

Esther: "One never knows how serious you are. So much of what you said sounded conveniently close to my husband's thesis." I smile enigmatically. "You are no longer in the employ of Rags Plante?"

I stare at her reproachfully. "I guess you haven't heard anything I've said all evening. I'm sorry about that. I'm really sorry."

Esther: "Has Rags learned that Otis is writing a book?"

Ackroyd: "I like you, Mrs. Kaufman. I want you to like me. That's the only reason I sit here and take this. I didn't know

116

before I walked in the door this afternoon that your husband was writing a book."

Esther: "Then why did you come?"

Ackroyd: "You're not going to believe anything I say so why should I say it?" We exchange stares in the darkness; it is like glaring in braille. "I like your husband. Plante has a way about him—particularly with young people. He can turn everything upside down and make it seem O.K. He gets you on the defensive and you don't know where you're at. I wouldn't work for him again for anything." I don't need to see her expression; I can smell that I am not going over well. "Quite recently he tried to hire me back." Esther's laugh is quick and vindictive. "The man's crazy. What he wanted me to do made no sense. I turned him down cold. I would have in any case. I couldn't stand the way people lionized him. Especially girls. When I saw what was going on at his house with girls—teenage girls!— I wanted nothing more to do with him."

Esther: "Are you saying that Rags conducts orgies? Really, now."

Ackroyd: "Well, then you haven't heard the rumors. The younger the better. They flock to him." She is so quiet I can hear Kaufman shuffling pages down the hall. She taps out a two-fingered beat on the table.

Esther: "Didn't you say you had run into Tina not long ago at a party?"

I manufacture a slow and reluctant "yes."

"Was it at Plante's?"

"I said I didn't remember which party."

"Is it that you don't remember or that you don't choose to?" I shake my drink and make it stir. I manufacture a frown.

"Mrs. Kaufman, I can't tell you how put off I was by that evening. Maybe I deliberately blanked it all out. Anyhow I assume Tina's old enough to know what she's doing."

I look up from my jiggling drink and Esther is gone. Kaufman, still gone, stays gone. Nor does Tina return. I hear the quiet closing of a door far down the hall. Muffled and intense

117

conversation followed by a long silence followed by more muffled and intense conversation. Fifteen minutes go by. I speculate on the propriety of leaving a note on the table. No, I will call in the morning. I let myself out of the apartment.

Home, at peace with a nightcap, I muse over the now predictable skill of that woman to pry information out of me.

March 8

First thing in the morning I call Plante to tell him I refuse to get him a copy of Kaufman's book and will have no complaints if he fires me. He is not home then or for the fifteen other tries I make at regular intervals until midnight. No better luck at the *Times*.

I dial the Kaufmans all day. No one home. Just as well.

March 9

The *Times* says Plante is on sick leave.

March 20

A note from Plante, postmarked Vienna.

The rumor of recent speculation has surfaced, small-bore, cretinous and altogether unimpressive, not without a taint of Comstockery but here too, dismally fainthearted. So laughable, in fact, that I have departed for foreign parts to gain suitable laughing distance.

In lieu of the bill you cannot send (since my travels allow no mailing address) I enclose a check which, if it does not discharge my debt, will in some small way compensate for that special service it is your custom to render.

As ever,
O.P.

The check is for $1,500. I call it even.

1966

May 11

"Even after he disappears he manages to run my life. So just get it out of your head that any of this is my doing." Annabelle Plante, looking strained, unhappy, older (What did I ever see in her?), stands in the center of the bedroom, swinging her eyes around the graveyard I call home, evidently looking for a chair to sit in.

God, she looks awful! Her long hair is sloppily pinned back, seemingly against its will; at any moment it may go—*sproing!!!*—in an explosion of lacquered blond porcupine quills. She wears a purple jacket that doesn't fit her and a brown knit skirt that doesn't go with the jacket and a yellow blouse that bunches at the waist; all in all, she is dressed for self-hate. "You're still in the detective business?" she asks. It is hard to ignore the slight curl of her lip.

"When it suits me."

"And now it doesn't suit you?"

"Working for your husband doesn't suit me."

She turns away, showing me her back. Her jacket is creased under the shoulders. "Oh, who cares! I don't want you at all if the truth must be told. I don't know why I bother to talk to you." She turns around to me with another face on. It is years younger, toughness gone, eyes bottomless and beseeching. "What am I supposed to tell him?"

I offer her a cigarette; she shakes her head no, then takes it.

"Tell him I don't want to work for him."

"He still has me running his errands. Isn't that a riot?" She holds out her cigarette, waiting for me to light it. I won't light it. We play at that game for a while but the outcome is never in doubt. Annabelle is one of the more easy people in my life to outlast. She lights up, blows smoke at me and says, "Well, he always did need villains in his life and I'm the convenient one. But get it out of your head that I'm in a position to tell him anything, because I can't." She rummages inside a giant suede handbag, pulls out a hairbrush with one hand and a letter with the other. With both hands occupied she tilts her head back to keep it out of the way of the cigarette smoke. "Here, read it for yourself," she says out of the corner of her mouth. She holds both brush and letter in her hands, apparently not able to decide how to get rid of either. In the meantime, cigarette smoke curls around her nose; her left eye begins to tear. I relieve her of the letter, thus somehow freeing her to drop the brush back into the bag.

"This is postmarked Orlando. Is this where he is? Florida?" Annabelle has out a Kleenex and is dabbing it against her eye.

"Florida, the moon! How would I know? Using his mother— can you imagine—as a mail drop! At his age!"

"He communicates to you through his mother in Orlando?"

Annabelle smirks. "He mails them to her, she puts them in an envelope with no return address and forwards them to me. Not that she'll admit it."

"How do you reply?"

"I leave a message with his answering service."

I hand her back the letter. "You can leave a message that I said no."

She acts as if she has not heard me. She scans the room, I guess for an ashtray. Having found none, she drags a stool full of dirty laundry out of the corner where I thought I had hid it. "May I?" What will she do with my laundry? I wonder. Will she put it on the floor, on the bed; will she fold it neatly; will she wash it for me? She does none of the above; she sits on it.

"He wants Josh. He wants him for the summer. But he won't come and get him and he won't let me bring him. He wants you. What's he so afraid of? That I'll find out where he's writing his precious novel? I'm no more anxious to see him than he is to see me! But what do I do with Josh? He hasn't seen his father in more than a year. Who does he blame? You can be sure it's not Rags."

"I can't help you."

She is a beehive of small actions: crosses her legs, hunches her shoulders, leans forward, points her cigarette in my face. "You've always looked down on me and I've never known why."

"It's not true."

"O.K., it's none of my business."

"It's also not true."

She grinds out the cigarette on the sole of her shoe. "I don't care what you think of me. I'm at my wits' end. Let *him* have a taste of those vengeful eyes for a while. I need a rest!"

Without planning the move, I pull myself off the unmade bed and stand over her. From this new vantage point she loses whatever limited interest I was beginning to convince myself I found in her. "I'm sorry," I say.

She does not budge. "You don't sound sorry."

"I'd sound a lot sorrier if I said yes."

May 12

True, that in this business you can't pick and choose your clients but there must be a wider choice out there than Plante!

Going over last year's diary: my obsessive, vindictive plotting against him. Childish. Degrading. All very far away from me now.

More trouble with Gloria. She's the only girl I can act normally with, so why do I always provoke fights with her? And why is it never important to me who wins?

May 13

Wildly drunk for the first time in nearly a year. Blacked out, but remember having a fine time with Ken Whiting, the English journalist who lives downstairs, here at the Excelsior. Desperately hung over but, other than my head, feeling no pain.

May 14

Suicidal.

May 15

Gloria dragged me to an Off Broadway production of *Three Sisters*. A boring, irritating play. Why critics idealize these stupid, selfish, smug, supercilious women I will never know. They emasculate their kid brother and then turn their backs on him when he cries for help.

May 16

Same old Larchmont. Same old Annabelle. Same old ingratitude. The less I have to do with her the better. I'm sorry I didn't tell her that. Looks good, but frigid, brother! She says I look down on her. Who wouldn't?

Kid is half-fag, half-monster.

Her eyes popped when I told her my fee. Best moment of the day.

Half hope Plante turns me down. Lots of luck!

May 18

Plante's counteroffer outrageous. Said as much to his answering service. They said he is due to call in for messages tomorrow.

I go downtown to Air India and buy a one-way ticket to London for the 30th.

May 20

Plante's service swears they gave him my message. So far no reply.

Gloria, of course, has found my plane ticket. She should be the detective, not me. The first drawer she opens—any drawer, it doesn't matter which, and she will find what I am trying to hide from her. She calls me a secretive son of a bitch and starts to scream at me. The more she screams the calmer I get. By the time she is screamed out I am practically in a state of meditation. It's funny how often the moves you make on impulse turn out to be the moves you've wanted to make all along.

May 21

Annabelle wants to talk to me about Josh. I tell her it's not certain that I'm taking the job, still haven't heard from Plante. She says it's typical. Sounds a lot warmer; asks if I want to take her to dinner. I say yes. She says, "I hope you mean it this time." I am halfway to the Algonquin to pick her up before I figure that one out. I broke a date with her two years ago; our one and only. Is that why she's so snotty to me? A two-year grudge?

We end up, after bitter recrimination, eating at the Russian Tea Room. With Annabelle it is a life-and-death struggle choosing a restaurant. She is expert at misinterpreting. She is also expert at making judgments, and they all seem to be against herself—or so they start out; then subtly, the line switches and I become the guilty party.

Dinner is tense, nerve-grinding and primarily a holding action. By the time I am back at the Excelsior there is no muscle in my body that doesn't require a month's vacation.

Three messages that Gloria called. Too tired to call her back and pay the price I will have to pay. Will try to get up early enough in the morning to call her before she calls me.

May 22

Call Gloria for an hour. She is either out or not picking up.

Call Plante's service and leave word that I am in New York for seven more days, at the end of which time, if our negotiations are not settled, I will leave for Europe. Call Annabelle to let her know my decision. She comes on warm, friendly, apologetic for last night. She acknowledges that she is a monster and invites me to take her to dinner.

We go to the Ginger Man, where, suffused in soft light, she looks kind; the one unvarnished face in the room. Says she feels out of place there, out of place everywhere, wonders if she'll ever reach a time in life when she feels comfortable in public. I tell her that she looks admirable, which she does. She indicates with a small wave of dismissal that she doesn't believe me. She hardly smiles, seems chronically disappointed. We don't talk much and I hold down my drinking. She tells me this pleases her. I put her in her car at midnight, glad that it's over and worried that she won't make it home.

126

May 23

Dinner at Gallagher's. I order for the two of us.

Her: "I envy you. You're so sure of yourself. You're self-sufficient. The one thing I wish—I'm always wishing—is that I were stronger."
Me: "Sorry, you don't strike me as being weak."
Her: "Don't I? Then I've fooled you. I'm glad."
Me: "Why?"
Her: "I don't know. If I can fool you maybe I won't be so afraid of you. You don't give very much, you know. I suppose that's part of being self-sufficient. But it makes you hard to deal with."

The phone is ringing when I get back to the room and I know who. Gloria. We have a tense five-minute conversation during which we agree to cool it for a while. I sound more regretful than I feel.

May 24

A message from Plante! He says he'll go up a thousand if I come down a thousand. I tell his service that I'll call in with my answer tomorrow. Actually it's a stall: he either goes all the way or no deal.

Dinner with Annabelle at Gino's.

Her: "Rags wouldn't talk to me unless he had a few drinks. It made me feel invisible."
Me: "What was he like when you married him?"
Her: "Very quiet. Very impressive. He could be terribly funny. When he decided to recognize your existence he could make you feel that you were the only person in the world. He was very gentle."

Me: "When I talk to him I often get the feeling he's off in another world."

Her: "I had to live with it. He never asked anything or expected anything. I could stand on my head and he wouldn't notice. It's not easy to face that he had to drink to pay attention to me."

I fall off the wagon in style. Roaring drunk. Annabelle very upset. Takes me back to Excelsior. I make a pass. Is that why I got drunk—to make the pass? She cries and walks out on me. Not even a farewell kiss.

May 25

Try all day to reach Annabelle to apologize. She won't talk to me.

Call Plante's service and leave word that I'd like to hear from him personally.

Call Gloria a couple of times. No answer.

Go down to Air India and get a refund on my round trip to London.

May 26

Annabelle calls, voice thin, concealed, nervous, wants to know if I'm free for dinner, seems to not hear my apologies though I run off enough of them.

The Ginger Man. No conversation during dinner. Air heavy. Unrelenting presence of quiet blame. She's through talking and I'm through apologizing. Had to be drunk, in no other state would I go near the woman. Over coffee steady maintenance of no contact.

Back at the Excelsior a note that Mr. Plante called at seven-thirty, no message. Call Plante's service, no message.

May 27

Annabelle wakes me at seven. Her turn to apologize. Doesn't know what got into her, it wasn't the pass I made, probably more that I did it drunk and that reminded her of Plante which made her turn me into Plante when she knows as well as she knows anything that we couldn't be less alike. When can she see me? Can she drive down now? Finally!

May 28

Incredible how natural we are together, as if we've been doing this for years. She makes love very quietly and it gives the act a dimension and dignity I never knew it to have before.

In the mail a check for fifteen hundred dollars from Plante and a brisk-sounding note of instructions. One thousand retainer, five hundred expenses. Further instructions await me at the Holiday Inn, Washington, D.C., where a reservation has been made in my name and Josh's for May thirty-first. I am to tell no one, including Josh's mother, our destination. If she will not release the child to my custody without a forwarding address I am to make one up.

Relay this information to Annabelle in bed. Do a short tirade on Plante's arbitrariness. She has lived through it all; in this we are one. The thought excites me. We make love.

Various post-love comments on Plante's attempted blitzkrieg. On his chiseling me out of my deal. On his contemptuous refusal to negotiate in the open. Hatred excites me. We make love.

Total hysteria. Annabelle and I concoct plans to screw her husband. Byzantine plots for betrayal. Ranging from bizarre to humiliating. Uncontrollable laughter. Conspiracy excites me. We make love.

Annabelle and I agree that the best way to handle Plante and all his bullshit is for us to go down to Washington together.

129

May 29

Six A.M.: Wake up Annabelle to tell her I can't go through
with it, that Plante is my client, that I have obligations toward
a client, that I can reinterpret these obligations but I cannot
blindly overlook them, that to succumb to temptation and take
her with me would be contrary to Plante's instructions and in
violation of my own personal code of ethics.

If I expected her to take it like a good sport I was wrong.
For over an hour her back is turned to me. It is a back that is
as stiff as a board. I try to imagine the face that is on the other
side of the back. I imagine it white, drawn tight, eyes squinting,
mouth rigid. I imagine it to be the face of the Annabelle at the
beginning, not the Annabelle of the last few days which is a
face so inexpressibly vulnerable that I can, if I'm not careful,
slip very easily into loving it. I cannot bear the substitution of
the old Annabelle face for the new Annabelle face. I cannot
survive the silent reproach. I will straighten out my ethics after
Washington.

May 31

Josh has grown in two years, but not more likable. He is
handsomer at eleven and more effeminate. He is foppish, expects things to be done for him—and they are—by his mother.
His wrists bend annoyingly. His little white mouth spits orders.
Annabelle jumps. Frightened out of her wits by the kid.

She and Josh have a chicken and egg thing going. It is hard
to spot who's at fault in a particular argument—on occasion
she will play the grownup, on other occasions he will—but in
the end it is their habit that he wins. Either by truce, negotiated
settlement or unconditional surrender. He chalks up his vic-
tories with no expression at all. The rest of the time that we are
together on the plane he wears a glower or a smirk.

"I'm not hungry."

"But you have to eat something, Josh."

"Why do I have to eat if I'm not hungry?"

"But you're never hungry."

His mouth twists in disgust at the dried tuna canape American Airlines has tried to foist on him.

"Aren't you going to eat when you're with your father?"

"What's such a big deal about eating?"

"It's for your own good."

"Is eating when I'm not hungry for my own good?"

An extended grim pause during which Annabelle gives my hand a surreptitious squeeze and then in quick reaction, as if we've been caught at it, begins to stroke Josh's head. Her touch is ponderously maternal.

The kid whines, "Stop poking me."

"I'm only brushing back your hair."

"You mussed it up."

"It *was* mussed up."

"I like it that way." He runs both hands through his hair, pulling it out in all directions. "O.K., is that better?"

"I just want you to look nice for your father."

Josh twists around in his seat and inspects the rear of the plane. "Where is he?"

"He's not on this plane and you know it."

"So why do I have to look nice if he's not here?"

"Why don't you show Mr. Ackroyd how well you can take care of yourself?"

"He tried to arrest me. Why do I have to look nice for him?"

Annabelle's eyes cross. "You only like to look dirty."

"Are these dirty?" He displays two small, immaculate hands. The fingers look vomitously virginal. "They're really dirty, aren't they? Aren't they?"

A matricidal glare. "All right, this time they're clean."

"This time!"

"I admit they're clean." Her complexion is blue from lack of oxygen.

Josh switches his glare from Annabelle to me. During the switch it stops being a glare and becomes a wide-eyed look of Annabelle-inflicted injury. His smile is a plea. If I hadn't witnessed the crime I might think he was the victim.

Holiday Inn, Washington: I have made Annabelle's reservation in Gloria's name—it was the first that came to mind. I check us in as Roger and Josh Ackroyd while Annabelle is Gloria Townsend. Our rooms are four doors apart. The arrangement is that Josh sleeps with his mother who, after Josh is asleep, sleeps with me.

As an act of fidelity to Annabelle I hold off opening Plante's sealed orders until after eleven, when we are in bed, rubbing bodies. I love lying next to her; shoulder to shoulder there is a sense of her flesh fusing with mine.

Plante's instructions are to proceed to the Holiday Inn at the Atlanta airport and await further instructions. Plane tickets and a room confirmation slip for the first are enclosed. We are one short on each. I correct Plante's oversight by phone. Annabelle picks her own name this time: Nora Charles. Her eyes twinkle as she says it. She asks, after I hang up, if I think her choice of names is clever. I say yes.

"Rags always made me feel stupid. Whatever he accused me of I believed. Does that make sense?"

She complains of a backache and I give her a massage.

"I know why I'm tense. I think you think I'm a bad mother." She looks at me as if I might hit her. "I'm glad Josh is a boy. I didn't want another one like me."

"Are you that bad?"

"Everyone seems to think so. He hates me." She takes my right hand and pulls on the fingers. She measures her hand against mine. It is whiter and smaller. "Does our difference in age bother you?" she asks.

"It bothers you I bet."

She laughs. "You're on to me. Do you think I'm a bore?"

"No."

"Do you think I'll always be this way?"

Here lies Annabelle: terminally vulnerable. Self-destructive to the point of vindication. I become aware for the first time that I have a plan: to seduce, charm, cajole, intimidate and fuck her out of self-destruction.

Gloria sees me the way I see Annabelle. Does someone see

Gloria the way she sees me? Is everyone in emotional hock to a smarter friend with an overview?

June 1

Holiday Inn, Atlanta. Instructions from Plante: same instructions; this time, Holiday Inn, Charlotte, North Carolina, on the second.

Conversation with Annabelle at Holiday Inn.

Her: "Josh knows what we're up to."
Me: "O.K., so he knows."
Her: "Maybe we should stop."
Me: "Why?"
Her: "The way he looks at me."
Me: "He always looks at you that way."
She seems suddenly embarrassed.

June 2

Charlotte, North Carolina. Plante's instructions—are you ready?—tomorrow: Holiday Inn, St. Louis, Missouri.

Annabelle appears tired, cranky, eases me off her. "I'm sorry. I can't."

She sidles away from me. Soon she will be off the bed. "You must think I'm terribly neurotic. Is that what you think? I bet basically I'm happier than you are." She seems to be shrinking in size; everything but her eyes which get larger as she gets smaller. "I want to give of myself! I have so much to give! I feel it to the core of my being. But no one gives back. You give more to Rags than to me."

"I took you along with me. I didn't have to."

"You run his errands."

"It's my job. You asked me to do this."

"Don't try to say you're doing it because of me."

133

"What other reason would I have?"

"You and Rags are so much alike. You turn everything back to me."

"Annabelle . . ." For a long time, no answer.

"Rags always said 'Annabelle' in that same fed-up way. Two peas in a pod."

June 3

Annabelle is a no-show at breakfast. Let her sulk. I have a sneaking awareness that the mean age of the crew on this mission is nine, possibly ten. Josh, the senior member of our party, sits across from me studying the menu. It is the same menu at every Holiday Inn and he gives it the same, exhaustive study. I now doubt that he reads it; my guess is that he hides behind it. It is his barricade against food. The only food I have seen him shovel away is French toast. Anything else that approaches on a plate is an enemy.

Not that he is in outright rebellion against the enemy; he is too canny for that. He knows that, nutritionally and socially, one is expected to eat, so what he does is present his gifted impression of a boy eating. Unless you watch him carefully you would swear that he eats. You would swear that the food goes into his mouth where it is chewed and swallowed. You would swear that he cleans his plate. But nothing of the sort; it is an imitation. The food goes into his cheek. The napkin goes up to his mouth when he thinks no one is looking. The food goes into his napkin. Josh leaves behind him, cross-country, a trail of stuffed, wadded napkins. His napkins are better fed than he is. So what keeps him alive? My guess is resentment. Whether he appreciates it or not: his mother's child.

Josh puts aside his menu and orders his French toast. He looks down with furrowed brow at his fork, probably trying to remember what it's used for. "I know what she does at night," he says in a guarded voice. I lean forward and wait. "She goes to you." He presses the prongs of the fork against the palm of his hand. "And I know what you do." He turns the fork over

134

and runs his thumb across it. "You talk about me." He looks up at me for the first time, a startling resemblance to his father. His figure is on the way to being Plante's, his posture as automated, his demeanor as unruffled. "That's why I stay awake all night. Because then you can't do what you want to do."

"What's that?"

"Leave me. But I stay awake so you can't. But I don't care anymore. So you and she can leave any time you want. I'm gonna go to sleep from now on because what do I care. I'll hitchhike to my father."

"Have you asked your mother what we do at night?"

"I don't have to ask her a thing. Why should I have to ask her? Who is she that I have to ask her anything?"

"We don't talk about you. We talk about her. I try to cheer her up. Have you ever tried that?"

"Boy, are you a liar."

"One of these days you should take a stab at cheering her up."

His expression is that of a banker refusing a loan.

It is a somber threesome on Braniff's mid-morning flight to St. Louis. We all look and sit like cardboard cutouts of ourselves, everyone afraid to break up the threesome lest the remaining two get an edge. Josh is the first to break—the spirit is willing but the bladder is weak—and fifteen minutes out of St. Louis turns on us with a betrayed-looking glare and hastens off to the john. He moves like Plante: that appearance of coming and going at the same time.

I take Annabelle's pale hand, lean very close and sketch, in a subdued voice, the highlights of the breakfast conversation. She grows, if it can be believed, more tense. Her eyes are bright with suffering. "Thank you," she says in a tone of consummate ambiguity. Does she mean "thank you for your loyalty despite our fight last night" or "thanks a lot for informing me that I have one more cross to bear"?

Josh starts his way back down the aisle looking leisurely out every window, indicating to the world at large that he

135

couldn't care less what his mother and I have had to say about him.

Holiday Inn, St. Louis. No instructions from Plante. His first slip-up. Can his imagination at long last be failing him in his choice of Holiday Inns?

I find that I am no longer troubled by the ethics of my Annabelle decision. When Plante signals that he is ready to be serious about taking possession of the kid I will ditch Annabelle. There is a certain degree of forbidden pleasure in the idea of her waking up some morning to find Josh and me long gone.

Dinner in the motel dining room is subdued and anonymous, as if we are three strangers seated by accident at the same table. Josh begins by not wanting anything, then wanting only water, then after some anxious prodding on Annabelle's part, agreeing to take a chance on a sardine sandwich. I order a double Scotch and a fried chicken; Annabelle orders roast beef, blood rare. It will come back well-done, she will complain to the waitress, who will offer to take it back; Annabelle will decline the offer —she has declined the same offer three nights running—and will eat her roast beef with an expression that will indicate that she is swallowing live coals. The more I see her at dinner the more I have the impression that the eating ritual has been reversed; that Annabelle herself is on the menu and, bite by bite, is being devoured by the roast beef. If I were Josh and were forced to sit and watch my mother eat I would also hate food.

"Is that good, Josh?" Josh doesn't answer. "Josh?" Nothing from Josh but the sound of small teeth making niggling bites.

"It must be good; he's too busy chewing to talk." A sprig of levity from Ackroyd.

Annabelle smiles. "My roast beef is good too." She cuts herself a slice and snaps it into her mouth with transparently false passion. "In fact, this is about as delicious a roast beef as I've ever eaten." She chews with enthusiasm. "It's awfully good. Would you like to try a slice, Josh?" Josh nibbles away with his little rat teeth. His eyes give off no interest in roast beef. Annabelle starts to cut peanut-sized slices. "I'll tell you what, I'll just leave this on your plate and you can try it if you like it and if not, don't, but at least it'll be there for you to try if you think you're in the mood." Her words, while reasonable, are said in a voice of such restrained hysteria that one might be led to believe she has poisoned the roast beef. She spears the meat samples with her fork and delivers them like a gift to Josh's plate. Josh gathers them up on a soup spoon as if they are live organisms and returns them to Annabelle's plate. Annabelle brushes them onto her fork and deposits them on the edge of Josh's plate. Josh uses a bread knife to knock them off the edge onto his soup spoon and puts them back on Annabelle's plate. Annabelle's fork stabs, snares and flies them back to Josh's plate. Josh, flicking his bread knife like a fly swatter, spatters the meat all over the tablecloth. Annabelle snatches up the scraps in her bare hand and slams them on top of his sardine sandwich. Josh turns over his plate. The game ends with the roast beef scraps and the sardine sandwich smeared on the dining room table.

"I suppose you think that's funny. I want you to clean up this mess!" hisses Annabelle.

"I thought you said it was delicious," Josh says.

"It is delicious!"

"Then how could it be a mess? I don't get it. Is it a delicious mess?" He looks at me, eyes twinkling like Plante's. "A delicious mess? I don't get it."

"You will clean up this mess on the table and then you will apologize to me and to Mr. Ackroyd for your very bad, bad, bad manners. Have I made myself clear? You will this very minute, this very second clean up this mess!" Expressed in a vibrating hiss within which I detect a note of pleading.

Josh reaches over to the center of the table and tears off a hunk of sardine sandwich.

"What do you think you're doing?" demands Annabelle.

"What does it look like? I'm eating."

"I told you to clean up this mess."

"I can't do two things at one time. Do you want me to eat or don't you? You always say you want me to eat and then when I want to eat you don't want me to. Boy!" His hands nervously tear away at the sardine sandwich. Frantic, actorish chewing which looks fake but, for once, isn't. Nervous ripping at the ruined sandwich.

"Do you hear me, Josh? I am going to let you finish eating your dinner and just as soon as you are finished you are going to clean up this mess. You think I'll let you get away with this but you can eat from here to doomsday and then you will still have to clean up this table."

"I'm thirsty," says Josh, and gulps down a glass of water with bits of toast and roast beef in it. Some of the flotsam apparently catches in his throat. He gags, coughs, rolls his eyes, slaps his own back. Annabelle does not move. I lift his hands in the air and give him a hand-slap between the shoulder blades. He stops gagging; his breathing returns to normal. His eyes shoot roast beef at Annabelle.

"Now clean up this table," she says.

Midnight: Annabelle is a no-show in bed.

June 4

Nothing from Plante. Now what is he up to? Annabelle, in a good mood for once, appears unconcerned, decides to treat the extra time as a holiday, goes into St. Louis shopping. I am stuck with Josh. It doesn't occur to her that if I knew where Plante was I could spirit the kid off. Annabelle's good moods seem to operate on a fixed biological schedule, the conditions of her life notwithstanding.

June 5

Nothing from Plante.
Conversation by the pool: "We got on my street a kid with a cleft palate. He talks like this, 'Nyuhh, nyuhh, nyuhh.' "

Josh starts into an imitation of a kid with a cleft palate but cannot finish because he cracks himself up.

"That's not funny," I remonstrate. "I used to have a cleft palate."

"Big liar!" Josh cracks up.

"It took twelve operations to make me normal."

"You call that normal?" He cracks up again, calms down and starts a rambling monologue in imitation of a punch-drunk fighter. "That's the way they really talk, I'm not kidding," he informs me when I again announce that I am not amused. "My father used to take me to see the fighters work out in Pompton Lakes, New Jersey, and that's the way they really talk. He took me to see Floyd Patterson. Do you know him? He doesn't talk like that though."

"I don't know him."

"He's not so big. I met him. You know George Chuvalo?"

"Never heard of him."

"Gee, you don't know anybody. I'll give you an easy one. Johnny Carson."

"Pitcher for the Yankees."

Josh slaps his forehead with his hand. "You have to have heard of him! He's one of the most famous people in the whole country! He's a friend of my father. He told my father he could be on his show any time he wanted. You know Cannonball Adderley?"

"The General?"

Josh screams with laughter. "He plays in an orchestra! My father took me one night to hear him. He's Negro. What would you rather be: white or Negro?"

"Chinese."

Josh makes a face. "Me, a Negro. They're the best athletes and musicians. I could be a writer but my father says it's too hard and he doesn't want the competition. He could be kidding though. With my father I can never tell if he's kidding or not. She never kids though. And she never knows if I'm kidding or not; I always have to tell her and that takes the fun out of it. Does your wife have a sense of humor?"

"I'm not married."

"You're lucky. Wait till I tell my father."

We lapse into trapped silence as Annabelle puts in a surprise appearance by the pool. She discards a terry-cloth robe with a carefree toss aimed at Josh. Before it lands, Annabelle ascends. Midway into her dive she hangs like an avenging angel, frozen in time, space and animosity. By the time she cleaves the water she has also cleaved our sanctuary. She surfaces and spreads her glistening arms in a wingspan that threatens to encompass the pool. "Josh, darling, it's delicious! Go change and come on in!" No response. Annabelle pretends not to have uttered a word. She upends herself. Her slender ankles and perfectly arched feet are all that are visible for a moment. I see in them an abstract of Annabelle: her biography can be told from just the sight of her ankles and feet; her face can be seen in the manner in which they hang out of the water like floating closet hooks, suggesting her crossed eyes, her tentative smile, her unrequited needs . . . She dives to the bottom of the pool, swims a brilliant lap underwater and surfaces to what she evidently hopes and expects to be applause.

"Nyuhh, nyuhh, nyuhh," says Josh.

A two A.M. knock on the door. I irrationally hope for Plante but it is Annabelle. Her hair is uncombed, eyes sunk in hollows, complexion waxen and pulpy. She wears a thin, blue silk robe with cotton puffed sleeves and a rip in the right shoulder. Her feet are bare and in mules. She looks at me as if she's waiting to be hit. I kiss her as a matter of form. She responds but I don't.

"How do I change?" she says into my open shirt. "Help me!" Her arms around my neck feel skeletal. "I'll die. All I think of is dying."

I prop up her nearly limp body; she appears to have shrunk in size, ten pounds lighter since afternoon. "Annabelle, where's Plante?"

"Nowhere when I need him." Her eyes narrow. Crow's-feet

sprout. "Laughing up his sleeve. Predicting Rags? Try astrology." Her voice loses substance, sounds reedy.

"I think he knows you're with us."

"I'm nearly a dead woman. I warn you, be careful."

I hug her with ferocity; the idea is to give her strength but instead I feel mine going. "If you want me to help, you have to listen. I mean seriously listen."

"I will. I'm grateful. You should have been his father."

"First of all we've got to identify the problem and then isolate it. And then we can discuss what to do about it."

"What is there to do? There's nothing to do!"

"That's because you see it as one enormous problem. You don't see it as Josh and Annabelle, you see it as Annabelle and her entire life. It's too enormous to handle, solving your entire life. But solving one problem at a time . . ."

"He thinks I'm a monster."

"That's not the problem. That's your self-pity speaking. To solve the problem—are you interested in solving the problem?"

"I must!"

"We take one step at a time. And when we hit self-pity, we go back and start over again."

"One step. No self-pity. Right." Her body stiffens. She pushes me away and stands shakily but unsupported.

"Why are we here?"

"It's some trick of Rags'. He's a sadist."

"Start again. Why are we here?"

"Because I thought a son should be with his father. What's wrong with that?"

"Why are we here?"

"Now I don't know. I mean I know but to you it will sound like self-pity."

"You wanted to get him off your hands. What's wrong with that?"

"Have it your way. I'm a bad mother. You know it, Josh knows it, the whole world knows it."

"Self-pity. Let's start again."

"Right."

"Why are we here? Black and white facts."

"I couldn't take it anymore!"

"You wanted some time for yourself."

"What's wrong with that?"

"Defensive. You needed time off. You agreed to send the kid to Plante. It was your chance to be free. Why didn't you just turn the boy over to me and leave it at that?"

"He's not a fit father."

"Is that why you wanted to track him down?"

"He has his hide-away and now he'll have his son and what do I have?"

"You're envious. Isn't that it?" No answer. "Cut your losses."

"What losses? You don't make sense. You talk too fast."

"Leave. Leave today. Go away. Go anywhere you want to go. Leave Josh with me."

"You want me to give up my son."

"I want you to take a vacation from your son. Isn't that what *you* wanted? Leave him. Go out to the pool with your bags packed. Say goodbye. Say it cheerfully. Now he's got a game going. You refuse to play. It'll be the first time you've ever refused to play."

"Just go to the pool and say goodbye?" Her eyes cross.

"Cheerfully."

"Where do I go then? Another motel?"

"Where do you want to go?"

"He'll hate me."

"Go to Paris."

"He'll never forgive me."

"Self-pity."

"Self-pity can also be true."

June 6

Josh passes the morning poolside, setting traps that his mother unerringly walks into. He does not want to go back

142

to the private school Annabelle sends him to. Annabelle, trying to sound agreeable, tells him it is too late to get him into a new school for next year but that she will be happy to look into the situation. Josh says, "She says it but she doesn't mean it." Probably true. Annabelle, still agreeable, insists that she will look into it the minute she arrives back in Larchmont. Josh says, "She won't take me out because my father wants me to go." Thus Annabelle is made the villain of Plante's desires. Annabelle tries to point this out by suggesting—still agreeably—that Josh discuss this with his father and that she will be happy to comply with their mutual wishes. "See?" says Josh, "She always listens to him."

June 7

At lunch Annabelle informs me that Josh has made a decision that he wants to room with me. I tell her, all things considered, it is probably not a bad idea. She says she has thought it over and agrees. It will give her more time to do things—for example, read—she has been months getting into *The Red and the Black* but Josh constantly interrupts. "He plays these games and I can't help myself, I get caught up. I think it's time I put a stop to it." She eats her eggs too fast, leaving yolk on her chin. I have an urge to wipe it off. The urge possibly communicates, Annabelle plugs into my stare and wipes her chin. "But won't all this be unfair to you?" she asks. "All this time you'll be spending with Josh. There must certainly be other things you want to do."

"What I have to do is wait for Plante."

"That's not a life. All we ever talk about is me. What about you?"

I restrain the temptation to tell her to go back to Larchmont to read *The Red and the Black*. When we get up from the table she surprises me by formally extending her hand. We shake hands.

"Did you two have a nice day?" Annabelle asks at dinner.

143

Her smile says: Hit me. "Well, I had one of those afternoons. I was shameless. I indulged myself. I don't care. You don't know how long it's been. I gorged myself. I had a banana split for lunch. A walnut sundae for a late afternoon snack. I must have put on five pounds. Who cares? Not me! I took two naps. You know how long it's been since I've had the luxury of that much free time to enjoy a nap? I watched television. Don't ask me what I saw. I watched in bed. Sheer heaven. I fantasized. Oh, wouldn't you love to know about what!" She winks at me, then digs into her roast beef. "Mmm. Much better!"

Josh looks as if he wishes he were at another table, reminding me of how often, as a kid, I was embarrassed for my parents in front of my friends. "Josh, your hamburger's getting cold." I realize, with amazement, that I said that.

"What if I like it cold?"

Annabelle chatters on, increasingly hard to listen to, like being tuned to two radio stations at the same time. She read *Cosmopolitan* from cover to cover, took an hour-long bubble bath, began constructing plans for the remainder of her summer "when I'll be free," Paris, Venice, Madrid . . . "I feel like a new woman." In a disjointed motion she brushes back Josh's hair from his forehead; his face disappears under her hand.

"Don't," he says.

" 'Don't. Don't,' " mocks Annabelle, brushing invisible dandruff off Josh's shoulder. "Finished. Now was that so terrible?"

Josh squirms. A tinkling laugh from Annabelle. "Isn't he a joy to be with?" She rolls her eyes. "You know what we must do? I must take you to the Mediterranean someday." She puts her hand on my hand. "It's very different. I think you'd like it although I never can tell in advance what you will or won't like. What I think you will, you disapprove of, and what I think you won't, you appear to cheerfully accept. You know where else I must take you someday?"

I try to slip my hand out from under hers but she holds tight. Josh has not moved for minutes, looks like a decal of a boy pasted onto a chair.

144

"Upper Malibu has some wonderful beaches. Do you know Trancas? I'll show it to you, you'll love it."

"I do know it. I come from near there. I don't like it."

Annabelle lets out another tinkling laugh. "See, you've just proved my point. Didn't he, Josh?" She squeezes my hand in a manner suggestive of rape. With my hand pinned to the table she turns on Josh, flashing a smile of high-frequency dissonance.

"I don't want to go back to that darned school. I don't see why I have to," Josh mumbles.

Annabelle's body tenses. "Do you really think this is the time?"

"Sure. Then later you'll say it's too late." His mouth twists bitterly.

"Josh, do you want to ruin my day? Is that the purpose of this?"

Josh looks up at her expressionless. "You don't have to yell."

"I'm not yelling." She faces me. "Am I yelling?" Among our threesome a prolonged silence, during which time Annabelle's neck cords stretch to enormous size as if for a scream. The silence heavies the air, makes me yawn. Annabelle observes my yawn with obvious irritation, then leans her face very close to Josh (she still has my hand). "You know what I am going to do with you in the fall? I am not only going to send you back to that school that you hate—I have had to take him out of three schools; well, not again, thank you —I am not only going to send you back to that school but I am going to ask them to recommend you to a psychiatrist. That's right! Your father has wanted me to send you to a psychiatrist for two years and I resisted him, but now I am at my wits' end and I refuse to put up with your antics for one more day and so you are going to go, as soon as vacation is over. Do you hear me? And I don't care how much you whine and complain and I don't care how much you hate me for it—you will always have some reason to hate me—you are going to a psychiatrist and that's the end of it.

145

I'm certain that from the example of your behavior at this table, in addition to your other wild antics, that even Mr. Ackroyd would agree that I should have sent you to a psychiatrist two years ago." She turns to me. "Isn't that so?"

I am not given the chance to use diplomacy. Josh does not wait for that. "Come back here, you!" shouts Annabelle across the dining room to his fast-departing back. He keeps on going. His mother pounces, moving as swiftly and beautifully and with as much singularity of purpose as she does in a pool. She has him nailed within a step of the door, one hand on his forearm, the other on his shirt collar. Josh goes limp. Annabelle half-drags, half-carries his sprawled body back to the table. We are, by this time, a spectacle.

June 8

"I'm glad about last night. It's the truth. I know you're not. But I feel a lot better. I think last night was very important. You're angry with me, aren't you?" Annabelle, the early bird, looks bright-eyed and invincible, sits on my unmade bed chattering to keep my unmade mind at bay. I don't know what the hour is; too confused to check my watch when she knocked and woke me. Josh could have but did not get the door. He was sitting in the chair right next to it, fully dressed, wearing, in the morning, his famous no-face. But when the knock came he didn't move, nor did he respond when I mumbled from my bed burial, "Will you get that?" In fact, he acted as if he were not in the room at all, possibly not on the planet. Not that it did him much good. I let Annabelle in and she went straight for him, crushed his head to her bosom, held it there, locked, squeezing its different parts with her hands the way one tests a melon to see if it's ripe. She had on the green cotton suit she wears for traveling—I noticed this and my heart bleeped.

Now, after a time she relinquishes Josh's head, tries unsuccessfully to catch my eye and announces in a voice close to

146

singing that she has some things to say to both of us. "I know I was angry with you last night, Josh, I hated you but I don't now. Do you hate me?"

Once again I am astonished at what she is capable of saying to her son. All I can say is "Annabelle." She is good-natured about it.

"Oh my, we're back to 'Annabelle.' You must hate me, too, this morning. You're both such little boys. It's so apparent when you and Josh are together. You probably think you're being fatherly. Do you mind that I tell you these things?"

"Whatever you're here to talk about, you're not talking about it."

She puts a frail, gloved hand to my shoulder and my flesh goes dead. "That's just like you. You make it difficult for me to say anything, and then you accuse me of not saying anything. Well, I've made a decision that you're bound to like me better for. I've decided that you two boys get on so famously, there's no further point in my staying. It would have been cruel to send him out alone with you; how did I know how you'd take to his moods? But now that you've become friends —well, then, I can be on my way." She laughs playfully. "So I'm going to leave you two conspirators alone, for better or worse. Now what do you say to that?" She slaps both white-gloved hands together and beams maternally.

I marvel at her genius for clouding the issue, so that her reason for leaving town is not because of her continued humiliation by her son, but because Josh and I want to be alone!

"Now, Josh, don't think you're going to have your way entirely. I want you to be better behaved with Roger so that I can be proud of you, because you'll be here to set an example and if it's a good example—well, some of the plans you and I discussed at dinner last night can be changed. I think you know what I mean. But that's strictly up to you, my darling. Is that understood? I intend to be firm about this."

Josh says and does nothing. This irritates Annabelle; still in her musical voice she asks: "Cat got your tongue?"

Josh bares his teeth and says: "Meeow."

"Don't be silly," says Annabelle.

"Meeow, meeow," says Josh.

Annabelle laughs. "Have you got the sillies this morning, darling?"

"Meeow."

She flashes her bright eyes on me with an expression that suggests that I am to consider myself once again an adult and her ally. "He does have the sillies, doesn't he? He really has a case of the sillies this morning."

"Meeow," Josh says.

Annabelle maintains a face rich with humor. "You silly, act your age."

"Meeow."

She chuckles. It denotes homicide. "Well, fun's fun but I don't want to be late for my plane. Who's going to see me off?"

In the cab to the airport it is mostly silence interspersed with nervous reminders from Annabelle. To Josh: "Remember, Roger isn't your mother, he's not supposed to look after you and it's unfair to ask it of him. You'll have to look after yourself."

To me: "Sometimes he wets the toothbrush and pretends he's brushed and you have to look out for that."

To Josh: "I want you to try to think of this as a wonderful adventure. You've never been to camp, so think of this as a sort of camp except you're more fortunate than other children because instead of sleeping in crowded bunks you're in a comfortable double bed with a TV and everything."

To me: "Don't let him wrap you around his little finger. If you let him he'll stay up all night but you'll be the one to pay for it the next day. He'll bite your head off with crankiness."

To Josh: "You'll be fine. Call me at home any time; I'll be there. This is a special occasion. I want you to get the most out of it."

Accompanying Annabelle's list of instructions: an air of agitation and possessiveness, as if we are seeing her off to the moon. And something else: the supposition that the higher she will fly, the lower Josh and I will sink, that if Annabelle gets away, I will not. Arrival at the airport corroborates my apprehension. It is like descending into a tomb. Never before had I appreciated the power of this woman whom I had accustomed myself to see as weak, vulnerable, incompetent, self-pitying.

"Am I doing the right thing? Tell me I am," says Annabelle.

I manage to tell her she is.

"You don't hate me?"

I tell her I admire her.

"Do you or are you lying?"

I take it as a rhetorical question and do not answer.

"You do? Really?"

I say yep.

"I hope we're both not crazy. Do you think you can handle it?"

I nod in the affirmative, wondering when, in God's name, this plane will load.

"I don't really know you. I must be out of my mind. What do you think, Josh? Should I go or should I cancel my reservation and come back with you?" She giggles, actually flirting now.

Josh's eyes are fixed on his mother's 707 crouched outside the waiting room window. "If that's what you want," he says.

Annabelle drops theatrically to one knee and grabs Josh by the shoulders. "What do *you* want?"

Josh's eyes never leave the plane. "Whatever's most convenient for you."

Annabelle, still down on one knee, arches her neck up at me. I cannot miss the stretched age lines. "Does he mean it? Do you think he means it? Then I will go! Am I wrong? Tell me!"

She says goodbye and stays, hugs Josh farewell and hello, shakes my hand with a firmness that promises that this is only the beginning and that it is all over between us. When she

149

has boarded the 707 and the door has clunked shut, locking her away, she stands behind us waving goodbye. The power of positive attrition.

A mood of anarchy in our escape from the airport: Josh has the giggles in the cab, goes wild, grunts, beats his chest with his fists, sniffs aggressively until I get the idea that he is imitating King Kong. He starts climbing all over the back seat, makes a roaring sound that I recognize as an airplane, clutches at the air, short, lunging grabs of air with his fists, followed by explosions and then machine-gun sounds . . . he grabs his chest, staggers, falls back against the partition window, slides to the floor, mortally wounded.

Plante, of course, is waiting for us on our return. "I'm broke," I tell him. "Will you pay the cab?" The bastard shows no sign of aging but it does please me that he looks smaller. He has on a tan suede jacket over a navy blue polo shirt and —to my surprise—blue jeans; not your everyday, off-the-rack blue jeans, mind you; these blue jeans are custom-tailored, appropriate for wakes and weddings.

Josh's whole manner changes. He is now Plante as seen in a reducing mirror, catches instantly the apparitional sense that his father conveys, the sense that he has magic and will disappear before your very eyes. Plante scratches Josh's head the way he would a pet dog and pays off the cab. The kid shivers with suppressed excitement. My hunch is that, with Plante, it stays suppressed. Still, I am forced to admit the boy is ecstatic. It is communicable. My spirits, down from Annabelle, are suddenly very high. I arrange a grin for Plante when he finally turns away from the cab. "I trust I haven't kept you waiting long," I say.

He tilts his head at me, indicating, I presume, that I am not the kind of person he is prepared to take seriously. His eyes, with their soft, luminescent, turned-inward look, switch to Josh, whose eyes do a flip-flop in imitation. Plante casually loops an arm around his son's neck in a half-assed headlock and lifts him off the ground, giving his awkward impression of an American father. "You've lost weight, old fellow," he says.

"Sure, sure," Josh giggles.

"My, my, how you've shrunk!"

"Six inches," chortles Josh.

"You're losing your hair."

Josh points me out. "He never heard of Johnny Carson."

"He is full of surprises," says Plante with a parenthetical smile.

They go at each other in the style of a light-hearted, ad-lib comedy team: wisecracks and banter glazed over manly affection. All of which should be enchanting—it is meant to be enchanting—that I be audience to a fifty-year-old man and an eleven-year-old boy as they smirk, wink and elbow-nudge their way into an acquaintance.

"You and I have some business," says Ackroyd, the party pooper.

Plante looks up from his work, then slides one knee to the gravel and embraces Josh by the shoulders as if for a man-to-man talk. "Listen, old fellow, will you accept it with good grace if Mr. Ackroyd and I stroll off to complete our affairs? I'll tell you what: you start packing and with luck we shall be on our way in half an hour."

"I'll be back in a flash!"

"Make it a trice."

"I'll make it a jiffy."

"Make it a half hour." Plante winks again (my bet is that he is always winking at the kid) and releases Josh, who, in his punch-drunk fighter pose, stumbles over to me, his hand out. "Nyuhh, I need the key, mister." I pull the room key out of my pocket more vigorously than I intended, thereby spilling a dollar's worth of change. Neither Plante nor Josh could care less. Josh starts off, doing a not-bad buck and wing, as I am down on my knees, scrambling for what's mine. "We're in room twenty-six!" the kid shouts at his father.

When he has danced out of hearing distance Plante says, "You share the same room?"

"His idea." I smirk a little.

"Mm," says Plante. I feel I am back in the game.

Plante leads me into the bar; the initiative, so far as I can see, is still up for grabs but perilously close to moving his way. Accordingly, I filibuster. "No doubt you have your own idea as to what went on. Far be it from me to interfere with the workings of a writer's imagination—" I am talking to his back as he circles the bar, sniffing for exactly the right table in the right corner, his movements throughout typically shy and obtrusive. "But for what it's worth—probably not much as far as you're concerned—" He settles at a table under a yellow-lit painting of Lassie. "I want to lay this out for you the way I saw it." His eyes move briskly across the room sending out summonses to waitresses. "So you can figure this for a verbal report. To begin with, it may come as a surprise to you—"

Plante drawls, "A glass of white wine" to the waitress. I order Scotch. Plante leans back, appears bored. I murder a yawn and burrow on. "I expected you to be waiting for us when we got back from the airport and you did what I expected. O.K., why did I expect it?" I wait for Plante to ask a question. He won't, so I go on. "It wasn't really that hard to figure: the long layover in St. Louis with no further instructions . . . Of course, you could have gotten yourself sick or killed—that was one answer, but the answer I put my stock in was that you had learned that Annabelle was a member of our party." A forked line slits his forehead at my mention of Annabelle; the first time in his presence that I haven't called her Mrs. Plante. Now that I have his attention I build. "Once I reached that conclusion I realized two things. One: that you or an agent of yours was in the vicinity. Two: you thought I was double-crossing you.

"I suspected from the start that Annabelle was using me to get to you. I had her with me because it was easier to get rid of her that way than if she had tailed me. Or hired some-one else to tail me." Drinks come. Plante brings his glass up to his face and stares through it at me. "Recently I had come

152

to know her a little. We had talked, you know. For long times on several occasions." I sip my drink and watch for the implications to sink in. "I think I understood Annabelle; I think I understood her well enough to make it certain that she'd leave town any time I wanted her to. Of her own volition." This time, a longer, more pregnant pause. "But before I could do that I wanted to hear from you. I didn't want to be stuck with the kid in the middle of nowhere. But I never did hear from you, did I?" I finish my drink. "The sad part is, if you had trusted me more you could have had him a week ago. Too bad, you would have saved yourself some money." I can't be sure Plante has heard me. True, he is looking in my general direction but his point of focus seems to end six inches short of my face.

"You did your usual splendid job. I'm sorry that you are angry with me. I sympathize. This must have been a great bore to you." His chest heaves as if in commiseration with what I have had to put up with.

"I never said I was bored."

"You're being kind. I am sure you were bored."

"Not *all* the time."

"You are in the right; I didn't trust you and consequently let you in for a period of excruciating boredom."

"It had its compensations," I say, with something short of a leer.

"I'm glad you say that but I can only believe you are trying to make me feel better. It is kind of you." His eyes, still on me but not near me, begin to water.

I suck up the melted ice at the bottom of the glass. "I can't complain, mind you. For me a lot of it was like a paid vacation. And Josh and I got along. Annabelle said the only reason she thought she could finally leave us was because he and I had become like brothers." I flag down the waitress and order another round. "I've had worse times in my life." We share an uneasy silence until the new drinks come.

Plante is looking through his glass at me again when he says, "Well then, I'm glad you weren't bored." He puts down the glass and feels himself up for a minute before unearthing a cigar case from one of his pockets. Another body search produces a cutter. He clips and lights the cigar. By this time I have done justice to my second drink and restrain myself from ordering another.

"I notice the more time I spend away from New York the more I see the place as a crucible," says Plante, smoking. "No one, if he is white, ever quite fails. In New York almost everyone is, on one level or another, successful. At the top of a heap. Not much of a heap, perhaps, possibly a low-lying heap or a heap only inches off the bottom. What one sees, in fact, is an endless clutter of miserly heaps, a junk pile of heaps upon any of which one can sit with pride and declare: 'Look, here I am, only twenty-five or thirty and at the top of my heap.' " His expression right now is soft, almost angelic. "Others, living elsewhere, cling to old friendships, church and family as their mainstays, but in New York, which is, after all, where one goes to flee old friendships, church and family, one's mainstay is one's heap. And one's vision of higher heaps. Friendships are determined by the level of one's heap. Envy, alienation, despair are the byproducts of disparity among heaps. What we have, then, in New York is a case of a people's roots sunk not downward but launched ephemerally upward; the New Yorker is the one citizen who, by nature, sinks his roots above his head.

"What finally turns one sour on the practice is the current invasion of heap termites. They do not climb, they level, they do not build their own heap, they tear everyone else's down. Until all is equal. Prairie and heapless. Of course, they can and will be driven back. But for me they degrade and dishonor an institution to which I have devoted thirty years of my life. To fight and beat them would be to dignify them. So my heap has been removed to the countryside where, with some pain and not a little pleasure, I am learning to integrate it into the prevailing landscape.

"Away from the city priorities change. In the country, the elm just now in full bloom outside my study window counts

154

for more. My own work counts for more. All those luminaries who come to befriend and patronize when one has climbed his heap, they count for less. And the heap termites, they count for nothing. One can only pity them." Something strong stirs, not in Plante's eyes but behind them, as if the eyes I'm looking into are shells for real eyes.

He has out a checkbook and a ballpoint pen. "Now let me pay what I owe."

1967

March 19

Though he is the only friend I have in the agency I am not sure what Dorsey thinks of me; not even sure he likes me. What makes us friends then? Probably it's political. He needs allies in his power struggle with the Captain. In our section I am Dorsey's only potential recruit. The other agents: Flanagan, Mayfield, Armbruster, LaStanza and McGrath are pragmatic and unreliable. Basically don't give a shit. They are classic bureaucrats, except that they are louder, more leaden-fingered, more potentially violent than your average bureaucrat in that all are ex-detectives. All past fifty and heavy drinkers who give evidence of happiness only when it looks like one or the other of us has badly fucked up. Dorsey, being a former Assistant D.A., pretends to me that he's of a different stripe, but when he unwinds with booze his humor loses its charm and turns childish, foul-mouthed and dangerously repulsive: the humor of the vice squad. In other words, the others, while seeming closed off, are more out in the open with me; Dorsey, while seeming out in the open, is not to be trusted. Why then is he the one agent here I can talk to? The answer, I'm afraid, is snobbery. Dorsey went to college. He and I are the only private cops in the agency, outside of the Captain himself, with college educations. With the Captain you'd never know it—you are not meant to know it —part of his game is to be more of a peasant than the peasants in his employ. His background is certainly peasant enough: Chicago stockyards. But he is quick as hell, knows everything that goes on, knows even how to delegate authority without relinquishing it. He reminds me of a cross between our President and Mayor Daley, except that, unlike those two statesmen, he can only glare at you with disapproval out of one eye; the other, shot away in Tarawa, is covered with a patch. Dorsey doesn't stand a chance against him, probably knows it, but conceives of himself as upwardly mobile, and since he is head of our section there is no other place for him to move but the Captain's chair. So I am in his favor because I represent young blood, the new breed that large organizations recruit with the idea that they are keeping abreast of the times and revitalizing their image. But the new breed began and ended with me. The Captain quit after one. So much for tokenism. Poor Dorsey.

I love this job. After three years of Plante what a joy to be part of a system! What a joy to have colleagues! To be envied when I wrap up a case! Until I joined Lyman Ross, Confidential Investigations, I had forgotten the security of being envied. Not since my junior year at Yale.

And I am not inventing the envy. It exists! Armbruster, McGrath, LaStanza, Flanagan and Mayfield dislike me, not just because I am young and well-bred, but, more important, in my nine months with Ross I have consistently showed them up. I am close to being on a rampage of showing these sons of bitches up! At times it gets very tense around here. That's where Dorsey helps.

I don't know if he's a good detective or a good administrator but no question he is a gifted social director. He keeps the section under control and temperamentally in balance. Primarily his method is the needle. He knows by instinct where one's emotional bodies are buried, and when matters threaten to get out of hand, he starts making cracks. His cracks at the others, particularly Armbruster, have bailed me out any number of times. Armbruster can't stand it when I show him up. He is effusive in his praise of me for the first day or so, but it is not too long before he goes on the offensive: files missing from my desk, my coat lining ripped, dumb things like that, all presented as practical jokes. McGrath is almost as bad— he and Armbruster are buddies—Mayfield and LaStanza largely restrict themselves to bad manners and heavy-handed insults. Dorsey has his own rule of thumb on how long to put up with these acts of petulance. ("Let 'em get their rocks off," he tells me. "You don't want to nail them right away, it humiliates them.") Dorsey is a champ at bearable humiliation; I bow to his expertise.

A case in point: An appliance wholesaler named Wasserman was losing inventory—five thousand dollars' worth of merchandise in two months. He hired Ross because the three security men he had on staff came up with nothing. The Captain turned it over to Dorsey who turned it over to Armbruster who, with McGrath's and LaStanza's assistance, conducted surveillance, did personnel checks, the works. Three weeks on the job and two additional TVs, five vacuum cleaners, two stereo players and six toasters, among other items, disappeared down the drain. None of our team of sleuths came even close to learning how.

It is the routine at Ross that individual sections hold weekly meetings in the Captain's walnut-stained, corporately imitative conference room. Whatever cases we are on that week are reported, reviewed and analyzed. If little or no progress comes out of the meeting, a meeting of section heads is set up. The problem case is re-reported, re-reviewed and re-analyzed. In the event that the twelve section heads screw up, the Captain is called in, or rather a summons is sent out by the Captain to the implicated section. The section then meets

161

with the Captain in his monastic office—Dorsey calls it the Holy See. The case is once more reported, reviewed and analyzed while the Captain sits, all soldierly concentration, occasionally adjusting his eye patch and sticking filters into his pipe. After the Captain has listened to everything that has to be said on the subject (not for the first time, some think; rumor has it that our conference room sessions are wired), he invariably comes up with an angle on the case that no one else thought of. Sometimes the fresh angle works out, sometimes not, but what most impresses people around here is the Captain's trick of reaching into a bag of worn-out information and pulling out from the bottom his angle. Agents gather around him like children at a campfire. They are in awe of the ritual, apparently not minding that a basic ingredient of its buildup is the exposure of themselves as fools. If they can't be fools the Captain can't be brilliant at their expense and the ritual has lost its effect. The Captain likes to run his ship on the principle that the exposure of fools is necessary to keep the help intimidated, competitive and content.

At the section meeting on the Wasserman case Armbruster, who was in charge of the operation, did a rundown of the measures taken to stop the thefts, which proved his thoroughness if not his adequacy since the thefts continued unabated. Armbruster is as much over six feet and two hundred pounds as the rest of Ross's agents and uses his girth as body English, especially when he has little to contribute and knows it. At the Wasserman meeting he writhed behind the conference table, bellying up to it as if it were a pinball machine. Dorsey waited for Armbruster to run out of gas, refusing to cut in or add a word that would help move him off the spot with his dignity intact. Dorsey, the expert at the needle, knows how to apply it through abstention. When Armbruster eventually died, Dorsey let the silence run on to sadistic lengths, impressing on all of us the enormity of Armbruster's failure. It is through such unannounced signals that agents, anxious always to be on the winning team, learn how much room they have for comment and on whose side; a dicey situation in that the comments have to be framed not to offend Dorsey and therefore be brief, while sounding good to the Captain just in case he is tuned in on the wire.

Because I was the new man—less than six weeks on the job—my turn at the wheel came last. At the time I did not know about the wire and was mainly concerned with discovering ways to get my fellow agents to talk to me. Naive as it now sounds, the method I hit on was to show them how smart a detective I was: respect would win me the friends that my youth and middle-class background denied me. As I write this, it is hard to believe I was ever that stupid. Maybe I wasn't. Maybe I was pissed off that no one in that goddamned place had talked to me since I came to work so I paid them back by breaking the Wasserman case.

I asked Armbruster if he had checked to see how many new accounts Wasserman had taken on in the several months preceding the start of the thefts. Armbruster shrugged; why would he do a thing like that? I suggested that Armbruster get such a list and check it against a list of personnel employed by Wasserman, looking, in particular, for employees who were relatives of new clients, or friends, or neighbors. Armbruster looked irritated. I suggested that if such a connection could be established, future shipments of merchandise to this new client should be placed under surveillance because, in all likelihood, the stolen merchandise was going out of the warehouse smuggled inside crates of regular orders.

The thefts, I said, were not of the size to signify a large-scale operation, so a plausible assumption was that the merchandise was being moved through a single dealer who probably sold the goods off the floor as part of his stock. Since the thefts began two months ago it was a plausible assumption that this dealer was a new customer. Then, again, the scale of the operation was modest enough to suggest a connection between the thief or thieves and the dealer that transcended the profit motive alone. So we had better investigate prior existing relationships, such as relatives, friends or neighbors. All of what I had to say was bracketed in a glut of concessionary phrases: "I may be wrong," "it seems to me," "O.K., maybe I'm crazy, but . . ." The sullen silence that followed my analysis was the first and only heartfelt response I have ever received as a member of the Ross organization.

These days, now that they know what to expect, they are ready for me at the section meetings. They applaud, salute, whistle through their teeth, and toot imaginary foghorns. Every time I am able to come up with the key to a case it is taken as an act of aggression and standoffishness.

One last example: When the section was having no luck freeing a lady client from a blackmailer I, alone among my colleagues, thought of looking past his police record into his home life, found he had had a rigid, fundamentalist upbringing, had lived in terror of his mother and had run away from home at sixteen. When it came time for the next payoff I flew his mother up from Kentucky and brought her along for the rendezvous. The poor bastard gave back everything: prints, negatives, letters and every cent he had on him. Our client made a few dollars on the deal.

Did anybody throw a party for me? No! Armbruster started calling me Sigmund Freud. The others, except for Dorsey, picked up on it. At that, it was an improvement over what they had previously been calling me: snot ass.

I should have accepted it. Instead I tried doing something about it. To make me less of a threat in the hearts and minds of my comrades I started regaling them with stories about Plante. I inundated them with anecdotes to show that I was every bit as much a fuck-up as they themselves. I told them about Plante's missing notebook and how I set it up for Plante to entrap the thief as I looked on, except I did not look on because I got blind drunk. My comrades loved that story. I told them about Plante hiring me to find out why he was not getting invited to the right parties anymore. My comrades did not know how to take that story; they suspected I made it up. I told them about the expedition with Josh and Annabelle, from motel to motel, babysitting and wife-fucking. They ate it up, wanted more. I embellished it with details: Josh's eating habits, Annabelle's bed habits, parakeets, King Kong, anything to keep them amused and at bay. I regurgitated Plante's stories till we sat neck-deep in them. They became an office staple, something to brighten a sour day. "Hey, Ack," McGrath or one of the others is likely to cry out, "you're not shittin' us about that notebook thing, are you? How does that item go again?" My escapades with Plante are now regarded as classics and, to a certain extent, they have worked. My comrades do not fear and despise me as they once did; they now fear, despise and have contempt for me. But the contempt is not to be regarded as flat out negative: it has, in some ways, humanized me; these days I am tolerated.

A funny thing happened along the way: In the beginning I had to force the stories out; they were funny to everyone but me. To me they were more in the nature of confessions. A sense of shame and betrayal got in the way of my effort at shaping anecdotes. But after a number of tellings and growing audience approval the stories became more joke than truth; they got to be actually funny. Dumb. Absurd. They deserved to be laughed at. I joined my comrades in the hilarity. What in the world had possessed me to take this banal insanity seriously? Plante is not a serious person, but a clown. And I was even worse than a clown; I was a clown's flunky.

The more often I repeat the stories the more distance I put between Plante's Ackroyd and today's Ackroyd, the Ackroyd that I had intended to be from the beginning.

If I strictly believed all of the above I would not have had to make this entry. The last previous entry in this diary was made nearly a year ago in St. Louis. Since then other things besides the job at Ross have happened: Elsie's marriage, my father's death, his will which left me nothing but proud, my resumption with Gloria and final breakup. Not one of these events struck me as worth recording. My early successes at Ross did not strike me as worth recording. The restoration of a sense of pride and achievement: not worth recording.

So what is worth recording? Dorsey stopped by my desk

after lunch today and dropped a copy of the April issue of
Harper's magazine on my lap. Headlined on the cover in bold
red letters above the title:

BEGINNING THIS MONTH:
THE WORLD OF OSCAR PLANTE

"Here's your boyfriend," Dorsey said. "Pretty snappy stuff."
I sit here with a case of the willies.

March 20

It is not pretty snappy stuff; it is unreadable. If Plante did
not have a name *Harper's* would never have printed this crap.
I can't make head or tail out of what he's writing and I defy
Dorsey or the editor of *Harper's* or anyone else on God's green
earth to tell me different. His sentences have become so elon-
gated and clause-ridden that they disappear into another dimension; only little green men can read them. Dorsey is giving
me the needle.

What I don't understand is why I am back in the trap. No
question, I am badly shaken up. I hate Plante for being on the
cover of a national magazine. It makes shit out of all my ac-
complishments. It reduces me to the level of Armbruster. Here
I am, pinning medals on myself for my status in an office full of
brutes, while out in the world Plante is back to making hay
among the people who count. I now realize that much of my
good feeling about myself was based on the formulation that
while I was on the way up he was going down and was supposed
to stay down.

I am drinking very hard tonight. My life is a fraud.

March 21

I telephoned Plante to congratulate him on his new column.
He was pleasant, if not friendly. Somehow or other we made a
date for lunch. Basically it was my idea, but he didn't put me

off. He could have said no and that would have been the end of it.

March 25

We lunch at San Marino's. I arrive late. Plante arrives later. He brings Tina Kaufman. He is in sports clothes, looking casual, scruffy (is he letting his hair grow or does it need cutting?). Not nearly as well turned out as the Plante of memory. His shoes actually need a shine! She has put on weight, too much, no longer ethereal, verges on plumpness, tucked into a wool turtleneck and bell bottoms. I observe them in the business of glowing in each other's presence. She is diffidently solicitous, touches him infrequently; he doesn't touch back. Plante unquestionably has her devotion—he visibly blossoms on it— but to spot it you have to watch him, not her. She does very little for him that can be publicly identified as loving; if it *is* loving it is out of a dry, subliminal love, sly as a card trick. At one point she says to me, "Rags has talked to me about you," obviously not remembering the times she has met me. It is one of the few instances during the length of our lunch that she takes the trouble to look my way.

She carries his cigars in her bag, bestows them like small, thoughtful gifts: a panatella for cocktails, a corona for coffee. She clips them for him. "I'm the *mohel*," she says. I nod and grin, not understanding. Very early on in the conversation she says to me, "Rags has talked to me about you," or have I recorded that? Incredible! Oh yes, they are a twosome all right: that space Plante used to mark off for himself, as if inside a glass dome, that dome now holds two. Occupancy by more than two is dangerous and unlawful. Yes, yes, they put on quite a show. I am reminded of the show he put on with Josh: the imitation parent. This is another version: the imitation couple. They exchange quips, private jokes, repartee. Nothing is required of me, not a word; all they ask is that I be the target of their happiness.

What do we talk about? It's not worth detailing but I am obviously out of control re Plante. So here's how:

"The last time I saw you you had given up the city," I begin.

"Actually I was trying to steal Tina away from her generation. When I was her age—how old are you, Tina?"

"Twelve." Neither of them smiles. Plante's eyes sparkle a bit; Tina's don't do anything.

"When I was twelve the only certain knowledge I had in this world was of my own powerlessness. Now this may surprise you—it certainly surprises Tina—but I did not view my powerlessness with a sense of pride; it was not a bridge between me and others of my age, also powerless—as a matter of fact, I recognized no others of my age or kind. My very powerlessness made me, as I saw it, one of a kind; a veritable paragon of powerlessness. It was a sign of my separateness and uniqueness. And in a very real way it was a sign of my shame. Certainly not a point to rally around or use as the basis for an ethic, an esthetic, an entire culture. It never dawned on me to unite with others—what others?—and celebrate in song and guerrilla theater my inadequacy. Or demonstrate for or against it on the streets. Or make war on language as a form of metaphoric matricide: if you cannot eliminate the mother, eliminate the mother tongue."

It's hard to know who all of this is aimed at; he is facing me but his eyes continually flash to his side where Tina sits, unalterably deadpan. "Well, I don't know," she says, "but I think every generation has to find its own way to compete with the past generation."

"I am not past, I am simply older," corrects Plante.

She puts a long hand over his to dissuade him from further corrections. "Your generation went to college and learned wit and cynicism and turned it against your parents. My generation can't possibly be more witty or sophisticated than you guys. No way! So the alternative is, we talk Negro."

Plante looks at me with adoration; a cushion-shot off my eyes into hers. "I see," he says. "We have freed the Negro from domestic servitude only to have our children enslave him in cultural servitude."

"Absolutely true," says Tina.

"And yet it is my generation she charges with cynicism."

I find this byplay so debilitating that, to shift focus, I lie and tell him I liked his first column.

"It's kind of you to say you liked it but I wish to God I knew what I was doing. Having nothing to say in twenty-five hundred words—well, at least I hope I've learned to say it gracefully. As long as you don't think of it as writing. It's not; it's space filling. Think of it, if you must think of it—and God knows, I hope you have better things to think of—as an act of philanthropy on my part: Once a month I fill a space which, if it weren't for my willingness to die for the cause, would be filled with, God help us, something worse!"

Tina shows expression for the first time: irritation. "Did you really think it was that bad? You're lying, Rags. If you did, I don't think you should have printed it."

Plante flushes; his eyes turn watery; he licks his lips and smiles. "I have mouths to feed. And no, I admit I had a thing or two in there at the time—a thing or two, that I thought could be said; a thing or two not unsayable." He seems to be on the verge of laughter; he suppresses it.

"Even after you've written something you've liked—a week later you treat it as if it's junk." Side by side, arms entwined, hands gripped so tight that I can see the whites of Plante's knuckles.

"She will not be deterred," he says.

"Sometimes I wish you were a shoemaker. You'd do your weekly quota of shoes and not worry about the big shoe that you're going to cobble someday."

Plante laughs out loud, his eyes all but ordering me to laugh, too. I abstain. The indefatigable Tina goes on: "I just think that one thing leads to another. Writing leads to more writing; not writing leads to more not writing. What do you think?" she asks what's-his-name, i.e., me.

"I don't pretend to understand the creative mind," I say, too wary to get sucked in. It is the last time she directly addresses me during lunch.

What shocks me is that Plante, whom I know to be oblique and evasive, is, in this instance, uncomfortably personal. Has he changed or am I watching the influence of Tina? Can it be that she intimidates him? Under the thumb of a girl of nineteen? No, I conclude, that is not the answer. The answer is more devious and more simple: It is that she gives him the excuse and the sounding board to talk about the one subject of legitimate interest to him: himself.

Not once throughout our two hours together does he ask about me, not the slightest interest in what I'm doing, no particular interest in my being there at all except, perhaps, as a convenient audience for the dirty old man and his girlfriend.

March 26

Am I in competition with Plante? Why Plante? The question answers itself. He reminds me of my father. Why my father? They are not at all alike; my father wouldn't understand the first thing about Plante; he'd deride him as a pseudo-intellectual. As I write the word down I feel proud of my father's perception and, at the same time, defensive of Plante. So how can Plante be my father when I have barely introduced them and they are already in an argument?

My father was an extrovert, Plante isn't; my father was aggressive, Plante isn't; my father was almost offensively masculine, Plante seems to be above sex. (That was what was so embarrassing about seeing his act with Tina: not their age difference alone, but the impression it gave of near-vulgarity. My urge was to pull them apart, cry: "Stop! This is disgusting!" As if they were fucking in public. And they weren't doing anything! Maybe I see Plante as some sort of priest, an emotional celibate.) My father, to continue the comparison, was more sensual. Although Plante, in his own way, is sensual: look at the women who flock around him. (I'd better leave this point;

170

it's clear I don't know what I'm talking about.) My father was strong, independent, a law unto himself; Plante may or may not be strong—I don't know—but he is certainly more beaten up than my father, somewhere halfway between a winner and a loser; my father was either idolized or hated by people, would go into rages against friends, not speak to them for years, make up emotionally and wipe the fight out of his memory so that if you ever brought it up he'd deny it with a conviction that was irrefutable.

He tried to make a marine out of me. Because he was in the marines. Dragging me around to all those veterans' clubs. Hand guns. Thank God, he didn't will me his collection! No, I'm sorry he didn't. I'd have melted it down into junk.

And she was no help, even when they weren't married anymore, she still took his side against me. Elsie says I shouldn't be bitter. But I'm not. But you can't turn the past into what it isn't. Elsie's way of dealing with an old lie is to corroborate it by making up new lies.

No, compared to my father, Plante's a sissy, a lightweight. The only power he has is the power my neurosis invests him with. That's the only thing he and my father share in common: my response to their intimidation.

But if he's not my father, why do I react this way? Been drinking since nine o'clock. My head hums with booze. My need is more than need, it verges on lust. A passion for Plante to tell me how good I am, that I have made it, that he will stop patronizing me . . .

This is insanity. It is humiliating and it is insanity. I feel like burning these pages . . .

Good thing I'm writing this down because none of it will be remembered tomorrow morning. I can't remember what I was thinking ten minutes ago; it is a total blank.

March 27

I don't respect myself. I don't like myself. It was not a rejection of my family—my father—when I took on this joke of a

171

name, Roger Ackroyd. It was a rejection of *me*. Self-mockery. A recognition that I was not a serious person, so did not deserve a serious name. Every time I take what I think is a positive step it turns out later to be disastrous. I have no psychic compass. My decision-making process is all screwed up. If I had any courage as a man I would painfully think a problem through, arrive at what I see as the correct solution and then do the opposite. Right now it seems to me the only solution is to kill myself. So I won't. Is this the right decision or merely self-serving?

March 28

My instincts tell me to forget Plante and bury myself in this job; to give him up as a lost cause, a battle I can't win. Because I want to, I won't. My new code: Don't do what I want, do the reverse.

The truth is I am suffering from a disease. But I have no real knowledge or information on the germ that infected me. Who and what is Plante? I'm not talking about the Plante I have invented who may or may not be my father or partly my father and partly my Uncle George, who in some ways resembles Plante (the only one in the family I liked, or, more to the point, liked me). The Plante who is driving me crazy with self-hate plainly does not exist. I have made him up. O.K., I could go to a psychiatrist and just possibly unmake him up. But, to me, not to be able to handle one's own problems is an abject admission of failure. The one thing holding me together at this point is my professional pride: I am a good investigator. To fob that investigation off on a psychiatrist is to confess that I am nothing. My instincts tell me that I am setting myself up in one more trap, that I should quit and put myself in another's hands. Because my instincts tell me this, I know it is wrong.

As a detective, I am taking myself on as a client. My assignment is to build a dossier on the authentic Plante, check out his past and his present with friends, enemies and, eventually, if I think I am up to it, the subject himself. Once I have a book on the flesh and blood Plante there is a very good chance that the Plante in my head will not be able to stand up to it. It will be like daylight in a haunted head—I meant to write "house," but let it stand.

Where to begin? A check of my files informs me that he has a mother who lives in Orlando, Florida. She is an important source and I will have to figure out a time to fly down and interview her. Maybe next weekend. But I want to move before then. There is a lot of waste time at Ross; other agents take advantage of it, why can't I? I should be able to put in at least two hours each working day—sometimes more—plus nights, plus weekends. The obvious person to begin with is Kaufman, his oldest friend. But every time I have faced Kaufman, Esther pushed her way into the picture and I am, frankly, afraid of her. I will get to the Kaufmans at some future time but my self-confidence is, at the moment, in such disrepair that I know it is sheer folly to tackle Esther at the start. Who then? Annabelle? How can I go back to Annabelle? The answer is I can't. To volunteer myself into more of that madness—and how could I trust her information? She is so crazed on the subject of Plante she's liable to say anything. Scratch Annabelle. Who's next? I guess Tina. Almost as depressing a prospect as Esther. And since she refuses to even recognize my existence how am I to extract any information out of her? And she will immediately tell Plante what I am up to. So scratch Tina. Who's left? Burden and Cornwall? I've tried pumping them before. A dry well. Who's next? The names on Plante's Ten Best party list? All superficial acquaintances. Scratch everybody. It would be funny if it weren't so fucking serious.

March 30

You'd think my obsession with Plante would cut into my efficiency at Ross, but not at all. I broke a mail fraud case this morning. It had been hanging fire for two weeks, and this morning I re-examined everything we had and dug out the piece of the puzzle that fit. The Captain actually came by my desk to congratulate me. That's a first. Not even Dorsey liked that one. He came over to me later and said, "How much you pay me not to tell him about Plante?" My heart jumped. Then I realized he was referring to the old stories I'd been using around the office. Dorsey and his needle. I am through providing him with material.

I am now of two minds on the Plante matter, don't know whether to pursue it or not. My instincts run in both directions, so I am not sure which I am not to follow.

I keep coming back to the Kaufmans. Kaufman has known him the longest and best, has obviously very mixed feelings about him; no doubt a gold mine of information. Tina loves him, could be informative on what makes him attractive to women. If I superimpose their two pictures maybe out of it will come something close to a real picture. On paper it reads like sense, but I hate the idea of going near either one of them.

A weird temptation to hire another detective for the job.

March 31

She has been in Gucci's for nearly an hour looking at leather handbags. I have been strolling Fifth Avenue, from Fifty-fourth to Fifty-fifth Street and back, on both sides of the street. I stroll leisurely, as if I am enjoying myself. Needless to say, on the last day of March it is snowing. But I don't mind. What I have learned to like best about myself as a professional (next to my perceptiveness) is my infinite capacity for discomfort. It is as if harsh winds and slush confirm my existence. It is kind of a collaboration: nature beats on me and I outlast it. I see it as a metaphor: if I can outlast the weather I can presumably outlast anything, meaning guess who?

It also gives the lie to the armchair detective reputation I am building up for myself at Ross. Somehow it is a mark against you if you are able to wrap up a case without putting in legwork. Even Dorsey has begun to sneer at me as if I'm some sort of aberration: Joe College Smartass, never leaving his desk, exploiting the hours of shit work put in by his colleagues, to swoop in at the last minute and steal someone else's case. The assumption is that if I didn't horn in they'd manage to wrap it up themselves. The fact is that I have vastly improved the efficiency of our section and only once or twice have I gotten credit for it. The Captain himself periodically praises Dorsey for our successes, meaning, in most cases, *my* successes (a detail Dorsey used to needle the other guys with but, interestingly enough, now uses to needle me). Our increased efficiency is seen, magically, as proof of my unwillingness to work with others. What's worse is that after a time I myself tend to accept the general view of me as a prima donna. I find as I trudge up and down slimy Fifth Avenue that I wish, over and over, that Armbruster and LaStanza and the others could see me now; they would hate me less.

I have been tailing Tina since eleven this morning when she left Plante's apartment or, more correctly, the one they now share together. The apartment is in a white, limestone highrise on East Eighty-third and the River. The wind was from the west and not strong, but in three hours of stakeout it had nibbled through the fibers of my coat, suit, shirt, T-shirt and shorts, to leave me chilled to the bone. My original plan was to confront her directly, but at the moment of truth, she shot out of the building too fast for me, loping west in her seven-league boots, her open suede jacket beating behind her like parade streamers. I took off in slow motion, a half block behind, silently mouthing—and forgetting—my carefully rehearsed script, my agitation and shortness of breath due to the fact that her physical appearance had an effect on me I was not prepared for. In the five days since our lunch I had come to believe she was fat, complacent, no longer attractive. But here, with her head cramped between her hunched shoulders, her stiff arms buried half in her pockets, her appearance suggestive of a wildebeest butting its way across town, I was inexplicably worked up.

Now staked out on Fifth, snow-drenched and bitter cold, I try to remember my plan to win her confidence so that she will talk to me about Plante. I cannot. I can't separate the plan from my interest in Tina from my problems at Ross. Fed up with the snow, the waiting and the ineptitude, I cast aside all illusions of competence and push on into Gucci's.

Fags, chic shops and foreigners who speak faultless English with Continental accents automatically put me on the defensive. I am instantly impaled on shards of immaculate taste. Tina stands tall among the sculpted handbags and preening luggage, nature's gift in a hothouse of handcraft, her unattractive fat and arrogance of five days ago now appealing as full-bodied womanhood.

I have a sudden inspiration as to how to proceed: I grab up the most ornamental purse on display and take it to Tina. "Am I glad to run into you. I wonder if you'd mind helping me decide?"

Her face, alive with empathy a moment earlier while studying handbags, takes on the veneer of the store when she sees me. To be expected: non-recognition. "Roger Ackroyd," I say.

"Right. Hi," she says, and then, "Oh, you know Rags."

"We had lunch last week."

Her expression undeadens. "Right. I never expected to see you here."

If the truth must be told she never expected to see me anywhere. "Listen, I'm looking for a bag for my girl. A present for her." Tina's expressionlessness is so powerful that in and of itself it is an expression. "Look, we've had a fight. My girl. I want to make it up to her."

"By buying her a present?" The smile is faintly ironic, reminding me of her mother. "You mean people still buy presents after they have fights?" She is incredulous.

"This seemed to be the thoughtful, the most thoughtful—"

"Buying her off with a present?"

"The idea was I was apologizing."

"Why don't you just apologize?"

"When I give her the gift I'll apologize."

"She won't accept your apology without the gift? Maybe you've got the wrong girl."

"That's what she says." I drop my eyes to the floor, noticing her suede boots; I get a rise out of them. "I guess you're right, it's probably over anyway. I really don't know what to do." I look at her, intending to convey controlled and manly misery. "Anyway—"

Her face is suddenly serious, revitalized. "You probably have other things to do," she says, "but if you want to go get a cup of coffee and talk, it's my treat, Roger."

In a Madison Avenue bar and grill empty of life but a definite spiritual uplift from Gucci's, Tina brilliantly cross-questions me while in the act of downing six coffees, two cheeseburgers and a tuna salad. I keep abreast with three Scotches to thaw me out, black coffee to sober me up and two more Scotches to seduce me back into the spirit of the false confession I am making. I improvise my confession to satisfy the thrust of her questions so that when she alludes to problems in communication, I give her problems in communication; when she alludes to problems in feeling, I give her problems in feeling; when she alludes to sexual power struggle, I give her sexual power struggle. I base my improvisations on data culled from my checkered past dating back to college, concentrating mostly on Gloria and Jeanie, combining all into the body of a single woman whose name I give as Deborah.

Tina takes to personal crisis like a duck to water. For the first time I find our relationship off and running.

"How long have you been together?"

"A year."

"Do you live together?"

"Yes. But lately she's been sleeping at a friend's."

"For how long?"

"Couple of weeks. She's jealous, she notices me staring at girls. Sometimes in the street. Or restaurants. It makes her mad. But it doesn't mean anything. Everybody stares."

"If you know it makes her angry why do you stare?"

"I can't be on my guard all the time. Anyhow, it doesn't

mean anything. She gets totally irrational and accuses me of, well, you name it. Anyhow, that's the point of the present. She says I never give her presents. But when I do she takes them back and exchanges them."

"I don't know, the way you talk, I get the feeling that—is this a possibility?—you don't like her?"

"Sure, I like her. But does that mean I have to make all the concessions?"

"Have you told her you feel this way?"

"Does everything have to be spelled out? Do you spell out everything with—well—Rags?"

There! We have finally gotten to it. Tina bites, doesn't even bother to slow down. "If something is bothering one or the other of us we talk about it until we find out what it is."

"But do you always know? I'm not sure it's possible. If you could give me an example—"

"I don't know what you want me to say."

"I mean I've told you all this personal stuff but you don't tell me anything about you."

She looks at me with a directness that is nearly blinding. "Maybe Deborah reacts to you the same way I do; maybe she's put off by you."

I have an urge to slap her face. Instead I rattle the ice in my Scotch glass and smile.

"I'm sorry, Roger, I didn't mean to hurt your feelings." She fleetingly puts her hand on my wrist. "Maybe she thinks the only way to keep you around is to let you have your way and then she gets mad and makes you pay for it with presents."

We are going so fast that I am in danger of losing control of Deborah, as if she is now Tina's invention, not mine.

"I'm pretty lonely." I hide my face behind clasped hands.

Lonely seems to be the operative word. She wads her napkin into a ball and places it in the center of her tuna plate. "Rags knows that I don't judge him. And he doesn't judge me. I didn't know very much when Rags and I got together—in fact, I was illiterate and stupid, I'd never read anything—but Rags didn't put me down or treat me with contempt or be funny at my expense. He has a way of listening that makes you feel very important. And with you—I don't want to make comparisons—it's as if you're gathering evidence."

I sigh involuntarily. It is not the first time I have heard this horseshit.

"You still haven't told me the things you and Rags talk about," I say, scowling behind clenched hands. "Does he ever talk about me?"

She shakes her head sadly, "Come on, Roger."

"Does he talk about his family?"

"Why is it important for you to know that?"

"Because if I'm to fix things up with Deborah I need examples, not generalizations."

"I really feel you're trying to wheedle things out of me."

A long impasse.

"Maybe I'm wrong," she eventually says.

With my bowed head I watch the last slivers of ice melt in my glass. "Can I call you sometime?"

She hesitates. "Or I can call you. Give me your number."

Back at Ross I type out a memo on what I've learned: Plante is her guru; they talk a lot; he has a way with her which makes her feel smarter and cleverer than she is, which may indicate why young girls go for him: he flatters them.

April 3

"Roger. Are you awake? Can you talk?"

This at 8:00 A.M. when I am barely functional, should, as far as Tina is concerned, be sleeping with Deborah.

"I woke up worrying about you."

"I'm fine," I say, knowing as I say it that it is the wrong thing to say to her. No matter. She accepts it as a lie.

"What's the matter? Anything new with Deborah?"

I try to imagine where she's calling from. Not their bedroom. His study, the door closed? Is she in pajamas? Don't see her wearing nightgowns. "Well, in fact, it's been rough."

I pause a long time, trying to clear my head so that I will know where I am leading. "Can I see you?"

"I can't today. Can you talk now? What's going on with Deborah? Did you get anything settled?"

"She's not here."

"I didn't think she would be. You didn't talk to her, did you?"

I surmise she wants me to say no so I say it.

"You know how I knew you weren't going to talk with her?"

I pretend to be interested.

"Because of all the questions you were asking about Rags and me. And I didn't realize—I should have, but I didn't— until I got home that you were doing that to get us off the subject. You'll have to be watched every minute. Seriously, do you intend to talk with her?"

"Uh—look . . ." I am ready for another seven hours' sleep.

"You sound like you're falling asleep. Are you sure I didn't wake you?"

I tell her no.

"Then it must be anxiety."

"You may be right." I am gradually learning that it is best to agree with her no matter how wrong she is. She has all the arrogance of her mother with none of the experience to back it up.

I spend the morning at Ross working out a scenario for Tina. It requires a degree of concentration not usually available at Ross. Dorsey is being a particular pain in the ass this morning, hates to see me typing away, makes him think I am stealing a march on him. The more I learn about office work the more it convinces me that most men are unable to work together beyond a certain level of mediocrity, that to exceed that level is to declare yourself an enemy of your fellow worker and therefore an exile, always open to envy, suspicion, subversion and attack.

Dorsey has succeeded in making me regard myself not unlike a communist agent working inside the U.S. Embassy.

Fortunately, he does not look over my shoulder to see what I'm typing: That would betray an interest that he can't openly admit to, so my notes are safe as long as I don't leave them lying around for inspection, not even when I go to the john. However, I must leave some notes around to prove I am doing my share of work. These notes I have prepared earlier and substitute for my scenario on Tina, so that Dorsey has material to check out when I am in the john, at the water cooler or out to lunch.

The notes I leave these days for Dorsey's light reading concern my surveillance of a broker named Perrini whose company suspects he's involved in stock fraud. Perrini is a flamboyant character whose flamboyance is as predictable as clockwork. He takes long, expensive business lunches, always in one of four Wall Street area restaurants. They never end before three. Four times a week he takes parties of six and up to one of a couple of Italian restaurants midtown, or one of three Italian restaurants down on Mulberry Street. His parties never arrive before nine, never leave before midnight, usually closing the joint. If I miss him at any of these places I can safely pick him up after midnight at P. J. Clarke's. There is no problem filing reports on Perrini. I could spend my days in bed and still make them sound convincing.

The unpredictable part of Perrini's life is his dates. Similar as they are in appearance: tall, leggy, fashion-model types (he would go crazy over Tina if she lost a few pounds), I have yet to see him with the same one twice. My one approach to the case is that somewhere Perrini has a steady girlfriend—or boyfriend—whom he is keeping under wraps. If I can get him to lead me to either one it is remotely possible she or he can be bribed or threatened into turning informant. All very iffy and not particularly satisfying. In all probability, when Perrini gets his it will be because Armbruster or Flanagan, who are also on the case, browbeat one of his business partners into informing on him.

I use my time in the john, in part, to review my morning conversation with Tina. It becomes oppressively clear that openness is a one-way street with her. She intends to volunteer nothing. As long as I pretend to collapse she will continue to show interest in me. Whatever information I get from her is going to be squeezed out. But by what means? Perhaps by offering her episodes in my relationship with Deborah which will suggest to her strong parallels to Plante. So if she wants to progress in her self-appointed role of psychiatric social worker she will have no choice but to tell me more about Plante, to cite evidence drawn from her knowledge of him, to cite parallels out of her own experience.

But how do I do that? Where do I get my material?

I have one titillating idea: it centers on Annabelle.

April 4

"She says I'm too self-sufficient, that when I drink I'm mean; I don't care about anybody but myself. Also I keep her from doing things she's interested in."

She laughs. "What does she say are your good points?"

I shrug into the phone. "Your guess is as good as mine. She's very vulnerable. She needs to be protected and she's mad at me because I don't protect her enough."

"What do you see in her?"

I make an attempt to envision Annabelle but get Tina: Where is she in Plante's apartment? I continue to wonder. And where is Plante? "For one thing, I respond to her vulnerability. You say I should talk to her more directly, but every time I try she treats it like an attempted assassination."

"It sounds like she's really in bad shape."

"She thinks I'm the one who has the problems. She thinks she's the best thing that ever came into my life and I must be crazy not to appreciate her more."

"That sounds familiar."

"Why does it?" I pause to see if she will respond to my lead.

"It doesn't matter. Get her into therapy."

"Are you in therapy?"

"You'd better believe it!" She laughs.

"O.K., why are you in?" I sense her hesitation. "If you're recommending it I need a little more information, although I realize I'm the only one around here allowed to be personal," I say with fully felt reproach.

"My mother put me in, if you must know. For all the wrong reasons. She found out about Rags and me."

"I've got the impression your mother doesn't think much of Rags. Is that a bone of contention between you?"

"Roger—" Her voice is brittle.

"Is it because of you, or does her dislike predate that? It must make it rough on your father."

"Let's not worry about my father." Now she has virtually no voice at all; I might as well be picking up sound waves.

"Is Rags anything like your father?"

I half expect her to hang up on me. Instead she guffaws, "Roger, you are a crazy person!"

I am a little offended by her fast recovery. "Sometimes I think he's a little like me. Or am I wrong?"

"Now that you mention it, there are some strong similarities. Do me a favor, don't dwell on them."

"Why? What's wrong with Rags?"

"Rags? I thought you meant my father! You're not at all like Rags."

"I'm not like your father!"

"I said there were similarities."

"You said strong similarities. What similarities?"

"First of all, you're both hung up on Rags."

"What gives you the idea I'm hung up on—" Her laugh is overbearing and irritating. While waiting for it to subside I work out a sudden excuse to get off the phone.

April 8

She is saying (the part that gets through) that she has some ideas about me and Deborah but doesn't want to talk about them over the telephone. She doesn't have to be at the studio until 10:30, can she come over now and talk to me? I pull my watch out from under the covers. It is 7:30. "Not up here. There's a coffee shop in the lobby. I can be there in half an hour." I give her the address.

Tina is becoming a nuisance, I decide in the shower. She has told me next to nothing about Plante and has screwed up my efforts to analyze the little she has told me since much of my spare time is now consumed with the invention of new Deborah episodes. She is too cocksure, in many ways the exact image of her mother. Small wonder they dislike each other. Are all Jewish women domineering, or is it just the ones I've run into? She treats me as if I'm an abstraction, as if my problems with Deborah are more real than I am. The recognition of this irony compels me to smash my fist into the shower wall.

What has always struck me about fashion models is their artifice, but Tina is wearing no makeup, her hair is carelessly brushed, her complexion is chalky with green fatigue welts under her eyes. On the basis of all existing rules she should look a mess. All that prevents her from looking a mess is that she doesn't know it. She has an air of regal certitude. That plus being young and tall and well-built and owning a good posture . . . all together she looks terrific. She is wearing a tight-fitting blue turtleneck that elongates her already long torso almost unnaturally. It takes a toasted English and two black coffees to dispel the image that she is looking down on me.

"I could be wrong but I think the problem is she wants to get married."

"To whom?" I say.

"You're not being funny." Tina has come to assume a proprietary manner toward me. "Has she ever talked to you about marriage?"

How am I to answer? Yes? No? What pops into my mind is what Jeanie used to say to me about marriage. "She says she knows I'll never get married, that I'm basically an unreliable character. I wish you wouldn't be so bossy."

She dismisses it with a nod of her head and a hunching of her shoulders. "Don't let it bother you. Well, what are your feelings about marriage?"

"If it happens, it happens."

"But not to Deborah."

"What about you and Rags?" I counter.

"He's already married."

"Maybe he's satisfied with the situation the way it is."

"And maybe I am too. I'm not Deborah. You're beginning to sound like my mother."

"Do you and Rags ever talk about marriage?"

"I don't believe in marriage. You're a very devious man. You've gotten me off the subject again."

"Are you sure you don't believe in it because you know he'll never marry you?"

She reaches around the coffee cup and takes my hand in hers. Her fingers are longer than mine and very skinny. Some sort of fusion takes place between them. In any case I feel a severe energy drain.

"Look, I may be wrong but if you clear the air—discuss the unmentionable with her—it seems to me a lot of these fights are cover-ups for her thinking that she's come to a dead end with you."

"You mean I should bring up the subject of marriage in order to tell her I'm not going to marry her? Tina, that's crazy."

"You're not listening."

"Just because I don't agree with you doesn't mean I don't hear you."

"If you are listening, you're not thinking." She draws away her hand. "You know I'm right."

The bags are gone from under her nagging eyes. She stares me down with an authoritarian righteousness which, considering the ages of the people involved, verges on the ridiculous. In order not to strain the ties that bind us I promise to give her proposal more positive consideration.

April 12

In slow dribbles, through countless excruciating conversations, I begin to get the picture:

1. Plante takes her more seriously than anyone she's ever known.

2. He can be very loving, but is never focused for long on any one particular person. This sometimes engenders misunderstandings and hurt feelings.

3. He's the least selfish or egocentric person she has met in her entire nineteen years.

4. He is driven about his work but does not appreciate its worth.

5. He has a very special relationship with Josh.

6. He is more generous and forgiving than he should be with Annabelle.

7. He sees few friends but remains loyal to even those friends with whom he has lost contact.

8. He is wonderful, practically a saint.

All of this out of an offensively domineering young woman who pretends to be perceptive. Clearly, this exercise is hopeless. The girl is a complete fool.

April 17

"Why have you been avoiding me?"

"I've been busy."

"You've been busy avoiding me."

"That's not completely true."

"However, it's partially true. Or am I wrong?"

I *have* been avoiding her. The last two times she called I said I was in conference with clients. "In bed?" she asked, not unnaturally since it was 8:00 in the morning.

This morning she called again and either because of the lack of humor in her voice or my early morning defenselessness I agreed to meet her in the coffee shop. It struck me, as I got dressed, that though I have not laid a hand on the girl I am acting like a man trying to extricate himself from a messy love affair.

As usual she made it crosstown before I am able to make it

downstairs. She waits for me at our regular table. She has even ordered coffee. It is with cream. I take it black. I find this more irritating than if she had not made the gesture at all. "I had a long talk with Deborah. Now this has been coming for some time so I don't want you to think it's your fault." I stare into her eyes. They are, as they often are, bright and demanding, but her morning green welts help curb their willfulness. "It's all over," I tell her.

Her face goes blank. "What happened?"

"O.K., so long as you realize this was bound to happen and you had nothing to do with it."

She nods, as if something else is on her mind. "O.K., it's not my fault. Now tell me what happened."

"It was a couple of nights ago, Tuesday. I told her I'd done a lot of thinking about us, about how well we used to get along. I said I wanted us to get back to that. I said I loved her more than anyone I had ever known."

She is wearing the same blue turtleneck she wore the last time I saw her. It crosses my mind that this is her uniform for me and that for Plante she has another uniform and for her parents a third and for modeling assignments a fourth, fifth and sixth. Typical, I catch myself thinking as she says, "Go on."

"I asked her right out in the open if it was possible that she thought it was time we got married. Her face lit up, so I had to say very quickly, 'Deborah, I can't get married. I'm probably not marriageable, but that doesn't mean I don't love you and that we can't be together.' The next thing she asked was if I was tired of her. I said no. She said too bad, because she was tired of me. She said that she had gotten used to the idea that I would never marry her and she was beginning to accept it, but she couldn't now because of my gross insensitivity to her feelings. She said it was pointless for us to see each other again. Then she cried. There was more, but that's as much as I can remember right now."

Tina looks at me as if my head's not screwed on right. "And you haven't talked to her since?"

"Is there a reason?"

She slaps a hand to her head. "I can't believe you could be this obtuse," she says in high spirits. "Call her right now. Do you have a dime? Call her from here." She fishes into her giant bag and brings out a dime. She sticks it in the palm of my hand and folds my fingers over it so I can't lose it. If I asked, I am sure, she would dial the number for me.

"Why do you want me to call her?"

"Because, dummy, she had a fit and she's been waiting since Tuesday for you to bring her out of it! Don't you know anything?"

I hand her back the dime. "It won't work."

Her eyes lock into mine. "There's something you're not telling me." She nods her head. "I can feel it. You're leaving something out, Roger."

I shake my head as she nods hers. "What you feel is my nervousness about telling you what happened because I was afraid you'd blame yourself."

Her face contorts as if I'm speaking broken English and she can't quite make it out. "Why should I do that?"

"No reason at all. But I was afraid you would."

She hunches her shoulders. "You said that. This is interesting. Why were you afraid?"

It's as if we are two doctors in consultation over a case. "Because you were the one who told me I should bring up the subject of marriage."

"So?"

"So nothing. I just didn't want you to blame yourself."

"But I don't."

"Well, that's fine then."

She takes my hand. "You wanted to get rid of her."

"Tina, I can assure you I didn't." I put it firmly; it is the only way to put things to her.

"I can tell by the way you've talked about her from almost the beginning. As if she's not really a person. You don't talk that way about someone you care for. Seriously. You know I'm right."

I take my hand away. "You're very transparent. You don't want to blame yourself, so you blame me."

Her laugh is genuine. "God, you're obstinate! You must be furious with me! Roger, really, I'm not to blame, so stop being angry at me. You wanted out and now you've maneuvered it so you are out. You just want it to look as if I pushed you into it."

I can barely keep my voice down. "I know if I hadn't listened to you I'd still have Deborah."

She grins. "You're not going to be budged, are you? I'll tell you what, if you don't stay mad at me I'll buy you breakfast."

Where does she get off treating me like a nine-year-old? I wonder as I eat my scrambled eggs. She looms larger than life across the table nibbling at a slice of toast, playing with her third cup of coffee.

"I may be wrong," she says, "but an idea occurs to me. Is Deborah at all like your mother?"

I glare at her and say, "Is Plante like your father?"

She puts her cup down and leans forward. "No, really, Roger, try to listen. It's like you can only take action when you can rationalize that you've been forced into it. Or am I wrong?"

I bow my head nearly into my coffee cup. "Tina, I think it's time you got out of analysis."

But she, who accuses me of only half listening, is half listening. "I'll give you my own example. I wanted to get out of the house, all right? But I turned it into a fight between my mother and Rags, so that when I left it wasn't my doing, I was innocent, it was Rags' doing. But Rags wouldn't put up with it. He made me deal with my mother on my own. I don't mean without his support. Yes, I had his support and his advice and his love—he was terrific—why do you look so funny?"

I have no idea what she's referring to.

"But basically he made me see—and so did my therapist—that for the first time in my life I had to deal directly with this woman: my mother. Because I never had. I always evaded her, a million things, horses, modeling, boys. But once I came to grips with her, sat down and had a real honest to goodness talk—our first!—I found she wasn't this cold, withdrawn, disapproving monster. I mean she's a terrific woman. I really admire her! And once I liked her and I knew she liked me it was easier to leave. I know she spits nails when she talks about Rags. And that's O.K. It's her privilege. I'm not bothered, because she believes in me now, I know that, and she has confidence in me and if I need help I know I can go to her. And I will. I didn't know that before. Neither of us did. It's really a sensational thing to know." Her face is radiant, angelic, close to tears. I am surprised at how unnerved I am.

"I wish I could live in a dream world. But I know your mother and that isn't the woman you describe—" Tina is smiling at me, shaking her head. "And I know Plante. That's not the man you describe."

Tina has broken out laughing. Her hand goes out to touch my forearm but I pull myself back against my seat, away from her. "You're really having a shit fit," she says with an expression of wonder which I find insufferable. It suddenly flashes in my mind that I am going to tell her about Plante and the missing notebook, tell her how her father stole it, tell her the role her mother played, tell her how Plante hired me to find out why he wasn't getting invited to the right parties, tell her all the stories I'd been rehearsing for this very moment all these months at Ross. Shatter that absolute certainty, that smugness. Do her a favor; let her see the real world.

April 20

She must suspect something; otherwise, why hasn't she called me? She must know, with that uncanny smart-ass know-it-allness of hers that I have a rock aimed right at her dream world. And she is not going to let me get close enough to throw it. Well, if she won't come to me I'll go to her. But not with a bunch of stories she can deny or pass off as meaning-

190

less anecdotes or turn into jokes as they do at Ross. No, I will have documentation. I take out my complete Plante file and go through it, digging out choice selections. It will take days to type up all this stuff. But I have patience. It is my gift to Tina. With this she can enter adulthood.

April 21

I decide that typing all that Plante junk is too depressing. Also, it's overkill. If she's not going to believe me when I tell it why will she believe it when she reads it? Anyhow, it is impossible to get through to her, so what makes me think this will work? A waste of time.

I tried calling her this evening. Plante answered. I hung up.

April 22

I stake her out as she leaves the apartment. Don't have too long to wait now that I understand that she goes out on her jobs at about 10:30. I am not sure at what point I will go up to her or how I will convey my Plante information. I now see it as imperative that I let her know the truth. At least about him. I have revised my opinion on telling her about her parents. Needlessly cruel. When she learns about Plante she will need some place to run and it will doubtless be home. I can't foreclose that exit. As insufferable and highfalutin as she is, I don't see myself as wanting to hurt her.

April 27

A week of following Tina, the bouncing ball. Her energy is frightening. She bounces along the streets like an ad for spring. An adverse comment on how old, stale and pitiful the rest of New York is getting.

Warm today, in the high 70s. This sort of weather, especially early in the season, usually has me tingling, but not now. Tina's tingling has eviscerated my own. The more I tail her the more I feel literally like her shadow, insubstantial, not even organic in her presence. I feel tied to her lifeline, totally dependent on the connection made by the distance I maintain between us. I find myself increasingly indecisive—one might even say cowardly—about making my move. No question in my mind that she should be told. But there is also no question that she will hate me for it and turn against me, focus that faster-than-a-speeding-bullet mind of hers on an examination of my motives. I will be dead as far as she is concerned.

April 28

She has spotted me. Did I get careless? You can't tail someone as regularly as I've been tailing her without eventually getting caught at it. I expected her to come right over and make a scene. Or, at least, to ask why I'm following her around. But she hasn't. Yet.

What does she make of it? As often as not, when I think she's going to blow up at me she laughs at me. Is she laughing now? Does she think I'm a little ridiculous following her around? Not for the first time do I wonder how much she has told Plante about us. Do they sit home telling Ackroyd stories the way I tell Plante stories at the Ross agency? No, Plante is easily capable of such cruelty, but not Tina. She is without malice.

What she should do, if I understand her at all, is to come right over to me and ask why I'm following her. Which apparently she is not going to do. Makes me uneasy. What must she be thinking?

What does she think of me? She treats me as if she's fond of me but, to be brutal about it, it's my problems she's fond of, not me. Without my problems, I don't exist. And they are invented problems. The thought of her analyzing my character in the Excelsior coffee shop on the basis of a completely fabricated case history! And yet, look how close she came. She is a scary young woman.

I would like to keep her as a friend. I'm sorry she spotted me. It compromises any chance I would ever have with her.

April 29

8:00 A.M. phone call. I know who. "Why are you following me?"

"I love you."

"You don't love me, you're furious with me."

"Stop telling me how I feel. I'm not mad at you anymore. I want to see you."

"You've been seeing me! And I don't like it. It scares me! I want it to stop. Do you hear?"

"I don't mean to scare you."

"Well, you do! That's very spooky behavior. How would you like me to follow you around?"

"I wouldn't mind."

"Don't laugh, this isn't funny. You're not funny. You're spooky. You frighten me."

"How could I frighten you?"

"By following me around, you idiot!"

"How can I believe you're frightened of me if you call me an idiot?"

"What's your being an idiot got to do with my being frightened of you? Roger, I warn you, stop."

"I can't stop. I'm in love."

"You sure have a funny way of showing it. I'm going to tell Rags."

"You've already told him. Who cares?"

"What do you mean I've told him? What's the matter with you? Do you think I'd do that to you? What's the matter with you? He doesn't even know I've been seeing you! Christ, what makes you so thick?"

"Stop insulting me."

"Stop following me!"

"Maybe I'm on a case. Maybe saying I love you is a cover-up because you spotted me. Maybe I've been hired to tail you."

"You sure do a lousy job of it."

"Maybe I had a bad conscience about it."

"Roger, you really are beginning to scare me. Are you telling the truth? Has anybody hired you?"

"I can't say."

"I warn you, you're going to force me to do something about this if you don't stop."

"Listen, don't threaten me. I don't like being threatened."

"I don't like being followed, you dope, you idiot!"

"You're so sure of yourself."

"I'm a wreck, what are you talking about! And it's your fault!"

"I could tell you a couple of things that would ruffle that sweet composure of yours."

"Roger, will you somehow try to get a grip on yourself?"

"I could tell you but I won't. Not that it means a goddam thing to you. I haven't done any harm. Compared to what I could tell you. I haven't come near you. What the hell are you complaining about? Fat chance I scare you. I'm on a case, goddammit! I'm protecting your welfare! Now stop interfering with a law officer in the performance of his duty."

"You are not to be believed," she says, her voice sounding smaller than I've ever heard it.

"See you tomorrow."

April 30

Staked out in my usual place at my usual time.

I don't expect her to leave the house but to my surprise she does. And right on time. She has dressed up for me, not in her usual baggy off-to-work clothes, but in a plaid jacket and skirt. I have never seen her in a skirt, never seen her legs. Wonderful legs. She wears loafers, looks like a schoolgirl, fragile, in need of protection.

She casts a glance where I am standing, nailing me with a directness that sends chills down my spine. She starts off across 83rd at a faster stride than usual. I am her shadow. Whither she goest . . . We are off.

In retrospect, I am not totally happy with our conversation of yesterday. Rereading my notes I am alarmed at how reminiscent of Annabelle I sound. Skirting the thin edge of manic hysteria, particularly the last couple of minutes. It worries me.

Or it should worry me. But nothing right now worries me. I mean something to her. She said she is afraid of me. That Tina should be afraid of me! Through the simple move of following her—and in following her thinking myself a fool, indecisive, a coward—I have caused her to see me in a new light. Why would she lie about it? She is afraid of me.

I know, that given time, I can take her away from Plante. What she loves in him is the mandarin. That will go in time. It will go by itself. I will not have to say a word. It would have been a bad mistake to blow the whistle on him. She would not have forgiven me. And there is no need to blow the whistle. He is her past.

May 1

May Day! The sun shines, the haze lifts, Tina and I took a walk in Central Park today. She hasn't gone into the park before. She strolled. She didn't try to get away from me. Did she go into the park and stroll because of this day? Because she wanted to share it with me? A signal? At one point I thought she was going to come up to me. But she didn't. And I was glad. There is something very close to love-making about this thing we are going through. Words would destroy it, especially her words; they are too explicit.

It is as if—unless I am crazy, and that's always possible—as if we are learning each other's private ways by my pursuit of her. It is not so much a tail job now as it is a subtle courtship, something age-old about it, medieval. . . . It has a ritual simplicity and a dignity and, at the same time, undertones of conspiracy. It is easily the most heady and passionate experience I have ever undergone and I haven't even touched the girl. But why did she go into the park? She didn't have to.

May 2

I am being followed. Can't prove it yet but I have no doubt. If I am right, it began yesterday on leaving Central Park. A cloud came over my mood—I remember when it happened precisely—on the corner of Sixty-seventh and Fifth. I wrote it off as sadness that our brief idyll was over. But maybe it wasn't that. Maybe I sniffed betrayal. Tina or somebody is having me followed. I am very down tonight.

May 3

I spotted one of my tails. It is hard to believe: LaStanza. If LaStanza is my tail it means at least two others in the section are assigned. Armbruster is no doubt one of them. But why? And on whose instructions? Are they trying to prove that all my time in the field is not agency work? But why should they be suspicious? I am well covered.

Perrini the broker's unimaginative night life leaves me perfectly free to follow Tina around town. I can pick him up at almost any hour, day or night, when I am bored tracking Tina. My tendency is to pick him up later and later, often not until after Tina has gone home to Plante. I treat myself to a leisurely dinner and then do a round of Perrini's favorite restaurants until I find him. The perfect cover, no chance of a slip-up. So why are they tailing me?

May 4

Spend the entire morning at the office. Everyone behaving, if anything, too normal. No cracks. No put-downs. Something definitely going on.

My first thought was that Dorsey is out to do me in. But I don't know, I suspect more than office politics goes on here. I think there's a client. But who? I smell Plante.

At 2:30, having learned nothing and lost Tina for the day, I leave to track down Perrini. LaStanza, I note, is not far behind.

May 5

Won't let them put me on the defensive. Stake out Tina this morning as usual. The hell with them! Let them do their worst. The best theory I am able to come up with is that Tina ratted to Plante, Plante went to the Captain, the Captain ordered me checked out. I suppose if she was as scared as she claims I can't really blame her, but I blame her. She shouldn't have betrayed me. I yearn to do violence. Can't think of a target. Not Tina. Not Plante. Maybe the Captain.

I feel more betrayed by the agency than I do by Tina. After all I did for them.

My tail, this morning, is Dorsey.

The spirit of the hunt fails me so I go back to the office at 1:00. Or maybe it's curiosity. Something is about to pop, I know it. And I'd just as soon get it over with. Dorsey stayed with me no more than a half hour. No one replaced him. That can only mean that the case they are building against me is set.

I smell the change as soon as I walk in the door. The normally garrulous receptionist and switchboard operator know what's up. Zipped lips. No question: I am walking the last mile. I couldn't care less.

If I go out I intend to go out every inch the smartass they loathe. Here it is one o'clock and no one in the section has left for lunch. I amble to my desk whistling something classical, probably Mozart. The chair seems a long way down. The section resonates with unreleased malice and anticipation. I straighten out yesterday's report on Perrini. It is out of order (who's been at my desk?). I mentally compute the assemblage of hooded, wrathful, beady eyes drilling into the back of my head. I swing my chair around and confront the assemblage. Not as I imagined; they are all immersed in paper work. No one stares back at me.

Dorsey interrupts the phone before it has had a chance to finish its ring. Very quietly he says, "Yes sir," barely pauses to listen, then hangs up. He starts making notes. His face is the color of the note paper. "Oh yeah, Ackroyd, the Captain wants to see you," he says while making notes.

In the past eleven months this will be but the third time I have been invited into the Captain's sanctum. With my record! The injustice of it inspires me. I knock, do not wait to be admitted, walk in and feel my bowels congeal at the sight of Esther Kaufman. But I was waiting for *Plante!* My posturing of the last few minutes now appears ridiculous, as do most of my actions when I come face to face with Esther.

She is in her perpetual black, correctly dressed at all times for whoever's funeral, today mine. She and the Captain set up two rival polar forces. Enormous waves of energy pulsate out of both of them. She should be married to him, not Kaufman. The perfect couple. It brings to mind a production I saw in college of Strindberg's *Dance of Death*.

I obey the Captain's instructions to take a seat, although I don't really hear them, I only see his lips move. Also moving are huge vans in my head loading and unloading furniture, making a hell of a racket. It is a miracle that I am able to hear the Captain say, "I am as mad as a wet hen." Through the roar in my head of smashing furniture, pneumatic drills, buildings going up and coming down, the gist of the message breaks through. I am on the carpet. I have put the Captain in a position that, in his thirty-five years as a private agent, he has never known the like of before. I think I hear the word "perversion."

It is hard to get. I am too busy dispossessing Plante from my brain and moving in Esther.

She is speaking. Her voice, clear, precise, low, resonant, has the effect on me of a needle shower or the sting of a jellyfish. Not that I can give what she says coherence but there's no mistaking her meaning. I hear the words "common decency," "harassment," "psychopathic behavior," "infantile charade," "rapist mentality." Her voice is edited of all emotion. She sits so straight in her chair she seems to be holding it up. Light from the table lamp by her side accents her short, thick black hair and her small squarish shoulders. She comes across, even more than in memory, as an act of conscience and retribution.

I can't get over it. Tina told her mother on me!

As an alternative to Esther I center my sights on the Captain. Both his good eye and his patch glare at me. I can hear him now, not that it matters. ". . . reluctant to give credence to this story of harassment she reported to me because it involved one of the best men in my organization. I told her I did not believe there was a grain of truth to it. Well, what can I say? Words fail me." He looks remarkably like Lyndon Johnson in miniature, his face a ravaged hollow of sorrow for the human condition. "You are responsible for besmirching the reputations of myself, the Lyman Ross Agency and every private operative in my organization, every private operative throughout this city, throughout this state." Both his good eye and his patch signal shock and bereavement. It is as if I have undercut the ground on which he has single-handedly, stone by stone, built the confidential investigation business in America.

"You are responsible for an expenditure to this office in time and manpower that goes into four figures. You are responsible for my owing this good lady an apology. You are certainly a new one on me."

Something interesting starts to happen: the more the Captain chews me out the more I come up for air. His dense, regulation rhetoric acts as a buffer between Esther and me. Her presence and her disdain are the real indictment here.

I exclude Esther from my field of vision and focus entirely

on the Captain. His loss of stature gives me a second wind. "Am I judged automatically guilty or do I get a chance to defend myself?" We match glares; mine is intended to convey outraged innocence. Esther hovers on the periphery of my vision. I narrow it so that I see no one and nothing but the Captain. His complexion is gray, his suit is gray. He appears two-dimensional, a black-and-white reproduction of himself.

"He is an accomplished liar. Don't believe a word he says," warns Esther from outside my field of vision.

"I have been slandered," I nearly shout to drown her out. "If these malicious charges injure your reputation, they injure mine considerably more. I have been under surveillance from agents out of my own section. My situation is the talk of this office."

The pit that the Captain's gray face has become deepens and darkens. It is as if all his features are in flotation over a dark gray mass. "That is contrary to the facts. This matter is being treated as highly confidential."

"I beg to disagree. There is not a secretary, typist, receptionist or switchboard operator who isn't informed. Call them in! Ask them! And who knows who they've spread the story to? This damage done to my reputation is irreparable. It may also be legally actionable. I am going to check with my attorney to see if the damage this woman has done to me is not actionable." The pit remains impenetrable; no sympathy from the Captain. "All I am guilty of is doing my job." I stop, wait for the Captain to say something; he bears few outward signs of life. "I am not about to violate the confidence of a client," I say at last.

The Captain turns his dead eye on Esther. "Are you charging this good lady's daughter has a connection with the case presently under investigation by your section?" A flicker of light in the pit.

"I would like to go into this in detail. I think I deserve the opportunity to clear myself. But this is official business. I can't discuss it openly in Mrs. Plante's presence."

"Mrs. *Kaufman!*" she all but shouts.

"Of course, Mrs. Kaufman." I try to keep my focus on the

Captain. Where Esther is concerned, I only make mistakes. If I can convince him to get rid of Esther . . . I have a story that may get by the Captain, but not her. Nothing I say or do will ever get by Esther. I have figured out a way of making Tina part of the Perrini case.

Tailing Perrini, I get a glimpse of him leaving a restaurant with one of his look-alike fashion models. But this fashion model looks familiar to me. I cannot get close enough to get a positive make on her, but she bears a striking resemblance to Tina Kaufman, whom I know in connection with a former case. If it is Tina, my previous acquaintance with her and her family may be useful in convincing her to turn informant. So my reason for tailing her is to confirm whether or not she's the girl I saw with Perrini; if she leads me to Perrini we are in business. Eventually she spots me and I try to sell her a story about a failed romance in an attempt to divert her suspicions and gain her sympathy. But her suspicions are not diverted for long. She tells her mother, who runs to the Captain. I am a wronged man.

The story has its shortcomings but is plausible enough. And I haven't actually libeled Tina. I am not alleging that she is the girl in Perrini's life. All I allege is the resemblance. If anyone is at fault it is Tina for not letting me tail her long enough to satisfy myself that she is not implicated.

One problem: Once I connect Tina to Perrini, however tenuously, her name goes into the files. She will have a dossier.

"I do not intend to leave this office until this matter is settled." Esther speaks with a calm that makes ripples. "If there is a question of confidentiality it is easily dealt with. Simply eliminate the names of the concerned parties. I have no interest in detective agency gossip. I am interested in seeing that justice is done, as ironic as that statement may sound in this place under these circumstances."

I had almost forgotten her premeditated manner of speech, as if she says the sentences first in her head.

The Captain mechanically pumps his pipe and weighs his decision. "I don't see any problem," he says funereally. "Just leave out the name of our client and the nature of the case.

Refer to the subject as 'the subject' and not by name. That will satisfy this good lady and it will satisfy me and it will satisy you."

No, I can't throw Tina into the files. Once her name is in the files she is there for life: a suspected associate of suspicious characters and, if Perrini goes to jail, a suspected associate of known criminals.

"I will want to question him," Esther says. Her voice carries such moral weight that if it had substance I could stick a knife in it.

The Captain smiles from out of his pit. "After his story." He screws his pipe back together and fills it with tobacco. He sticks it in his mouth and lights it. "Why don't you proceed?"

I look directly at Esther for the first time. Her coldness has the force of gravity. It is as if a thin steel band extends between my eyes and her face.

"Don't waste our time," says the Captain.

I look away from Esther, but the steel band between us pivots her face wherever I turn. Right now she stares at me from the Captain's pipe. "I can't talk with her in the room."

If she would just get out of here I know I could come up with something: mistaken identity? Tailing the wrong girl?

Esther snorts. The Captain removes his pipe from his mouth. "I'd make the effort if I were you."

"I won't talk with her in the room."

He pushes his face forward at me but it does not make it through Esther's face. "Are you aware of the consequences?"

"I'm not going to say another word until she leaves the room."

"Are you aware of the consequences?" repeats the Captain with Esther's head on.

"You get her out of this room. I'll talk."

"You will talk now if you know what's good for you," says Esther's head.

"You get her out of this office."

"You are wasting valuable time," says Esther's head.

"I'll only talk if she goes."

"The cheek!" says Esther, out of sight.

"You are a new one on me," says Esther's head.

Let them rant. What can they do to me?

May 6

Tina calls at eight to say she's not speaking to her mother, that she repeatedly made it clear to her she didn't want me fired: she only wanted to get me to stop following her. She asks what I'm going to do now, sounds racked with guilt. About time. To shove it into her a bit more I tell her I am doubtless blacklisted in the agency business and I will have to find another profession. "Oh no," she moans, "what will you do?"

I tell her I have been thinking of joining the army. Her response is satisfying. She spends over an hour trying to talk me out of it.

1969

August 5

It comes as no surprise that Plante, who has never had a
moment's thought for anyone's interest but his own, is trendily
sympathetic over the plight of the Viet Cong. Scratch a cold
heart and find a bleeding heart. He has haunted my office at
CID for three days now, trying first to seduce and then to intimidate atrocity stories out of me. Our atrocities, naturally,
not theirs. Plante couldn't be less interested in the mutilation
and slaughter of the innocents in Hue, that's our side; it's
Thieu's atrocities that work him up, and, even more than Thieu,
General Westmoreland's. Having lately arrived at political consciousness, he has chosen to out anti-war the anti-warriors. His
problem is that his ambition, while overweening, conflicts with
his qualifications which are nonexistent, so that he lets himself
fall victim to every lame, bullshitty, poor excuse of a Saigon
resistance movement he stumbles on. And he believes everything they feed him. The more horrific the bullshit the more he
believes it. Then he comes running to me at CID and demands

to know what the U.S. Army intends to do about, say, the imprisonment and torture of Buddhists, or U.S. officers throwing VC POWs out of helicopters. And when I sit him down and tell him the boring, factual truth he takes it like a drunk on an overdose of black coffee: it disquiets and irritates him.

He is also insistent on seeing my files on drug addiction among GIs. He is determined to find something to say that's rotten about this war, and he is determined that I am going to be his source. I have done everything I know how to get him off my back. (This has gone on for three weeks, ever since he stumbled on me—if, in fact, he did stumble on me: I suspect he knew I was here all along. But how could he? He didn't know my real name.) I have sent him around to countless Quaker groups, Concerned Clergymen groups, pro-Cong students, disgruntled journalists, you name it, but he keeps coming back to me. He hangs on like the bad news he is. Lederer can't handle him. (No surprise; he can't handle anything.) So as soon as he learned Plante and I were acquainted he threw me to him, a human sacrifice. Lederer is the exception around here, a total incompetent who made Major through politics and connections and is interested only in protecting his flank. But he happens to be all flank, so what you get out of him is deviousness and evasion. Child's play to Plante, who saw through him in a matter of minutes and broke him down into an incoherent glob, scared shitless of what his superiors will do to him after Plante writes him up in the *Washington Post*. (What's he doing in Washington? He won't tell me. Is Tina still with him? He won't tell me. Not that I've asked but, based on our long association, you'd think he'd volunteer a minimum of information without being pressed. But no, all he talks about is Saigon's corruption. With Plante it's a one-way street.)

Christ, they shit green for him around here; you'd think he's Joseph Alsop—unless you read him—you'd never guess they're writing about the same war.

I admit that he's cleaned up his purple prose. Or his editors have. What's scary is his passion. His column is full of moral outrage which, in Saigon, comes off as simpleminded, but back in the States doubtless makes our presence here sound wrong-headed, if not criminal. If I were back home and didn't know Plante for what he is and didn't know the facts, I might easily be taken in by his reports. I can imagine the effect he has on draft-age kids.

Until Plante arrived on the scene I was having a good war. Not at the beginning—it took almost a year to lose my civilian irony—but as soon as I came under Colonel Trowbridge's command it was uphill all the way. In or out of the army I have never met a man better qualified, a more natural leader. He pulsates power but doesn't push it, you just feel it expanding beneath the surface like a tidal wave. He has the best interrogative technique I have ever seen; I love to be around him when he's interviewing a suspect. It's a work of art.

I tell him he's the next senator from Kentucky. He takes it as a gag; I know he likes me to kid him about it. He kids right back, tells me he's going to make me his legislative assistant. We banter about it a lot but, underneath, I'm deadly serious and, my bet is, so is he.

You can kid with Trowbridge, he doesn't pull rank. Of course, there are unstated rules and I abide by them. He has no sense of humor about negativism: at the point where my cracks begin to derogate the war or the military, or even the very bureaucratic horseshit of which he constantly complains, he puts me down hard. "Where are you, Lieutenant Hollister?" he will ask at such times. "I think you must be in Manhattan." Manhattan is his euphemism for smart-assed negativism. Negativism, he says, is acceptable among the troops because it keeps the bodies in their cages, but it is treasonous among the elite, it is counterproductive. (In the beginning I found his candor hair-raising: unabashed references to GIs as "bodies," or, as their hair grew longer, as "hippie-bodies," or even "foes." We, the officers, are always "the elite." His frames of reference are contagious and I find that I have appropriated, sometimes against my will, much of his language. But it sounds harsh coming out of me; his softer Kentuckian accent makes terms of opprobrium sound reasonable and graceful. I find that when I'm drinking I have an off and on tendency to speak in Trowbridge's voice. It is very effective with women.)

No question, our styles are complementary. A sort of non-conversational shorthand has developed between us: fewer words, more communication. He will begin a sentence and I can complete it. But when I slip into what he calls "vocabulary" he cuts my legs off: "Say it in half, Lieutenant."

He is, in every sense of the word, a professional; what Lyman Ross tried to pass himself off as but really wasn't. In addition, Trowbridge has the physical equipment: the looks and build of an athlete. (I think he played some football in college.) He occupies space in a way that demands attention.

He is not a man you want mad at you. He won't explain why he's mad, merely announces: "You're on the shit list, Lieutenant," and until the shit list is taken down not word one will he say to me. It can take a day or it can take a week.

He despises incompetence, has a low tolerance level for any mistake whatever, including his own fuck-ups. "My turn on the shit list," he will say. He can be in a bad humor for days after that.

He thinks the war may have been "America's biggest fuck-up," but since we're in it we'd better do everything in our power, short of nuclear warfare, to win it.

I wish he'd get back from Tokyo; he'd kick Plante's ass.

Plante refuses to call me "Hollister" or "Robert" or even "Lieutenant"; he keeps calling me "Ackroyd." His little dig, I guess, not that anyone particularly notices. As far as the personnel here are concerned he's just another civilian, in other words, a martian, a type not expected to behave rationally.

Still I have a difficult time expressing myself in his company. First of all, I'm always afraid he's going to end up quoting me—or misquoting me—and undermine all the gains I've made in the last year and a half. And, second of all, his moral outrage outpoints my moral outrage. Here the bastard is selling his country down the river and treats me as if I'm the bad guy. And gets away with it! That's what pisses me off! As always, he manages to put me on the defensive. He literally forces me into a hard-line position equally as dopey as his. Eventually I abandon all attempts at sophisticated analysis and start arguing like Curtis LeMay.

So I try to stay off the subject of the war. No one here more than a year theorizes about the war. As Trowbridge would put it, "That's bush."

August 10

Plante cannot resist baiting me with provocative conversational openings: "As a humanist with a deep ethical sense—" meaning, of course, "You bloody war criminal!" And then, typically, he will go on to ask why the most powerful nation in the world involves itself in the middle of a civil war in Southeast Asia, and just as typically I reply that it is not a civil war but an invasion from the north, and so on and on and on. He insists on using terms that he knows raise my hackles, such as "U.S. imperialism," and when I ask him to stop talking like a Berkeley student, he tells me he will make a deal: if I stop using the terms "power vacuum," "surgical strike," and "pacification," he will stop using "imperialism," and I tell him, as kindly as I know how, that he is tragically misinformed, and he smiles innocently and begs me to overlook his ignorance on the grounds that he lacks the access to classified information that I am privy to, but he would be more than happy to see that oversight corrected and—who knows?—it might turn him around on the war, and I say, to get him off my back, that I will consider his case if he will promise not to publish the information I feed him. (Not that I'm serious: Plante's promises are to be taken with as much credulity as he takes press releases from MACV.)

But he cannot restrain himself from using my joke as the excuse for a self-righteous diatribe on what he calls the inside-dopester journalist who lusts so hard after secret information that he will do almost anything to get it, especially not print it, and that a reporter who censors himself is not a reporter at all but, at best, a sycophant to power and, at worst, a conspirator at suppressing information which rightly belongs to the American people.

The above is a small sample of an ordinary night's conversation. The high moral ground Plante occupies is muddied somewhat by our surroundings: one or another dismal honky-tonk on the Catinat, where we compete with ear-shattering rock and the din of drunken U.S. service personnel, their whores, their guests, their clients, and their dope dealers who sit, stacked together, mouth to ear, alternately shrieking and pretending to listen, just as Plante and I. We have discovered, through excruciating trial and error, that we have little to say to each other unless a noisy mob is on hand to drown us out as we say it.

He is back on the booze—heavily—and much of what he has to say is conversation for the bottle. The only noticeable difference between him drunk and sober is that drunk he does not demand eye approval for his monologues.

August 13

Plante's latest column hits a new high in demagoguery: I'm surprised the *Washington Post* printed it; it is more in the style of the *New Republic*. He got some asshole of a Quaker to take him to a refugee camp fifteen miles north of Saigon, where he insinuated himself, Plante style, ingratiatingly enough to convince the camp commander (obviously one more asshole) to let him have the run of the joint. He interviewed a small handful of refugees, but in his account that handful symbolizes all refugees, all Vietnamese, all of Southeast Asia under the yoke of Yankee imperialism! And what's their problem? Only American bombing runs. Without our war criminal bombers the Vietnamese have no problem.

His perverse determination to see everything as its opposite is truly staggering. I get nowhere with my objections. It is hard to be frank with him and not play his game, slipping into "language." The bluntness I have learned from Trowbridge makes not a dent on Plante. His ear is not attuned to it. So in order to make myself heard I have to elongate and convolute my sentences, stuffing them with parenthetical, ironic asides, precisely the sort of negativism that would get my ass reamed if I tried it on Trowbridge. But Plante only takes you seriously if you act as basically clownish as he. It is a New York style that is very much out of place over here.

One item of good news: Trowbridge got back yesterday from his R and R in Tokyo.

August 14

Plante continues to push hard for me to leak him classified stuff on whatever happens to be his latest interest: this week it is the torture of civilian political prisoners by CIA, or is it CID, or is it the Phoenix Program? He doesn't care. As long as it's us. He has no concept of loyalty, and I tell him so outright; egged on, perhaps by the contradiction between his politics and his style of dining: he is, unfailingly, drawn to the fanciest and most expensive restaurants—tonight it's Ramuntcho's! This gives him the opportunity to challenge my own concept of loyalty which, being Plante, he takes full advantage of: he starts digging up some ancient Ackroyd horrors, totally irrelevant to this time and place. I tell him he is way out of line but, I must confess, his reworking of the past, however distorted, has its effect on me.

I am confident for the first time that there is an enormous difference between Roger Ackroyd and Robert Hollister; I am not just making it up. Ackroyd served his purpose as a transitional figure but, thank God, he's dead and buried and Plante's insidious influence is buried with him. Not that I am totally immune to the man—I am a realist, that may take years—but I no longer feel like a creature of his will.

I hate to sound callous but if it took a war to cure me, it is one war I am not going to knock.

August 15

Plante had his first appointment with Colonel Trowbridge today. That's one I would like to have been in on. I can just hear Trowbridge saying, "Say it in half, mister."

Amazing how this office has settled down since Trowbridge's return.

August 16

This morning Trowbridge called me into his office and for the first time since I've known him sat me down and simply bullshit. Football stories from his days at Duke. Difficult to make head or tail of, but I laughed in all the right places. He did not volunteer any information on his meeting with Plante, so I guess I will not find out what went on between them.

August 17

Trowbridge stopped by my desk this morning to ask me to dig up copies of Plante's columns in the *Washington Post*. I get no sense that Plante has said anything to him about our friendship. If it can be called that.

August 19

Trowbridge and Plante whooping it up together in Trowbridge's office, in there for over an hour, the door closed, but gusts of laughter breaking through. He obviously has not had a chance to read Plante's columns yet. I stick around out of curiosity. They come out at eight, and I hear Plante saying: "And to this day he will argue for hours that he caught the ball." Trowbridge says: "That reminds me—" and then stops being reminded when he sees I am still there. Plante suggests I join them for dinner. Trowbridge appears surprised by the suggestion. "If you've got something better to do, Hollister . . ." Does he or doesn't he want me along? I decide that he wants me, and see from his shit-list glare, as we leave together, that I have misread his signal.

It is immediately clear what they have in common. Football. Trowbridge was a star at Duke. It figures that Plante would have heard of him. Either that, or he did some fast research. Anyhow, they are, amazingly, asshole buddies. What gets me is the deference Trowbridge pays Plante, calls him "Mister Plante" and "Sir" while Plante calls him "Trowbridge." Their conversation is not once an exchange, simply a succession of mind-wearying anecdotes that exclude me totally. I am not a member of the club: I don't know any amusing sports stories. Both are acting high even before we get to our destination.

Trowbridge is going all out for his guest. We are taken to the Cercle Sportif, a fancy private club where Saigon war profiteers mix with Americans who have gotten themselves a deal. It is a chance for us all to talk French to Vietnamese waiters. Trowbridge begins by reciting the entire menu in French and then translating it into English. The waiter stands over us without ever quite seeing us. I speculate on the loyalty of the Vietnamese serving class as Trowbridge translates and analyzes the wine list, periodically checking with Plante but not with me. To all intents and purposes, I am not here. When the double Scotches arrive I begin to feel a little more here but keep it to myself. Trowbridge has quietly made it clear that I have been allowed in only to audit the dinner.

It is a lamentable part of my character that I am a conformist drinker; whether I am in the mood or not, when the gang drinks I drink. The booze induces bodily contact. When either Plante or Trowbridge wishes to take over the monologue he grips the other's forearm as an early warning signal. That gives the storyteller thirty seconds to a minute to wind up. Longer than that and he's liable to bang head-on into a competing anecdote.

Trowbridge is positively garrulous. Very much out of character. Is that what three weeks in Tokyo does to a man? "We had a running back the size of a semi, easygoing colored fellow named Moses," says Trowbridge. "Talent every which way. A born crowd-pleaser. He'd run with the ball, the crowd'd cry: 'Go down, Moses!' " Trowbridge flashes a glance at Plante to see if he got it. Plante's return smile signals yes. "The crowd destroyed that boy. He lost his concentration. Crowd'd cry: 'Deliver us, Moses,' and he'd prance up and down like a leaping goat, more yardage gained in the air than on the ground, like a fucking ballet dancer. The crowd'd yell: 'Divide the Red Sea, Moses!' " Plante laughs. Trowbridge chuckles in appreciation of Plante's laugh. "He always got nailed, though, Moses. Showboated too much. And he had trouble holding on to the ball. Got too busy orchestrating the crowd. He'd come out of a pileup empty-handed, the crowd'd shout: 'Golly Moses!' They never got mad at him, though. And him, he loved it! He'd lose possession and come out of that pileup, wide-toothed, grinning, waving his big, empty meathooks at the crowd. Don't you know they took to shouting commandments at him? 'Thou Shalt Not Fumble, Moses!' Actually, some rumors circulated at the time that down at the bottom of the pileup when he found he still had possession he handed off the ball, gave it away. 'Thou Shalt Not Fumble, Moses!' "

Underneath the joint laughter I sense terrific tension, alleviated somewhat as more drinks arrived. It is Plante's turn for a boring story, but Trowbridge won't be stopped. "We had a ferocious offensive tackle named Dawson, monster of a man, beautiful to watch, no wasted violence, just consummate destruction. He got mixed up with a pretty girl poet, though. Samson and Delilah all over again. She shorn his locks. He was useless on the ball field after that, a pacifist. Waltzed away from linemen like a ballet dancer. The ball carriers were getting smeared!

"Somehow someone made the discovery that Dawson be-

216

came his old, violent self again when he got drunk. So we started tanking him up before games. But that was only good for about a quarter, so we instituted a policy of feeding him bourbon out of a water bottle during his times on the bench. It worked wonders. It was the same old Dawson. Everybody knew, after a time, that when they carried Dawson off the field the last five minutes of play, it wasn't that he was hurt but he was passed out."

Trowbridge is almost dog-like in his eagerness for Plante's approval. Plante smiles distractedly as if he's still waiting for the end of the story, then quietly says: "Incredible." He brushes his glass against his lips but puts it down without drinking. All that saves us from still another anecdote from Trowbridge is the arrival of twenty tiny roast pigeons on a platter. Trowbridge digs in like a wild man; he is extraordinarily anxious for Plante to say something nice about the pigeons. Instead, Plante moves into his story. "I like your Dawson. It seems to me that each of us must have a Dawson in his past. Mine was named Carmichael. I met him in my salad days when I covered sports and local esoterica for *The Glens Falls Orator,* a small, unpretentious weekly whose main reason for existence was a pseudo-Winchellian gossip column assigned the by-line Willie Warbler and called 'The Opinionated Orator.' It is, I suppose, far enough behind me now to confess that I was Willie Warbler. My friend, Carmichael, was as exceptional on the football field—he played semi-pro ball—as he was hopeless with the ladies. I, who saw no reason why so admirable a halfback should not be rewarded in fancy, if not fact, advanced Carmichael, by way of *The Orator,* into a ladies' man. I ran items linking his name to that of a local beauty queen, Miss Glens Falls, though, for all I knew at the time, they had never met. Small matter, I awarded her to Carmichael.

"It was then that I first discovered the tendency of life to imitate artlessness. Reading that she was interested in Carmichael, the beauty queen became interested in Carmichael,

217

and he, no less, in her. They were inseparable for a year, and might have been to this day had I not, in a bored and reckless mood, run another item, this time hinting that Carmichael, unbeknownst to his beauty queen, was quietly squiring around a high school English teacher. The beauty queen threw over Carmichael who, out of his naive belief in the printed word, developed an interest in the English teacher. Now, mind you, I have nothing against English teachers but this was hardly the best example of her grade. She was inferior to the beauty queen in every respect but English.

"If I could go this far with Carmichael, I wondered, to what limits did my power extend? And could I resist finding out? I could not. I announced his impending marriage to the English teacher. Carmichael stormed into my office, stupefied with terror. He pled with me to retract the item: He did not love the girl, she was a tartar and a tyrant, and having read the item and being no less literal than he, had set a date for the wedding. I owed no less to my friend than to write him out of his misery. I published a string of items linking his name, in humiliating ways best left unsaid, to various voluptuaries about town. And Carmichael, as ever my creature, could do no less than date them. It did him no good. The English teacher, too familiar with the written word to heed it when it went against her best interests, refused to abide by the rules of the game. She would not go the way of the beauty queen. She made the poor lout marry her. A year later, on my way to no bigger but less shameful work in New York, I ran, as a last-ditch effort on Carmichael's behalf, word of his imminent divorce. But I had lost the old magic. Soon after, they had the first of their five children. My former friend is now a car salesman in Schenectady, a martyr to yellow journalism if ever one existed."

Trowbridge rears his head back and gives the finale a louder laugh than it deserves. Plante, in a quietly theatrical motion, as if he is taking a bow, wipes his lips with a cocktail napkin and launches into an encore about a New York Mets ballplayer who went zero for sixteen and was cured by

218

a guru. This somehow reminds Trowbridge of a quarterback who was so extravagantly boastful of his sexual prowess that the entire team financed an out-of-town hooker to come to Duke, entice the stud, and then publicly reject him. This is followed by another story by Plante, and another by Trowbridge, and I assume another and another and another, but I can't be sure because somewhere along the line I make the wise decision to stop taking notes, sensing that momentarily I will be in a condition of blissful blackout and, without notes, will not remember another word tomorrow.

August 20

Plante comes by hung over, pasty, waxen, acts even more evasive than usual, wants to know what went on last night, reluctantly admits he blacked out and is afraid he might have behaved badly.

His anxiety fairly makes him twitch as he waits for me, for the umpteenth time, to dig him out of his hole. The temptation is strong to dig him in deeper, but I resist it; I have learned that Plante is like the tar baby: playing with him gets you stuck. So I tell him the truth: that Colonel Trowbridge came in this morning happy as a lark, saying the three of us had to do it again real soon.

"Do what again?" asks Plante, and insists on a report of the conversation during dinner. His tone irritates me; it implies that I still work for him. I make it clear that I am not obligated to tell him a thing. He actually apologizes! A *first!* So I relent and tell him that he and Trowbridge entertained each other with sports stories.

"What stories?" Plante wants to know. I say I am too busy to go into it. He insists, almost pleads. I tell him I don't remember the stories because sports stories bore me silly and I did not listen. Plante looks at me suspiciously, possibly because he cannot believe he could bore anyone. I've got news for him.

August 25

Plante has become so chummy with Trowbridge that I can hardly expect him to be interested in the stuff I've come up with in the course of just one afternoon's browsing in the Military Region I files.

A certain amount of corruption is to be expected in war; it is not only forgivable, it is, undoubtedly, essential. But there are limits.

It seems, however, that the limits—if they exist in this war at all—have escalated beyond belief. Can't say more here. Material is too hot. Also I could be overstating the case.

August 27

This diary is no place for details on the results of my research thus far. The stuff is too hot.

Not that there haven't been rumors—I'm not a total innocent—but the sources for the rumors have always been the same predictable cranks and special pleaders politicking up and down Tu Do Street or the Caravelle Bar. How can you take them seriously? I still don't. If you spend all your free time making up the wildest charges imaginable some are bound to be true just by the law of averages.

Still it's hard to believe the Vietnamese Navy running armed escorts for boats carrying cargoes of rice to the Viet Cong. And that's the least of it. All neatly buried in a file labeled: "Import Monetary Oversight Control."

Trowbridge will go through the ceiling when he sees what I've found.

August 29

I left another big, fat present for Trowbridge on his desk this morning out of the IMOC files. Red hot stuff. "Import

Monetary Oversight Control" apparently means when you decipher it: "Who Got Paid How Much When for Stealing What and Selling It to Whom."

Trowbridge has yet to say a word to me about my findings. Plante, of course, has not been around to see me in days.

August 30

Trowbridge stopped by my desk on his way in this morning, looking very stern, almost haughty in his seriousness. "I appreciate your bringing that material to my attention." That's all he said; that's all he had to say.

I am gleeful with anticipation.

September 20

I learn slowly, but I now realize that I have embraced the army too uncritically, its shabby side with its good. I understand why: I required a refuge. But that doesn't excuse me for overlooking acts in the conduct of this war which, if it is to remain a war on behalf of the Vietnamese people, must be brought to light and punished. But because it was important for me to believe in the leadership, to identify with army officers as a class, as a group which has dealt with me more fairly and with more respect than any other, I allowed a shameful series of criminal acts to slip by me, unnoticed. And I am a law enforcement officer.

But I wanted to be more than that. I wanted to be one of the boys. And I became one of the boys. I was held in respect, still am. Well, tough shit, it is over.

The army is riddled through with frauds like Trowbridge. They insinuate themselves everywhere, build their careers, first in service and later out, on the bodies of the good and brave men who have fought and died here, many not knowing why. Certainly not to return Trowbridge to Kentucky a chicken colonel so he can run for the U.S. Senate.

The Trowbridges of the army use this war as a job application and use the dead and wounded as references. They exploit innocents like Plante who have come over to exploit them. They suck up, seduce, charm with the age-old political weapons of camaraderie, palmanship, getting along. The society of jocks, that closed corporation with its private signals, boring codes in the form of monologues, that society strong enough, insular enough, to bring together men who, by rights, should despise one another. But not if they belong to the club. Principles have no meaning once you belong to the club. You can be on opposite sides of the issue and it's not important; nothing is really important between asshole buddies who belong to the club.

I am not singling out Trowbridge, I have nothing against him, he is a symbol. More and more, as I go through the classified files these last weeks, I discover the differences between the upright career officer and the fakes, the bullshitters and the opportunists: the unserious men who, through connections and wit, achieve sensitive positions on or near the top where the corruption they take part in, the crimes they cover up, are incalculable. They will do anything to keep their records clean. They bury their mistakes; they bury issues that could become politically touchy and damage their careers. They treat the uniform code of military justice as a convenience, dependent on the rank and connections of the parties involved. They treat high crimes by ARVN officers, crimes that lead directly to the deaths of U.S. and Vietnamese soldiers, as non-events. They do not exist, did not happen, there is no proof, no record. The record is buried in the files, stamped "Classified," or "Top Secret," or "Cosmic."

And I am expected to sit at my desk and build a criminal case against some poor slob of a GI who has been caught smuggling cigarettes! This is a country where you can land in the brig for cigarette smuggling and get promoted into the high command for smuggling weapons to the enemy.

Shocking crimes pass for standard operating procedure, but does Trowbridge care? No, because it will endanger his future! Does Plante care? No, because his bleeding heart is not equipped to deal with issues larger than conditions in refugee camps or the occasional torture of VC prisoners; he is not able to face the large-scale sellout of the Vietnamese people by members of his own privileged club. No, he is not even a member: a monkey on a leash, an entertainer; they keep him around for diversion and laughs. No wonder they let him write against the war; all he does is blow hot air, not lay a glove on them, because he doesn't have the real information.

And if he had it, if I put it in his lap, would he do anything with it? Yes, he'd do something: he'd check it with Trowbridge for confirmation. And I'd spend ten years in the brig for giving away secrets.

1971

January 5

The original idea was to get up instantly on awakening, before resistance set in, and put in two hours on the book. Before orange juice, before coffee, before I knew what was really happening. Because if I do not sneak up on the typewriter, nothing gets written. If I wait till I am alert, or it is past ten, nothing gets written. If I have taken a phone call, or read the papers, or am in any way, shape, manner or form, close to real consciousness, nothing gets written. I have to slip into writing like a paraplegic. Nothing originates organically. I need artificial and mechanical aids in order to function. Not simply the typewriter, but the factory of locked filing cabinets in my living room where I work, the reel-to-reel tape recorder, the cassette tape recorder, the Xerox, the three-button telephone with buttons that don't connect anywhere, even the desk at which I presumably work, as imposing as the instrument panel of a jet: clocks set for Washington time, because it is where I live; central time because I am to lecture next week in St. Louis, Chicago, Cleveland and Kansas City; mountain time because I am to go on from the University of Missouri to testify at the trial of the Denver Six, who are Quakers charged with burning a draft office; pacific coast time because I am to go on from Denver to testify at the trial of the Sunset Ten, who are Yippies charged with blowing up a draft office; Vietnam time, in support of the illusion that it will inspire me with a sense of appropriate place in my struggle with the book; plus a barometer, a second barometer to check on the first barometer, a dud fragmentation bomb sent to me by an anonymous vet after he saw my Mike Wallace interview, a loaded mauser to fend off real and imagined patriots coming to get me, plus an instrument resembling a minesweeper that, it is claimed, will detect bugs—if I knew how to work it and I trusted it (I suspect it may be bugged)—plus three rough-hewn stacks of CID, ARVN and MACV releases, denials, explanations and counterattacks, in other words, lies, which are supposed to prod me into productivity, but more often lull me into a stupor.

I have already missed one deadline and Simon and Schuster is suspiciously sanguine about my missing another: the army has informed them, unofficially, of the penalties for publishing classified material, and it would not surprise me if they weren't quietly hopeful that I missed all their deadlines so that they could save themselves an expensive time in court.

Up till now I have been able to respect writers without taking seriously what they do as work. I suppose it is the fault of the diary. In a half-assed way I must think that the diary, though not for publication, is every bit as legitimate a literary effort as Rags' columns. And I spend no time on it at all. That is, until lately! Now that I am a writer under contract for a book, the diary is damned near as hard to write as the book, which is not being written at all.

For a month I managed to get up early enough to catch the book napping, got ninety pages done that way, but then the book caught on. Now, as early as I rise, the book is up before me, fighting me from the moment my eyes open. I haven't

228

been able to outfox it, so I am ignoring it. Thus I have re-sumed the diary, hoping it will make the book feel bad.

But I am now as self-conscious on the diary as I am on the book. I have to control myself from being literary, have to *fake* a relaxed tone. This entry is a *second draft!* The first draft read like Rags wrote it. Maybe if I ask him to take over the diary I can write the book.

Will I ever learn to trust him? I doubt it. Any more than Tina will learn to trust me. Not that she doesn't like me—I know she does—but in the same nebulous way she likes Rags' other friends, or the rest of the crowd of distinguished and not so distinguished visitors who pour in and out of that house, which is fast becoming a landmark on Twenty-first Street. (How does he get his work done?) I am not on special terms as a friend; only as a possible enemy to Rags. I notice that she tries not to leave us alone. She will leave him alone with politicians, congressional aides, reporters, cronies like Cornwall when he comes down from New York; but the two people she does not trust him alone with are her father and me.

Why is Tina so disturbed by her father? In his presence she becomes irritating as hell; protective, almost motherly of Rags: Kaufman has to virtually climb over her to get at him. Father and daughter rarely, if ever, talk directly to each other. They do talk at each other a good bit, using, as mediums, Rags or Josh or me. Around her father Tina grows gawky, clumsy and adolescent. It is as if her awesome poise is an unfair weapon against someone as lacking in poise as Kaufman, so she vol-untarily disarms herself. Together they come across as two stammering, incoherent fatheads, Tina the more offensive of the two because her fatheadedness is unbecoming, unnatural; an obvious damper on other emotions I can't begin to identify.

But Kaufman is rarely there. In the six months that I have been in Washington since my barely honorable discharge I have seen him only twice; I, on the other hand, have prac-tically moved in. Sometimes I walk into that house and can tell from the atmosphere that they have been arguing about me. I am the mouse in the walls of Tina's home life, not dangerous but discomforting. As much as she likes me, I know she would be a lot happier if I were nowhere around. And this pains me. I admire her inordinately.

So to keep our relationship on an even keel I try to confine my visits to Rags to periods when she is at home. (She has quit modeling for reasons of girth and now does free-lance photography, of what nature I do not know, because she refuses to show me her work, and she refuses to talk about it. When *I* talk about it, ask her innocent, often innocuous questions, she is likely to flush crimson and say, "Robert, why are you trying to embarrass me?" It is the only way I know to put her on the defensive.)

January 6

New York is more humane in winter than Washington. In New York people go out to meet the cold, hate it, but are somehow energized by it, walk into it, whale into it, overcome it. But Washington is still basically a Southern town; it treats winter like Sherman's invading army: it caves in and goes underground, becomes one vast sniveling fallout shelter. Snow and cold dictate the terms by which people live; no one argues. Washingtonians wear expressions of childlike hurt and abandonment. They take winter personally.

"Where have you been?" demands Tina. No matter what time of day or night I arrive, whether expected or not, she always makes me feel I am late. She and Josh are sitting at the oak dining table in the living room. It is covered with books, as is every other surface in the room. The room is enormous and badly lit. Rags always complains that there is no place to read, though lamps abound: floor lamps, table lamps, wall lamps. The dark green walls drown the light, even sunlight, making that room on even the brightest of days dark and cave-like. The furniture, spread everywhere in no discernible pattern, is puffy, shapeless and, in the half-light, resembles large, unkempt, sleeping cave animals. The entire room gives the impression of slowly settling into the earth. I always expect, on my next visit, to see only the tops of sinking tables and chairs.

Tina, now on her feet, moves in close to get a better look at me. I have noticed that she often does this with Rags and Josh too when they first come into a room or when they react in a way that puzzles or disturbs her. Her habit is to station herself within inches and beam her large, unwavering eyes into mine, invariably compelling me to confess what I have done since I last saw her that I know in advance she will not approve of.

"I am not going to write that damned book. Everyone knows it. I don't know why I bother to go through the motions. Anyhow, I've got four speeches to give next week and two trials to testify at. Where am I going to find the time?" I hate the way I sound; she brings out the latent whiner in me. I break out of her eye-lock by jamming myself into the chair next to Josh. Looseleaf paper, obviously homework, is spread out all over the table. I look over his shoulder to see what he is doing. He covers the papers with both hands and says apologetically, "It's a first draft." Josh and I are constantly apologizing; Tina *never* apologizes, and, on those rare occasions, when Rags apologizes, it is a riposte, not an apology.

At sixteen Josh still looks eleven. All right, twelve. He seems to have genetically chosen to avoid the awkwardness of adolescence by not going through it. I have seen his physical type before: men who look like boys into their fifties, and, overnight, become old men. He dresses like an old man: dark blue suits, grey sweaters, conservative striped ties, black oxfords; the only wild note in his dress is his socks, acrylic argyle, which he covers with his hand when he crosses his legs.

He crosses his legs like Rags, that is, slightly dandified. Tina crosses her legs more like a man or a peasant or—let's face it—a lady wrestler. She has gotten as big as a house, damned near as big as her father, but seems not to be self-conscious about it. She is carefree, sometimes I think careless, about the use of her body, which, depending on how far she carries it (or my mood), I find alternately vulgar or provocative. Her uniform dress is a tent-sized, floral patterned shift that could be a maternity dress for an entire baby ward. No, that's cruel; she's not that fat; actually, I don't think of her as fat at all, just overpowering, intimidating, not to mention voluptuous. And I don't usually go for large women.

"I know why you're having trouble with the book. Do you want to hear?"

"No, I don't want to hear. I know what you're going to say."

"What am I going to say, smart-ass?"

"You're going to say I've got writer's block."

"No, dummy, you have to be a writer before you can have writer's block. And you haven't written anything. No, the reason you can't write the book is you feel disloyal to the army."

"Bullshit!"

"Come on, Robert, you know they still have a hold on you. The question is why."

"The answer is you're wrong."

"Then why are you smiling?"

"Does Rags secretly like the army? Then why can't he write his book?"

"Not only are you smiling but you're being evasive. Robert, you're caught. Admit it."

Josh: "His book is harder because it's fiction. All you have to do is write down the facts. It's not real writing. There's no comparison." I am good at conning Josh into my evasions; never Tina.

"You'll never get those guys off in Los Angeles," Josh says out of nowhere.

"Who said I was going to Los Angeles?"

"You said you were going to testify at two trials. It's obvious: Denver and Los Angeles. In Denver they're pacifists so maybe there's a chance, but Los Angeles? Forget it!"

Tina smiles proudly at Josh. "Is he right? I bet he is."

We both laugh and Josh, noting that it's all right, joins in. If Annabelle had known he was going to have such a good time down here I doubt if she would have been so fast to surrender custody.

232

Josh leans back in his chair and folds his arms, in solid enough now to not worry about his exposed, classified school assignment. "What are you going to say in court, Ackroyd?" Like his father, he persists in calling me Ackroyd. I uncap the plastic humidor in which Rags keeps his illegal Havanas and filch a Partagas. "I say what I always say if the court allows it. Sometimes they throw out my testimony as irrelevant."

"Irrelevant? That's a laugh!" snorts Tina. At times, her open and direct support irritates and depletes me, as opposed to her back-handed support (wise cracks, for example) which somehow strengthens.

I often switch sides when Tina is on mine. "As far as the law goes the morality of the war has no bearing on criminal cases. So if these nuts go and blow up a draft board, my testimony that, at that time, half the South Vietnamese general staff was smuggling arms to the NLF while the other half was smuggling dope to GIs is, in plain fact, irrelevant. It's only relevant if the defense convinces the court that it's a political and not a criminal case and therefore the background behind the acts of the defendants should be taken into consideration. Most judges throw out that argument, and maybe they should. What do these Yippies know about the background of the war? They were just trying to get their rocks off."

Tina bristles, as I expected she would. When she bristles she balloons: her head looks like it will expand to the ceiling.

"You're not being funny," she says, displeased by an argument she can't refute and the grin I can't hide. She leaves the table for a cigarette. She smokes only when she's angry or in the company of people she's not at ease with. In my case, it is possibly both.

Josh, the little opportunist, always buddies up to the winner of the argument; he asks me to look over his class assignment. For half an hour we talk Plato. Josh hates Plato. His teacher admires Plato. In this dispute, I am on Josh's side. I think Socrates was a supercilious, game-playing, sadistic little fag, interested exclusively in scoring debater's points. He would do

233

very well at Georgetown cocktail parties. Josh is made euphoric by my diatribe, which I must say, involves a certain amount of overkill. (I had no idea I held such strong opinions on Socrates.)

Tina's only comment when she reappears from wherever she's gone to sulk is, "I just wish that for once in your life you'd try to be serious." Her petulance has the effect on me of a warm bath.

January 7

Tina does have a point: I still do feel loyal to the army. And I still do feel that in Xeroxing those documents and leaking them to Rags I betrayed a sacred trust. All right, "sacred" is excessive. Possibly I am the last respecter of institutions of my generation: the army, whatever its mistakes and failures in the war, is an institution that accepted and embraced me. That is no justification for the cover-up of criminal acts, but it is a very good reason to not gloat over their exposure. I take no pride in those last eight months in the service when every last CID, CIA and intelligence officer knew damned well who the fink was, but could not raise the hard evidence for a court-martial. Not to say I escaped prosecution; I was prosecuted by my closest friends, men who I shared good and exciting times with: they never spoke another word to me.

The difference between Rags, Tina and me is that after my prolonged agony I remain a patriot, while Tina, who has had the best of everything, takes her line from Rags and professes to be a cynic. And Rags continues to hide his substance from those nearest to him as if it's not chic.

Still, I would be doing five years in the brig right now if he hadn't protected me as his source: not just with CIA and CID, who are military and could not hurt him, but twice before a federal grand jury. He was threatened with jail for contempt, survived months of legal and extra-legal harassment finally to break the story in his column in the *Post* on the day of my honorable discharge. He treats it now as if it's a joke, one of his anecdotes for cronies like Cornwall, but as hard as he tries he can't turn it into something less than it was: an act of dignity and courage that puts me forever in his debt.

January 8

On the walk over to Rags' I sidestep the cold by thinking about Lieutenant Calley. I have learned that it is not a bad idea with Rags to have a preworked-out topic for discussion. Not that we are as stiff with each other as we were in Nam. That has all changed; we are on an entirely different footing. But I can't escape feeling that I have to brilliant up for my visits. Not with Tina: with Tina I confess; with Rags I perform; with the two of them together I simply try to hold my own.

I am pissed off at the Calley case. First, I am pissed off that he is being singled out while his superiors, all the way up to Westmoreland, are let off the hook. But, more basically, I am pissed off (and it took a long time for me to admit this) because Calley broke just before my case broke and Calley got all the attention. I am convinced that my case, while less dramatic, is more significant. But because Calley coincided so perfectly with our national self-revulsion against our role in the war, Rags' columns, while hardly ignored, didn't get the amount of serious attention they deserved and, as a result, the incidence of corruption in the Vietnamese high command continues unabated. Another result: Rags lost his Pulitzer to Seymour Hersh.

I am further pissed off that I was too easily scared off in my research of secret documents. Had I continued my small excursions into the classified files, I might have been the one to dig up the Calley case; it must have been there somewhere. Maybe part of it was my state of mind. The press, Rags included, bugged me so relentlessly on rumors of atrocity stories that, out of perversity, I may have blinded myself to them. It is possible that had I come across Calley in the files I might have ignored him; it's even possible that this happened and I don't remember it.

The house, as I approach, seems to embrace me in all its rotted shingled, battered, horror movie campiness, and my anger dissipates; my mood always improves at the sight of that house.

"Where have you been?" Tina asks, as I walk in. Her long, dark hair hangs loosely about her shoulders; the flowers on her shift today are green and yellow; she looks absolutely marvelous. She is sitting at the oak table eating a cup of yogurt. She waits for me to take the chair opposite her, but I don't. I can barely talk I am so mad at her.

"Is Rags working?" I ask.

"Still mad at me?"

"What makes you think I'm mad at you?"

"If you're not mad at me why is your voice an octave higher?" She is in a good humor. She is always in a good humor when I am mad at her.

"I'm mad about Calley, smart-ass. You think you know everything." I proceed at unnecessary length to explain why I am mad at Calley.

"I see. And the other day you were mad at Plato."

"I don't know what's the matter with you today." I start upstairs, dissatisfied with my end of the exchange. Halfway up the squeaking, uncarpeted stairs I am suddenly outraged that, after all these years, she is still not married to Rags. I don't know for a fact whose fault it is, but I blame it on Tina; I'm sure it is Tina. It is one thing to be independent—everyone wants to be independent—it is another thing to be so independent you give your friends a sense of abandonment even when you're with them. And if it's true with friends, it must be doubly true with Rags. I am strongly tempted to go back down and tell her she is a selfish bitch. But that would only start a fight, and fights with Tina never get you far.

January 10

It is very unsettling driving in a car with them: first of all I am invariably consigned to the back seat where I find myself playing audience to their act and claque to whichever one needs my support the most or subliminally demands it the most. Tina always drives because, if you are to believe her, she doesn't trust Rags behind a wheel and, if you are to believe Rags, he enjoys the freedom of being chauffeured. I don't know why they own a car—it is not used to get them anywhere, destination being the last thought they seem to have in mind; sight-seeing is the next to last. Their car, a '69 blue Chevy, appears to play the part of mobile living room; when they run out of material for banter in the house they go for a drive to find new subjects for banter. It often sounds like acrimony but it is not, or it is mostly not; it is their perverse method of communicating closeness.

"You missed the exit," says Rags with satisfaction.

"How would you know?" retorts Tina.

Rags turns to me in profile. "Tina makes the assumption, Ackroyd, that, the world being round, we cannot fail to be moving in the right direction."

"How can I take you seriously when you get lost on a road map?" says Tina.

"Road maps are abstractions; they are only understood by bureaucrats and technicians."

"And your sixteen-year-old son," says Tina, taking her eyes off the road to confront him full-face with a triumphant grin.

"He will mature out of it or he is no son of mine."

"*I* can read a road map."

"You read a road map not unlike the way you read a detective story: an overload of false hunches and confused guesses."

"But I get us there!"

"Proving, after all, that the world is round."

"This is our exit, know-it-all," hails Tina as she cuts over to the right and off the George Washington Memorial Parkway.

"It is *an* exit," concedes Rags.

"And there is our restaurant," points Tina.

"They have moved it since last time."

A dispute in the parked car follows. Rags will not get out; he denies that this is the right restaurant. Tina insists that he leave the car and take a look inside. Rags refuses—as he puts it—"to authenticate the obvious." Tina calls him "impossible" and "a pain in the ass" and drives off.

Now I know that neither one of them honestly gave a good goddam whether we ate in that restaurant or not—back on the highway, they chat amiably—but my stomach is a mess; at times I have to accept it on faith that their routine abrasiveness is underlined with good will.

Later on in the drive the topic they pick to fight over is children.

"The boy does not resent me for leaving his mother, he resents me for marrying his mother."

"He resents you for not being open with him."

"He resents me because it is the prerogative of a child to resent his parents and Josh, being a conservative and a traditionalist, honors the prerogative."

"He also resents you because you intimidate him."

"Intimidation is modern man's last viable weapon against being devoured by his loved ones."

"You've got a good case there: Josh is incapable of devouring a good meal, least of all you."

"He has violent silences."

Tina giggles. I can tell from the flush spreading on the back of Rags' neck that he is pleased.

January 15

We are alone in Rags' study talking about guilt. The room is dark and spacious but appears small; it is cluttered with furniture, almost all of it tables and desks. The tables, of various sizes and heights, are repositories for more books and papers; the desks—there are two of them—are his columnist desk and his novelist desk. His columnist desk is smothered by the sort of debris that overflows the surfaces in the rest of the room. The novelist desk is neat, only an electric typewriter, a stack of paper and a couple of books. I have yet to see him sit there.

It rests on an Oriental carpet and looks a bit like a shrine, in fact, it appears to be levitating.

"My last six months in Vietnam it was impossible to find anybody guilty. If we nailed a suspect with a kilo of heroin on him he'd act as if he hadn't done anything wrong. The concept of guilt has ceased to exist over there."

Rags is sitting up straight in his God chair, always an indication his interest has been aroused. The chair is a tan leather monster, close to the size of a bed. A visiting Russian journalist on seeing the chair for the first time commented, "This is a chair a great man should be buried in." Right now the great man *seems* buried: papers, magazines and books six inches high line both arms of the chair. I wonder if he knows what any of them are.

"A couple of years ago I might collar a T3 on a black market rap. Well, he'd be furious he got busted but in his heart he'd know he had broken a law. But it's not that way anymore. The concept of law, the concept of a specifically definable set of rights and wrongs has stopped being acknowledged by criminals."

Rags laughs out loud.

"I'm perfectly serious," I say, swallowing my smile. "Effective law enforcement depends on a generally recognized agreement between law officers and criminals that determines what a crime is. If you commit what is defined as a crime you get busted and, if convicted, you go to jail. But what seems to have happened in Vietnam is that that agreement has been dissolved. Today there is no way, absolutely no way, of convincing a drug dealer or a currency smuggler that he has done anything wrong. To them it has become gang warfare. If they are taken into custody, they are not lawbreakers, they are prisoners of war."

"Are you saying that Vietnam, being such a monstrous crime, has converted all crimes short of mass murder into legitimate business operations?"

"I don't know. Am I? Or are you trying to trap me into sociology?" I am having a very good time, hampered only by the lingering fear that, at any moment, Tina will barge in.

239

Rags ends my good time by saying, "Why don't you put it in the book?"

"What book?"

"Really, Ackroyd. What you said just now is fine stuff; it should go in the book."

"I'm not sure I know which book you're talking about."

"Be serious. You should get back to work and, just perhaps, make that pithy observation of yours the overarching theme." He leans forward in his God chair and rubs his hands together. "You're not simply exposing corruption in high places, you're providing the social and moral context which explains why such corruption is tolerated and covered up."

"Is that what I'm doing?" I reach for a cigar, unasked. He is making me nervous.

"Certainly what you should be doing. The question is why aren't you and why won't you?"

I light the cigar and then remember to look at the label. It is a Don Diego. I feel victimized that I am not smoking a Havana. "I'm not a writer."

"Wonderful! In that case you are miles ahead of the rest of us; you needn't worry about prose style."

"Look, I don't know the first thing about what I'm doing. It makes no sense." My previously prepared observations on guilt are carrying us much further than I had intended.

"I am not unacquainted with the problem," says Rags dreamily.

"How do you solve it?"

"My first rule as a novelist is: no improvident haste. A seed is somehow planted and one trusts to God it will manage to grow. But it will not grow if it is watched, and it will not grow if one makes oneself sick about it. So I leave my seed in peace. I go on to other duties elsewhere. Once a year or so, I check on it to see how it is growing and if it still lives.

"But that is the novelist's way. As a journalist I have the responsibility of a deadline. So I publish, whether it makes sense or not. Some of my very best columns do not make sense.

"But your situation lies somewhere in between. You are

neither journalist, novelist, or writer. This book of yours should be no more of a burden than writing those detective reports I was once so fond of. There's your answer! Write your book as if it's a report!" He folds his hands behind his head, obviously delighted by his own suggestion.

I am less delighted. "I'd be self-conscious."

Rags grins. "It sounds as if I've given you all of my bad habits."

"What's your novel about?" It is the first directly personal question I have ever asked him, and it lowers the temperature in the room alarmingly.

"We are talking about your book, Ackroyd." He brings his hands down from behind his head and places them, fidgeting, atop the stack of books on the arms of his chair. The stack is thick, so that his arm-reach is high while his body is low: it looks as if he is sitting in a high chair.

"But you know all about my book. I don't know about yours."

His smile is wary. "You know nearly as much as I do, I'm afraid." He waits as if he's expecting some sort of agreement from me. "But perhaps it has slipped your mind. My notebook."

For a very long moment I don't know what he's talking about. "You don't mean the one that Kaufman swiped? *That* notebook?"

Rags smiles as if I'm playing a game with him that he is on to. "That very notebook."

"But I never read it."

He continues to look as if he's waiting to hear the punch line. "You didn't read it?"

"Of course not."

"But surely you did!"

"I never read it." He appears to be offended, so I add, "It would have been an invasion of privacy." He blinks, seeming not to understand. "It would have been a violation of ethics. My own overarching social and moral context," I add with a smile.

His return smile is uncertain, as if I am tricking him. "You actually didn't read it?"

I can hardly suppress the growing excitement. I am almost certain he is about to show it to me. "I swear to you, I never looked past the first page."

"You really didn't go past the first page?" He is leaning all the way forward, his hands clasped and massaging themselves.

"I didn't go past the first page."

His hands clench and unclench. "What you missed!" A gray smile. He is out of the chair, moving stiffly and in slow motion to his novelist desk. It is the first time I have ever seen him go near it. He reaches into the bottom drawer, removes a 3 by 5 spiral memo pad and carries it over to me in a manner that might pass for casualness, except that his shoulders are up around his ears. "See for yourself." He flips the notebook open and places it in my lap, and then resumes his seat in his God chair. He stares at me as I read the page. It consists of two lines. The first line reads:

"Big Chief Little Shit"

The second line reads:

"Opposites"

I turn to the next page. Blank. I turn to the page after that. Also blank.

"Keep looking if you like; tell me if you find anything," he says dryly.

Foolishly, I go back and forth through the entire notebook. But all there is is "Big Chief Little Shit" and "Opposites." I smile down at the page, "A lot of work . . ."

"For nothing?" Rags quickly puts in.

"I didn't say that."

"You weren't going to say, 'For nothing'?"

"No," I lie. "What does it mean?"

"It is raw seed."

I take a mental leap. "You don't know what it means, do you?"

"I know a raw seed when I see one. You are looking at an unspoiled example of an idea for a novel. Unembellished, unexpurgated, and unwritten." Rags has a curious, drained color to his face. He looks as if he's about to blend into his chair.

"Why don't you give yourself a deadline?"

"The journalist in me has asked that question; the novelist in me refuses to dignify it with an answer."

"So you've been waiting seven years for this to grow?" I speak in astonishment but I see by the stricken look on his face that I am being cruel.

"I have nursed it some. I have danced around it." He points to his novelist desk as if he's introducing a stranger. "In those drawers lie five hundred single-spaced typewritten pages. Perhaps seventy-five of those pages are usable if I had a book to put them in. They are how I keep myself in shape while waiting for the book."

I hand him back the notebook. He is very tired on rising, very slow in returning it to the novelist desk. He stands behind the novelist desk, his hands stuck rigidly in his pants pocket. "Ackroyd, why don't you let me get a start on your book for you?" he says, suddenly animated. "I know it's presumptuous. But perhaps if I begin it you will be able to get into it. If you give me your research and we tape a few interviews—who knows? I am a gifted mimic. It will sound incredibly like you." He smiles broadly. Is this a joke?

January 16

I can't decide where my interests lie. Should I say the hell with it and let him do it? Oscar Plante, my ghost? Shouldn't I be flattered, *honored*? So why can't I make up my mind? And why do I feel insulted?

Tina is not to be predicted. "You're kidding me," she says when I break the news to her.

"He was putting you on." She is flushed, agitated.

"Ask him yourself."

"If he wants me to know I guess he'll tell me." Her voice is little more than a growl.

"Why do you think it's such a bad idea?"

She looks at me as if I'm crazy. "Because he's got his own book to write."

"He showed me his notes." She folds her arms across her chest and clutches her shoulders. I wonder if she has seen the notes.

"You're not going to let him do it, are you?" she asks—virtually demands—putting me on the defensive.

"I think it's a rotten idea. But maybe he thinks working on my book will goose him into working on his."

Tina's face elongates, almost as if it's made of wax, becomes an ominous, barren waste, devoid of features, devoid of everything. "You do want him to do it."

"No, I don't."

"I can tell you do."

"All you can tell is I'm overwhelmed by the suggestion. And why shouldn't I be?"

"I'm not going to let him do it."

"I haven't said yes, you know." It is like having an argument with the landscape of the moon. And why are we arguing? We both agree on this! And who is she that I should want so desperately to prove to her what doesn't need proving?

January 18

More out of anger with Tina than real interest in Plante's proposition, I drop off my ninety pages—all that I've written in five months—at his house on my way to National Airport. "Is it in English?" Plante asks as we stand in the hallway, the front door open, my cab ticking away greedily at the curb.

"Barely."

"Not in verse, I hope?"

"Iambic pentameter."

A thin sliver of a smile. "I will lead your iambic to slaughter." He rattles the clasped manila envelope. It seems appallingly slim. "Is it possible I will surprise us both and like it?" He unclasps the envelope and removes the manuscript, making me nervous. He starts reading the first page, making me more nervous. Just as I begin to wonder if he intends to read all ninety pages with my cab ticking away, he looks up. "Seriously, Ackroyd, I'm glad you're permitting me to see this." He doesn't look glad; he looks apprehensive. I can't stand another second of our act, and I'm scared shitless that Tina will catch us at it.

Plante stands in the doorway, still in his pajamas and bathrobe although it is eleven-thirty in the morning, and waves me off with my own manuscript; a reflection of either style, thoughtlessness or contempt.

I am relieved to be getting out of town.

January 26

As it turned out, my preconceptions were wrong: I despised the pacifists; too one-dimensionally self-righteous. I enjoyed the Yippies: funny, unpompous, abusive, cynical and hopelessly innocent—in fact, not so different from some of the guys I knew in service. Not surprisingly, my testimony was stricken after voir dire examination in both Denver and Los Angeles, but my presence and support evidently cheered the defendants. I put it down to a deficiency in character that I resent cheering up pacifists. I am as opposed to pacifism as I am to Vietnam. I often wonder why I can't find a group that represents my side.

Forgot about the book until the flight home from Los Angeles. Now, all the way home, I can't get it out of my mind. I really must get to it. It is important that I get to it. My four speaking dates were convincing proof, if I needed any, of the amount of ignorance that continues to exist on the war. (Kid in Chicago: "Isn't it idealistic not to expect a certain amount of corruption in wartime?" A girl graduate student in St. Louis: "Isn't your violation of your oath by stealing classified documents as morally reprehensible as the corruption you're denouncing?") Nothing right now is as important as writing that book. I will work on it if it kills me. And well it may!

Plante likely hates what I've written but it's not literary merit that counts here, it's the clear presentation of the record. I am not about to be detoured by his bullshit professional criticism.

Maybe he hasn't even read it yet. I hope he hasn't. I am sorry I gave it to him and it will make it a lot easier taking it back.

8:00 P.M.: The phone is ringing as I unlock the door. "Where have you been?" Tina asks, and I am immediately on the defensive.

"I just walked in the door this second!"

"Have you eaten? Come have dinner. Rags is dying to talk to you." My heart leaps. At the same time I resent it that he hasn't called me himself. He never calls me. Tina is in charge of invitations.

"Robert, you don't have to bring anything, O.K.?"

She refers to my habit of never going there for dinner without two bottles of wine. I wonder if I can manage not to bring it; will I feel that I haven't earned my invitation?

I am the star of the dinner: Plante pumps me with questions about the Denver and Los Angeles trials, drags opinions out of me on the usefulness of our system of criminal justice in arriving at the truth of a case—a subject I didn't know I had strong ideas on. But I do, apparently, and they are impressive. I am certainly impressed and, according to the voice vote, Rags' and Tina's, so are they. I am giddy to give something in return for all this acceptance. When Rags treats me as an equal, uncritically—or, if critically, with the eventual acknowledgment that I have passed all tests; when Tina laughs— but more than that, basks in my wit as if it is Rags making the joke, not me; when the two of them embrace me in a warm Dickensian glow, I am transported. The experience is absolutely spiritual: I would sacrifice much for them at times like these. An idea dawns on how I may serve them. It is not yet an inspiration but gives promise of becoming one. "Listen, I've been doing a lot of thinking about your notebook."

"Fine," grins Rags impregnably. "You write my book. I'll write yours."

"Not exactly what I had in mind," I say, but before I can finish the sentence with a joke he has left the table with his mug of black coffee and tramps upstairs. What now? I am afraid I've cut into the glow, but one look at Tina, who is staring at me with manic anticipation, instantly replaces that fear with another. Rags bounds downstairs carrying my manuscript and his coffee mug in one hand and, in the other, fifty or sixty typed pages. He retains the manuscript and offers the typed pages. "You may hate it. See what you think."

Tina rises and yawns, stretching to the ceiling. "I'll make more coffee."

"No, I'll make it," says Rags.

"You can help," says Tina.

"No, you can help," says Rags. Like Siamese twins they sidle off into the kitchen.

At first I have the impression that I am reading a more neatly typed, somewhat more readable version of my own draft, but then I realize it is Rags' revision, written in my style: not the style of my manuscript, which is devoid of style, but the style I would write in if I knew how to write. And it sounds, as Rags promised, exactly like me. The feeling is spooky: hearing my own voice, or, rather, an idealized, clearer, more concise version of my own voice coming at me in words I did not say or write or make notes on. But they are incontrovertibly my research and my conclusions. Page after page, phrases come at me that I recognize as mine but sound too natural to be in the book, so where did he get them? He doesn't have access to my notes; I doubt that my notes read this naturally. Conversation? Has he remembered verbatim our every conversation on Vietnam over a two-year period?

Reading becomes slow going; my mind hopscotches over high and low points in my relationship with Rags, too obsessed to concentrate further on the distant business of the war. I read on out of fealty to Rags: He wants me to read and approve of our book, for it is unquestionably *our* book now: He is a far more gifted spokesman for myself than I am; of the two of us I am the ghost. But I am a grateful ghost: rather than depleted I am added to. I have to choke back the desire to humiliate the two of us by my, now dangerously close to the surface, idolization of the man. I engage my cool and skim the remaining thirty pages.

I can't break into the kitchen where they wait for the verdict without pouring myself a drink, finding in the process that I am acting like a one-armed man because I will not put down our manuscript. It is not safe to put it down. The table is packed with dishes and glasses and my empty Beaujolais bottle; it will surely get stained if I lay it on the table. If I put it on an end table or the coffee table it will be surrounded by published books and be swallowed alive. If I go into the kitchen without it, it will disappear without a trace; I will never see it again. So I carry our work in one hand, my Scotch in the other, and butt my way with a shoulder through the swinging door that leads into the kitchen.

Tina alone registers her awareness of my presence. She is sitting, her chair tilted back from the kitchen table, her legs crossed under her shift in her off-putting masculine style. She is not drinking coffee, but Scotch and, unlike Rags, who is drinking coffee, appears very, very nervous. Rags apparently doesn't know I'm there, so busy is he at the stove masterminding the Chemex. I say, "Hi there" to Tina, and sit next to her at the table, both of us facing Rags' back. "You know it's wonderful to get out of town for a couple of weeks," I begin, as Rags turns around to face me, a slow-forming grin on his face. "It gives you a whole new perspective on your work. For example—" I hold up our manuscript. "My writing seemed absolutely incomprehensible when I left town but it's amazing how much better I like it after a two-week layoff." I note in a side-glance that Tina has switched her focus from me to Rags to see if he gets the joke or is taking me seriously. Rags now leans with his back against the old-fashioned iron stove, his legs crossed elegantly. His coffee mug is cradled in the palm of his hand, his thumb hooked over the rim. I have yet to see him hold a cup by its handle. (I sometimes practice the thumb-over-the-rim hold but it is not natural to me.)

"I couldn't agree more. The longer one stays away from one's work the better it reads. If one stays away long enough it takes on the dimensions of a classic. Of course there is that inevitable letdown when one goes back and rereads. But that can be cured by either progressively longer absences or, if one is a purist, resisting the temptation entirely."

A low growl emanates out of Tina. She slides her chair discordantly away from the kitchen table. "The two of you are cute as pigshit." She whirls on me. "Do you like it or don't you?"

I smile into the threatening storm, appropriating Rags' cool. "I'm surprised you're interested. I assumed you were against this project."

Tina slams herself down in her chair and folds her arms across her chest. "I am not speaking to either one of you ever again." She is quiet like a ticking bomb. "Frank and Dino!" she snorts. Rags' face is crimson with contained affection.

I place my hand lightly on her shoulder. (A first!) "Tina, I don't like it—" The muscles in her shoulder spasm. "I love it." Her shoulder relaxes but she will not look at me.

"Why tell me? Tell him!"

I let my hand slip off her shoulder and turn my attention to Rags. "Rags, it is not without promise."

Tina unwinds a growl which turns into a baritone scream. "You are both so insufferably precious I hope you both choke!"

By way of shifts and starts, we manage to loiter in the kitchen until daylight, all of us drinking heavily, Tina most of all. Once every hour or so she disappears into the living room, stretching out on the couch for a short nap. Each time she leaves the look of distrust she throws at me is bloodcurdling. Rags and I are so intent on backing obliquely into an agreement that I am only dimly aware of her absences; dimly aware, also, that when she naps she snores lightly. I find this as disturbing as the way she crosses her legs.

January 27

Tina calls at ten-thirty, waking me. "Did I wake you?"

"No, I had to get up to answer the phone."

A long pause during which I think she has hung up. "Look—" she finally says.

"I thought you'd hung up."

"I very nearly did. I am desperately hung over and feeling extremely angry at myself. I want to apologize for my behavior last night. I know how extraordinarily difficult this is for both you and Rags and it drives me crazy that you can't be out in the open with each other but it's wrong of me, it's obtuse of me to think I can force either one of you to act contrary to your natures. I've already apologized to Rags."

"I accept your apology. I also apologize to you."

"Goddammit, I don't want your apology when I'm apologizing! You know more ways to make me furious at you!"

"Do you think Rags will really write the book?"

"Better and better!" Tina snarls piercingly, causing my head to cannonade with hangover. Even her apologies end up putting me on the defensive.

In the shower, which has no effect on my condition whatever, I conclude that the best time to hit Rags with my scheme for a quid pro quo is right away, while neither of us is able to think too straight or react cleverly. I fry and eat a couple of eggs which I recognize, too late, as an error. I correct the error, douche my system liberally with Empirin and black coffee, and head for Rags' without telephoning, afraid that if I phone he will put me off. If he puts me off I will lose the courage to confront him.

He is, as it turns out, in remarkably good shape, already

dressed when he greets me at the door although it is not yet noon. "Good, you've brought everything!" he says with a grin, rubbing his hands together; it seems to me I detect a small tremor in them. The "everything" he refers to are two fat briefcases of files which represent barely one percent of everything. The two briefcases are my excuse for stopping by without phoning. They will get me upstairs to his office where Rags will invite me to sit and visit for a while. At least, that is the plan.

"Let me give you a hand," Rags says, and relieves me of both briefcases, giving me the feeling I am not doing my share. His eyes are bright and his step quick; I trail sluggishly upstairs after him.

My reaction as I step into the office is unexpected and shameful: I compare the clutter of the journalist desk to the surgical sterility of the novelist desk and think irritably, "Of course, *I* get the journalist desk."

Rags dumps the two briefcases on the wheeled stenographer's table next to the journalist desk. He grabs up a sheaf of pages from beside the typewriter and waves it at me. "Twenty more pages this morning!"

"I don't believe it!"

"Neither does Tina. She insists I'm working well only to make a fool of her," he cackles. He melts into his swivel chair, waving an arm at me in invitation to take a seat. The chair he points to is the God chair. I have never been in the God chair; I didn't know anyone but Rags was allowed to sit in the God chair. As I recline into its soft, womb-like leather and feel its arms swell to embrace me, I can't help but fleetingly wonder, who among his other friends has occupied this chair. The fresh wave of shame that follows the thought revives my hangover.

It fades during Rags' dissertation on our book: on the unexpected ease with which he finds himself able to write in my voice, on the singular importance of the writer's voice in fiction and nonfiction, how the credibility and authoritativeness of voice decides for the reader from very nearly the first page if a book can be trusted. He speaks with an intensity and live humor I can't recall having seen in him before. He sprawls in his swivel chair with an unconcerned casualness that is also new to me. He fairly bubbles with contentment. I cannot interfere with it; I go home without dropping my bomb.

9:00 P.M.: My second shot at it. This time I tackle Tina, a bit tricky because it takes forty minutes to clear Josh out of the living room. He wants to hang around and talk about Gene McCarthy, whom Rags had to lunch today. The kid is attractive in many ways but much too much of a name-dropper. The awful part is that I can't stop myself from competing with him. I mention all the celebrity-Yippies I ran into at the Los Angeles trial. I win that one; he is really impressed. Why must I give to others, regardless of age, intelligence or capability, the right to decide the level of my conversations?

The kid goes, leaving Tina and me and the muffled thumping of Rags' typewriter upstairs. Sounds like twelve hundred words a minute.

"Seven years ago Rags got drunk in a bar in New York with three of his friends," I begin without prologue. "He blacked out most of the episode but what he was able to remember later was that during the course of the evening one of his friends—he couldn't remember who—mentioned something which set off a spark in his head. He went to the john and wrote what he remembered to be dozens of pages, the outline for his new novel, on a memo pad. He was very excited. He considered it to be a very special idea. I suppose you know all this?"

Tina responds without enthusiasm, "I know it. Why are you talking so fast?" Only then do I realize that I've been competing verbally with Rags' typewriter.

"Do you know that the memo pad was stolen that same night and that he hired me to get it back?" She releases a sigh and half smiles. "Do you know who stole it?" I ask.

She grimaces. "Why are we talking about this?" Her eyes narrow. "Robert, what are you up to?"

252

"Tina, for once can you stop treating me as if, (a) I'm an incompetent, or (b) I have ulterior motives, or (c) both?"

She catches me in her all too familiar eye-lock. "Do I do that?"

"All the time!"

"*All* the time?"

"A lot of the time."

"Then I'm sorry. I didn't know I did it that often."

I am moved by her quiet directness, as I always am when subjected to it. "Have you ever discussed this with your father?"

"Neither Rags or I is very good at talking to my father. Rags is better at it than I am; I'm impossible. You've seen us: can you imagine what would happen if I brought *this* up?"

She embarks on a meandering speculation on her relationship with her father, doing a short tirade on his lack of moral support—his disappearance whenever she needed him. She talks longingly about how different he acts towards her sister whom she knows he likes better, thereby undermining any possibility of a friendship between the two women.

It is irritatingly clear that the purpose of her confession— executed movingly, by the way, with long pauses, emphatic head shakes, tantalizing contact or near-contact between her hands and mine—is to distract me. "What about the words on the pad, Tina? Do they seem worth all that fuss to you?"

She glares at me for my lack of interest in her problem.

" 'Big Chief Little Shit' and 'Opposites,' " I say to egg her on.

"You don't know that's all that was on the pad," she says in obvious bad humor.

"You think your father might have torn out the incriminating pages?"

Her shoulders rise and fall expressively.

"I had the same idea so I counted the pages in Rags' memo pad. And I dug out of my files a similar memo pad of my own, purchased at about the same time. Exact same number of pages."

"He thinks he wrote more," she says firmly.

"He's wrong." I meet her slow, simmering stare head-on. "Rags can be wrong, you know."

She lifts a corner of her mouth in a wry smile.

"He thinks he wrote more because those words meant more at the time he wrote them."

Tina begins scratching her head furiously, as if massaging her brain. "O.K., I know what you want to do and Rags won't let you do it."

Why does she always have to anticipate me?

"Anyhow, you'd never get past my mother. Why are you dragging all this up, Robert?"

I ignore her question. "Your father has to know what those words mean."

Tina throws both hands in the air. "Well, it's not going to do any good to go ask him. Anyhow, I know what some of it means. A lot of good it does us." She proceeds to scratch the back of her neck, then her left shoulder.

"You know what what means?"

"Oh come on, everyone knows what 'Opposites' means. But what does it mean to Rags is the question." She scratches her right shoulder. She is making me itch all over.

"Tina, I don't know what you're talking about."

"Don't be dense. You played 'Opposites' as a kid. Everyone's played 'Opposites.' "

"I haven't played 'Opposites,' " I say, irritated that once again I am losing the initiative to her.

"Yes, you have, you just don't remember. Neither does Rags. What a team!" She catches my scowl and says quickly, "I'm sorry. I hate this conversation. It's that game we all played—you did too!—where you say just the opposite of what you really mean. Like 'I hate boys' means 'I love boys.' You have to know it."

I shake my head no. "And 'Big Chief Little Shit'? Another game we all played in childhood?"

"Oh, fuck you, Robert! I don't have to put up with your

254

sarcasm. Since you brought the subject up you can try to be helpful."

"I am trying," I say in a manner which suggests that while I am she is not.

"And stop accusing me!"

I heave a heartfelt sigh.

"I'm sorry," Tina says, with a weak laugh. "Look, it's perfectly obvious that those words refer to something in Rags' and my father's childhood that Rags remembered when he was drunk and forgot when he sobered up. And my father remembers and is scared shitless by. Don't you think I know all that? I've known it for years!"

I am beginning to get the same sense of diminished presence from Tina that I typically get from her mother. It never occurred to me till now that they were alike.

"O.K., you're way ahead of me," I say, as if I don't mind. "But how about doing something about it?"

"Robert . . . ," she says ominously.

"Rags and your father share a knowledge of some childhood episode that threatens them both. It is remotely possible that they don't share it alone, that other friends from back then share it with them. Or relatives. Or adults. I want to check on it. I want to dig up those people Rags knew back then and find out what, if anything, they know about this."

"Who's going to remember after all these years?" She sounds astonished. "You act as if none of these people have their own lives."

"You act as if anything I have to suggest isn't worth bothering with."

She shakes her head wildly and lets out a muffled growl. "Will you please stop feeling sorry for yourself."

"Will you talk to Rags about it?"

She puts her hand on mine; I get the clear indication it is to stave me off. "Robert, he is having a good time."

"He's writing my book."

"And he's grateful."

"I want to do something for him, Tina."

"You are doing something for him!"

"Maybe I can help him."

"Why can't you hear what I'm saying?" she says, exasperated.

Obviously the wrong person to talk to. Like it or not, I will have to take it up with Rags.

January 28

Tina stands filling the door, large and grouchy, bundled up to her nose by the fur collar of her belted, tan mackintosh. A bulky camera case dangles off her right shoulder, a smaller sized handbag dangles off her left. She shoves a Medaglia d'Oro can at me and says: "My turn to bring the wine. I suppose you have a hot plate?"

"An entire stove."

"Better and better," she snarls, and leads me into the apartment. I follow barefoot, half asleep, the pajamas I wore when Tina buzzed from downstairs not three minutes ago concealed beneath a sweater and blue jeans; no matter: my exposed feet are enough to make me feel inadequate to the occasion. She towers over me in three-inch boots which she whisks off before she is halfway to the stove. Her coat comes off in virtually the same motion. She drops it on the floor—or would, if I did not grab it before it hit and throw it on the bed, covering it almost as completely as a comforter.

"This place is a mess; don't you own a can opener?"

I run from the bedroom to the kitchen and locate the can opener, lying in plain view on a counter.

"It's a hell of a place to keep a can opener" she mutters, as she attacks the Medaglia d'Oro can. "You may have noticed, I'm in a foul mood." She turns her back on me to concentrate on the coffee. I watch her, intimidated by the notion that if I move, make any sound whatever, I will spoil her concentration. I back slowly out of the kitchen.

"Where are you going?" she snaps.

"I don't feel welcome here. I thought I'd go to a movie."

She turns away from my three-piece, perfectly impossible coffee maker and shoots a withering glance that nails me to the spot. "If you want coffee you'll have to make it yourself. You have the wrong kind of pot. Anyhow I've had mine. I was just trying to be nice."

Not until I see Tina sitting in it, sipping her coffee, do I realize I have only one chair in my living room. I lean against the archway dividing the living room and the bedroom.

"I want to know how you'd go about it," she begins, assuming that I know what she's talking about. I do.

"O.K., I would get from Rags a list of everyone he can recall from childhood, his friends, your father's friends, neighbors, relatives, teachers. If he has knowledge of their present whereabouts I would want that information. If not, I would want whatever old addresses he can recall, any information that might be of help. I would start tracking down some of the more reasonable sounding people on the list. I would interview them. Most of them will know nothing. Maybe all of them. Odds are it would be a waste of time. But whose time? My own. And I want to do it."

The longer I talk the more her face loses definition, until she begins to look as if she's wearing a stocking mask. "It could all be so simple if you could only talk to my father."

I nod encouragingly.

"Rags absolutely forbids it." She pulls herself out of her slump and reaches for her handbag. "I anticipated you'd need a list." She unstraps her handbag and fishes out a list. It contains thirty or so names written in longhand. I pretend to look over the list, but nothing registers. In response to my obvious confusion Tina says, "I told Rags this morning. I had no right to keep it from him. He will never cease to surprise me. He thinks it's a wonderful idea. It's a terrible idea but I'm not going to fight it. He's actually sorry he hadn't thought to hire you to do it years ago. He insists on paying you." She says all this flatly, as if she's talking of things that don't concern her.

"Out of the question."

"He insists."

"Can't be done. I'm out of the detective business. My license has lapsed. Besides, I value Rags as a friend. I always hated him as a client. Anyhow, he's writing my book. I'm insulted."

She lets the matter slide—temporarily, if I know Tina. "Rags doesn't want any interim reports. He doesn't want to know a thing until it's all over one way or the other. He wants to be free to concentrate on your book." She says this last with a bit more emphasis than I consider within the bounds of tactful behavior. "He doesn't want to see you or talk to you before you go." Her tone verges on command.

I laugh. "He's handling this a lot more maturely than you are."

She laughs too. "Don't rub it in." She gets up to leave, ineptly trying to organize herself into her coat. I can't restrain myself. I go to her and button her up. She falls into me, nearly knocking me off balance, one hundred fifty pounds of dead-weighted dejection. I hold her against my shoulder until it falls asleep. "Robert," she moans, "you have to let me know what's going on! You have to promise you'll let me know. Do you promise?"

She is shivering. I have never seen her helpless before; it derails me. I promise to report to her daily. I feel a shade guilty that I am happier than at any time since I joined the army.

January 29

Dear Tina,

The Hotel Van Dam in Saratoga Springs will be my headquarters for the foreseeable future. Address and phone listed on letterhead above.

On the flight from Washington to Albany I read over my 1964 reports to Rags re: the notebook. Nothing helpful. Did you know I had to drug your father to get the notebook back? I don't know why I tell you this.

I also brought along my diaries from that period—did you know I keep a diary?—and in it I have recorded a conversation between Rags and your father which I transcribe verbatim:

Plante: "Remember Tessie Toga?"
Kaufman: "I sure do."
Plante: "Tessie Toga, the girl of our dreams."
Kaufman: "That's right."
Plante: "That's right. You don't miss Tessie? I sometimes miss Tessie."
Kaufman: "Tessie's dead."
Plante: "Is she? Poor Tessie. No, Tessie Toga will never die. And her faithful Indian companion? You don't miss him? Now what was his name again?"
Kaufman: "Damned if I know."
Plante: "That's not right. Damned-If-I-Know is no name for an Indian. Poor Tessie. We used her when we needed her and now disparage her memory. It's hardly fair."

Question for Rags: Who is Tessie Toga and what is the meaning of the above exchange? Ask Rags to note particularly the reference to a faithful Indian companion. Big Chief Little Shit? I want to know anything he can tell me about it. It would be easiest if I called and asked him myself but I have agreed not to speak to him until this job is done. I have also agreed not to speak to your father. Before I have imposed on me a new directive that I cannot speak to you, I will get all I can out of you as my go-between.

My only good news for you thus far is that Saratoga is a lot colder and nastier than Washington. Air, clear and needle-sharp. Snow, high as an elephant's eye. That exhausts my descriptive powers. Picture postcards follow.

January 30

Dear Tina,

A day of reconnoitering. It turns out I am in Andy Hardy's America, not completely dissimilar to the Los Angeles of my youth, except less ostentatious—at least in the winter; in the summer there is the racing season. By January the temperament of this place is, according to my eyes, at low ebb. Not only snow but unemployment is as high as an elephant's eye.

It does not seem very cold today, although the Albany airport radio station reports the temperature to be down in the 20s. Still it is a dry, practically balmy 20, except for the snow in the streets and the lack of joy in the air. The scene reminds me of towns in wartime that I have read about or seen in movies which are drained of their vitality because all the young men have gone off to fight. Except the young men are still here; it's the horses that have gone off.

The only air of excitement—and this is not to be overlooked—are the Skidmore girls. They are everywhere, tall, attractive, open-faced and full of good, clean, unexotic sexual energy; the only entertainment in town.

Now that I'm here my mission appears idiotic. Maybe all I am is homesick.

January 31

Dear Tina,

Picked up and bought beers for a couple of Skidmore girls. They have not heard of Rags; one of them had heard of me, however. Her father says I am a traitor, but she is more open-minded about it; she thinks I am only betraying my country because I am a confused idealist. Both girls asked for my autograph.

I took a cab this morning out to the edge of town to the baths. They are open all year round but apparently no one but me and a half dozen sick, old men care enough to go. Neither of the bath attendants had heard of Rags or me.

I would like to hear from you but am embarrassed to call when there is nothing to report. Nothing, however, stops you from calling me, especially since I am anxious for information on Tessie Toga. I bet it is the key to the entire mystery and as soon as I hear from you re: it I will get rolling and solve this here now case.

The nighttime television schedule up here stinks.

February 1

Dear Tina,

Out of Rags' entire list of names I was able to find only one in the Saratoga Springs telephone directory. His name is Walter Muldaur; he is by trade a pharmacist and owns a drugstore on Broadway. I dropped by to see him this morning. I resisted the temptation to resurrect the late Roger Ackroyd's identity for the occasion although it made me feel odd, even uncomfortable, approaching an investigation under my own name. Nevertheless, I braved it through as the traitor, Robert Hollister. Muldaur, not being a Skidmore girl, reacted calmly to the name: he has not heard of Hollister, has possibly not heard of Vietnam and, to a certainty, has not heard of Rags.

"Oscar who?"

"Oscar Plante."

"I went to high school with him?"

"According to Mr. Plante."

"Plante?"

"Oscar Plante. Rags Plante."

"Rags?"

"Oscar 'Rags' Plante."

Muldaur is almost as big as your father but appears hollow from the shoulders down; he looks moldy beyond his years. "He says I went to high school with him?"

"He says you were friends in high school."

"He says that? What's he done, this fellow?"

"He's a writer."

"I thought *you* were a writer."

"I am a writer. I'm writing a biography on Oscar Plante." (Note: my cover story.)

"What's he done? Is he in trouble?"

"No. He's famous. He's a famous writer."

"He's not in trouble?"

"He lives in Washington."

"I don't want any trouble with Washington. Are you from the government?"

"No. He only does his writing in Washington. He wrote a book and he wrote a movie and he wrote a sports column. Now he writes a column in Washington for the *Washington Post*. He used to be on Johnny Carson."

"Well, what am I supposed to do about it?"

Following the above digest of our interview (which I have livened up for your benefit) I convinced Muldaur to meet me for lunch at an establishment of his own choosing, my treat. The establishment he chooses is called the Executive Restaurant, though mine is the only suit in the house. The rest of the clientele look like professional bowlers. Over chicken salad sandwiches we go at it again from scratch, making no headway whatever until, in desperation, I mention your father's name. Muldaur comes alive, his face and posture lose fifteen years and, before he can be contained, is reviewing his entire senior year at Saratoga High, after World War II the best time in his life. And who, according to Muldaur, made it all memorable? None other than that "prince of a fellow," your father, "Big O." I swear to you he goes on for forty-five minutes about that "big brute," "the first Jewish saint," to whom he would "happily give his right arm" because not only was he "the greatest all 'round athlete in the history of Saratoga High" (forty-year-old facts and figures are at Muldaur's fingertips), but, what's more, he was decent, he was regular, just one of the guys, not stuck up like other less regular big shots of the day (Muldaur names names). "That's the man you should be writing about!" I am told by Muldaur, who can't stop pointing a chalk-stained pharmaceutical index finger at me. I am then told what to write: about the time O . . . or that other time when O . . . or, even better, when this girl who . . . or, wait a minute, the big game with . . . Tears, actual tears, glitter in Muldaur's eyes. He is having such

262

a wonderful time I wonder if I shouldn't let him pay for the lunch.

Determined not to leave lunch without some useful information I hurry Muldaur through Rags' list of names, asking him to check off the familiar ones. He knows nearly all of them, quite a few in grisly detail: war dead, death by drowning, death by automobile and airplane, death on skis, death by stroke, cancer, hunting accident, death by suicide, plus two surviving suicides, plus a half dozen alcoholics. The rest still exist so far as he knows but none within reasonable reach: Hawaii, Japan. The closest is California. A lull suffused in depression follows; Muldaur suddenly wants to get back to the store. Before I allow it I badger him into supplying me with a list of your father's friends from high school; almost an entirely different list made up of names Muldaur refers to as "the old gang." Two are located locally: one in Saratoga, another in Glens Falls, a half hour's drive from here.

I try "Tessie Toga," "Opposites" and "Big Chief Little Shit" on Muldaur. As expected, no response.

February 2

Dear Tina,

Wasted an entire morning trying to convince the bureaucracy at Saratoga High that I did not mean to compromise the integrity of their records by my request to go through back issues of the school paper. I name dropped that noted graduate, Oscar Plante, and that other noted graduate, Otis Kaufman. They informed me—and by they I mean faculty advisors, guidance officers, assistant principals, you name it—that mine was a virtually unprecedented request which they could not accede to lightly and if I put the matter in writing they would take it under advisement.

It was easier to steal classified documents from the army.

As consolation, they allowed me freedom of the library where I unearthed Rags' yearbook, starring your father. Action photographs everywhere: baseball, football, basketball, track. Underneath his class photo is a list of clubs and credits that is so Joe High School it makes you want to punch him in the nose. Rags' class picture is lonely by comparison, the single notation being that he was on the staff of the school paper, *The Oratoga*. He is very skinny in the photograph and wears his hair well greased and parted in the middle like George Raft.

I tried calling the two local names Muldaur supplied me, but so far no luck.

February 3

Dear Tina,

It was good to hear your voice last night and I apologize for being drunk. If I had known you were going to call I would not have been drunk. Though it is four in the afternoon and I am cold sober I do not know even now what you object to in the tone of my letters. The tone represents the way I feel when I write the letters; if you want me to affect a tone that is false to the way I feel I suppose I could do that, but I thought we were good enough friends to not have to bother with that horseshit. After all, you are the one who likes to be direct and open.

If my tone sounds too flippant to you, then that is tough shit: flippancy happens to be an integral part of my personal style just as irony is an integral part of Rags' personal style. You take Rags seriously when he is ironic, and I expect equal treatment for my flippancy. Heavy-handedness does not always indicate seriousness.

Which reminds me: at times, my girl, you can be heavy-handed. Yes, you too can miss the point. I am not confining my activities up here to picking up Skidmore girls and proving how famous I am. I am not and never have been competitive with Rags. (O.K., that's a lie, but not anymore I'm not.) I admire and am grateful to him; I admire and am grateful to you. It pisses me off when you misread my motives.

The reason I am having a hard time getting on with this case is because I am a slow starter. I have always been a slow starter.

264

It does not mean I am uninterested or unserious or frivolous or sadistic.

If you don't want me to tell you things about your father, I won't, but I don't approve of the restriction because it has not been our habit (certainly not my habit) to keep things from each other. Either we are friends and trust each other or fuck it! I am sick and tired of your putting me down! Especially when you have been no help at all in this entire affair.

I do not accept Rags' statement that he does not know what I am talking about in regard to Tessie Toga and that I must have been drunk at the time and misheard what he said. I know what I heard and he did not say "a depressing joker" or "a blessed ogre" or "a mess of yogurt" or any of the other suggestions he suggests I might have heard him say. (How come when Rags is flippant you don't put him down for it?) Rags was no less drunk and no less blacked out than I when he said Tessie Toga. The difference is that I happened to be the one taking notes.

What becomes increasingly clear is that neither one of you has any intention of helping me.

I have other news but the hell with you, you don't deserve to hear it.

Yours truly,
Frivolous

February 4

Dear Tina,

I have decided to continue. All I ask is one small favor: Do not communicate with me again. Just leave me alone to do my job as I see my job. If you don't like my letters don't open them, burn them. (I keep carbons.) They are not for you anyhow. They are for me. They clear my head; help me think straight. So much for your accusations of posturing.

Two days ago I visited the local paper in town, *The Sara-*

togian, where Rags claims to have worked as a reporter. No one can remember Rags anymore than Rags can remember Tessie Toga.

However, it is not my habit to let other people's memories slip by as fact, unchecked. I spent the entire morning in the files going through back copies. And came upon fifty-eight sports stories in the fall and winter of 1940–41 written by Oscar C. Plante. No doubt there are a number of other stories not by-lined. The stories are all straightforward, eager-beaver reporting, no hint of Rags' present style, in other words, unmemorable; but it is still a bit surprising that no one recalls him working here.

Of course Rags was just out of high school in '40; your father had already gone on to college (an athletic scholarship to the University of Michigan, lead sports page story in *The Saratogian,* May 15, 1939, accompanied by a three-column photograph).

Tried again to make contact with the two names given me by Muldaur, the dour druggist. One of them, Mrs. Carrie McWhinnie, of Saratoga Springs, alternates between being busy on the phone or not answering. Mrs. McWhinnie was a cheerleader forty years ago. Dr. Robert Poole, Muldaur's other name, was a quarterback. I give up on the cheerleader but finally nail the quarterback.

"Are you *the* Robert Hollister?" Dr. Quarterback asks on the phone.

I admit it. "I'm doing research on a biography of Oscar Plante."

"*The* Oscar Plante?"

I admit it. "I'm here in Saratoga researching his high school years. That's why I want to talk to you."

A delicate pause. "Well, who referred you to me?"

I tell him.

"Walter Muldaur? But I went to high school with Walter Muldaur. I don't understand what this is all about but I can see you at eighty-thirty tomorrow morning."

Doesn't he remember Rags either?

Dear Tina,

Woke up to find three inches of snow on the ground. Still coming down. Nevertheless, rented a Hertz and drove in blind lunges toward Glens Falls, which the Hertz car rental lady told me I couldn't miss but I did. It is a depressing, sprawling Edward Hopper of a town; the snow doing little to bring joy, inspire youth or all those other things that snow is alleged to do. Saratoga's snow is more cheery.

Dr. Poole is in his office at eight-thirty, as promised, with his lawyer, who was not promised. Poole is short, thick-set and full of energy and, despite the presence of legal counsel, a man of apparent warmth and good will. Perhaps to make up for the formality of the lawyer he is in shirt sleeves. The lawyer, whose name is Sturdivant, is in a three-piece gray suit, as elegantly turned out as Rags. A scary face, smooth as glass on the surface, tensed, shivering muscles beneath, reminiscent of the facial characteristics of certain psychopaths I did business with in CID.

"I find this situation a little uncomfortable," Poole begins. "You don't look very dangerous—" He chuckles self-consciously. Sturdivant frowns. Poole examines me with twinkling eyes and an uncertain smile. All this non-verbal give and take takes place on back-breaking, squeaky leather chairs in Poole's private office, the doctor having had the good grace to remove his squeaky chair from behind his desk so that he is out in front with Sturdivant and me, the three of us positioned as equals.

"You needn't be embarrassed, Dr. Poole. I'm not. I know my reputation. I know what the government says about me. I know it's an act of courage on your part to see me."

Poole shakes his head vigorously. "I was one of the earliest anti-war activists in the Glens Falls area. It wasn't a popular position, you better believe it." He bends his barrel chest forward and places a heavy and hairy hand on my knee. I resist bolting, telling myself that this is not a homosexual pass but an example of bedside manner. "I think what you did took an enormous amount of courage. All I want to make clear is that I am fighting the war in my own way."

"Dr. Poole, it should be made clear, works within the definable legal parameters of dissent," intones Sturdivant.

"Doctor, I am not here to fight the Vietnam war."

A final squeeze and Poole releases my knee.

"I don't at all compare the scope of my activities to yours," he says.

"Why are you here?" harumphs Sturdivant.

Poole slaps the question aside with a short, openhanded chop. "Mr. Sturdivant is a friend of many years and an attorney of considerable standing in the community. He is also one of our leading hawks." Poole grins awkwardly at Sturdivant, who does not smile back. "We long ago agreed to disagree. I have asked him here in an advisory capacity that works against his own political interest. Whatever reason you're here, people are going to find out about it. If I had interviewed you alone or had invited a fellow dove, it would have been no sweat to link my name and the peace movement we laboriously built up to a position of respect in this community to your activities."

"No one wants that," I say.

"Forgive my bluntness. I would be discredited. My usefulness—if I am useful—would be at an end. So you see Mr. Sturdivant is here to protect what I consider to be our common goal. Neither of us has any illusions about the time we live in."

"I wish to take exception to that remark; I am not bound by its assumptions," admonishes Sturdivant.

I sense myself sinking into a sea of quasi-legal sludge. "Look, can I tell you why I'm here?"

"I think we've said enough, Charley. Dammit, let the man speak!" Poole growls at Sturdivant.

Sturdivant twitches his face muscles and sits back in his chair. It creaks.

I creak forward. "I have another career besides traitor to my country."

"Your interpretation, not ours," objects Sturdivant, who is

overruled by Poole: "He's joking, Charley." Sturdivant creaks back in his chair, his face muscles jangling.

"Before I went into the army I was a private investigator. It's in that capacity, more or less, that I've come to see you. Oscar Plante, who as you may know I have some connection with—"

Both Poole and Sturdivant nod.

"I'm a great admirer," says Poole. Sturdivant twitches.

"Oscar Plante is working on his autobiography. He has one serious limitation. He is gifted with a near total lack of recall. I have offered to use my investigative talents on his behalf as a friend, not a client—I am not being paid—"

"Dr. Poole cannot associate himself with your client; his case is before a federal grand jury."

"He said he wasn't a client," Poole admonishes Sturdivant.

"The term of that grand jury has ended," I add.

"Has it indeed?" Sturdivant inserts into the record.

"You don't have to take my word for it."

"Your word is good enough, don't let Charley get your goat."

Sturdivant clears his throat in objection.

"Look, all I'm here for is to ask your recollections, if any, of Oscar Plante in high school. That's all I want to know. Nothing else."

"What would I know about Oscar Plante in high school?"

"Saratoga High, class of 1939."

"Oscar Plante?" Poole turns to Sturdivant for counsel.

"How about the name Otis Kaufman?"

"What is this?" snaps Sturdivant. "First you say you're investigating Plante and now this new name!"

Poole rubs his hairy hands together, a gesture reminiscent of Kaufman. "Otis Kaufman was my best friend in high school. We were on the football team together."

"Not another word!" advises Sturdivant.

"Plante and Kaufman were close friends in high school," I interject.

"Oscar Plante?"

"I don't like this, Bob," snaps Sturdivant to Poole. Poole ignores him. Sturdivant twitches. "I knew all of O's friends. I would have known—you mean *the* Oscar Plante?"

"He was called Rags. He still is."

"Rags?" repeats Poole.

"I think this has gone far enough," objects Sturdivant.

"I really don't know what you're getting at," sustains Poole.

"If you are trying to link the names of your client and Dr. Poole in any activities let me warn you—"

"You don't mean the Rat," mumbles Poole reflectively.

"Right now I don't know what I mean. Who's the Rat?"

"That can't be him, can it? No, it's impossible. The Rat?" Poole looks to me for the answer, and not finding it looks to Sturdivant, who, thank God, withholds his objection. "We can't be talking about the same—he was a little creep, a hanger-on. I think maybe he did some reporting for *The Oratoga*."

"The school paper?"

"He was a little suck. A nobody. If that was Plante, he's come a long way. Is it possible? Well, if that's who we're talking about, I can't help you. He just hung around. Sort of O's mascot. Sometimes we sent him on errands. You know, to buy Cokes or beer." Poole grins maliciously. "Fools' errands just to get rid of him. He says he was O's best friend? That's a load of— Talk about credibility! I'm certainly going to have to read that autobiography!"

"You say he and Kaufman weren't friends?"

"If you want to know about O, I can tell you all about O. Christ, O was—"

Sturdivant cuts him off. "You're very clever, Mr. Hollister, but I can't allow this to continue. Of course we both know it's this man Kaufman you're interested in."

"I don't give a damn about Kaufman!"

"Come now, I may be a small town lawyer but I'm not a child. I will give you an E for effort, however." Sturdivant grins nastily.

"I have not the slightest interest in Kaufman!"

270

"Why can't I tell him about Kaufman?" Poole, now bursting to talk, asks of Sturdivant.

"I don't want to hear about Kaufman!" I protest for the nth time.

"I fear Tom Sawyer is just a little too eager to whitewash Aunt Polly's picket fence," smirks Sturdivant.

"Does the name Tessie Toga mean anything to you?"

"What the hell ever became of O?" Poole asks me, his face suddenly boyish, back in high school.

I am determined not to talk about Kaufman. "Tessie Toga," I repeat.

Sturdivant is on his feet, outraged. "First it's only Plante, then it's this man Kaufman, now it's Tessie Toga!"

"He was the greatest," Poole says quietly to himself, a small smile on his face.

Sturdivant stands over Poole. "If you insist on falling into this man's trap, I refuse to continue to be a party to it."

"Tessie Toga?" Poole at last responds. "Yes, it's familiar. Tessie Toga. Sorry. No, I can't place it."

Sturdivant stomps out of the office.

"Thank you, Charley!" Poole calls after him distractedly. "Tessie Toga, no, doesn't mean a thing."

"O.K., Big Chief Little Shit?"

"Big Chief Little Shit. Big Chief Little Shit? No, I can't say—Big Chief Little Shit." Poole leans so far back in his chair I am afraid he will topple over. He folds his thick arms behind his thick neck and smiles at the ceiling. He is silent for a long time.

"Big Chief Little Shit," I prompt. No response. I might as well have left with Sturdivant.

I find my retreat from Glens Falls slowed by a snow jam. Cars made by the snow to resemble children's drawings of cars crawl mutely, bumper to bumper, as if in procession through a cemetery. Twenty minutes into the pilgrimage I spot, coming up slowly on my right, the offices of the Glens Falls *Post-*

Star. I have ten minutes and more to wonder why the sight of the newspaper office strikes a chord. I am just about to inch past it when a small charge goes off in my memory bank: Rags used to work here; one of his first jobs; he told me so years ago! By the time I have pulled over to a snowdrift and parked, my memory bank is issuing clarifications and partial denials: it is not altogether sure that Rags worked on this particular newspaper, though it is willing to go on record in asserting that Rags, at one time or another, told me that once in his youth he worked for a newspaper in Glens Falls. But that was thirty or more years ago. Who knows if the paper is still in existence? And what does it have to do with the business at hand? Nothing other than the fact that if I can trace Rags to Glens Falls, if I can find anyone here who remembers him, any source of information whatever—I will even accept more names. . . .

But no! Everyone on the *Post-Star* is over seventy, or so it seems, but not one of them can recall Rags, whose name and reputation they deplore, having ever held a job there.

Back at the Van Dam in Saratoga, thawing out on Scotch and trying once more to break through aging cheerleader Carrie McWhinnie's busy signal, I am suddenly made dopily aware of the panic Dr. Poole and attorney Sturdivant would now be in if they were to know that the moment I left the doctor's office I went directly to the local newspaper.

February 6

Dear Tina,

Carrie McWhinnie, the veteran cheerleader, apparently is not anxious to see me. Called her repeatedly last night and again this morning. The two times I got through I got a man who sounds like he hates telephones and has a bad cold. Mr. McWhinnie, I take it. He is exceedingly polite and exceedingly finicky, asking me each time to spell my name which he spells back to me and give my number which he reads back to me. Because his voice is gravelly and unclear, I want to make sure he gets my name and number right. So we go over the whole thing again. We have now done this twice and I am not looking forward to a third try.

Called the high school. Another runaround. I am beginning to get the idea that they know who I am. It was a lot easier being a detective before I made it as a disloyal American.

Having nothing better to do, I wander the streets of Saratoga. There are some odd and lovely homes at the north end of Broadway; millionaires row: habitat of the racing gentry for August and white elephants for the rest of the year. The houses look like Currier & Ives nestled cheek by jowl with Charles Addams.

February 7

(Written, but not mailed)

Dear Tina,

A desperation midnight call to cheerleader McWhinnie produced results. The lady herself! Sounding distracted and wary. Instantly recognized my name but claimed not to have received word of my previous calls. Couldn't imagine why I wanted an interview with her but was interested in meeting with me in order to persuade me to talk to her political science class. Cheerleader McWhinnie teaches poli sci at Skidmore! At her suggestion: breakfast at seven-thirty this morning to give us plenty of time before her nine-thirty class.

The only thing remotely fiftyish about her are her hands. The backs of her hands are heavily veined, the fingers textured with fine wrinkles. Other than that, I might be eating eggs with a woman no older than you. To my inexperienced eye in this sort of thing, she has not had a face-lift and does nothing at all to enhance her beauty (if it is beauty; on first acquaintance it is hard to judge: it may simply be presence but, whatever it is that she has, one has to fight not to be intimidated by it). There is not a wrinkle on her face—a very expressive face, though masked. She is wearing a teacherly tweed pantsuit, the one unacademic note being a ruffly, white silk blouse worn within an inch of a plunging neckline.

"I better warn you I'm very ill at ease." She speaks with a controlled but amused drawl, in a voice that quietly resonates with self-assurance.

"Why is that?"

"I don't often meet celebrities. The ones I have met have usually disappointed me. They are often not very nice people."

"I'm a lot nicer than J. Edgar Hoover," I say, as our eggs arrive.

She laughs. I spot laugh lines around the mouth; first signs of age. "Are you nicer than Joseph Alsop?"

"I don't know him."

"He's my husband's hero," she says in a way that suggests that she and her husband do not share the same heroes.

"I'm sure it's a toss-up which of us is nicer."

"Are you nicer than Oscar Plante?"

"I doubt it."

"What's he like?"

"I have a feeling he's changed a lot since you knew him."

"Since *I* knew him? When did I know him?"

(Here we go again.) "I was under the impression he knew you in high school."

"Everyone knew me in high school. I was captain of the cheerleading squad."

"Plante was on the school paper."

"He was? I don't remember him."

"He covered sports."

"Well, then we must have known each other. But I don't remember him."

"He was called Rags."

"No." She looks away; I get the impression I am boring her.

"How about the Rat?"

She frowns; I spot wrinkles on her forehead. "That doesn't sound very inviting."

"You never heard of the Rat?"

"No, I missed the Rat. I knew quite a few rats but not *the* Rat."

"You remember Otis Kaufman of course."

"Why 'of course'?"

"Everyone remembers Otis Kaufman."

She smiles at that. "Do they?" I spot crow's-feet.

By the end of breakfast, despite all sorts of questions asked in all manner of ways, I feel like a teenaged kid who has struck out on a date. But I can't be a complete failure because she asks me to cocktails at five. I accept, though more than a little cynical about the invitation; I can't believe it would have come if she didn't want me for her political science class.

Spend the afternoon combing my diary for the entry in which Rags talks about his days as a young reporter in Glens Falls. I finally locate it in Saigon. Rags, Colonel Trowbridge and I at the Cercle Sportif. The name of the paper was *The Glens Falls Orator,* the name of Rags' gossip column was "The Opinionated Orator." I call Glens Falls Information. They have nothing listed for *The Orator.* I call the *Post-Star.* They are less receptive than yesterday (have they too discovered my identity?); they firmly and succinctly let me know that no newspaper exists now or ever named *The Glens Falls Orator* and that no gossip column on any newspaper exists now or ever named "The Opinionated Orator."

I accept their assurances about the paper but am unconvinced about the column. I am at the point where I am not willing to accept as definitive anybody's memory about anything.

5:15: The McWhinnies'. A rambling two-story turn of the century white brick and wood front house on Fifth Avenue, one of the fashionable streets in town. Gabled roofs flare off at different angles like a cubist painting. A chimney puffs smoke. The snow is banked in clean, unsoiled borders on both sides of the white-columned porch as if it's been trimmed by garden shears. One hard look and I begin to feel a nostalgia for a past not my own.

I can't help but scrutinize Mrs. McWhinnie for signs of age the moment she opens the door. She is now in a ski-type turtleneck sweater, so I am unable to spot the stretch lines on her neck that I forgot to look for this morning at breakfast. As I follow her into the living room to meet her husband, I study her ass. It is tight, well-formed, appealing in white bell-bottoms. From the rear, she could pass for eighteen.

McWhinnie could pass for seventy. I am distressed by his appearance. Their situation strikes me as a marital version of Dorian Gray: he does the aging for both of them. He is big, well over six feet tall and broad in the shoulders, but stands with a stoop and walks with a shuffle. He comes at me like some great ship docking, his huge slippered feet making loud hissing noises on the carpet—I am afraid he is not going to be able to stop himself in time and will bowl us both over. "This is a great pleasure," he says, after introductions, but instead of hoving to and shaking hands he slides right past me to an antique end table two feet away. He takes a bulging briefcase off the table, turns and circles around me through an arched doorway, giving Mrs. McWhinnie all the time in the world to ask me what I am drinking. By the time I answer, McWhinnie shuffles back—this time, I think, to shake hands—but no. He says, "One more moment, if you please," and chugs off to the piano at the far end of the room. On the piano are a stack of notebooks. He bundles the notebooks under one arm and shuffles on past me, smiling brightly but without humor. He had to have been terribly handsome once; he still is but in the manner of a patriarch: a mane of white hair and a face so fragmented with tiny lines it looks like a jigsaw puzzle about to decompose.

Mrs. McWhinnie hands me my Scotch as McWhinnie reappears empty-handed and heads, this time, off to my left to a glass coffee table on which lie an assortment of typed papers. "One last moment, sir, and you will have my undivided attention." He clutches the papers to his chest and slides on out. Mrs. McWhinnie brings two more drinks over and sets them on the coffee table. Her silence contains tension. She motions me formally to a seat on an old-fashioned, tufted couch, which I take just as Steamboat Willie starts coming 'round the bend again. "Now then," he says, and lowers himself with extreme caution into a rocking chair directly across from me. His eyes focus on me claustrophobically; they are a brittle, cold Kennedyesque blue. "Now that the classified papers are locked away, we can have our chat. No need to tempt the fates."

I realize slowly and stupidly that I have just been the victim of an elaborate insult. I stare at Mrs. McWhinnie, who will not meet my eyes.

"If you will spare me a moment to answer a question that by now must be repetitious and boring: What is it like?" His voice is grainy and indistinct and takes a little tuning into. "Before the fact, I mean. What are the steps? How does one arrive at a state of mind that makes criminal acts heroic and unethical acts selfless and high-minded?"

"Philip, Mr. Hollister didn't come all this way to plead his case with you. Now come on, be good. Knock it off."

"I see. I see," McWhinnie says meekly. "I assumed he had come to educate and enlighten." He turns his icy, bright eyes on his wife. "Then *you* must enlighten me. Mine is but a poor, benighted eighteenth century mind hopelessly trapped in the age of reason and not conversant with the more metaphysical moral climate of urban guerrilla warfare."

All of this obviously means something to her because she reddens. All I get out of it is that he is also a teacher. Also political science? At Skidmore? Is that how they met? Great-looking student falls for great-looking teacher? Mrs. McWhinnie sits straight and rigid and sips at her drink as if it's a hate potion. "I can tell you another reason he didn't come here, Philip; he didn't come here to be drawn into an intra-family row over politics."

McWhinnie slips his rocking chair six inches closer to me. "Well, now you've got my curiosity good and worked up. He is not here to plead his case and he is not here to plead your case. What is he here for? Does he suppose I am in possession of classified documents? Is he reduced to raiding the meager files of the political science department of Skidmore?" He rises out of his chair slowly, evidently in some pain. He hoists his hands in the air over his head, one of them holding a martini glass. "If so, let us get on with it. You may search me, sir."

Mrs. McWhinnie is also out of her chair. "Philip!" she barks.

McWhinnie ignores her. "I insist you search me, Mr. Hollister. I want to prove to you that I am hiding nothing. Then when I have proved it to your satisfaction, you may prove to mine that you are hiding nothing. No less than a fair shake, don't you agree?" He hovers over me, the martini glass trembling in his large, freckled hand. "You have my permission to search me, but I ask as a favor, do not trash me. I have done a little research on trashing and I understand that it is as moral and revolutionary an act as stealing documents or burning down universities. But I ask, if only because you are a guest in this house, that you make an exception in my case." His martini glass trembles violently. I notice wet spots on my lap. All that is on my mind as I stare up at this overwrought, geriatric wit is: Is he going to keel over and die on me?

"Oh my God, the time!" cries Mrs. McWhinnie. "I'm late for my Molotov Cocktail class. Can I drop you, Mr. Hollister?"

I deposit my untasted but terribly needed Scotch on the coffee table and slide off the couch to the right; it is the only way I can get to my feet without knocking over McWhinnie.

"I've driven you off," he says in mock sadness. "I am always driving Carrie's friends off." Mrs. McWhinnie gives me a forceful little shove toward the hall; good thing too since his seething by-play has frozen me in place. McWhinnie calls to us at the door. "When you return you must bring your Moscow gold. I have always wanted a look at Moscow gold. Do they spray it red?" His hands are still in the air as Mrs. McWhinnie shuts the door, parting us.

The bar she has picked for us to go to is less than a mile away but she nearly kills us getting there. "I'm inviting you to have dinner with me," she says in a shaky voice as we order drinks. "I think I am about to do a lot of drinking so I am going to need food. I'm hoping you'll join me."

I join her. It is nothing but chitchat during our first martini. Her poise is remarkable, no scars of combat. I look for wear and tear, spot a few gray hairs among the black; that is all. I wonder how old she actually is.

"He's not really a troglodyte," she says halfway through our second martini. "He does that to—well, he likes to use the Socratic method. I have a lot of peace people out to the house and—well, he's more sinned against than sinning. What the hell am I apologizing for?"

I can't believe she's much over thirty.

"This war," she says—and nothing further for a long time. "At times I really hate the peace movement."

"Hawks and doves. Opposites attract."

She tries to smile. "You seem like a nice kid. Are you married?"

I say no.

"Do you have a girl?"

I say no.

"How old are you?"

I resist the strong temptation to add ten years to my age.

"God, you're just a baby, aren't you? And what you've been through! I bet you've done more in your thirty-one years than Philip and I have done in our lifetimes." Her body has the suppleness and fluidity of a teenager. I can't believe she's much over forty.

"I can't believe marriages go wrong just because of Vietnam," I say.

"You're lucky to think so."

"It sounds screwy to me. I had a girl once who claimed her marriage broke up because she hung her husband's picture of the Brooklyn Dodgers in his bathroom."

To cheer her up, I start telling her some of my private detective stories. Before very long, I have her laughing into her fourth and fifth martinis. It is disturbing to be in her company, to be that sexually aware of a woman who must be— how old must she be? At least ten or fifteen years my senior. Or twenty? Twenty-five?

Perhaps out of guilt to Rags—he has been the unnamed butt of my stories—I start telling her about him. I tell her about his life in Washington. "You should meet him." I tell her about Rags and Trowbridge in Saigon. "You should meet him." I tell her about his years in New York. I am about to say "You should meet him" for the fifth, sixth, or dozenth time when it dawns on my befogged, booze-addled brain that she went to high school with him. "I find it astounding that no one here remembers a great guy like Rags, but a nobody like Kaufman is—"

She glares at me. "Don't talk about what you don't know about."

"I forgot. You're a cheerleader."

"You're all alike," she snarls. I can tell by how drunk she is how drunk I almost am.

"I am not all alike," I say.

"No, absolutely correct, I apologize. But I don't like you when you're stupid. Please don't be stupid."

We are at a conversational impasse. Neither of us says a word for a long time. The gulf that has opened between us yawns wider, so wide that in my alcoholic state it takes on close to realistic dimensions: I see her growing paler and fuzzier before my eyes. To bring her back into outline, I ask, "Does Tessie Toga mean anything to you?"

"No," she says after a long time. "Is it a new song?"

"How about Big Chief Little Shit?"

"How about— You don't— What are you trying to do? Humor me?" She looks on the point of crying. Not being able to think of anything better to do, I order two more drinks. I know I would be doing much better with her if I could forget about her age. She can't be over fifty.

"He must have been a late developer," she says.

"Who?" I ask.

"Your boyfriend."

I see red. She sees I see red. "Well, Jesus Christ," she protests, "the way you talk about him. I mean no wonder I don't remember him. I didn't know any pansies."

The accumulated martinis allow for an outbreak of fanta-sized violence. I civilize it by saying: "The simple fact of the matter is Rags the Rat is a success and famous and popular and people come from all over the world to see him and Kaufman is fund raising for the Jews in New York."

Her face breaks into ugly blotches. "On top of being stupid, you're anti-Semitic."

A surge of joy that I've gotten a rise out of her. I hold on to the advantage by saying calmly, "I feel sorry for you."

By now her face has turned the color of strawberries. "He wasn't supposed to make it in the first place and he did! And now he didn't. So I hope you're finally satisfied," she says in tones of moral outrage so out of keeping with the topic under discussion that I have to resist laughing. "They wanted him to run for senior class president! That's how popular he was! Jewish kids weren't supposed to make it on his level in those days. Don't you know anything?" She looks near tears, and I am pleased. "For me it was easy, the line of least resistance. Nobody knew I was laughing at them because it was so stupid, what I could get people to do for me. But he made it look easy, but it wasn't easy for him. We were such phonies! 'The royal couple' they called us. Everybody envied us. 'The royal couple.' " She scrounges around in her bag for a tissue and blows her nose. When she finishes blowing it, the tip of her nose is bone white while the rest of her face is blotched red. "Boy, that sure went down well with his parents. And I thought they liked me. Well, you don't want to hear this. You're a supercilious prick and I bore the pants off you and my husband probably has got the right idea about you in the first place."

Thank God the steaks come.

We eat numbly, each bite sobering us a bit more and widening the breach between us. Our state of hostility has about it a sense of déjà vu; gone before I can place it.

"And I won't listen to a word against Esther," she says out of nowhere. Uncanny!

"Don't tell me you know Esther?" I say.

"Don't tell me you know Esther," she says.

"She's the scariest woman I've ever known!"

"It's another Esther," she says. "Esther Weill."

"I meant Esther Kaufman."

"That's right! That's her name. I introduced them!" She smiles gratingly at me. Smiling, she looks her age. "She was my best friend. If I couldn't have him—" Her face, ossified in a smile, wrinkles and thickens like grooves in a sheet of corrugated board. I know it's the booze I've drunk but I am no less horrified. For another hour we engage in intense conversation and I don't hear a word: My mind is off somewhere negotiating with her age.

The next thing I hear her say is: "I'd better make a note of this or I'll forget it tomorrow. You sure Tuesday's all right?"

"Right," I say noncommittally, not having the slightest idea of what she is talking about. I read her note pad upside down: "Hollister Lecture. Poli Sci Tue. 10:30."

"I can't tell you how much they'll appreciate this," she says warmly.

We seem to have become friends again while my head was out of the room. I fix that by squabbling with her over the check. By the time we finish we might as well be on different sides of the moon.

She insists on driving, so I insist on riding in the back seat. Probably to get my goat, she drives beautifully despite the fact that half the time she spies on me in the rearview mirror.

"Why do you keep looking behind us?" she asks, irritatingly. "Are you afraid my husband is following us?"

We glare at each other's reflections in the rearview mirror. There is no question in my mind that we are short steps away from heartily disliking each other.

February 8

Wakened at eight by Carrie McWhinnie. "I'm just leaving the house and you'll never guess!"

My head resonates with hangover and this woman sounds as if I drank alone last night.

"I couldn't sleep after I got home. God, were you as drunk as I was? So I thought I might as well get to the attic before I sobered up and thought better of it. And my memory was absolutely dead right! I found a whole stack of them!"

What in the world is she talking about?

"A lot of them after O and your friend Plante had graduated—I was two years behind them—but some from 1938 and 1939. What do you think of that for results?"

"I can't believe it!" I say too loud, in hope that an energy level rivaling her own will get her off the phone.

"I'll drop them off at the hotel on my way to school, but remember, these are precious mementoes to me; I want them back."

"You have my word."

"I'll leave them at the desk."

I go back to sleep, not even vaguely curious to find out what this obnoxious woman is talking about.

I pick up *The Saratogian* to read at my twelve o'clock breakfast and it reminds me of my thwarted search for Plante's high school newspapers. I have been up here for ten days and cannot find anyone who remembers Plante and cannot dig up a lousy copy of the newspaper he worked on in high school. My ineptitude is enraging. I skip coffee, leave the hotel dining room and walk in a rage of self-loathing down Broadway to Muldaur's pharmacy. I wait with throbbing head and growing impatience while he makes a perfume sale to a Skidmore girl. When I finally have him alone he makes it clear that he is not happy to see me. He has learned who I am and he wants me to know that he is a loyal American, a patriot, a veteran of World War II, a Bronze Star recipient for action in the Italian theater, and that he would prefer that I get out of his store. Under the circumstances, I find it impossible to ask him if he has any copies of his old high school newspaper lying around.

I make a decision to find reasons to stop despising myself and go back to my room to call Dr. Poole. The doctor is out.

I take a nap, wake up and discover, despicably, that I am despising myself again. I call Dr. Poole again, who remains out. I leave word that I called and will call back, and take a second nap. I wake up to find it is five o'clock and that I do not despise myself anymore. I call Dr. Poole and actually get Dr. Poole. He sounds relieved to hear I only want to ask him if he has copies of his old high school newspaper. *He* doesn't but his father once owned a treasure trove of his high school mementoes and he will check with him at the nursing home to see if he has maintained any of his collection.

Early dinner without drinks followed by a movie in the only movie house in town. *The Sound of Music.* I doze through most of it and walk back to the hotel totally paranoid and again despising myself: I am sure I am being followed. At the desk the night clerk, who has a bad complexion and looks like he knows I am *the* Robert Hollister, hands me a message from Dr. Poole. He says the papers I want are in the possession of Mr. Oliver Poole, who is expecting me at ten tomorrow morning at the Margaret Faye Nursing Home in Glens Falls.

On my way up in the elevator rereading the note, I am reminded suddenly of Carrie McWhinnie's package. She called me this morning! She was going to drop off a package. The elevator shudders to a halt on three, my floor. I push the lobby button.

The night clerk knows nothing about a package. There is no package in my slot. If there was a package it was picked up earlier when the day clerk was on. On my way back up in the elevator, I try to remember if Mrs. McWhinnie said what was in the package. All I can remember her telling me is that she wanted it returned because it was a precious memento. Why would she be giving me a precious memento? What went on between us while I was drunk last night that she should give me a precious memento?

A wave of nausea overcomes me as I unlock the door to my room. Blacked out again, you son of a bitch! Was it sex? I drop onto the bed, my legs unsteady. I am sure it was not sex. With a sixty-year-old lady?

I go into the bathroom, vomit, brush my teeth and wash my face. My diary lies on the bathroom floor. I run through last night's entry for clues. A lot of games going on; not very proud stuff; a long interlude in which nothing is recorded except idiotic conjecture about her age. I come out of the interlude to discover I have made a date to speak to her political science class on Tuesday. *That's tomorrow morning!*

I rotate back to the bedroom and sit down with my head cradled in my hands. What the hell am I going to say to a political science class? I don't know anything about political science. Anyhow, I'm not prepared! And according to my notes, it's scheduled for ten-thirty. And I have a date with Poole's father at ten to pick up the high school papers.

The high school papers! That's what she called about this morning! That's what we must have talked about in that unrecorded interlude when I was worrying about her age. She was going to look for her copies of the school paper. And, in gratitude, I agreed to talk to her class! And she found them! And I lost them! And I don't want to talk to her goddamned class!

I repress, with considerable effort, a fresh tidal wave of self-loathing. What could have happened to the papers? Yes— I definitely remember now—she said she would drop them off on the way to class this morning. But there are no papers. Did she forget—or not have time to drop them off? But then she would have dropped them off later. Or she would have called and left a message. Unless the woman is totally unreliable.

I play for a while with the possibilities of blaming it all on Carrie McWhinnie. But I can't make it stick. Whatever I may think of her—and I have not the slightest idea what I think of her—unreliability does not strike me as one of her traits. If the woman said she would drop off the papers, no doubt she did.

So they were here. At the desk. And now they are not. Which means what? It means someone picked them up. But who would care a damn about old high school newspapers? Could the explanation be as simple as an ordinary hotel mail thief? He breezes through lobbies, grabs what's in sight? In that case I should go to the police, I can place an ad in *The Saratogian,* I can offer a cash reward. . . .

Someone has been following me! I am sure of it now. I suspected it last night driving back with Mrs. McWhinnie, but she smart-assed me into doubting myself. I was sure of it tonight coming out of the movies but, in my orgy of post-alcoholic despair, dismissed it as paranoia.

No, it was no hotel mail thief. Whoever has been following me took those papers. And I know who. Philip McWhinnie! It has to be McWhinnie. No one tailed me before last night, and last night I met McWhinnie, and last night McWhinnie went into his song and dance about Moscow gold and classified papers. And here is his wife giving me papers! Christ, how he must react to that! "You will not give that traitor your papers," he screams. "These are only old high school papers," she reasons. "Who knows what use that radical pup will make of them!" he screams. And she tells him to fuck off and proceeds to bring me the papers and he proceeds to follow her to the hotel. And steals them. Steals his own wife's papers! This eighteenth century refugee from the age of reason.

February 9

Get a wake-up at seven to give me time to concoct a talk for the political science class. It is one thing to speak from a prepared text to a general audience of several hundred people who, because of the size of the room and the formality of the occasion, tend to cancel out each other. But it is another matter entirely—or so I fear—talking to a small classroom of students who, being on their own turf, will not hesitate to talk back.

And a classroom of rich girls! Why would they give a shit about the war, or corruption in Saigon? In five or ten years they will be going to fancy dinner parties with the very people I depict as war criminals. I am not up to crusading against the war today; I am up to facing down that son of a bitch

McWhinnie; I am up to finally getting my hands on those god-damned high school papers!

I pull an armchair over to the window and stare down on boring Broadway. Two full hours of staring, sipping coffee and not an idea in my head. I have but one thought for a lead-in and that is to ask, "Do you have any questions?" If I did not feel bad about losing Mrs. McWhinnie's papers I would find a way to back out of this.

The phone rings at nine. Carrie McWhinnie. Very cheerful, very up. We make arrangements to meet. She does not mention the papers and neither do I. I call the Margaret Faye Nursing Home in Glens Falls and postpone Dr. Poole's father until four o'clock this afternoon.

There must be more than 150 students waiting for me, a third of them male. Every seat is taken, in some cases two in a seat. Students sit in the aisles, stand shoulder-to-shoulder in the back and on the sides, form a wall against the blackboard behind me, sit in front of the desks at my feet staring curiously, aggressively, impersonally, and to my eyes, inhumanly: a sea of mutants. "You should be very pleased," whispers Mrs. McWhinnie. She wears a yellow cashmere sweater, gray skirt and loafers, looking no older and easily more beautiful than her students. "I've never seen such a turnout!" She begins to reach for my hand to squeeze it but thinks better of it. I think better of her for it. I can't bear the thought of letting her down.

I begin by attacking the illusion that the U.S. is on its way out of Indochina. I quote figures to show how much money and material we continue to pour into South Vietnam, Cambodia and Laos. I go on to describe the official reasons for our commitment. I then describe the corruption that makes hash of those official reasons. Ten minutes into my talk scattered coughing begins. In another five minutes, a noticeable bobbing of heads in the back of the room and rustling of papers in front. A side-glance at Mrs. McWhinnie reveals her smiling defiantly.

"There's a story we used to tell in the CID," I say, using the subject of corruption in Saigon as the context for a short joke about drug smuggling. The laugh comes in a loud whoosh, an enormous release. That one drug joke reminds me of another drug joke. It breaks up the room. That leads me into a money-smuggling joke. It is received with applause. I take time during the ovation to take a second look at Mrs. McWhinnie. Her expression is the one I've seen her wear with her husband. I switch to a lurid account of the interrogation techniques employed by South Vietnamese police on VC suspects under American supervision and guidance. The room quiets; it hums with tension. I hold their interest for another three or four serious minutes before the head bobbing, paper shuffling and coughing begin to build again. I let them have a Saigon hooker joke. I am paid back with a rousing ovation. I go into a story that may or may not be factual about a touring Congressman on the line who shoots a round of artillery into our own troops. Screams of laughter. Several girls seated down front are hugging each other in uncontained hysteria. I tell them sternly that, all kidding aside, lives are still being lost out there. They react with appropriate gravity and low murmurs of assent. I tell a joke about the way ARVN beefs up statistics on enemy body counts. I am awarded with grateful squeals of laughter. I throw open the floor to questions. There is not a single one. Mrs. McWhinnie, looking still beautiful but considerably older, thanks me for my informative, first-hand report. I receive a standing ovation. Anything Bob Hope can do I can do better; I have access to classified jokes he doesn't have.

Mrs. McWhinnie comes up with a lie to cancel our lunch (a relief to both of us), so I am at the Margaret Faye Nursing Home two hours early. It is a one-story, institutional, brick-front ranch house which tries but fails to not look like a hospital. The interior is airport modern, done in Los Angeles pastels. If I were a resident of seventy-five and a stranger to contemporary design I think I'd be afraid I was in a crematorium.

288

Dr. Poole's father, Oliver Poole, meets me in the dayroom, an expansive, sunlit room which is disturbingly reminiscent, because of the green plants on the windows and the crayon drawings on the walls, of first grade. He is a frail, tiny man, years younger in appearance than McWhinnie, an almost unlined baby face which when it isn't looking stupefied is sodden with self-pity. All my time with him I am desperately apprehensive that he's going to play on my emotions and make me take him out of there.

But it doesn't happen; he is too well-behaved for that. He sits in his neat pin-striped suit, gray shirt and tie, his white, polished hands clenched in his lap, his legs nailed together in a familiar pose of polite fear which I tend to think of as the mature man's fetal position.

As I turn the pages of his scrapbook, he watches where my eyes go, wetting his lips nervously. It revises an image of my teenage dating years when the girl's parents often acted as if the purpose of my visit was to judge them. "That's a good page," he says from time to time, or "I love that page," or "That page I used to think was a good one but I don't think so anymore." He has no idea who I am or what I am doing there. He doesn't ask. The only question he asks—and that is at the very beginning—is, "Are you Catholic?" I tell him no. He says, "Most people think this is a Catholic home, but it's not. This is an interdenominational home. I'm not Catholic."

The scrapbook is made up almost entirely of borrowed clippings from *The Oratoga* sports pages reporting on the ups and downs—mostly ups—of the football team called the Blue Streaks. The earliest stories are dated 1937 and are written by someone named Pinky Collins. Beginning in 1938 the by-line changes to Oscar C. Plante. At every mention of Dr. Poole—called Barreling Bobby Poole by Plante—his name is underscored in red ink with an exclamation point next to it in the margin. If not for the underscoring it would be easy to think this was Kaufman's scrapbook. Oscar C. Plante gushes like a schoolgirl: Big O saves lost ball games, intercepts bullet passes, stampedes through the opposition to score touchdowns—all to the hysterical screams of unbelieving fans. The prose style is unadulterated hero worship. Ass-kissing sycophancy. I can't get over it; am lost in another world with another Plante and another Kaufman, brought back to the nursing home only at intervals when Mr. Poole butts in to say, "Don't waste your time on that page," or "That page is a particular favorite of mine."

Also included are clippings of gossip columns from the inside pages of *The Oratoga,* containing a mess of blind and not so blind items about big wheels on campus. Here too Barreling Bobby Poole is underlined and exclaimed over but again takes second place to the affairs of Big O, who's repeatedly seen huddling or scrimmaging or running plays with captivating or curvaceous or constant Carrie Stevenson.

My attention fixes on two interesting aspects of the gossip column. It's title is "Oratoga Oratory." To the right of the title is printed a cartoon of a girl's frizzy head poking out of the top of a wigwam, the wigwam drawn to look like a gown. Each column concludes with the line: " 'Nuff's plenty, *satis verborum,* Tessie Toga."

The ride back is a dream. There's not an iota of my being not operating in a state of overwrought joy. I even have a hard on. I am too excited by my windfall to bother right now with analysis. Reason waits while I gloat over the raw material: "Oratoga Oratory," "The Opinionated Orator," Tessie Toga, Willie Warbler, Kaufman, Carmichael. . . . Rags and his secret codes! God, do I find that man interesting! He invented himself from scratch! Kaufman was a finished product in high school, finished for life after high school (peaked too soon, to use Nixon's phrase), but Rags—that's the wondrous part of it, the psychic embodiment of the American Dream—he didn't merely raise himself by his bootstraps, he materialized himself from nonexistence. Small wonder he haunts my soul! 'Nuff's plenty. *Satis verborum.*

He is so much on my mind, I am so inextricably interwoven with him, that I should not be as startled as I am to learn from the room clerk at the Van Dam that a message waits from Mr.

Plante: He is in town, registered at the Van Dam, Room 327, I am to please stop by when I come in. Can it be for real? I don't have the patience to wait for the elevator; I jog headily upstairs to three. I am at his door before it dawns on me that 327 is next door to 325 and 325 is my room.

"Ah, there you are, I was getting anxious about the time!"

I don't know what I expected—I suppose a different Rags from the one I last saw in Washington, a composite molded out of the mental play dough I was giggling over on my way back from Glens Falls. But it is the same old Rags, the same old diffident friendliness, the same old ironic restraint, the same split down the middle between effeteness and elegance. Here I spend days dragging him, kicking and screaming, from out of the collective amnesia of everyone's past, and he acts as if nothing has changed. "What are you doing here?" I ask, hoping he doesn't notice the sense of personal injury I am unable to keep out of my voice.

"Ruminating," he answers. But he is not ruminating, he is dressing. He glides between the cramped bedroom and bathroom, mirror images of my own quarters next door, knotting his tie and inserting his cuff links with a cool but ceremonial grace appropriate to a magic act. "Saratoga induces in me a tendency to ruminate or drink or both. Help yourself." He shoots a cuff and, in the same motion, indicates with the hand inside it an open fifth of Scotch on the bed table. On the bed table opposite lies a neat stack of newpapers. Other newspapers are spread open across the bed, the only inelegant note in the room. Orderly as the place may be, I have the impression he did not just move in.

"When did you get here?"

"Did you ever stop to consider what a despicable line of work I'm in?" He begins to collect the newspapers off the bed, folding them neatly, stacking them on the table, turning this too into a ceremony. "And how very much I enjoy it?" He pauses and smiles at me contemplatively. In a complete change of tempo, he says, "'I spoke to Tina a few minutes ago. She sends her very special regards." Then, without a hitch, he resumes his ironic tone. "The indecent amount of righteous pleasure I take, the sheer, malicious joy—good lord, Ackroyd, what would we all have done without Vietnam?"

I find it hard to see him; I see multiple images: my own imposed image shimmering over the visible image.

"Do you think we would have gone into Negroes without Vietnam? But it's too late for Negroes: Before your time and before my politics. And Negroes aren't nearly as reasonable victims as the Vietnamese. They're too close; they're right on top of us. No, if there is a Vietnamese equivalent of an Eldridge Cleaver or a LeRoi Jones, he is too far away to seriously humiliate us. The essential rule in arguments over exploitation is that the exploited are not to be allowed to take part in the debate. The traditional practice is for the exploiters to argue the issue amongst themselves; the traditional practice is self-humiliation." Much of this comes from the bathroom as he ceremoniously buffs his black Oxfords with a shoe cloth, resting one foot, then the other, on the closed toilet seat. I can't help wondering what all this has to do with why we're here. I am impatient to cut in but can't find an opening.

"The English were cleverer about these matters. Nothing went well with the English until they moved mass exploitation off their own territory and colonized it, first with Ireland, then points east. The English learned early that if you are going to exploit a people and not be brutalized by it you must do your exploiting away from home."

"And what better place than Southeast Asia where lives are cheap?" I chime in, blending my ironic tone in harmony with his.

"Yes, we are fortunate to have come across Vietnam. I would guess it is the most satisfactory crisis of conscience to engage the liberal community since Hitler's persecution of the Jews."

"Or the Spanish Civil War," I add, but Rags dismisses it.

"Too special."

"The Depression wasn't bad."

"No, despite the fables your mother may have told you of

the Depression, it was a total flop as a crisis of conscience. It didn't alter anyone's conscience except a half dozen Hollywood script writers, and twenty years later they regretted it and turned in their friends."

What are we suddenly doing in Hollywood? How the hell did we get here?

"The Bomb very nearly succeeded as a crisis of conscience but it petered out," Rags says in mock sadness, as he buttons himself into a gray tweed vest.

I peter out. I drop onto the bed and try to analyze why I surrender to Rags' judgment that his discursive conversation takes precedence over my news. On the floor half hidden under the bed lies a newspaper he forgot to be neat about. I lean over and pick it up. It is the sports page of *The Oratoga* dated December 9, 1938. The headline reads: "STREAKS DEMOLISH SCHUYLERVILLE 24–6 AS BIG O SCORES 2."

Rags sees me staring stupidly at the headline but doesn't blink an eye. "Why aren't you dressed?" he asks, buttoning his jacket. "We are due at the McWhinnies' in half an hour."

He stole the papers! It takes me another ten minutes— until I am away from him, in the safety of my own room— before I am willing to admit it. Not McWhinnie but Rags stole the papers! Not McWhinnie but Rags has been tailing me! Tailing me for what reason? To see what I have come up with. And when it looks like I am about to come up with something—the papers, no less!—Rags steps in and steals them. But why? Why would he want to do that?

Apparently I was not intended to come up with anything. All the names on Rags' list were useless except for his one mistake, Muldaur. It was Muldaur's list that came through, delivered Dr. Poole and Mrs. McWhinnie. It's conceivable Rags could forget Poole, but Carrie McWhinnie?

No, I was sent here to fail. He sits in Washington writing my book while I'm sent on a wild-goose chase in Saratoga. Talk about exploitation! Is that what that coded conversation was all about?

By the time I am dressed I have made my decision: Tonight,

dinner with Plante at the McWhinnies'; tomorrow, I go back to Washington.

I understand that I am dealing with neurosis: I have no right to blame him. It's none of my business, anyway; it was presumptuous of me to interfere.

En route by cab to the McWhinnies, I cannot resist telling him that throughout the length of my investigation I did not find a single person who remembered him. I omit, not without inner struggle, Dr. Poole's recollection of "the Rat." Too cruel. Besides, it was not a positive identification.

Plante pretends to be amused. I am sure he is not really amused. And I regret my cheap shot as soon as I note his coded reaction. I now know how to read him: When he acts happy he is not happy; when he is ironic he is also not happy, he is disturbed or angry or hurt or something; when he is diffident he is possibly furious or possibly hurt or possibly even happy. Whatever he is on top he is assuredly something else on bottom.

I try to undo some of the damage: "All these assholes remember are the jocks. I.Q. doesn't count, ability doesn't count, wit doesn't count. I think adolescence must be the worst time in a person's life."

Plante smiles, but not at me, at the back of the neck of the driver. "Don't knock it, Ackroyd, until you've tried it."

Squelched, I feel better. I hope he does too. How is one to know?

He appears irritable as we wait at the door for someone to answer. What does it mean? Is he mad at me? At himself? Or is he pleased that he got back at me? Or is he pleased to be invited to dinner at Carrie McWhinnie's? Or bored?

If I went back home to L.A. and saw my boyhood friends—but she doesn't even remember him! Then why are we here? How did we come to be invited? How would I react to being back in L.A.? I make an effort to empathize and draw a blank. The blank is filled by Mrs. McWhinnie opening the door.

"How nice that you're here," she says in a manner that gives one reason to doubt. She has on the same smile I left her with

294

in her poli sci class. It looks weary. She looks weary, looks old tonight, not her age but within striking distance, unimpressively dressed in an orange blouse, an olive green cardigan sweater and dark brown slacks. Her bare feet, their veins showing, are in pink ballet slippers.

Because she seems to have trouble looking at me, I say "Hi." It succeeds in getting her to look at me coldly.

"I wish you had let me know that Mr. Plante was going to be in class today. I would have introduced him." Halfway through the sentence, before I understand its meaning, she starts us inside where McWhinnie stands watch over the archway to the living room—bow tie, pin-striped suit, both hands extended in greetings.

"The visiting firemen!" he announces. His voice has the sound of cracking ice. He makes an extended display of shaking hands, first Plante's, then mine, reciting to both of us in turn how fortunate we are to be in out of the rain.

Like a fool, I respond, "It isn't raining."

"Oh, don't tell me that. Don't tell me that. I was all set to say: 'Let me help you out of those wet clothes and into a dry martini.' But it needs to be raining for that, doesn't it? It doesn't fit when it's not raining. I was hoping for rain."

"Next time," says Plante.

"You are too kind," says McWhinnie.

"You could have said: 'Let me help you out of those cold clothes and into a hot toddy,'" says Plante.

McWhinnie nods thoughtfully. "Yes, I should have thought of that."

I am offended that for Plante's benefit McWhinnie behaves like a different man tonight. He is charming, he is winning, he stands straighter, walks instead of shuffles, he is amusing without being acerbic, he is years younger in appearance. While he is off spellbinding Plante, I join Mrs. McWhinnie at the bar. "I *was* invited, wasn't I?"

She flushes but doesn't look at me. "Of course."

"When?" I ask.

Now she does look at me; I was better off before. "I'm sorry, I don't understand you." The implication is that it is more than my question she doesn't understand about me.

"I don't remember being invited to dinner tonight. But I do remember that you didn't remember Oscar Plante. And yet here we both are, guests for dinner."

She smiles wearily. "You put things so strangely," she says, that simple statement carrying with it more than its normal weight. "Mr. Plante introduced himself to me after you had left. He is very paternal toward you. You should be very pleased by how much he thought of your talk."

I begin to get it: Plante praised my talk, meaning in all probability that he hated it, or didn't bother to listen; she hated my talk, which made her think that much more of Plante for his loyalty to his friends.

"I had no idea he was there. He's supposed to be in Washington."

"My students adored you; you were a big hit."

"Was it that bad?"

She tries and almost succeeds in smiling. "I'm sorry. I know I'm being ridiculous." She must feel a little better toward me because she asks me to help her carry the cocktails over to the coffee table.

Plante slowly circles the coffee table and the two overstuffed armchairs that face it.

"Mad as a hatter. Sober as a judge. Drunk as a lord," says McWhinnie, rooted in his rocking chair, turned obliquely away from Plante's cruising path. "I have often wondered," he goes on, his voice breaking to denote that this is an exercise in wit, "if one can be mad as a judge, drunk as a hatter and sober as a lord."

Plante, not listening, not registering the fact that he has just been handed a drink and downed half of it, says to Mrs. McWhinnie, "I used to wonder what the insides of these houses were like."

She sits in one of the overstuffed chairs. "That's right, you come from Saratoga. Where did you live?"

296

Now that she is seated, Plante sits. He fidgets with his glass, the creases in his trousers, the knot in his tie. "Oh, Elm. I prefer this. Where did you live?"

"Union Avenue."

As she answers, Plante shifts toward her in his chair; a surprisingly awkward motion, as if he is trying to turn himself over. "Odd, I remembered you living on Circuit."

"I was born on Union and lived there my first twelve years, then we moved to Circuit—"

"You were in high school."

"That's right. How did you know?"

"We went to the same school."

"On Lake Avenue?"

"You lived at 461 Circuit."

"That's right! How did you know?"

"Don't be impressed too easily. I also know baseball statistics. I wonder if we had any of the same teachers?" he says slowly, watching her carefully. "Who did you have for English?"

A pause that Old Man McWhinnie is about to fill; his mouth creaks open but the words come from Mrs. McWhinnie. "Mr. Monroe."

"That's who I had. I bet you don't remember the period."

She laughs. Plante smiles along with her laugh. When she stops laughing, he stops smiling.

"You mean you don't remember what period you had English?"

"You're not serious, are you?"

He leans back in the chair, stretches out his legs, one ankle over the other, his arms behind his head. "You sat in the front of the room. You didn't understand why we had to read *Return of the Native*. I was astonished at how you talked back to Mr. Monroe."

She breaks into a buttery smile. "He was afraid of me! I never did finish *Return of the Native*," she laughs. Plante smiles.

"You always cut class," he says.

"No, I didn't."

Plante tips forward in the chair and, with his drinking hand, points a mock-accusing finger at her. "Quite often you did. I was astonished." Mrs. McWhinnie flushes a deep red, I can't tell why. Plante reacts by sitting bolt upright. "My most fervent fantasy in those four years spent on Lake Avenue was to some-day work up the minimal courage necessary to cut one single class." He speaks slowly and formally, as if it's a recitation. "Finally, in my senior year I cut gym. I thought with my un-impeachable credentials as *The Oratoga*'s star sports corre-spondent no one would complain. I was mistaken. Mr. Gaffney dressed me down in the locker room in front of the entire class. I was enraged at the injustice of it all. The athletes were cutting gym all the time. . . ."

"But they spent hours after school training," she protests, giving Plante a chance to take his first breath in a minute.

"That thought didn't occur to me until much later. In fact, this very moment. I was convinced some people were destined to get away with murder and I . . ."

She smiles. "Poor boy." It is the duplicate of his ironic smile.

"Shall I freshen that up for you?" chuckles McWhinnie. I wonder why Plante does not answer him, when I come to my senses and realize he is talking to me.

"I got away with murder all the way through school," re-sumes Mrs. McWhinnie about an hour through dinner, follow-ing a series of McWhinnie monologues on: (1) scientific polling, (2) student self-government, (3) the Warren Court.

"How very cruel of you to say so," says Plante ironically.

"Wait." She holds up a hand. "This works out well for you in the end. I never picked up a book! Was I surprised in col-lege: one moment so arrogant, the next so dumb! What a shock to discover teachers existed who were actually on to me. I felt so transparent. What a comedown!" They exchange tenuous, ironic smiles; they seem bound together by one long string of a smile.

"I lived in hope of committing some small crime. And get-ting away with it. My nerves failed me until that day in gym."

298

"You probably looked so guilty it was an invitation to be caught." She says it as if she's making an important point in an important conversation.

"No, I would have been happy and proud to have gotten away with it. The class I really wanted to cut was science. I hated Mr. Fisk, cutting gym was a consolation for not having the nerve to cut science. And I got caught!" Said without a trace of self-mockery.

"*You* had Mr. Fisk?"

"You did too. I know." Plante restrains a grin.

"Oh God, don't tell me you were in my science class?"

"I was the lad in the gingham shirt, purple tie and baggy blue corduroys. Surely you remember?"

"How could I ever forget?" She slaps a hand across her brow and laughs. Plante laughs with her. I laugh out of loneliness. McWhinnie smiles on us benevolently, as if he is responsible for our laughter.

"Mark Twain once said," says McWhinnie, " 'I wouldn't belong to a club that would have me as a member.' What do you think he meant by that?"

Mrs. McWhinnie flushes dark brown.

"It sounds like a remark made by somebody who's just been blackballed," I say, smiling to Mrs. McWhinnie.

"He possibly meant," drawls Plante, "that he wouldn't belong to a club that would have Groucho Marx as a member since I think you will find it is Marx who is credited with that remark, not Mark Twain."

"I stand corrected. I am not as well read in light humor as I should be."

"You haven't been reading your Marx," I say with pride. "I guess you confused your Mark for your Marx," my mouth continues, seriously out of control.

"What was your worst subject? Mine was math," says Mrs. McWhinnie, a hard edge to her voice.

"You had Mr. Graham, too?" Plante's expression is cherubic; I have never seen him cherubic before.

"How do you know I had Mr. Graham?" she all but shrieks.

"If you hated math you had to have had Mr. Graham." Plante laughs. She laughs. He stops laughing. She looks at him and this makes him laugh again. She laughs too. "Do you remember Loretta Davis?" asks Plante.

"We used to double date together! Did you date Loretta?"

"No. She was too beautiful."

"She was a terrific kid."

"Whatever became of her?"

"Oh, we lost contact more than twenty years ago."

"Who was the girl who was dating Mr. Appleby?"

"You're kidding! A student?"

"Yes, I can see her face but I can't recall her name."

"Dating Appleby?! Everyone wanted to but no one had the nerve. Christ, he was cute! Are you sure?"

"Everyone talked about it."

"Not to me! I would have been jealous as hell. I had a crush on Appleby. Even I didn't have the nerve to date a teacher."

"You were pretty wild."

"I sure was. All I cared about was having a good time. I was crazy!"

"I was too cautious. I had a pretty good time. Astonishing how it all comes back."

"Where did you go to college?"

"Columbia."

"You're kidding! I went to Barnard!"

"You're not serious! You did?"

"Yes, Barnard. I went to Barnard!"

"Isn't that astonishing? I didn't know that!"

"God, my first two years in New York I thought I really discovered heaven. I wouldn't go back now if you paid me. You live there, don't you?"

"Washington."

"Oh, I thought you lived in New York."

"I did. For many years. I moved to Washington a few years ago."

"Isn't Washington dull next to New York?"

"It's a very insular town. But so is New York after you've lived in it for thirty years."

"So is any place."

"Perfectly true."

"What's Washington like?"

"I suspect it depends on which party owns the White House."

"You mean the party sets the tone?"

"Oh, absolutely. It's astonishing."

"So every four or eight years it changes."

"So I'm given to understand."

"Have you met Nixon?"

"I met him, he didn't meet me. We shook hands. He has wet palms. Johnson had an enormous paw that functioned like a rabbit trap. Once you were in his hands it was up to him whether you were ever to be released or not. He was astonishing."

"Did you ever meet Kennedy?"

"Before my time. I used to see him in bars around New York when he was a kid Senator. Couldn't believe he'd ever make it to President. I was astonished."

"I had a crush on Kennedy."

"Not as cute as Mr. Appleby." He smiles gently.

"No one was as cute as Mr. Appleby. He was pretty cute, though. Did you know Bobby?"

"I didn't like him. He was always holding back. You could never tell what was really on his mind."

"But isn't that par for the course with politicians?"

"But Bobby gave the impression that it might have more to do with Freud than politics."

"You mean he was neurotic?"

"At the very least, repressed. You never knew what was really on his mind." He smiles naughtily. "He reminded me of Raskolnikov."

She whoops in an explosion of laughter that seems to me out of keeping with the comment.

"I didn't trust him," Plante goes on, his eyes extraordinarily bright. "There was an astonishing picture in *Life* a few months ago. A two-page color spread of Rose Kennedy seated at her

301

piano in Hyannisport. And her fingers are on the keys." Plante poses at an imaginary piano. "And she is grinning triumphantly into the camera—" Plante grins toothily. I have never seen him so animated. "Reminding one, for all the world of Jimmy Durante about to break into a solo of 'Inka Dinka Doo'—"

She doubles over, clapping her hands three times in fun-struck approval. Plante raises his voice to a near shout. "And on the piano in black-bordered frames are photographs of all her dead—of Jack, of Bobby, of her first son Joe—"

"—who got killed in the war!"

Plante nods and lowers his voice. The sudden contrast is spooky. "Lost on a bombing mission. And her husband, Joe, still alive but paralyzed by stroke."

"Astonishing!" she says.

"And at first blush there is something monstrously satiric about that picture. This matriarch, triumphant at the piano, surviving it all."

"Astonishing," she whispers.

Plante's eyes shine with compassion. "But the longer I looked at it the less amusing it became. It stayed in the mind. I found it in the end admirable. Even heroic."

"It *is* fantastic. The Church, isn't it?"

"Yes, it is undoubtedly the Church. It struck me for the first time how much non-believers lose when they give up obses-sional religion for obsessional rationalism. Or obsessional prag-matism. Or obsessional self-analysis."

"It's true. It's absolutely true. How do we ever manage to survive?" she asks, childlike.

"Alcohol," says Plante.

"Obsessional alcohol," says Mrs. McWhinnie.

They roar for each other, out of control.

February 10

At breakfast I break into a Plante monologue on the basi-cally bad character of successful American novelists to tell him that I have made a reservation on a 1:52 Allegheny flight back to Washington.

"I'm sorry to hear that," he lies.

"I don't see that there's much more I can do here except to go through Mrs. McWhinnie's *Oratogas* and you know what to look for better than I."

Plante's smile is infectious. "Are you sure you don't want to delay your departure for a day or two?"

"I don't know what for. If I had the papers—"

"They are depressingly revealing."

"I'm glad you've learned something."

"I've learned that I was utterly devoid of talent at a time in my life when I imagined myself in training to be the American Balzac."

"Since I'm not going to have a chance to look at them," I say pointedly, "let me suggest a shortcut that might lead you somewhere."

"I need your help, as always," he lies.

"The Tessie Toga gossip columns that you ghosted. I have a feeling you might find a lot in those."

Plante laughs. "You've done it again, Ackroyd. Completely puzzled me. What Tessie Toga gossip columns?"

"It's called 'Oratoga Oratory.' Look for it, you'll find it."

"That I ghosted?"

"You may have forgotten," I say diplomatically.

"What makes you think I ever ghosted a gossip column?" He presents a picture of earnest bafflement.

"You didn't?"

"I may have been an atrocious sports writer in my youth but I was far too pretentious to ever lay hands on a gossip column."

"What about 'The Opinionated Orator'?"

"What about explaining yourself?"

"The Willie Warbler column? 'The Opinionated Orator'?"

"Ackroyd, you are quite right, it is time for you to go home. You have been stricken with a bad case of Plante's Disease: a broken field memory. Soon you will have my past confused with pieces of old movies. I sympathize. I am subject to bouts of it without warning, particularly when I imbibe. I'm given to revealing significant data out of my past which are altogether false: cribbed either from a friend's life or from a recently read fiction—or sometimes made up entirely out of whole cloth. I can be so convincing in the telling of these stories that I will temporarily convince myself. No, it is time you got away from me: I am clearly a carrier, an insidious influence."

Not having my Plante code book on me, I go on to other business. "But you will return the papers to Mrs. McWhinnie? I'm responsible for them."

"I envy your being responsible for any possession of Carrie McWhinnie's," he says with a sobriety that strikes sparks.

"You will return them then?"

"You can depend on it."

The tension that was building between us now dissipates. "How long are you staying on?" I ask.

"Until I complete the work that you have begun."

"You don't know anything about what I've begun." I cannot keep the exasperation out of my voice. "We haven't spoken a word about it."

"Which is my fault, not yours," he says generously.

Before parting in the lobby, Plante says: "You must remember to call me as soon as you have read the manuscript."

For a moment I think he has gone completely mad: otherwise, why is he calling the high school papers a manuscript and why ask my opinion of them when he refuses to let them out of his hands? Then I realize he is talking about the book, our book, his book. I had forgotten any such book.

"I was at the typewriter at six every morning. You know the last time that happened?"

"I'm anxious to see it." My turn to lie.

"I am more proud of it than any work I've done in a long time. Wouldn't it be peculiar if my best writing turns out to be under your name?" Rather than resentful, he sounds pleased. He stands close to me, looking conspiratorial and sounding pleased.

304

I know who is on the other end of the phone before I decide, on the tenth ring, that it's time I picked up.

"You're hiding from me," barks Tina.

"I just got back," I say, instantly out of breath.

"You've been back for days, you rat. If Rags hadn't told me I still wouldn't know. Why are you hiding from me? I'm furious with you!" She doesn't sound furious, she sounds lonely.

"When did Rags get back?"

"He's not back, that rat. He's mad at you too. He wants to know why you haven't read his book."

His book!

"He has to stick around to give some stupid talk at Skidmore. When am I going to see you?" she demands.

"How about right now?"

"If you mean it I just might forgive you."

It takes an hour to get me over there. I am unable to move. Tina catches me in the act of not moving twice more: once, when I am trying to decide which blue shirt to wear and twenty minutes later when I can't locate my keys. As I climb into a cab I have the insane impulse to give as my destination National Airport.

"Where have you been?" Tina attacks, wild-eyed, at the door. The floral pattern on her shift today is green. Her hair looks like it has had a brush pulled through it once in honor of my arrival and, before that, not for days. Her skin is puffy and gray. The house is every bit as much of a mess as she is.

"When did you start smoking?"

"When did you start being my mother?" she snaps at me while devouring a king-size cigarette—the first time I have seen her smoke in months; it makes her look hard.

The downstairs is darker and more disordered than usual. The paleolithic sofas and chairs do not appear to be sinking into the floor tonight, but edging away from each other in an attempt to escape through the walls. It leaves a great void in the center of the room. Josh sits cross-legged in the middle of the void, in his traditional mortician's wear, looking shockingly like his father at the age of fourteen. "Perfecto! You're all I need today! How the hell am I supposed to get anything done around here?" He slams shut a fat textbook that he was reading in the dark and swishes out of the room, his walk strikingly effeminate.

The single bright light in this nether-world comes from the ceiling fixture over the oak dining table. It spotlights an assortment of dirty dishes and three open cartons of yogurt with spoons sticking out of them.

"It's good to see you," I say. The complex levels of meaning that back up that simple statement impel me to take a deep breath. I inhale a toxic accumulation of Scotch.

"He's deserted me too!" Tina growls in reference to Josh. Her blown-up body is warlike in its formidableness. Her eyes are greedy with their demand for compassion. She reminds me of a Valkyrie Annabelle.

"What the hell has been going on around here?" I ask.

"What the hell's been going on up there?" she retorts.

"I can't talk in this mess."

She glowers at me. "Then go home!"

I don't know what to say to her and I am not at all that anxious to talk about Saratoga, so I start cleaning her house. I remove the dishes and yogurt cartons from the oak table into the kitchen. The kitchen is oppressive with cooking odors. Thickly crusted broiler trays, frying pans and pots overflow the stove and sink. The oven is baking away at 400 degrees and nothing is in it. It has obviously been on for some time because the temperature in the kitchen must be close to eighty. The dishwasher is stuffed, but half the dishes seem to be clean or at least rinsed, the other half soiled. The cold water is running in the sink.

I take off my jacket and begin work on the stove. I scrape the heaviest grease out of the broiler tray and the frying pans with a soup ladle and wipe up the residue with paper towels. I load the tray and the pans into the sink, after first emptying it of coffee mugs and yogurt cartons, and turn the hot water on full force. I roll up my sleeves and begin scrubbing.

"What do you think you're doing?" Tina shouts over the din of crashing pots.

"I'd appreciate a drink."

"Then wash out a glass," she says nastily.

I take a cocktail glass out of the dishwasher, sponge it with soap and rinse it off. I turn to hand it to Tina, who is sitting, sulking, at the kitchen table, a cigarette drooping passively from her lips, her head resting on her hand, her legs crossed: clearly no intention of moving. I plant the glass in front of her glazed, angry eyes and place my order: "Scotch on the rocks." I return to my scalding pots at the sink.

"We have no ice," Tina says as if it's my fault, then adds miserably, "I apologize."

"I don't try to be loved, I just like to be appreciated as a good homemaker."

"Why is it when I feel awful it never fails to put you in a good mood?"

As often happens, she strikes a chord. "I didn't ask to come, I was summoned."

She emits a loud parody of a scream that sends chills down my spine. "That's better," she says. "Now you can have your drink."

I finish scrubbing the pots and start clearing the dirty dishes, cups and coffee mugs off the kitchen table. Tina smokes in the middle of this mess, not budging. She has her cigarette in one hand and my drink in the other. For a long time she does nothing with either but by the time I have finished sponging down all of the table, but for the area blocked by her sprawl, she has put out the cigarette on the leg of her chair and drunk my Scotch.

Josh comes in scowling, carrying his fat textbook. He takes the chair across from Tina and without a word to either of us opens his book and starts making notes in the margin.

"You're all against me," Tina growls.

"Shhh," says Josh, "can't you see I'm working?"

I squeeze one more plate and two more glasses into the crammed dishwasher and set the remaining ten-inch-high stack of dishes on the drainboard. I start the dishwasher, scrub the stains off the top of the stove and prepare to evacuate the kitchen for the living room. The dishwasher roars like a bulldozer, drowning out the lack of communication in the room. A brief look at Tina and Josh before the kitchen door swings closed on them recalls to mind the general demeanor of Vietnamese refugees.

I grope about the living room turning on lamps. The green walls suck up light like a sponge but I have moved the sense of time up a few hours, say, from the middle of the night to daybreak. I am able to weightlift one window open an inch or two; the others won't budge. I go down the hall and leave the front door ajar, unleashing a small tornado of a draft that operates on the room like a transfusion of blood. You can almost see the gray mass of declined furniture resume breathing and sit up with straightened postures.

"What are you doing? I'm catching pneumonia!" screams Tina over the blast of the dishwasher.

I gather from the four corners a week's collection of the *Washington Post* and *New York Times* and move them into the kitchen.

"All I ask," I hear Tina demanding of Josh, "is that when you borrow film you replace it."

"You borrow things of mine all the time and you don't replace them. You borrow my socks."

"Bullshit I borrow your socks; your socks don't fit me."

"Stretch socks? Stretch socks don't fit you?"

"I hate stretch socks. I don't wear them."

"You wear my father's shirts."

"Don't try to bring your father into this; this concerns you and me only and it involves my professional tools, not shirts or socks but the tools I use to earn my living." Tina's voice rises shrilly, hitting a near-Annabelle pitch.

"Film's film, it's not a tool. You're pretentious."

"Film is a tool of my trade."

" 'A tool of my trade,' " Josh repeats to me. "Isn't she pretentious?"

"Where's the vacuum cleaner?" I ask Josh.

"How should I know? Ask her." Without looking, he thrusts a thumb at Tina.

"You do that again, I'll break it off," Tina snaps. Josh pales. I have never seen the two of them go at each other this way.

"Where's the vacuum cleaner?" I ask Tina.

"How should I know? In one of the closets. What do you think you're proving?"

"It's a tool of his trade," smirks Josh.

I open and close four narrow, stubborn doors until I discover the door to the vacuum cleaner.

"Do you ever intend to talk to me?!" shouts Tina over the grinding dishwasher.

"I honestly don't know what to say," I answer. I kick the wheeled cannister through the swinging door and plug the stretch-cord into a socket in the living room. I am about to connect the hose and commence cleaning the Persian rug when I hear Tina, no more than six inches behind me: "If you turn that machine on, I promise you I will stuff yor head inside the bag in that cannister."

Even in this unfocused underwater light, it is plain to see how desperately unhappy she is. "Who is Carrie McWhinnie?" she begs.

"A political science teacher at Skidmore married to an ass."

"Robert, please talk to me." It is practically a whimper. She is suddenly childlike.

I take her limp hand and guide her to the couch; I seat myself next to her. "Carrie McWhinnie went to high school with Rags and your father. But she does not remember Rags. She does remember your father. She was his girlfriend. She says she could have married him—"

Tina looks panic-stricken. "Rags?!"

I squeeze her two hands tightly. They are cold and clammy. "Not Rags, your father."

Green welts appear under her eyes. "Will you please stop talking about my father? Why are you doing this to me?"

"Tina, I am trying to tell you this in an organized way."

"Please. Just tell it. Let me do my own organizing."

I am suddenly aware of Josh sitting at the oak dining table. His skin is parchment yellow under the overhead light. His textbook balances on his lap, closed.

"O.K., no one I interviewed remembers Rags from high school; no one on the Saratoga paper remembers him although he worked there after he got out of school."

"Forty years ago? What's odd about that?" she asks irritably.

"They all remember your father."

Tina snaps her hands free. "You just will not quit, will you?"

"O.K., a doctor named Poole who was a quarterback on the football team thinks he may remember him but he is not sure. There was a kid who used to hang around the athletes, particularly your father." I slur that last, intimidated by her attitude. "He describes this kid as a flunky, someone the jocks sent out on errands and used as the butt of jokes. They called him 'the Rat.' "

Josh lets out a hoot, signifying what, I do not know.

"So what? So far you haven't said anything," Tina mutters.

"I read some of Rags' high school sports stories. They are embarrassingly sycophantic."

"As are all sports stories in high school!" She looks at me as if she does not know why she let me into her house.

"Even more so. They are—I hesitate to say it—most embarrassing in reference to your father. You'd think he was describing the second coming," I say in a fast, needlessly reckless finish.

"You hate him, don't you?" Tina says, her eyes blazing, the green welts under them fading back to pink.

"Do you know what this is like? It's like walking through a mine field."

"But you do hate him."

"If you really want to know what I hate it's your behavior right now."

310

"Because you got him cornered!" Josh sneers.

"In two minutes I'm going to get up and walk out of here."

"I just want you to tell me straight: Why do you hate him so?" she asks calmly.

More than anything else, I am surprised by how little of this gets to me. I am slightly depressed, in a way waterlogged by the aquatic morbidity of the surroundings, but the depression is minor compared to the bubble of excitement inflating within me.

"Mrs. McWhinnie saved her old high school newspapers. I thought they might hold some relevant information, so I asked her to dig them up. She left them for me one morning at the hotel. By the time I went down to pick them up they were gone. Someone had swiped them."

"Don't tell me who, let me guess," says Tina.

"Rags arrived in Saratoga at least two full days, possibly three, before he made me aware of his presence. He tailed Mrs. McWhinnie and me for one entire night. He tailed me to and from a movie on the following night. He observed me giving a talk to Mrs. McWhinnie's political science class on the following day. Don't you find that just a little odd? That he should be standing in the back of a classroom watching me and not let me know he's there? Yes, he stole the newspapers."

"What'd he do on the seventh day?" yells Josh. "Bomb Hanoi?"

"How do you know he followed you? Did you see him follow you?"

"I used to be a professional investigator. I have a pretty good notion when I am being tailed."

"And your pretty good notion tells you it was Rags."

"What is so threatening to him in those papers that make them worth swiping?" I ask her.

"You are paranoid," is her reply.

"He's making the whole thing up," crows Josh.

"Do you want to know where I found the newspapers?"

"You broke into his room and searched it, didn't you? Is that what you're about to tell me?" Her lip actually curls.

"In fact, I did not. I was an invited guest," I say in a tone far more defensive than I want it to be. "I could hardly miss the papers. They were on his bed. They were on the floor. The bed table. Obviously, he had been going through them very thoroughly. Looking for what? What was he so afraid I'd find that he had to find it first?" Viewed from Tina's position, the question seems to me unanswerable. She proceeds to answer it.

"He didn't bother to hide the newspapers, did he? He was so afraid he didn't bother to deny he had them, no, and he didn't care that you knew he had them, now did he?"

"That much is true," I concede with what I intend to be good grace.

"Maybe Rags made the mistake of thinking that you and he were working on the same side in this so-called investigation you cajoled him into. Maybe, since he knew what to look for and you didn't, he thought he could expedite matters—considering the amount of time you usually waste—if he examined those papers first."

"If he knew what to look for why hasn't he found it?" I ask.

"It is remotely conceivable, Robert, that you could be wrong. Maybe there isn't anything in those newspapers."

"O.K. There is a gossip column in those papers. It is called 'Oratoga Oratory.' The name of the paper is *The Oratoga* and the gossip column is called—"

"I get it," Tina snaps.

"The gossip column is ghostwritten under a house name. The name on the gossip column is Tessie Toga."

Tina smiles contemptuously. "If you think you've just dropped a bomb, I'm sorry to say it's a dud. I don't know what you're implying."

"You don't recall my asking Rags about Tessie Toga?"

She groans and rolls her eyes in mock-exasperation. "Criminentlies, Robert, you've really got your teeth into something this time! Rags didn't remember a forty-year-old gossip column from his high school newspaper. What perfidy!"

Josh giggles.

"If Rags didn't remember it where did I get the name Tessie Toga?"

"From the newspaper."

"Long before I saw the newspaper I asked you about it."

"That isn't true."

"I quoted to you from my diary!"

"I see. Your diary is the source material for your own research. In other words, you are your own corroboration. That's very good, Robert, even for you."

"You can't squirm out of it, Tina; Rags and your father talked at some length about Tessie Toga in May of 1964 and it is recorded verbatim in my diary. Yet Rags later denies any such conversation."

"He was drunk."

"Agreed. But he further denies any memory at all of Tessie Toga."

"Because, dummy, he was drunk! He blacks out! You know that! Where's *your* memory?"

"O.K., he denies any knowledge of Tessie Toga. Then he opens those newspapers he has confiscated. What does he find? He finds Tessie Toga. Now, you said it yourself. We are working together. Wouldn't it be natural for him to come to me and say, 'Look, look what I found! There *is* a Tessie Toga!' "

Tina stretches and yawns. It goes on for a long time.

"Am I keeping you up?" I ask.

"No," she smiles pleasantly. "You're better than Seconal."

Josh drops his head on the dining table and makes loud snoring noises.

"I get the distinct impression that you don't want to hear what I have to say."

"Do you?" Her smile is pitiless.

"So if you'll please excuse me—" I pull myself off the couch, every muscle aching.

"Not bloody likely," Tina says.

Notwithstanding, I excuse myself.

February 17

Her unpredictability is becoming predictable. I expected to hear from her all day yesterday, so she didn't call; I expect her to call today, so at four, without calling, she shows up at my door.

"Rags wants to know why you haven't read his book yet. He's very anxious to hear from you." She hands me a bulky envelope.

"Thank you," I say, still not inviting her in. She comes in anyway; I either have to step aside gracefully as if it's my own idea or get into a shoving match. I pretend grace. I wave her to the chair in which she is already sitting.

"He's never coming back," she says, exasperated. "What's he doing there? Why won't you tell me?"

"You don't want to know anything from me. You've made that crystal clear."

"Robert, please." First sign of emotion.

"You've treated me with utter contempt."

"You're so disloyal."

"You're still doing it."

"Well, aren't you? You know you are!"

Her stare of betrayal is so outrageous I want to hit her. If I hit her where would I hit her? She has a strong-looking jaw. I decide that if I ever hit her it will be on the jaw.

She takes a deep breath. "Robert, if you want to tell me what you think you've found, I will listen. I'm ready to listen."

"Without interruption?"

"You know me better than that."

"Tina, you're incredible: you make it sound like an unreasonable request."

"It's blackmail."

I sigh. It is a sign of surrender. "O.K., remember Tessie Toga?"

"Christ, you're not going to start that again?"

"The Tessie Toga gossip column was ghostwritten by Rags."

"So what? Anyway, you have no way of knowing that."

"I know it's hard, but try to listen. In Saigon Rags and I got drunk with my superior officer, Colonel Trowbridge. I made notes of our conversation and entered it into my diary."

"Jesus Christ, Saigon!" she moans. "Why are you being so evasive?"

"We will spend a lot less time in Saigon if you can manage to shut up!" I wait for her to go on attacking, but this time she surprises me: she nods, giving me permission to proceed.

"Rags and Trowbridge started exchanging anecdotes about the days of their youth. Rags told a story about his time as a reporter on a Glens Falls, New York, newspaper called *The Orator*. He ghostwrote a gossip column called 'The Opinionated Orator.'" Tina closes her eyes in impatience.

"I checked in Glens Falls. There was never any such paper as *The Orator*."

"Did you bother to check with Rags?" Her tone indicates that she knows I did not.

"Yes, I bothered to check with Rags," I mimic her own surliness. "Rags' response was that I should never believe stories he tells in bars, they are all untrue."

"But you choose not to believe him."

"Look, do you want to hear the story he told or don't you?"

"But if it's not true—"

I rise. "Goodbye, Tina."

She doesn't budge. Instead, she waves me back into my chair. "Stop being a prima donna. Go on."

I am too irritated to go on. Instead, I show her the extract from my diary.

"The famous diary," she says under her breath, just loud enough for me to hear. I point out the significant sections.

". . . I, who saw no reason why so admirable a halfback should not be rewarded in fancy, if not fact, advanced Carmichael, by way of *The Orator*, into a ladies' man. I ran items linking his name to that of a local beauty queen, Miss Glens Falls, though, for all I knew at the time, they had never met. Small matter, I awarded her to Carmichael.

"It was then that I first discovered the tendency of life to imitate artlessness. Reading that she was interested in Carmichael, the beauty queen became interested in Carmichael, and he, no less, in her. They were inseparable for a year, and might have been to this day had I not, in a bored and reckless mood, run another item, this time hinting that Carmichael, unbeknownst to his beauty queen, was quietly squiring around a high school English teacher. The beauty queen threw over Carmichael who, out of his naive belief in the printed word, developed an interest in the English teacher. . . . I announced his impending marriage to the English teacher. Carmichael stormed into my office, stupefied with terror. He pled with me to retract the item: He did not love the girl, she was a tartar and a tyrant, and having read the item and being no less literal than he, had set a date for the wedding. I owed no less to my friend than to write him out of his misery. I published a string of items linking his name, in humiliating ways best left unsaid, to various voluptuaries about town. And Carmichael, as ever my creature, could do no less than date them. It did him no good. The English teacher, too familiar with the written word to heed it when it went against her best interests, refused to abide by the rules of the game. She would not go the way of the beauty queen. She made the poor lout marry her. . . ."

Tina hands back the diary. "It means absolutely nothing to me."

"Look, one fact you have to accept if we are going to get any place. Rags often talks in code."

"Not with me!" she flares.

"I don't know how he talks with you, but don't ask me to believe you haven't seen him do it with others."

Her expression hardens. She is not about to concede anything.

"*The Orator* is not *The Orator*, it is *The Oratoga*."

"I was waiting for that," she sneers. "So what?"

"Then who is Carmichael?"

"You're going to say he's my father."

"Very good. And who is Carmichael's beauty queen girl-friend?" Tina won't look at me. "Carrie McWhinnie," I say softly. "And the English teacher who won him on the rebound?"

Tina sighs. "Robert, this is so far-fetched—"

I put out a hand to stop her which actually stops her. "You won't tell me so I'll tell you. It's code for your mother. Not an English teacher but probably an English major. A student in Saratoga rather than an adult in Glens Falls. Your father was going steady in high school with Mrs. McWhinnie. His parents didn't approve because she was gentile. So Mrs. McWhinnie decided if she couldn't have your father, who would never marry without his parents' approval, she would pick the Jewish girl he did marry. And she did. She picked her best friend, Esther Weill.

"That much is fact. It comes from Mrs. McWhinnie. The rest is conjecture. Your father wanted to break off with Esther Weill but didn't have the courage. He prevailed upon his flunky friend, the Rat, to print gossip about him that would turn Esther Weill against him. You can see how well it worked out."

"This Mrs. McWhinnie has really done a job on you, hasn't she?" If eyes had teeth I would now be clamped between Tina's.

"These are my conclusions. Mrs. McWhinnie has nothing to do with them."

"Who is she?" Tina demands, as if I am a captured spy from the McWhinnie camp.

"She is a political science teacher at Skidmore."

"I know that," Tina roars. "What does she want?"

"Tina—" I extend my hands in a plea for friendship.

"You tell that harpy to stay out of my life!" Tina is on her feet, suede jacket fluttering, pants legs spread wide, high-heeled boots biting into the floor. I am afraid she is going to raise one heel off the floor and run me through with it, nailing me by the chest to the back of the chair. "You were sent to

317

find out the meaning of 'Opposites' and 'Big Chief Little Shit'! You weren't sent to find out about *Oratogas* or Tessie Togas! You have twisted this thing— You have fucked up totally, you have fucked up everything! Everything! Everything!" Her complexion is pasty white, her forehead sweaty, her eyes feverish.

"Tina," I say calmly, "I wasn't 'sent.' No one 'sent' me. I am not working for—"

"Shut up, fuck-up!" she screams. She raises her right fist. I am sure she is going to hit me. I close my eyes, hunch my shoulders and position my elbows to protect my face. I decide, moments later, that this is an undignified position for a man under attack from a woman.

No matter. Tina is gone. The front door stands open.

February 18

"Don't say anything," she says in a quiet but firm plea. "I realize that I've been on a tear. I'm still on it. Not this moment, but I can go off again at any moment and you seem to trigger it so let me talk first and then I'll listen. If I *can* listen to you. I don't know that I can. I think I want to kill you. But I'll try. But first you have to listen to me."

I am about to say O.K., but she orders my mouth to stay shut with a frantic wave of her hand. "Don't say 'Yes' or anything. Just nod. Please indulge me, Robert."

I nod.

She says, "Thank you."

It is two in the morning. I am in my pajamas and bare feet, standing against the door to the bedroom. She sits on the edge of my bed in a bulky coat made of some monstrous, deranged fur that seems to spread like a fungus as you stare at it. Her face has aged years, she could be older than Mrs. McWhinnie. The drink I mixed her when she and Josh marched in on me sits trembling and untouched in her hand. Josh stands next to her, his right hand resting on her right shoulder. His face is pinched and corpselike. He reminds me of Richard Widmark when he played psychotic killers pushing old ladies in wheelchairs downstairs.

I had been sitting in bed reading—or trying to read—Rags' book. I don't know whether it's me or the book but I cannot get into it. Shortly past the section he had previously shown me the style shifts from mine to Rags'. It shifts back and forth for a dozen or so pages and then takes on a glib, knowing tone more in keeping with *Time* magazine than either one of us. None of this can I be certain of—I am not in good shape right now to read anything—but when it comes to documentation there is no doubt that Rags has gone off the deep end, has embellished the facts or distorted them deliberately to make points that, if true, are not demonstrably true and which can easily and legitimately lead to charges of falsifying documents.

"Josh and I have been talking things over, and this is what we think—" She pauses. Josh tightens his grip on her shoulder. She places her hand on top of his and leaves it there. "That awful gossip column. Tessie Toga. That story Rags told in Saigon. He didn't want to marry my mother. I think he loves her now. I mean he's devoted to her. I'm sure he has never played around. But I could never see them as a couple. I couldn't. So that story makes sense. He didn't want to get married. So he planted those stories. They were engaged in high school. My mother has told me that story over and over till it was coming out of my ears. The childhood sweethearts! Maybe by now she believes it. He didn't love her. He loved this Carrie woman. He's very weak-willed. You come back with these stories about what a big shot he was and what a nebbish Rags was. I don't believe it! It doesn't make any sense! Anyhow, that has nothing to do with anything. Rags and my father were friends. Rags was writing, ghosting this silly column. As a favor to my father, he wrote all those terrible stories about him and other women, girls. I mean they couldn't be that bad, the stories, raunchy as Rags made it sound in Saigon, because it was a high school paper, you know, it couldn't be that bad. But can you imagine my mother, you know how she is, going steady or actually engaged to my father, and this is a hundred years ago when the morality at the time—and him the big catch, the big star." Venom in her voice here. "And she reads in a gossip column that he's going out with this or that girl. You know how possessive she is! She must've blown her top! And of course he wasn't. He was too scared. The big man on campus. My father, the pussycat. So he's too scared of her to break off, which is what he really wants, that's what it's all about, you see, he wants to back out, so he tried to set it up where *she'll* break off, get mad, pissed off enough, but it doesn't work. I'm sorry, I'm incoherent, I know. Those words —I don't know what they mean—in the notebook, Rags' notebook, they refer somehow to that. 'Big Chief Little Shit.' 'Opposites.' I don't know how or why. But it's the only thing that makes sense. Rags was going to base his book on that and he told my father and my father couldn't, he must have felt desperate, the humiliation—I don't know—it must have opened, reopened an old wound because my father doesn't steal, so he stole the notebook knowing that Rags blacks out and he might not remember. I'm sorry. Does any of this make sense to you?"

I am impressed and I am touched that, despite her far heavier emotional involvement, we have come up with similar explanations. "It makes enormous sense," I say. "But what about Rags? We know what your father is hiding but what's Rags hiding?"

"There he goes! Didn't I tell you?" She leaps off the bed and whirls on Josh, scaring the shit out of him. "I knew I couldn't talk to you! Josh said so and I didn't believe him!" Josh squirms uncomfortably and backs against the wall. "You're out to get him. I should have listened to Josh! I give you the answer to this whole business and are you satisfied? Are you ever satisfied? Will anything short of Rags' head on a platter satisfy you?" She stretches one long arm from where she stands by the bed to where Josh cowers by the wall. She clasps a hand around his wrist and sweeps him past me out of my bedroom, out of my apartment.

"I'm sorry," she says weakly over the phone.

"I know you are."

"Don't be pompous," she says, her voice strong as ever.

"I really bring out the best in you, don't I?"

A weary laugh: "I don't know what you do but you know how to do it. I have to go to Saratoga."

"O.K."

"Why do you have to say it like that? Christ, you know how to make me furious."

"Tina—" I say in warning.

"I apologize." Her voice is weak again. "Rags is giving that all-important talk of his to Mrs. Childhood Sweetheart's class."

I have never heard her sound bitchy before; I didn't know she had it in her. "And he asked you to come up for it?"

"Is there anything wrong with that?"

I have decided not to answer when her tone is vicious.

"I'm sorry, Robert. He didn't ask me. I miss him. I just want to see him. I'm catching a 10:30 plane."

I bring my watch hand up from under the covers. She woke me at nine. "You don't have much time."

"I just decided. Look, Josh is in school, he doesn't know. I know I should wait and make arrangements, but I can't. Listen, say no if you want to. Will you stay with him until I get back?"

"I have no place to put him up."

"At my place. You can stay in our room."

"No thanks."

"Well, Rags' big chair, the one in his study, it opens into a bed. Robert, I can't even promise to change, but I promise I'll try."

"Even if I don't move in?" She doesn't answer, thank God. Her unusual restraint in the face of my provocation robs me of any choice. "Sure, I'll stay with him."

"I had no idea how much more punishment you were willing to take," she says meekly. Her laugh is so defenseless I want to reach through the mouthpiece and pull her through the cord into bed with me.

"What should I say to Rags about the book?" she asks, businesslike, dispelling my fantasy.

"Tell him not only does the book need work, but his last few columns need work. He'd better get back here."

"That's what I think." She sounds grateful. "You do think his recent columns are bad? I wondered if it was just me. They are pretty bad, aren't they?" she says cheerfully. "I'll lay out our best bed sheets for you. I'm sorry the place is such a mess. Get in a maid. I'll pay for it. Stock the house with anything you want. I'll pay for it. When I get back I'll take you out to a fancy dinner."

I can't take much more of her pain. "You'd better get moving," I suggest in self-defense.

She has a hard time disconnecting. She hangs on for another two minutes: The keys will be in the mailbox and the mailbox will be unlocked; fifty dollars will be in the top drawer of Rags' desk; Josh hates food, don't worry about his not eating. . . .

By the time she rings off I am ready for my first drink of the day. And it is only nine-thirty.

February 20

Too exhausted to record this last night: Josh and I stayed up till three talking; when I awoke at eleven he was off to school, leaving behind a note in the kitchen telling me how excited he is that we broke the case.

I am a little embarrassed by what I see in the light of morning to be my act of deliberate seduction. Luring the kid into liking me again. Stepping into Plante's shoes. Why not? He's still trying to step into Kaufman's.

I dislike myself for justifying my actions by comparing them to Plante's.

The most noticeable thing about Josh is how much less effeminate he is without Tina around. It is as if her larger than life, dominating, almost masculine presence drives him in the opposite direction: into delicacy and passivity; not able to compete with her as a male, he will do it as a hybrid.

He is also less reluctant to talk about his father when Tina is not around. So it is not Plante he fears offending, it is Tina. "You have to know my father. I mean you keep asking Tina what he's afraid of. Well, I don't think he's afraid of anything. I think he's a terrifically cool guy. I think the only thing he might be afraid of is being embarrassed." We were in the kitchen preparing a frozen dinner: tuna noodle casserole. Josh will only eat soft foods and creamed vegetables. "He hates to be embarrassed. I mean when I was a kid and I'd do something to embarrass him, I mean I wouldn't eat my food in a restaurant and my mother, you know, always has to make a fuss—my father would just get up from the table and walk away. He'd disown us. What my mother calls 'your father and his famous walks.' She still calls them that. She still talks about him all the time and he never once talks about her. This is when I'm seven, something like that, because he's still living with us and we were in a restaurant and I must have embarrassed him or she did— let's say we both did—and he took one of his famous walks. And she finishes her dinner, you know, and he doesn't come back. And she says, 'We're not going to leave this table until he comes back.' Well, we must be there for over an hour and he doesn't come back, but I have to go to the bathroom but she won't take me because she won't leave the table but I'm practically doing it in my pants because I never took myself to the bathroom before. By now we're practically the last customers. So she calls a waiter and she asks him to take me to the bathroom, and he does and it's around the corner from our table and all the other tables are empty except one table and it's my father, all by himself. And he won't even look at me. I go in and out of the bathroom, right by him, but he doesn't look at me. The waiter couldn't guess in a million years he's my father. Boy, did he disown me that time!" Josh looked pleased at the idea of being disowned. "He was disowning my mother all the time."

"Does he ever disown Tina?"

Josh crowed with incredulity. "I'd like to see him try!"

After dinner we went up to Plante's study. Going upstairs without Plante or Tina in the house made me feel, for the first time that evening, like a burglar. I don't know why: Perhaps because the public rooms are downstairs and the private rooms, the bedrooms, Plante's study, are upstairs. With each step I became that much more of an intruder. At the first sight of Plante's study, minus Plante, I was certain I was not going to be able to sleep in that house that night.

I realized by Josh's high state of excitation that this act was more threatening to him than to me; he probably spent less time in his father's study than I; that to intrude there, to switch on all the lights, to fold out the bed from the Big Daddy chair were transgressions of such weight that he had to expect to pay for them someday, perhaps by a fatal piece of food caught in the throat.

The foldout bed was a skimpy affair considering the formidableness of the chair out of whose loins it sprung. Josh and I shared the making of the bed, getting competitive when it came to hospital corners.

"Do you get embarrassed easily?"

"What do you mean?"

"Like your father."

"I don't know."

"You think he got embarrassed in high school easily?"

"High school's the worst."

"You don't like it?"

"It's O.K."

"Maybe he disowned himself."

"What do you mean?"

"You said he was always disowning you or your mother."

"I didn't say always."

"When you embarrassed him."

"Not always."

"But a lot of the time."

324

"Who knows?"

"Maybe he was an embarrassment to himself."

"How can you disown yourself?"

"Maybe he couldn't stand himself. Do you ever feel that way?"

"Not particularly."

"You never hate yourself?"

"What do you mean?"

"Maybe he hated himself in high school because the guys he hung around with were the big shots—your Uncle Otis was a big shot—and he was a nobody."

"No he's not."

"Not now, but then. No one remembered him. He was a flunky."

"He was a late developer. I am too. My father says the guys who made it in high school don't make it in the real world."

"Did he say that?"

"You think I'm lying?" The protest was followed by a bowed head and a trapped smile. "Maybe I said it." He overrode my laugh with: "That doesn't mean it's not true!"

"He's made it in the real world all right. Your Uncle Otis was big in high school."

"But he didn't make it in the real world," Josh said proudly.

"Seems to prove your case, doesn't it?"

"My father's twice as big as he is, three times!"

"But he wasn't in high school."

"High school's just a racket. I only go because you need it for college. But it's a racket. It doesn't matter if you're not so big in high school."

"Your Uncle Otis was twice, three times as big as your father in high school."

"Now it's the other way around."

"The opposite."

"Yeah, the exact opposite." Josh stops. His eyes pop wide. His ghostly white complexion grows even paler. "You get it?" he cried.

"Get what?" I stalled.

"You get it? Don't you get it? They were the opposite! They were opposite of each other!"

"Opposites. I get it!"

"That's what 'Opposites' means!"

"Do you think it could mean that?"

"Am I right? Am I right? Do you think I'm right? What else could it mean?"

"You could be right."

"Did I solve it? Did we solve it? What else could it mean? We got it! I solved it! We got it!"

On closer examination I am not sure "we got it." If I really felt we got it, I know I would be exhilarated. But I'm not. I'm depressed. I'm angry at myself: I exploited Josh. I manipulated him into conclusions of my own in order that he think they were his conclusions; accept them as his ideas as much as mine. And as Josh blossomed on the results of my manipulation, acted eerily manic until three in the morning, couldn't sit still, tore up and down Plante's study, couldn't stop repeating our findings, treated that office as if it were his office, even deigned to sit in the novelist chair, I felt increasingly cold toward the kid, contemptuous: I wanted to be rid of him, irritated that he could be so involved in his own excitement that he was oblivious to my withdrawal.

So as Josh played detective, played me—taken into camp by me as he was five years ago in St. Louis—as he neatened the case, modified it, joined it by its separate parts, improvised connections of his own—totally immersed in investigative euphoria—I mentally played Tina to Josh's version of me: Tina scoffed, criticized, picked up the solution by its tail, turned it over and shook it so violently the separate pieces fell out and scattered, turning my neat solution into a silly-looking mess. Not even the beginnings of a solution, not halfway home.

Overnight I have turned Plante's bookish study into a pig-pen. The bed remains exposed and unmade all day, obscene within the context of asceticism that usually permeates the

326

place. Instead of making the bed or folding it back into invisibility, I muck up the rest of the joint. I go through the drawers of Plante's journalist desk, dig out my files and spread them over the desk, the bed and the visitor's chair, the one I usually sit in. In another drawer I find a carbon of the (our) book, and, without looking at it, set it next to the typewriter. In another drawer I find a sheaf of bond paper. I feed a sheet into the typewriter and, deliberately numbing myself to myself, start writing from scratch. I type blindly for over an hour, consult my research minimally and type, without pause, for two more hours. The phone rings downstairs three or four times but I cannot leave the room; if I leave I will never get back to the book. I type barefoot for two more hours; my shoes and stale socks defile Plante's muted, ocher carpet. My documents seem to be Xeroxed into my brain. At four or a little after I hear the sound of Josh home, moving about. I type until six, sweating buckets, the seat of the chair damp, the soles of my feet squished into the carpet.

I am afraid to leave the room, thinking the room is magic. I'm afraid to go downstairs for the drink I now desperately deserve. In something of a panic, I take the first step out of the study. The hall, the rest of the house are foreign to me, distances between walls, heights of ceilings have altered since yesterday.

Josh has altered since yesterday. He is cool, stiff, accusingly silent. He sits at the oak table, bathed in the subterranean glow of the ceiling fixture, at work on his math like a monk in a cell. I say "Hi" and he says "Hi" and I say "Did Tina call?" and he says "She's coming back tonight."

I dogpaddle to the kitchen and find a box of spaghetti. I cook it, melt a quarter-pound of butter into it and sit barefoot, pitching down great scoops, pouring Scotch after it. My appetite is insatiable.

I delay my departure from the kitchen long enough to allow Josh to disappear if he has a mind to. But he is very much in evidence as I push through the swinging door: spectral in his black suit and pasty yellow complexion. "She's really unfair, just because my father's not here she has no right to give me orders," he says as I pass by.

I stand for a moment, my real self very much upstairs. He waits for me to talk, I wait for him. Two minutes later I say, "My feet are cold."

Feeling like a fool and a victim, knowing for certain that the night is spoiled for further work, I trudge upstairs. I close the door. I sit at Rags' typewriter. I read the last two paragraphs, x them out and proceed to write six more pages in the unspecified amount of time it takes for Tina to arrive home and scare the hell out of me by quietly pushing open the study door.

She stands in the doorway, an enormous wraith, her fungus fur coat filling the space like a concrete block. "What are you doing here?" she says.

"How was the trip?" I am still in the book. And she is a million miles away.

"You have destroyed this room," she says.

"How was Rags' speech?" I ask, gradually making out the stone-cold expression on her face.

"Get out of this house," she says.

I can only react by laughing.

"I never want to see you again," she says.

February 21

Why is she taking it out on me?

I am up at six, slightly hung over, deliberately blank my mind to go to the typewriter, work for two hours, turn on the Today Show at eight for company while I fry a couple of eggs and brew coffee, work another two hours. She is certainly up by ten. I call. The line is busy.

I work two more hours, plowing ahead, not daring to correct or reread while I can still write. Try calling again at one. The line is busy. Is she trying to reach me? I hang up fast and wait.

I can't stand the injustice of it all. Rags leaves her, so she takes it out on me. I attack the typewriter. Two more hours and I no longer know what I am typing. The number at the top of the page says 55. I look away fast. I don't want to know the number. I go for the phone.

The line is busy. I accept it as a direct insult. I am her stand-in for Rags. He rejects her so she rejects me. I wonder if it is the first time in her life she has been rejected by a man. It wouldn't surprise me. That's what happens when you let yourself go that way. Same style dress month in, month out. Fearfully overweight. Why blame me?

At five I can't work anymore and I can't think anymore. The line is still busy. I try to reread. By the end of a sentence I can't remember how it began. If I keep on reading I will not be able to continue writing. I try calling. Busy signal. I hop a cab over there.

Josh eventually answers the door. The entire downstairs smells like a cave. "She's not here," he lies. I tell him about the busy signals. "The phone must be out of order," he lies. He seems angry, not at me particularly, but impersonally angry.

I lead him down the hall unable to restrain my eyes from the top of the staircase beyond which Tina secludes herself. I am struck with the flash mental image of my figure racing upstairs, and smashing into Tina's bedroom— It never gets there. It gets to the living room instead.

"That whole 'Opposites' business, you didn't believe that." Josh stares at me as if he's been defrauded.

"Did Tina tell you I didn't mean it?"

His face turns bright pink. "You leave her—she doesn't tell—" He waves his hands in disgust. "What's the use?"

"At the time it sounded like a plausible theory."

"You're backing down. I knew it!"

"Josh, do you know how many theories I used to come up with on cases before I hit the right one?"

"I knew it!" He refuses to look at me. He sits in his chair at the oak table, his hands between his knees. In his black suit he makes a convincing mourner.

"Look, what I'm saying is there are no shortcuts. We will

have to work through ten, maybe a dozen more theories, yours prominently included—"

"Don't bother!" he says curtly. Fired by another Plante.

February 22

If I could see her, if she would answer the phone which still rings busy all day, I would tell her, I would make her feel better. I could explain to her that Rags is finally making it with his high school dream girl. He has stolen Big O's love away. Up against obsession a straight relationship doesn't stand a chance. Tina has nothing to hate herself for.

Eight pages written today.

February 23

But was theirs a straight relationship? Who is Tina but Big O's daughter!

Line is busy, busy, busy. I feel like the innocent bystander in a Freudian nightmare.

Another ten pages written today.

February 24

Only five pages today. All I do is wait for the phone to ring.

February 25

Left the phone off the hook all day. Wrote twelve pages. Can't sit still. Too excited!

February 27

Phone off the hook all day, even during breaks. Don't want interruptions.

"Hello, Robert, this is Tina Kaufman." Stiff. Chilling.

"Where have you been?" I joke; it is her line but she gives no acknowledgment.

"Robert, I wonder if I could see you? I'm in town for a few days."

In town? "I didn't know you were out of town." I regret the words as soon as they are out of my mouth. Callous.

"Yes, well, I have been but now I'm here for a few days. I wonder if you have the time to see me?"

"I'll make time. Any time's fine, I do nothing but write all day." Pompous! "What's best for you, Tina?"

"Really, Robert, I have no preference."

"Good, because I welcome interruptions." *Interruptions*! Ye gods! "Look, Tina, why don't you come over now? We'll have lunch."

"Do you want me to come over there?"

"Unless you'd rather meet somewhere else? Your place?"

"I'm not there anymore. No, that's all right. I could go to you."

"We could meet at your hotel or wherever you're staying. Or a restaurant."

"Would you mind terribly?"

"What restaurant?"

She is either very silent or has hung up on me. "Paul Young's is all right," she says.

"That sounds all right. In an hour. In a half hour?"

"Thank you, Robert."

She has lost fifteen pounds or more but it does not help: she looks awful, a sickly Amazon. Her skin is sallow, the green welts under her eyes now resemble tire tracks, her posture, usually so erect, is stooped. She is not smoking, she is not drinking, she is not eating. "I'm a reformed woman," she says, smiling coldly. She is totally distant. We would be in closer proximity over the telephone. Even her mode of dress is distant: layers of tightly packed wool, ungiving as armor: gray wool sweater, green wool suit.

She has no small talk and no talk at all in regard to me. Her remoteness reawakens a memory of a Tina I had completely forgotten: ethereal, aloof, not remembering who I was from one meeting to the next. "Robert," she begins without lead-in, "we never finished our conversation of some time ago about Rags' notebook. I very much want to know if you've come to any conclusions."

One conclusion: She is on drugs. "About what, Tina?"

"I'm curious, you see, about the meaning of the words in his notebook. Perhaps you've forgotten——"

"No, Tina, I haven't forgotten."

"Out of curiosity, I would like to hear your opinion."

"Tina, what's going on?"

"On the other hand, if you and Rags have come to some agreement——" The temperature of her voice lowers twenty degrees.

"I haven't heard from Rags in over a month."

"That's no concern of mine, Robert." She acts as if I have violated an unspoken agreement between us.

"Tina, where have you been? What's going on?"

"I see," she smiles coldly. "You want your curiosity satisfied before I'm allowed to satisfy mine. Is that your bargain?" She is like some ghastly mannequin, a wind-up Tina: her speech has no texture, the words pop out computerized, disembodied, more her mother's speech pattern than her own. My drink arrives. I don't let go of the waiter without ordering another.

"I think Rags invented himself; that the Rags who existed in high school turned into another Rags. Turned into the opposite of Rags. I think the original model was your father; he wanted to turn into your father. I'm sure there were other models later on. But I think he's a total invention."

"You think he's a fraud."

"I don't think he's a fraud. He's an invention, an authentic creation: He didn't like the Rags he was born with so he put years of sweat and toil into building a better Rags."

"That, in your opinion, is the meaning of 'Opposites.' "

"In my opinion."

"And the second phrase?" She has become so tight-assed she can't say 'Big Chief Little Shit'!

"I'm less certain. I can speculate. Do you want me to speculate?"

"That's why I'm here."

Even if true, I resent her saying it. I do not exist solely for the purpose of defining her ex-lover for her; I have other qualities! I am writing a book! " 'Big Chief Little Shit' was probably a derogatory name he used on himself; a reminder that despite his grandiose dreams—for example, becoming the American Balzac—he was really a little punk. So 'Opposites' is at one end of the spectrum, 'Big Chief Little Shit' at the other."

"Perhaps," she says, after a thoughtful pause which I read to mean that she thinks I'm full of shit. I decide she is not on drugs.

"Where is Josh?" I ask.

"Josh?" she says as if she hasn't heard the question and is asking "What?" "I'm sure he's in good hands."

"Oh? Has he been put out for adoption?"

Her smile continues to lengthen the distance between us until I want to scream to be heard. On the other hand, I can't think of anything more I want to tell her.

"Thank you for being so cooperative, Robert." She opens her purse and lays out a dollar bill, either as my fee or to pay for her glass of club soda. My second Scotch arrives as she leaves. We haven't been there long enough for me to order lunch.

"Robert, I have some further thoughts on the subject we were discussing today at lunch. This is Tina Kaufman, by the way."

"Yes, Tina, I know."

"Am I disturbing you?"

"Not at all, Tina. I'm taking a break. I've been working on my book."

"I wondered if you'd mind getting together later. Is it an inconvenience?"

"Not at all. Would you like to come up here?"

"I'm staying at the Mayflower. Would the downstairs bar be convenient for you?"

"When?"

"At your convenience. Ring my room when you get here." She hangs up without letting me know the number of her room.

Maybe the dark bar atmosphere acts as a stimulant; in any case her vital signs appear to be functioning at a more life-like clip. She wears the blue turtleneck sweater that I have admired on her many times. And she is sitting up straighter. The room is too poorly lit to gather information on her pallor or her green welts.

"I found what you had to say very interesting this afternoon, but I think you are mistaken in one significant area. I don't believe my father was ever a model for Rags."

"I see."

"You're not to blame. It's only that I have more information on this than you, and I think since you've been so forthcoming with me it's only fair that I share it with you."

"That's very thoughtful of you, Tina."

"First, may I buy you a drink?"

"I'm not drinking tonight," I say, sensing from her Esther-like delivery that I am going to need my wits about me.

"How much do you know about Rags' childhood?"

"Not a thing."

"Very good!" She claps her hands to indicate she is pleased, the first expression of anything approaching emotion all day. "So you can't be blamed for your misinterpretation. You formed your opinion without certain facts."

334

"Please enlighten me," I say, doing a slow burn.

"Well, you know Rags comes from Saratoga?"

I look at her to see if she is kidding: she is not. "Yes, I do know that."

"But did you know his father ran a speakeasy during Prohibition?"

"No, I didn't know that."

"And that after Prohibition he went to work for a caterer. And that Rags had to assist him for the family to make enough to live on: catering parties for the rich during the racing season, working in those incredible mansions—"

"I've seen them."

"You've seen them as an adult. Rags saw them as a child, making deliveries, bussing at tables. . . . His whole idea of style and elegance developed on the basis of six weeks of catering to the rich every summer."

"So the rich at play were Rags' model, not your father."

"Do you see any relationship at all between my father's style and Rags'? Be serious for once, Robert."

I make a spot decision that it is now or never. "Tina, you are so full of shit it is coming out of your ears. If Rags did not use your father for a model, if your father is not in the picture at all, please explain to me what he's doing in Saratoga with Big O's childhood sweetheart, Carrie McWhinnie?"

Tina turns to stone, says nothing for a long while, says finally, "You're presumptuous," stands up and leaves.

The phone is ringing as I walk into the apartment. Guess who? "I understand what you were trying to do tonight. But you are not professionally trained. What you did was very dangerous to me. If I am to see you again to discuss what we need to discuss, you must promise me that you will not intrude on my personal life. You must allow me the right to arrive at my own solutions at my own pace and in my own way. Your melodramatics don't help. They hurt. Have I made myself clear?" She hangs up before I even get a chance to say hello.

335

"Look, Rags' entire life has been conducted in code. If he says 'A' he means 'B,' if he praises you it means he despises you, if he puts you down it means he likes you, if he's droll it means he's passionate, if he's passionate—well, he's not capable of passion, or is he? You'd know more about that than I."

"Robert, you promised."

"You hung up on me before I could promise. You and I have no contract."

She laughs. She actually laughs. Not only are we sitting in her room at the Mayflower—yes, I made it past the portals!— but Tina has laughed at me. She still looks god-awful, however.

"That childhood game of 'Opposites' you educated me about has been played by Rags his entire life."

She shakes her head vigorously in dissent.

"O.K., certainly since high school. Not that he knows it. He doesn't want to know it. That's why he pathologically scorned psychoanalysis all these years. Rags dare not go into psycho-analysis: there's the danger of finding out something about himself. So what does he do instead? He hires a private eye. He's in a position of control with a private eye, the amount of new information he will absorb is fixed by him."

"Robert, your exaggerated sense of your own importance overwhelms me."

"Thank God, you're back to directly insulting me."

"Rags did not hire you as his analyst. He hired you to find a notebook. Then he hired you to escort his child to him. If anything, the psychoanalysis was your idea."

"You left out the best one: He hired me to find out why he wasn't being invited to parties."

"No he didn't. He hired you to find out who was spreading malicious rumors about him."

"The rumors were about you and him. And they were true."

"Robert, I'm going to have to kick you out of here if you don't behave." Even her threats begin to sound more energetic.

Rags' column in the *Post* is improving. Today's was on the humiliation parents go through in order to get their kids into good private schools. I notice the dateline is New York. So I now know where Rags and Josh are.

April 1

We are at my apartment.

"By your compulsive fixation on Rags' personal life you overlook the entire social and political context," she says.

"I wasn't aware he had any politics until a couple of years ago." I hand Tina the bottle. She pours one more drink for herself and offers to pour for me but I shake my head no; I have had enough.

"When did he write in that notebook? It was April of 1964, wasn't it?" I nod. "And what was April of '64? It was barely six months after the assassination of President Kennedy."

"Tina, what in the world have 'Opposites' and 'Big Chief Little Shit' to do with the death of Kennedy?"

She puts a hand on mine to shush me. The first personal gesture out of her since her reappearance in the guise of Esther. "Bear with me. Take a look at Rags' career since 1964. His first novel, written before the death of Kennedy, is a trivial potboiler. After the death of Kennedy he plans a serious work of fiction."

"Which doesn't get written."

"Shut up. He loses his interest in sports, he begins to write long, serious magazine pieces, he begins a political column for the *Post,* he takes an unpopular position on the war, he defies a federal grand jury. Now where in his life do you see the background for this sort of growth before the death of Kennedy?"

"Tina, you can't make me believe that Rags' childhood model is John F. Kennedy. What happened to the Saratoga millionaires?"

" 'Opposites' and 'Big Chief Little Shit' refer superficially to his childhood. I don't question that. Why else would my father

337

be frightened into stealing the notebook? But maybe Rags wasn't thinking of his past in the narrow, autobiographical terms you insist on; maybe he had a larger canvas in mind. The contradictory role America plays in the world: Mom's apple pie versus napalm, a nation of do-gooders turned mass-murderers, big chiefs who are really little shits." Her eyes sparkle with self-congratulation.

"You're reaching."

"You're going to stay superficial to the very end, aren't you?"

After she leaves I take my first look at the book in days. While it has nothing to say about Mom's apple pie versus napalm or do-gooders turned mass-murderers it doesn't seem half bad to me. I will have to write Rags and let him know that I am not going to need his help.

April 2

We are at Rags' house, packing Tina's belongings.

"Look, we agree that Rags was a nobody in high school and Big O was a hero. I am going to call him Big O from now on. He is not your father. Forget he's your father. That doesn't happen for another twenty years."

"It doesn't happen ever," she says bitterly: the first note of Esther in her voice all day.

She hands me a large carton; I start packing it with books.

"Big O is everything Rags is not. He's popular. He's athletic. He's handsome. If Rags had a choice he would be Big O. So he decides, one day, he does have a choice. He will cease being Rags. He will become Big O."

"But he doesn't! You're wrong! How do I get that through your thick skull?" she says, sounding exactly like Tina.

"The fact is he tries. He makes an intellectual decision:

whatever Rags would do intuitively, the new Rags will do the opposite. He wills himself into another person."

"Who is not Big O," she says firmly.

"He wills himself into whoever is waiting at the other extreme of Rags."

Rags' column today was his best in months. Being back in New York seems to have revitalized him. Is he with Mrs. McWhinnie? I don't dare ask Tina. I clip the column. It is on the women's movement. Very telling. When I get the time I will try to decode it.

April 3

We are drinking Scotch in my apartment.

"What you don't understand is that Big O in high school was exactly the same as he is now: good natured, weak-willed, easily manipulated. The one difference in his life is who's doing the manipulating. That job is now taken by my mother."

"No loaded names, please. Call her Esther."

"And the person manipulating him in high school—"

"—was Carrie McWhinnie," I sneak in.

"Don't provoke me. No, it was Rags."

"How can you say that, Tina?"

"Because it makes sense. Big O was Rags' creation."

"But, goddammit, if Rags was so all-powerful, how come no one remembers him from high school?"

Tina may be looking and acting better but she hasn't given an inch. "Who do you usually remember? Dr. Frankenstein or the monster? If Rags lacked the physical attributes and the money to be one of the dashing, elegant young men he envied, he did the next best thing: he cultivated Big O, flattered him— yes, became his flunky, but all for one purpose: to manipulate him. Rags didn't need the limelight, Big O was his limelight! All his energies went into creating a creature under his quiet

339

control who was the opposite of everything he saw himself to be. Rags pulled the strings and Big O flourished. Then Rags matured, saw that he didn't need Big O anymore. He gave up Big O and became himself. Big O languished until my mother came along and filled the shell."

"And where does Carrie McWhinnie fit in this diagram?"

"Big O was Rags' Frankenstein monster. McWhinnie was my mother's."

I groan loudly and bury my head in my hands.

"You know I'm right," I hear Tina say in unflappable good humor.

April 4

We have just finished a late dinner at Solo's and are strolling back to Tina's new apartment on R Street. "We keep avoiding the main issue," I say. "What was Rags so scared about? He spends seven years hotfooting around a subject that he pretends is of vital importance to him."

I speed on past her opening mouth; she has been on her toes all night, looking and acting in top form. It warms my heart. "Rags wants to be taken seriously as an artist but he knows that won't happen before he's come to some kind of literary reckoning with himself. Here, look at this. I found this in my diary." I take from my inside jacket pocket the Xerox I had made yesterday and shove it under her nose because it is the only way to get her to read it.

May 4, 1964

Plante: "Otis Kaufman is my oldest friend. We date back to grammar school. In high school he was the star athlete and I was the star reporter. We made each other local legends."

"So in the end he goes back home but he doesn't go back to dig out the truth; he goes back to reinforce his big shot fantasies. So much for truth. So much for art."

340

April 5

My place.

"Your problem," she says, "is that you don't have the first understanding of how an artist's mind works."

"I don't have to. I don't have any artists I'm desperate to defend."

She sticks out her tongue at me. She is in a full white blouse and short gray skirt tonight. Thank God, she has given up her maternity shifts. Day by day and inch by inch she is coming to be more of a joy to look at. A joy that reads "hands off," but I don't care; I have solved that part of our relationship.

"You know as well as I do how Rags gets his material," she says. "He absorbs it from the air around him. His interests aren't visceral or psychological; they come from his surroundings. Why did he become a sports columnist? Because he was surrounded by sports figures. When did he start taking himself seriously as a writer? When he began to meet other writers and saw that they took him seriously. When did he get interested in Vietnam? When I dragged him off to a couple of demonstrations. You've seen the way he talks half the time. He doesn't have normal conversations: he talks in columns. His conversation is a filter for the raw material he absorbs around him. In all practicality, his conversations are first drafts.

"He went to Saratoga because that's what he wanted to write about. He took up with that woman because she's an important part of his past. He's not off on some ridiculous letch for a woman who's old enough to be my mother—give him more credit than that. My God, have you seen her? She dresses like a teenybopper—I mean, she's not to be believed, quoting Noam Chomsky with her legs spread apart."

It irritates me when she acts petty; it is not part of her character—or it is not a part of her character I choose to know about.

April 6

We are in my apartment. Tina is sprawled on the bed, playing with strands of her hair. We have been at it again for hours.

"Rags is lusting over Big O's girl, but is it really the girl he wants or is it Big O?" I manage to say, before she grabs my hand with both of hers and puts it over my mouth.

"It's the cheerleader he wants, dummy, the abstract symbol, the same thing he wants in Big O: the football player, not the man, not the sex, the symbol. The key to Rags is his symbols." She frees my mouth; I miss our hands making contact.

"Rags' entire life is in revised edition," I say, wondering if it would be all right to sit next to her on the bed. "Isn't that why he blacks out his past? In order to rewrite it? So that the elegant Rags, the charming Rags, the diffident Rags, the disarming Rags, the lovable but frustrated Rags—the Rags who's so puzzling because he makes you feel close and distant at the same time—Rags the celebrity has been substituted for Rags the flunky.

"Is that why he hired me to find out why he was not being invited to parties? Not such a frivolous assignment, after all: he was scared that his assumed identity was peeling away, that the Rat was surfacing. Not that he knew it consciously, but wasn't that the buried fear? The rumor that so worried him: it wasn't that he was living with a teenage girl—of high school age, I might remind you—" My spirits are lifted by the growl I provoke out of her. "But that the dead and buried Rags was threatening a comeback."

Tina slides off the bed and onto the floor, where, no doubt to shut me up, she does a headstand. My pleasure is barely containable.

"Why this strange Tessie Toga business? In his sports column he wrote like a sycophant; but given the protection of Tessie's Toga he wrote malicious mischief: knowing Big O's weak point to be his shyness with girls, he paired him in print with the most sought-after girl in school. Why would he embarrass his hero? Did he do it in innocence? If so, why did he try to break them up when his fictional romance became fact?"

I take up a spot on the floor three feet from Tina and sit, my legs folded under me.

"At that dinner party in Saratoga with the McWhinnies, Rags complained that in high school the jocks got away with everything, while he got away with nothing. He was referring to Big O. Hero worship can only go so far. Big O moved from an idol he worshipped to an idol he wanted to smash. He, who could get away with nothing, could get away with one thing: he could destroy the romance he created. He wrote it into existence—'life imitating artlessness,' as he said in Saigon— now he decided to write it out of existence." I stretch out on my stomach and cradle my head on my forearms. Our two heads, hers upside down, are inches apart.

I wait with exhilaration for my comeuppance from the upside down Tina.

"I think you're really Tessie Toga," she finally says. "When are you going to let me read that book you're supposed to be writing?"

April 8

4:00 A.M.: Fell asleep in the chair while Tina was reading. Wake up in bed. How come?

Tina gone. Discover my manuscript all over the bed. She has been reading in bed while I was asleep. Was I asleep next to her while she read? She has left a note.

> Rob—
> A lot of this is very good, terrific. Very clear. Very direct. You are at your worst when you're polemical.
> I want to talk to you about it at dinner.

April 17

Josh down for a weekend visit with Tina, little to say about his father whom he now resembles remarkably. He has lost much of his effeminacy but it is not an improvement—he seems incomplete now, like an amputee. His conversation when he got in last night was a junior-sized Plante monologue on urban violence. "I always carry five or ten dollars mugging money. If you give it to them right away they won't hassle you; if you give them an argument then it's your own fault whatever happens. It's like arguing with a cop. I mean they're the real cops, the muggers. They make the law, like where you go and where you can't. You obey their rules and it's no problem. You fight back, it's the same as the regular cops, they walk on your face; you pay them off, it's no hassle. It's like paying taxes. I mean they're no different from regular tax collectors except you don't have to fill out a form. It's actually more convenient."

Neither Tina nor I got in a word edgewise. It may be nothing more than his lack of ease with his new living situation.

He's obviously trying to figure out what, if anything, goes on between Tina and me. What a life he leads: musical relationships.

Go for a drive today. Tina, as usual, behind the wheel. She won't let me drive, says my spotty concentration makes her nervous. I don't mind. I get a charge out of her appearance behind a wheel: vibrant, self-confident, in control for once. She has a knack for observing things on the road that I will either miss or spot too late: exit signs, patrol cars, breakdowns. . . . I concentrate on concentrating but still she is the first to say, "Oh look—" and point a finger at a spot I was sure I had my eye on, clearing my vision to see a vintage-model Ford or two nuns hitchhiking or a smoking 747 landing at Dulles. My willful blindness infuriates me!

Josh is more at ease this morning—I can tell because he conducts an old-fashioned tirade against his mother. He sits in back, his feet lodged annoyingly against my headrest, cataloguing Annabelle's deficiencies: She is pushy, a know-it-all, a phony who can fool his father and all his friends but not Josh, a selfish woman who fakes generosity, an old lady who dresses as if she's still in high school. I find his catalogue riddled with false notes; few of the items remind me of the Annabelle I knew. Tina, as usual, hears the same false notes I do, but hears them first or, at least, objects to them first. It is a surprise to hear her speak in Annabelle's defense. "You've got to remember you're living in a new city and in a new home and it obviously is going to create tensions you can't even begin to be aware of," she says. "You complain about her lack of generosity but I don't get any feeling of generosity coming from you," she says. "Try to be less judgmental, otherwise whatever you set up is likely to happen, it becomes a self-fulfilling prophecy," she says.

This exchange fills me with unease. I watch the Shenandoah River sliding by outside the window, wondering what it is I'm missing. Tina points to a circling parakeet, a three-car pileup, Pat Nixon hitchhiking.

Eventually it dawns on my sluggish brain that I have been missing the code, that poor Annabelle is no more part of the conversation than I am: she is the beard. The real subject is Carrie McWhinnie.

Josh spots a dead chipmunk on the side of the road. Now he's doing it to me.

May 14

Josh down again for the weekend. I get the distinct feeling that Plante is using us as sitters. He is basically a nice kid—we both feel sorry for him—but hours go by when his presence is excruciating. Tina and I will look at each other, our eyes screaming to escape. He is of no help at all when it comes to Rags' current life. We are more informed on his father than he is.

Rags has become a home movie to us. We run him forwards

and backwards, freeze frames, run him in slow motion, do as we please with him.

May 15

Tina, Josh and I celebrate the book. At Tina's insistence. "It's not finished," I say for safety's sake.

"Shut up," she says, leaving me no choice by shoving a lobster claw in my mouth. "If they loved the first 150 pages they will love the rest." She makes me take out my editor's letter and read it aloud for the third time. Josh agrees with Tina that it is unequivocal. I sense some between the lines foot dragging. We analyze the letter, particularly the last paragraph, line by line.

Fifteen minutes of this is as much as Josh can take. "Jesus, you guys," he says in exasperation. "Who wrote that letter? My father?"

The three of us nearly fall off our chairs laughing.

At 4:00 A.M., with Josh asleep on the couch in the living room, we make love for the first time. Have to do it quietly for fear of waking him. The letter makes a hell of a racket in my inside jacket pocket.

May 16

Rough day with Josh. Couldn't wait to get him on the shuttle back to New York. Snipes at Tina and me all the time. Claims that one of us swiped his camera. Tina attempts to convince him that he didn't bring down a camera. I ransack the apartment. No camera.

It becomes more and more clear that Rags has dumped him on us—and with summer coming along it wouldn't surprise me if I had an uninvited guest for two months. Not that I really mind. Tina, I know, welcomes the idea.

Before he boards the shuttle home, I browbeat out of Josh

346

a list of all the places he visited without us this weekend. "What's the point? You're not going to find it. My only good camera."

Back in the apartment, Tina dashes to the refrigerator for ice for drinks. It's somehow risky being with her without Josh present. I sit down on the bed with the telephone directory, looking up the House of Pancakes, the Orpheum theatre, the National Gallery. . . .

"What in hell are you up to?" asks Tina, handing me a Scotch.

"I'm going to find his camera."

She plunks herself down next to me on the side of the bed. "God, are you obtuse. Don't you know what that was all about? The camera is a metaphor. He must have been awake while we made love. He's blinded himself. It's an act of sheer, willful blindness."

We go at it for an hour before bedtime, neither of us giving an inch. A fight over a camera is not at all what I had in mind for tonight.

2:00 A.M: Why don't our arguments have the charm of her arguments with Rags? Rags has been on my mind all night: As we made love I wondered for the first time how Rags did it with her. I wanted to ask: Does Rags do this to you? Do we do it the same way? Do you want to tell me how he does it? Do you want me to do it that way?

And so I awoke at two, afraid that Tina might feel that I'm not holding up my end of the bargain: I don't argue with her the way Rags did. I'm not as witty, I'm not as articulate, not articulate at all. I'm often surprised at how well my arguments sound considering the amount of difficulty I have getting them out.

Do I love Tina? Do I like Tina? Writing out the words brings forth no emotion weightier than apprehension.

Does it all come down to the shabby fact that I am after Rags' girls (first Annabelle, now Tina) just as Rags was after Big O's girl? But Annabelle wasn't Big O's girl. No—but she lived with a professional football player before she married Rags. Loved by a jock and therefore lovable?

Here I am back again on Rags' case, when the case I should be working on is Hollister's.

Disguises.

Even asleep, her beautiful, scary body draped in a light sheet, Tina maintains a distance between us.

We talk even less about Tina than we do about me. She won't even talk about her photography. She won't show me her work; I don't even know if she's good.

This awful suffocating game the two of us play! It makes me so angry I want to rush over to the bed and shake her awake.

At the moment I wrote it down she heaved a sigh and turned over, away from me. She reads my mind even when she sleeps. I would like very much to think of that as love.

I am a lousy observer. I see like a cop; I see prejudicially; I collect evidence; what can't be included as evidence is not seen; doesn't exist.

I only collect significant prejudicial data. How do you establish your true feelings in relation to a collection of significant prejudicial data? Do I have the foggiest notion of who this woman is that I'm sleeping with?

I am not too surprised to hear the telephone ring or to hear Plante's voice filtering through. He congratulates me on the acceptance of the book and tells me how good it is to be speaking to me. His voice is warm, exuberant; how am I to take that? "Only the first 150 pages," I am quick to correct him.

"One of your many enviable traits, Ackroyd, is that you are an obsessive finisher."

What's behind this effusiveness? Or was that a crack? Persistent but pedestrian, is that what he means by obsessive finisher?

"We drank a toast in your honor with hot chocolate tonight."

We? Who's we? Josh and him alone? McWhinnie, too? Hot chocolate? Is that an innocuous remark or a put-down?

"How's New York?" I ask, my stomach churning.

"Beyond belief but not without redeeming social content."

Why can't he ever say what he means to me?

"You are better off where you are."

Is that supposed to mean that I couldn't make the grade in New York? Or does he mean I am better off with Tina than he is with McWhinnie? What?

I ask how his book is coming along, wondering as I ask if I ask out of curiosity or sadism or pushiness to be accepted as a peer.

"Better and better. When you get to these parts we will have to celebrate."

Meaning, I am sure, that he hasn't touched a typewriter in months. After minutes more of cramped conversation he gets around to the purpose of his call; he asks for Tina.

If I deliver Tina to him, am I once again acting as his operative? If I tell him she's not here, am I once again acting to sabotage him? What would Tina want? Do I have any right to decide?

I observe Tina in sleep. In the midst of my observation she rolls over toward me. Or toward Plante? She groans and stretches out a long beseeching arm toward me. Or toward Plante?

"Ackroyd, are you still there?" Plante asks.

I wedge the receiver into the pillow against Tina's cheek. "What?" she says crankily, still asleep.

"For you," I say, not needing to say more: she locks eyes with me and speaks into the receiver.

"Rags?" Her voice denotes . . . Pleasure? Anticipation? Coolness? Praying God that the correct clue is coolness, I go into the kitchen to make myself a drink; no, not a drink, a sandwich; no, not a sandwich. I stare at the white wall of the refrigerator hoping to come up with a clue to what I want to make myself.